BRIGHT DAY

JOHN BOYNTON PRIESTLEY was born in 1894 in Yorkshire, the son of a schoolmaster. After leaving Belle Vue School when he was 16, he worked in a wool office but was already by this time determined to become a writer. He volunteered for the army in 1914 during the First World War and served five years; on his return home, he attended university and wrote articles for the *Yorkshire Observer*. After graduating, he established himself in London, writing essays, reviews, and other nonfiction, and publishing several miscellaneous volumes. In 1927 his first two novels appeared, *Adam in Moonshine* and *Benighted*, which was the basis for James Whale's film *The Old Dark House* (1932). In 1929 Priestley scored his first major critical success as a novelist, winning the James Tait Black Memorial Prize for *The Good Companions*. *Angel Pavement* (1930) followed and was also extremely well received. Throughout the next several decades, Priestley published numerous novels, many of them very popular and successful, including *Bright Day* (1946) and *Lost Empires* (1965), and was also a prolific and highly regarded playwright.

Priestley died in 1984, and though his plays have continued to be published and performed since his death, much of his fiction has unfortunately fallen into obscurity. Valancourt Books is in the process of reprinting many of J. B. Priestley's best works of fiction with the aim of allowing a new generation of readers to discover this unjustly neglected author's books.

FICTION BY J.B. PRIESTLEY

Adam in Moonshine (1927)

Benighted (1927)★

Farthing Hall (with Hugh Walpole) (1929)

The Good Companions (1929)

Angel Pavement (1930)

Faraway (1932)

Wonder Hero (1933)

I'll Tell You Everything (with Gerald Bullett) (1933)

They Walk in the City (1936)

The Doomsday Men (1938)★

Let the People Sing (1939)

Blackout in Gretley (1942)

Daylight on Saturday (1943)

Three Men in New Suits (1945)

Bright Day (1946)★

Jenny Villiers (1947)

Festival at Farbridge (1951)

The Other Place (1953)★

The Magicians (1954)★

Low Notes on a High Level (1954)

Saturn Over the Water (1961)★

The Thirty First of June (1961)★

The Shapes of Sleep (1962)★

Sir Michael and Sir George (1964)

Lost Empires (1965)

Salt is Leaving (1966)★

It's an Old Country (1967)

The Image Men: Out of Town (vol. 1), *London End* (vol. 2) (1968)

The Carfitt Crisis (1975)

Found Lost Found (1976)

★ Available from Valancourt Books

BRIGHT DAY

by

J. B. PRIESTLEY

*It is the bright day that
brings forth the adder . . .*

With a new introduction by Alice Ferrebe

VALANCOURT BOOKS

Dedication: To MY WIFE for September the Fourteenth

Bright Day by J. B. Priestley
Originally published in Great Britain by Heinemann in 1946
First American edition published by Harper & Brothers in 1946
First Valancourt Books edition 2019

Published by Valancourt Books, Richmond, Virginia
http://www.valancourtbooks.com

ISBN 978-1-948405-37-9 *(trade paperback)*
ISBN 978-1-954321-25-0 *(hardcover)*

Also available as an ebook and audiobook.

Set in Dante MT

INTRODUCTION

J. B. Priestley (1894-1984) has proven a difficult writer to classify. Reviewing *Bright Day* in the *Observer* newspaper in 1946, Norman Collins jokes, "There are about half a dozen different Mr. Priestleys. And for some time I had been wishing that one or two of them would meet each other."[1] "They didn't know how to pigeon hole me," Priestley later remarked ruefully of the critics and dons who presided over English culture between the Wars, "so they left me out altogether." As a novelist (even more so than as a prolific playwright, broadcaster, journalist and essayist) he has remained rather marginalized, and as a transatlantic novelist he languishes unconsidered. Yet *Bright Day* is a revealing transatlantic novel. It is also a deeply un-American one. "It is the bright day that brings forth the adder (and that craves wary walking)," Brutus warns his co-conspirators in *Julius Caesar*, lending Priestley's novel its title and epigraph. Crowning their leader, Brutus believes, could change Caesar's nature, wrenching their general from his roots, and making him cruel and proud. The doleful conviction that success cannot but corrupt rings more English than Roman, and far more English than American.

Priestley's protagonist, Gregory Dawson, fifty years old as the novel opens, and born in Bruddersford in the north of England, has made himself a big success before the Second World War, living and working as a writer in the archetypal dream factory of Hollywood. Returning home when war broke out, his work is still bankrolled by American money—holed up in a Cornish hotel, he is finishing another script starring another transatlantic export, Elizabeth Earl. She is both his friend and also his Pygmalion product, whom he has cannily styled for the American market, maintaining her mythos with feisty roles like that leading *The Lady Hits Back*. When Liz arrives to meet him at the Royal Ocean Hotel, Gregory prescribes her easy radiance to having had "more than her fair share" of vitamins—her agent, he tells her, is "the type that makes Americans so unpopular on this side of the Atlantic. There they are—energetic and helpful, generous and rich—and hardly any of us poor half-starved Europeans can stand 'em." Rationing was rife in Britain after the Second World War—in fact, it became more restrictive than during the Blitz. The hotel's food is brown and "dullish, and it was doled out in exact and inadequate portions, as if there were physicists at work in the kitchen." Yet as Gregory completes the script, his need to renounce what he calls the "gigantic doped jam-puff industry" of the American studio system is rising.

In half-starved Britain, which "threw all we'd got into the kitty" (and had to borrow much of it back via Marshall Aid), America provokes complex and contradictory hungers. The masses gather in the dark to gaze at its myths projected onto lighted screens, willingly sacrificing pub after pub in preference of the hokey glamour of roadhouses serving "bogus Martinis". Gregory evokes the USA only as a negative example, as replete, imperialist and founded in its turn upon the defining opposite of a picturesque fief across the Atlantic. He notes of his temporary residence, "the entrance hall and the vast lounge were full of bogus lances and battle-axes, shields and suits of armour, lions rampant and leopards couchant; and the general effect suggested that Metro-Goldwyn-Mayer were around there, doing *Ivanhoe* as a B. picture." London, in "the flimsy and treacherous South", he claims, has become like "the shabbier side of some third-rate American city." "At least they're alive," counters Liz, piqued by his relentless antagonism towards her Hollywood colleagues, "and half the people in this hotel are dead." "How would you like to play to zombies every tea-time and evening?" one of the Royal Ocean's resident, recalcitrant, musicians asks him. But Gregory would rather be creating moments that, like the trio's lounge-room performance of Schubert, rouse him from his zombified state. Other than during the fleeting transports provided by art, Gregory recognises, "As a real man, as a planning, struggling, hoping, loving human being—I was dead." *Bright Day* is driven by his quest to produce work about "life, and not the movies".

John Boynton Priestley volunteered for the British Army in 1914 aged twenty, and, unlike so many of his generation, saw the First World War out. By the Second, he was well established as a writer, and his most gilded national service came in the form of his *Postscripts* radio broadcasts, with their audience of around 14 million Britons. On 6 October 1940, he looked at his nation and announced:

> We are floundering between two stools. One of them is our old acquaintance labelled 'Every man for himself, and the devil take the hindmost', which can't really represent us, or why should young men, for whom you and I have done little or nothing, tear up and down the sky in their Spitfires to protect us, or why should our whole community pledge itself to fight until Europe is freed? The other stool [...] has some lettering round it that hints that free men could combine, without losing what's essential to their free development, to see that each gives according to his ability, and receives according to his need.[2]

Postscripts is often cited as one of the prompts of the postwar mood that routed Churchill's Conservative wartime government in the 1945 General Election. In a swing still unrivalled in postwar British politics, voters moved in favour of the Labour Party's vision of a Welfare State that eschewed quick amelioration for the universal (and largely enduring) provision of social services. Yet though on that bleak October night Priestley was paraphrasing Marx ("from each according to his ability, to each according to his needs"), his was always an idiosyncratic socialism that shunned established political parties. In *Bright Day*, 1914 Bruddersford Councillor Fred Knott represents, for Gregory, "that earlier and more innocent phase of the Labour Movement, when it was still uncorrupted by power, [...] still lit by the sunrise of simple and noble aspirations"; a time before the light "brings forth the adder". Priestley's own wary walking led him through a range of causes in search of such a sunrise, most notably, from 1957, in the Campaign for Nuclear Disarmament (CND). "Perhaps because of my upbringing, my 21st birthday lost in the Flanders mud," he later claimed, "I could not be entirely serious about anything except the well-being of our society itself."

For all he decries his current profession, Gregory comes to

discern that his eighteen-year-old self, who was "a lonely boy and rather sentimental and romantic, and enjoyed making things up" was on an apprenticeship to become one of Hollywood's resident mythologists. His training begins with the Alington family. Like Priestley's native Bradford, Bruddersford's trade is centered upon wool, and Mr. Alington is Gregory's boss in the company Hawes and Co.

Too kindly for an increasingly ruthless managerial industry, Alington introduces his orphan employee to a family life bustling with sociability and culture, and centered upon his three daughters and one son. Like heyday Bradford, Bruddersford is crammed with cosmopolitan culture—with theatres, orchestras, libraries, and music halls. When Councillor Knott lists his citizens' basic rights, he includes being able "to read some books worth reading—to go to a theatre or to listen to some music." Postwar British society committed to a vision of broad access to the arts as a human and humanitarian right, as well as a restorative tonic. The 1945 Labour government empowered local authorities to tax sixpence on the pound to fund cultural activities, a scheme historian Arthur Marwick has identified as "culture as a form of social welfare."[3] The Alingtons, their lives full of music, books, skits, picnics and apparently unconditional love, transform Gregory's life, and are in turn transformed by him into an lingering myth of perfection. The Last Edwardian Summer is by no means untrammelled as a literary theme, but here Priestley offers it to us anew and affectingly as an intensely personal memory of a sun-dappled day ending in an unexpected death.

Sequestered in Cornwall, his script nearing its end, Gregory spends more and more time "going Bruddersfording" back to 1914, trying to free himself from his current personal and political stasis. Yet the novel's time scheme far exceeds the binary. Priestley was fascinated by the work of John William Dunne, soldier, aeronautical engineer and philosopher, who, prompted by his own experience of pre-cognitive dreams, published *An Experiment in Time* in 1927. Many of Priestley's plays of the 1930s and 1940s play with Dunne's ideas on how we move freely across time, inhabiting past, present and future simultaneously. In 1964 Priestley had produced his own treatise, *Man and Time*, arguing that linear time as a concept was bafflingly incomplete and creatively incapacitating. One of *Bright Day*'s most intriguing characters is Jock Barniston, also part of the Alington circle, who "always gave one the impression that he had just returned after a long and probably very strange journey, from Patagonia, from the moon, from some other solar system." His sister Dorothy has "second sight", a power harnessed by the novel's narration to provide unsettling forward flashes of characters' fates, their bodies lying broken on sunny rocky outcrops, or reduced to "so much bleeding meat in a sandbag". Time-traveller Jock gives the young Gregory advice that it will take him years to understand; that he "can go a long way—and give us something good—if you travel easily and lightly, seeing people as they are, just as people and not as symbolic figures, and not leaving parts of yourself behind, frozen in some enchantment." The novel's time machinery whirrs on beyond both Wars, setting out most of the literary concerns of its subsequent decade: a perceived lack of, in Jimmy Porter's words, "good, brave causes"[4], the pursuit of authenticity, a rejection of transatlantic "invitations to a candy floss world"[5]. Gregory's quest anticipates so many of the qualities that will burnish the New Left writing of, for example, Richard Hoggart and Raymond Williams; it is for the real, the rich, and the plain—a dappled shade, rather than those artificial studio lights. Older and wise, Priestley offers us more hope than anger.

Alice Ferrebe
Liverpool John Moores University

NOTES

1 Norman Collins, "Priestleys", *Observer*, 16 June 1946, p. 3.

2 J. B. Priestley, *Postscripts* (London: Heinemann, 1940), p. 90.

3 Arthur Marwick, *Culture in Britain Since 1945* (London: Blackwell, 1991), p. 70.

4 John Osborne, *Look Back in Anger* [1957] (London: Faber & Faber, 1989), p. 84.

5 Richard Hoggart, *The Uses of Literacy: Aspects of Working-class Life with Special Reference to Publications and Entertainments* [1957] (Harmondsworth: Penguin, 1958), p. 169.

ONE

It was Brent, the film producer, who suggested that I should go down to Tralorna and stay at the Royal Ocean Hotel. I was doing the script of *The Lady Hits Back* for him, and when, after wasting months, he suddenly came screaming for a full shooting script to be completed as soon as possible, I told him I should have to go away and do it. It was then he suggested Tralorna and the Royal Ocean. He had stayed there when they had been on location in Cornwall, the year before. "That's the place for you, Greg," he said. "Nothing to do but work. They'll give you a room about the size of Stage Four. The food's dull and there isn't much of it, and most of the people there are just waiting for death. So you'll be hungry and bored, and you'll have to work. Don't mention my name—they hate my guts. The bar's quite good and don't spend too much time in it—I want that script by the fifteenth of next month."

So down I went. And Brent, who always sounds as if he must be wrong about everything, surprised me once again by being right. The Royal Ocean Hotel was just what I needed. And they did give me an enormous bedroom that wandered off into a turret, where I worked, high above the glittering sea, like a man in a lighthouse. And the food was dullish, and it was doled out in exact and inadequate portions, as if there were physicists at work in the kitchen; and most of the people there were what he said they would be, although some of them who were waiting for death in his time now looked as if it had arrived since and they were now haunting the place. So I was hungry and bored, and I had to work. And the bar was quite good, and Brent and the boys of the unit were remembered there as an invading army is remembered in a sacked city. The hotel was much larger than I had expected; it stood on a high cliff, with gulls mewing at the dining-room windows and the Atlantic grumbling and shuddering far below; and the entrance hall and the vast lounge were full of bogus lances and battle-axes, shields and suits of armour, lions rampant and leopards couchant; and the general effect suggested that Metro-Goldwyn-Mayer were around there, doing *Ivanhoe* as a B. picture.

My own programme of work and play in that hotel was as simple and tedious as a helping of tepid porridge. All morning I did my two-finger typing in my turret, going down for a late lunch. In the afternoon I pottered about, strolling to the village or mooching along the cliff walks. After an early cup of tea I returned to my turret and slogged away until about eight, when I hurried downstairs to the bar for a quick pink gin and then went to my solitary meal in a corner of the dining-room. I was always in the lounge in time for the nine o'clock news, which rattled the animals rampant and couchant with its false bright certainty, its blind-man glimpses of promised lands; and then when the trio (of which more later) got busy with Eric Coates and Cole Porter again, either I escaped to the bar or I went up to my room, sometimes to take a telephone call from Brent or George Adony, who was to direct the film; often to make some notes for the next day's work; and always, sooner or later, to read some American detective stories, the hard-boiled and irascible kind, some of them written by drunks I had known in Hollywood. It was full spring down there in Cornwall; and I noticed the dramatic alternations of slashing rain and sunshine, the tattered sails of cloud, the green fury of the sea, the gorse along the cliff walks and the cushions of primroses in the deep lanes; but it all seemed to be happening a long way off and to have nothing to do with me. My schedule, which did not include spring, was dreary enough, as Brent had promised, but it was certainly good for work. I pulled scene after scene, sequence after sequence, of *The Lady Hits Back* out of the bag. This bag, no doubt, was a bag of tricks, but this does not mean that the work was not real work. For these film scripts you use only part of your mind but you keep that part very busy: the old unconscious is not much help with these things; no treasures come up from the deep; you have to plan and argue and sweat it all out in the front of your mind. Which I did.

Let me add here—and it has its place in the story—that *The*

Lady Hits Back had rather more in it than met the eye or that would be included in our hand-outs to the trade and the press. It was something more than ninety minutes of light comedy with a pinch or two of easy sentiment in the final sequence. It was essentially hard and cold; its toy figures existed in a world of black ice. It was really a private message from a few of us, from Brent and me, who had planned the story, and from George Adony, who would turn it into a moving picture, to our millions and millions of customers, all relaxed in the dark, telling them quietly to expect nothing from such a world as this but the worst, imploring them not to be fooled again by anybody; and though we never mentioned what we were up to, not even to each other, we knew what we were doing, and we all knew that we knew. Although publicity men, distributors, exhibitors and critics do not know it, this is the innermost secret, the real sorcery of film-making—this whisper in the dark to fifty million people. And therefore I may be wrong in saying that the unconscious played no part here, though the fact remains that every scene, every line of dialogue, had to be coolly and consciously invented and set down. And this is work.

There were about forty people staying in the hotel, and apart from a few young couples, discovering each other all over again after the war, most of them were elderly. I exchanged a remark or two every day with some of them, chiefly in the bar, but I deliberately kept aloof, refusing to be dragged into any group, simply because, unlike them, I was there to work and was not on holiday. I was particularly careful about this at first, before I had really got going, and after that, when it did not matter very much if I became sociable, I remained aloof because nobody there interested me very much. But there was one couple, who arrived a few days after I did, about whom I was mildly curious. They sat only two tables away from me in the dining-room. They were a prosperous-looking pair, probably quite rich, and both in their sixties, both fairly tall and thin and rather bloodless. Like so many elderly married couples they appeared at a casual glance to be extraordinarily alike. They were about the same height, had the same dry, grey, papery look, and both had rather small heads and flattish faces. But I soon noticed that he had light blue eyes, cold but flickering, whereas she had dark eyes, restless and still rather fine. She had obviously been a very handsome woman in her time, but now she seemed to be one of those elderly women who suddenly begin to pay a heavy price for having played too many tricks with their faces, so that she looked older and more ruinous, in her face if not in her figure, than other women of her own age who have never had the same time and money to squander on their appearance. He was spruce and pink and seemed to have an easy pleasant manner, but there was about him a certain air of cold self-indulgence, common among many well-to-do elderly Englishmen, that I always find repellent. I was not sure about her, but I was quite prepared to dislike him.

What made me curious about these two, however, was that from the first I felt I had seen them before somewhere. Then I felt that they reminded me of two people I had once known. But where had I seen them before? Alternatively, who were the people they reminded me of? Time after time at lunch and dinner I stared hard at them, trying to force my memory, but it was useless. The little unsolved riddle was like a buzzing gnat. It soon became a nuisance. So after a few days I decided to make some enquiries about this irritating pair, who incidentally had shown no interest whatever in me. I asked a question or two in the bar, and finally learned that they were Lord and Lady Harndean, and that he was a wealthy City man who had been given a peerage just before the war. This meant nothing to me. I had never heard of Lord Harndean.

"That wasn't his name before he took a title," said the man I was talking to, a fellow called Horncastle. "But I can't remember what his original name was. He's been doing some job for the Government during the war—one of those controls. Chucked it now, of course. You may have run across him on some war job."

I knew I hadn't. "If I ever did know him, it was before that. And I didn't get back from America until early in 1940, and I'd been out there ten years—mostly in Hollywood."

"Hollywood, eh?" cried Horncastle, brightening up at once. It is surprising how many people brighten up like that as soon as you mention Hollywood—men old enough to know better too.

They don't know the name of a single producer, director, script writer, but nevertheless Hollywood lights them up. Famous profiles! Blondes with million-dollar legs! Orgies! Horncastle almost smacked his lips. "You in the film game, Dawson?"

"Yes. I write scripts."

"Invent all the stuff they have to do and say—what?"

"Some of it." But I didn't intend to stage a juicy brains trust about Hollywood for him, so I said I had some work to do, and left the bar. On my way out I decided not to waste any more time wondering about these Harndeans. After all I was not looking for finance, so why should I bother about rich titled types from the City? It was not as if they had shown the slightest curiosity about me. So from now on, I told myself, the Harndeans were out.

And so they might have been—and I think they might have left without my remembering who they were—if it had not been for Schubert. And this is where that trio comes into the picture. The pianist, who was worthy of better things, was a baggy-eyed old Czech called Zenek; and it happened that I had known his brother, who was a smaller and neater edition of him, in Hollywood where he toiled as an assistant director at Paramount. The other two members of the trio, Susan the violinist and Cynthia the 'cellist, were two untidy but pleasant girls from the Royal College who were filling in a few months, and getting some cheap bathing, by sawing away at Coleridge-Taylor, Eric Coates and Jerome Kern and the rest. Susan was small and fierce and Cynthia was very long and mild, and they amused me, not only because of this contrast, but also because they both had an unfathomable contempt for the Royal Ocean Hotel and for almost everybody who stayed there. After talking to Zenek about his brother, I had got into the habit of exchanging a few remarks with the trio every tea-time, and I used to chaff the two girls, who took themselves very seriously, about the kind of stuff they had to play. I told them that they couldn't play a real trio even if they tried, which annoyed the girls, especially the fierce one, little Susan. And that is how they came to play some Schubert, and how I came to recognise the Harndeans.

I had come in rather late for tea one afternoon, just as the

three of them had finished banging and scraping away at a selection from *Show Boat*. I looked across at them to see that Susan
was staring at me—and she had dramatic dark eyes—in a curiously significant and challenging fashion, while the tall Cynthia,
wrapped about her 'cello, was looking particularly demure,
and old Zenek, who was sorting out some music, was grinning
away. So I came to the conclusion that the next item, whatever it
was, must be specially meant for me. The trio was determined
to show me what it could do if it tried. I glanced around. Most
of the guests had drifted out; it was much quieter than usual.
I noticed that the Harndeans were still lingering at a table not
very far away, and because their two faces, very clearly seen,
raised the old tantalising question, I told myself sharply that I
had stopped bothering about them; and I waited for the music,
which I suspected had been not only specially chosen but also
specially rehearsed for my benefit. And then, after a final flashing *Just-you-listen-to-this* look from young Susan, they began.

It was the slow movement of Schubert's *B Flat Major Trio*, as
I knew at once when the 'cello began the exquisite quiet tone,
slowly and gravely rocking in its immeasurable tenderness. A
few moments later, when the 'cello went wandering to murmur
its regret and the violin with its piercing sweetness curved and
rocked in the same little tune, I was far away, deep in a lost world
and a lost time. I was back again—young Gregory Dawson,
eighteen, shy but sprawling—in the Alingtons' drawing-room
in Bruddersford, before the First World War, years and years
ago, half a good lifetime away. The thin ribbon of sound pulled
back curtain after curtain. People and places that I had thought
had dwindled and faded to the dimmest shades of memory, to
smudged scrawls in an old diary, came flashing back, burningly
alive, as the music went winding through my heart like a slow
procession of fire-raisers. The Alingtons' house ... the office
and warehouse in Canal Street ... and the cottages on the moors
... and all the Alingtons—Oliver, Eva, Bridget and the rest—and
their friends ... Uncle Miles and Aunt Hilda and the whist-
players ... and Ackworth and Old Sam and the others in Canal
Street ... and the wool samples in their blue paper seemed close
to my fingers ... and somehow I could smell lilac and the bitter

scent, so long forgotten, of summer dust pitted with raindrops
... and over the ling on Broadstone Moor the larks were rising
again. When the music came to an end, which was soon enough
because they played only the one short movement—I had to
make a sharp effort, breaking out of my waking dream, to smile
at and applaud the three musicians.

But already I had recognized Lord and Lady Harndean, still
sitting there stiffly, not talking, not listening to the music (they
had never cared anything for music), but just resisting the vast
somnolence of the after-tea lounge atmosphere, still on guard.
I was astonished then that I had failed to recognise them earlier,
for now it was quite obvious, beyond any shadow of doubt,
that they were Malcolm Nixey and his wife Eleanor, who had
arrived so unexpectedly that night at the Alingtons' when we
were listening to this very movement of the Schubert trio. More
than thirty years ago, of course, and we had all changed; but
how could I have been so dense these last few days? Of course
they didn't remember; it would have been all wrong, so unlike
them, if they had remembered. There they sat, with 1913 probably not causing the least flicker in the smallest brain cell, stiff
and brittle, creatures of the Wooden Horse that we drew into
our besieged city. Malcolm and Eleanor Nixey, who descended
on us so suddenly from London, to take what they could from
us, perhaps in order that one day they should be Lord and Lady
Harndean, sitting rigidly in the Royal Ocean Hotel, Tralorna,
wondering what the devil to do with themselves.

I didn't really want to talk to them; I knew very well there
could be no genuine communication between us; yet I couldn't
resist going across and confronting them. "For days," I told
them, "I've been wondering where we'd met before. And now
I remember."

They were polite but couldn't conceal a certain blankness.
The rich have to be careful.

"My name's Gregory Dawson, and over thirty years ago we
knew each other in Bruddersford. In fact," and I turned to him,
"we worked together for a time—Hawes and Company—you
remember?"

Yes, now they remembered, and glanced at each other and

smiled reminiscently and then looked at me and gave me a nice reminiscent smile too, dead certain I would understand how faraway and quaint and absurd those Bruddersford days were. After all, I was staying at the Royal Ocean Hotel too, wasn't I, and a solid middle-aged type, eh? Well, we must meet for a cocktail or for coffee and a liqueur and have a chat about the good old days. That was the line, as I might have known it would be.

"Let me see," he said, still smiling, "you joined up, didn't you? What happened after that? You never went back to the wool business, eh?"

"No, I got a job in Fleet Street after I was demobilised in '19, and then after a few years of journalism and magazine work, I wrote a novel or two and a play, and finally landed in Hollywood."

"Ah—films, eh?"

And I saw that she rather liked the sound of that too. Young Dawson hadn't done too badly for himself, it appeared. Films were smart and there was big money in them.

"I remember now," she said slowly, with one of those flattering glances from her pretty eyes—and they were still the same pretty eyes—that immediately annihilated two world wars and all the muddle between them, "you were a clever boy and were writing even then."

"I was talking about it. Now I have to do it and not talk about it. And I must go up and do some now. I'm working rather against time on a script. See you later—perhaps."

Far more impressed now than they had been when I had first reminded them of our time together in Bruddersford, but a little uneasy, for of course they could not make up their minds about writers, who might be mere triflers but then again might be sinister magicians, they begged me to join them as soon as I felt I had a little spare time. (They were, I suspect, rather bored and lonely.) I promised that I would, and then hurried away, brisk and already busy, as if I had not found myself suddenly supporting an astonishing burden of memories, as if the past were as dead and gone to me as it clearly was to them, as if Schubert had not whispered out of the grave.

TWO

There are some advantages in being fifty and an old hand. I went upstairs to my room to work, and I did work. Bruddersford and the Alingtons and Uncle Miles and the rest might be clamouring for my attention—as indeed I knew they were—but I made them wait. The scenes I wrote were neither better nor worse than those I had done during the morning or the day before; they required rather more effort, a sharper edge of attention, that was all. But when I went down to dinner I decided that I could not spend any time talking to Malcolm and Eleanor Nixey (and I could no longer think of them as the Harndeans) without first clearing and sorting out and reassembling my recollections of that Bruddersford period. For instance, I might discover now that I had been wrong about them then. On the other hand, if I did not first try to re-live the past, if I did not meet them in Bruddersford all over again, then in an atmosphere of coffee and liqueurs and middle-aged chit-chat and social success I might easily join them in condescending to and patronising our youth and the past, might accept their values out of sheer laziness, and then that great stir and challenge of life which had come flashing out of the Schubert slow movement would have meant nothing. And I wanted it to mean something. I knew that I needed it, just as most people now needed something of the sort. I had to go back, so to speak, before I could take another step forward.

So when, after dinner, I entered the lounge, to find the Nixeys staring expectantly and Malcolm even beckoning, I went across and told them I would have to go up and do some more work. They said they were disappointed, and I believe they were. Tomorrow, perhaps?

"Y'know, Dawson," he said, after a moment's hesitation, "I don't suppose either of us had given a thought to those old Bruddersford days for years. Such a long time ago, and so much has happened since—eh? But you reminded us, of course—so we've been talking about 'em—and some things Eleanor remembers, and I've clean forgotten 'em—and some things I remember and she doesn't. Names an' all that, y'know. Interesting in a way."

"We argued about some things," she said, smiling. She was wearing black now, had obviously taken a good deal of trouble before dinner, and in spite of ruinous sagging and that heavy make-up which emphasises rather than conceals age, in that flattering golden light she still looked quite handsome and not too hopelessly unlike the Eleanor Nixey who arrived in Bruddersford. "And you might be able to tell us who's right, Mr. Dawson. Unless of course—what with Hollywood and all that—you've forgotten even more than we have."

"We'll see," I said. "I haven't thought much about Bruddersford for a long time, but I've a rather good memory. You two carry on, and then I'll try to catch up."

Somebody came to ask them if they would like some bridge, and I was able to escape. Up in my room, which was so big that you could sit in it almost without noticing that it was a bedroom, I turned on the electric fire, made myself comfortable in pyjamas, dressing-gown and slippers, sank into an arm-chair, lit a cigar, listened for a moment or two to the wind screaming at the turret and to the dragging and rolling of the tide below, and then flew back through the night and the years to Bruddersford.

There are a lot of Dawsons in the West Riding, but actually Bruddersford was not my father's native city—he came from Kent—but my mother's. Her name was Lofthouse, and she met my father—I think at Scarborough—during his first leave from India, where he was in the I.C.S. My childhood and boyhood do not come into this story—I never gave them a thought that night—so I propose to skip them, simply explaining how I came to live in Bruddersford. I was the only child, and when I was old enough to go to a public school—a very minor one—my mother spent most of her time in India with my father. During my last year at school, in fact only a few weeks before I was due to sit for a Cambridge scholarship, my father, who was extremely conscientious and very obstinate, went down with a raging temperature, and my mother, who came hurrying from the hills to nurse him, fell a victim to the same epidemic; and

within a week they were both dead. Stunned and miserable as I
was, I could not possibly sit for the Cambridge exam. I seemed
to have reached a dead end. Sometimes during the remainder
of that terrible school year I felt I had died myself and was now
merely a ghost. As we grow older we are apt to forget that the
despair of the young is even more gigantic and immediately
overwhelming than its hopefulness: we never again face such
towering blank walls of misery. Since then I have lived for weeks
in waterlogged trenches, have been machine-gunned, gassed,
bombed, have been down to my last few shillings without a
job or a friend in sight, have seen good work of mine ruined by
others and potentially better work of mine ruined by myself,
but I do not think I have ever felt so utterly wretched and hopeless as I did during those last months at school. I mention this
because of what follows, because it may partly explain what I
felt, and still feel now, about the two years in Bruddersford that
came after that time. I climbed those West Riding hills out of a
morass.

The four hands that helped me out belonged to my Uncle
Miles, my mother's only brother, and his wife, Aunt Hilda. They
had never had any children, and they were as fond of me as I
was affectionately devoted to them. It was arranged between
us that when I finally left school I should go to live with them
in Bruddersford, where of course I had stayed before. If I still
wanted to go to Cambridge, they told me, then they would see
that I went there; which meant, I knew, that the responsibility
would be chiefly theirs, for my father had left me very little. But
I had told them already that now I did not want to go to Cambridge, that it did not seem to matter any more. I knew what I
did want to do, sooner or later, and that was to write—though
I was still uncertain what kind of writing it would turn out to
be. In fact I spent more time then imagining myself a writer, of
some vague but distinguished sort, than I did making clear to
myself what I would write, which is natural enough in a young-
ster in his teens although fatal in an adult. I dropped a hint of
two of this ambition to my aunt and uncle, and they pointed out
very sensibly that they could not turn me into a writer, I would
have to turn myself into one, and that in the meantime, if I did

not want to go to a university, I might as well learn something useful and also earn a little money. So we agreed that after the holidays Uncle Miles should try to find me some sort of job in the local trade, the wool trade. And that is how I came to live in Bruddersford, to work in the office of Hawes and Company, and to know the Alingtons and their friends—and Malcolm and Eleanor Nixey.

My new home was in Brigg Terrace, in a newly built and growing suburb of North Bruddersford, between the laurel-and-monkey-tree, detached-villa grandeur of Merton Park, where the rich wool merchants and manufacturers lived, and the long, dreary, tram-haunted Wabley Road. The house was unpretentious and very snug. I was given the large back bedroom, not merely to sleep in but to use as my own place. In two little bookcases I arranged and re-arranged, with the solemnity of some royal librarian, my *Everyman* volumes and *World's Classics* and the slender rest. I peppered the walls with my photographs and uncertain but hopeful reproductions of Masterpieces of Art. A noisy little gas-fire was installed. From the attic I brought down an old desk that had belonged to my grandfather and also two lop-sided leather arm-chairs; so that now it was a sitting-room too, and I could entertain a friend there, once I had succeeded in finding one. The room was lit by two angry little gas-mantles, white and trembling with fury. I recalled the view outside my two windows: first a rather melancholy prospect of back gardens and sooty privet and clothes-lines, and of some stacks of builders' timber in a ruined field; and then to one side there was a constant sight of the vast square chimney of Higdens' giant mill, the largest chimney and the largest mill of their kind, it was said, in the world then; and on the other side, above the clustered roofs, there was an occasional hazy glimpse of the moorland sky-line. I was delighted of course to have this room, and I doubt if any room I have occupied since—although I have ranged at some expense from Amalfi to Santa Barbara, California—has ever brought me such a satisfying sense of possession as that one did. But being young and restless I spent very little time in it, except in bed; and my chief pleasure came from knowing it was there.

If the house in Brigg Terrace seemed like home almost at once, that was not only because of my rather homeless childhood but also because my uncle and my aunt gave it that quality. I was equally fond of each of them, but they were so gloriously different that it was hard to believe they were not doing it deliberately, like an artful pair of comics. Aunt Hilda had no sense of humour at all, not the least glimmer. In the house she was extremely active, almost tireless: a passionate cleaner and indefatigable tidier-up, serving some ideal of spotlessness that was far beyond the sight or comprehension of Uncle Miles and me. But she was also a really superb cook, which was something we could understand. She had one maid, a plump and snorting lass called Alice, from a miner's family down Barnsley way; and there was also a charwoman called Mrs. Spellman, who was small and skinny but had one of those shatteringly loud Bruddersford voices not capable of being modulated at all, so that her least sarcasm rang through the house, and any observations she made while scouring the front-door-steps could be heard the length of the terrace. Aunt Hilda drove these two hard, but drove herself harder still. But in company, dressed in dark rich stuffs and wearing a few ornaments that always had an odd funereal look, handsome in a pale, stricken fashion, Aunt Hilda always appeared to be recovering slowly from some terrible bereavement, and arrived at a picnic or a whist drive as if attending the reading of a will. She had good features and a square pale face, with some hint of a marble monument about it; she was always pulling down her mouth, in pity and sorrow, and so lengthening her upper lip; and she had a deep mournful voice. Her favourite talk, when she was out to enjoy herself, was all of minor ailments leading to major ones, of operations and tragic breakdowns, of dissolution and death. But she was also fond of a gossip about house property, having inherited some herself (and I suspect that it paid most of our expenses in Brigg Terrace) and following a local fashion in talk—for in those days Bruddersfordians liked to discuss house property, and two oldish men, solid citizens, might easily go for a long afternoon's walk and never talk about anything else. Aunt Hilda liked to spend a fine Sunday afternoon walking round the huge cemetery beyond

Wabley Wood (as did thousands of other Bruddersford folk), and there she could lead the talk from puzzling early symptoms to grave illness, and illness to death and burial, and burial to wills and house property.

Behind her mask of woe was an unfailing store of kindness. She was a most lavish hostess, and she kept to the good old-fashioned feminine idea that the male sex, nuisance though it might be, should always be promptly, generously, gloriously fed. At the same time she was extremely fastidious. And when I remembered this, I remembered also, after forgetting them for thirty years, the two Miss Singletons. They kept a small corner shop, a confectioner's, not far from the Merton Park end of Brigg Terrace. It was my aunt's favourite shop, representing her ideal of shopkeeping. The two Miss Singletons were timid and shrinking old maids, forever blushing as they told you they were sold out (and their little shop always appeared empty of everything but these blushes and apologies), but they were so devoted to some high fanatical ideal of baking and confection-ery, which they shared with my Aunt Hilda and a few other fastidious matrons, that they only made and sold about a tenth of what was demanded of them. They would have driven all the recent advocates of high-pressure commerce and salesmanship to despair and suicide. In their determination to sell the best, and only the best, they turned that little shop into an uncon-quered fortress of taste and integrity. And if the universe is not simply an idiotic machine, grinding out nothingness, then in some queer but cosy dimension of it my Aunt Hilda is still trot-ting round to the Miss Singletons to secure the last brown loaf and the remaining six Eccles cakes.

Sitting there in my room in the Royal Ocean Hotel, with the wind howling at the turret and the Atlantic booming below, I heard again, after so many years, Aunt Hilda's reproachful: "Now, Miles—really!" But as she said it—and of course she was always saying it—there was often just the very ghost of a twin-kle in her dark hazel eyes. I can see now that while outwardly disapproving of so much he did and said, inwardly she must have relished and applauded every self-indulgent whim and caper; and he had a plentiful supply. As a boy of course I never gave their relationship a thought; it seemed to me then one of the great stable things of the world, companion to the Pennine Range; but now that I am about the age they were then, and move among the wrecks of marriage, I realise that it must have been an unusually good and happy relationship. They bickered now and then, but I never remember even the shadow of a serious quarrel. They were perfectly complementary. The hidden and unconscious life of each one was reflected on the very face of the other. The sad responsibilities, the sick-beds, the tombstones, all so airily banished by Uncle Miles, were the essential properties of Aunt Hilda's outward life; while all the easy self-indulgence and pottering and clowning so sternly suppressed by her were jovially flaunted by him.

Uncle Miles was a large comfortable figure of a man, steadily thickening, with one of those massively handsome heads, of a type often seen among old-fashioned American politicians, that promise more than they can perform. He had a fine mop of hair and an imposing moustache, dancing blue eyes and a fine pink shining face. (I have tried every shaving gadget that our recent ingenuity has contrived, but have never succeeded in being so exquisitely clean-shaven as he was with his single old cut-throat razor.) He had a mysterious little business of his own, something to do with manufacturers' remnants, that was perfectly contrived for an unambitious man who had plenty of other interests. If Yorkshire happened to be playing at Lords or the Oval, this business could take him even as far as London, and had always had nice little journeys for him; but if he wanted a week or two in Morecambe or Filey or up in the Dales, then apparently it never suffered at all; and even when he was attending to it, he had ample time for dominoes or chess in the various smoking-rooms of the cafés near the Wool Exchange. It was an ideal business for a happy-go-lucky man whose wife had some house property. And the textile trade in Bruddersford in those days, before the first war, seemed to be able to support hundreds of these independent lucky fellows. I can see them now, in their fragrant haze of Virginia and Latakia, at their dominoes and chess, or strolling towards tram or train to watch some cricket or to try for a trout in the Wharfe. All day Uncle Miles smoked

his pipe—always Exchange Mixture from Porsons' in Market
Street, and very good it was too: I wish I had some now—but
over his toddy at night, perhaps sitting up to read W. W. Jacobs,
he liked a good cigar. But then there were a lot of things he
liked: a walk over the moors and then bilberry pie and new milk;
an afternoon in the sun with a good view of Hirst, Rhodes and
Haigh; the clarinets and flutes of a Guards' band in the park
tootling away at Delibes and Massenet; the Bruddersford Choral
Society dealing roundly with Handel; Little Tich and Robey, the
Six Brothers' Luck or Fred Karno's knockabouts at the Imperial;
roast pork and veal-and-ham pie, tea with a drop of rum in it,
then playing what was regarded as a devilishly cunning game of
whist, perhaps followed by some riotous charades; and a grand
onslaught upon the Tories by Lloyd George or Philip Snowden
or the leader writers of the *Manchester Guardian*. There was
nothing of the bitter rebel about my uncle, and no revolution
could ever have been of his making, but nevertheless he held
strong progressive views, was always ready to defend them, and
often surprised me by showing much skill and tenacity in argument. He still lived in that early optimistic Labour atmosphere,
before anybody had sold out and before the party machinery
had grown too elaborate. In those days Merrie England, with
more good cricket and W. W. Jacobs and Exchange Mixture and
roast pork and bilberry pie and June mornings in Wensleydale
for everybody, still seemed just round the corner.

Some of my uncle's and aunt's friends, who joined them
for holidays or little expeditions up in the Dales, popped in and
out of the house and assembled regularly for vast high teas and
whist, came from the chapel, the Parkside Congregational,
which my aunt and uncle attended. Others of course were
neighbours, for in those days in Bruddersford—and it may
be the same today, though it certainly is not the same today
in other cities I know—it was easy for neighbours to become
friends, and people never dreamt of living that boxed-up lonely
life which left so many suburban housewives on edge during the
1930s. Modest and informal hospitality was easy then and was
taken for granted. Hence the popping in. And though my uncle
and his friends—or at least some of them—went to concerts

and occasionally visited the theatre or the music-hall, they spent far more time than people do now amusing themselves and entertaining each other. They made their own fun instead of having it concocted for them by film and radio experts. Perhaps it is against my own interest, as one of those experts, to declare that they were better off than the passive mobs of film goers and radio listeners of today; but I feel strongly that they were; and perhaps, after all, both films and radio would soon be compelled to adopt far higher standards if their audiences still mostly made their own fun, entertained each other, and so demanded from the expert entertainers only the very best. And here, searching among my memories that night in my room at the Royal Ocean, I had to call a halt, because I realised that if I began to recollect all the rum middle-aged characters who were among my uncle's friends, I should never reach the Alingtons. If later some of them popped up, just as they used to pop in, then it could not be helped; but I told myself not to encourage them.

But I had to set myself, a lad of eighteen, squarely in Bruddersford again. Snugly installed in my back room in Brigg Terrace, on the most affectionate terms with my uncle and my aunt, coming to life again after the numbing blow of my parents' death, not yet a man but a schoolboy no longer, I looked about me and began to explore this new world of wool and mills and moorland. Lost in its smoky valley among the Pennine hills, bristling with tall mill chimneys, with its face of blackened stone, Bruddersford is generally held to be an ugly city; and so I suppose it is; but it always seemed to me to have the kind of ugliness that could be not only tolerated but often enjoyed: it was grim but not mean. And the moors were always there, and the horizon never without its promise. No Bruddersford man could be exiled from the uplands and blue air; he always had one foot on the heather; he had only to pay his tuppence on the tram and then climb for half an hour to hear the larks and curlews, to feel the old rocks warming in the sun, to see the harebells trembling in the shade. And on the days when the hills were bright in the sunlight, the streets in the centre of Bruddersford underneath their shifting canopy of smoke, seemed to me to have a curious and charming atmosphere of their own, a pecu-

liar alternation of dim gold and grey gloom; so that even now I
rarely enter a large railway station on a bright day, to find myself
in its smoke and subdued sunshine, without thinking of Bruddersford and remembering myself there, trotting to and from
Hawes's office in Canal Street. At the same time I find myself
remembering lines of verse, lines from Yeats and Housman, de
la Mare and Ralph Hodgson, just because in those Bruddersford
days such lines used to go buzzing in my mind like fat golden
bees. I pondered over these and other poets in my room, carried
their more evocative and magical lines with me through the
streets, and sometimes shouted them idiotically—startling the
sheep—on the windy moorland tracks. I am told that the poetry
that is being written these days is very fine, but somehow you
never catch a youth bellowing lines of it on a hill-top, and indeed
I never find anybody wanting to quote it at all. I suppose it is no
longer that kind of poetry. But the kind I admired in 1912 you
could mutter over and over to yourself like a magical rune or
could take out and wear like a gaily coloured scarf.

At the time when verse becomes magical to us, there is also
another sorcery, created by glimpses, brief and tantalising, of
people we do not know and at first hardly ever expect to know.
It is as if in the stone forest of the city, through which we
wander in youth, we catch sight of brilliant creatures belonging
to unknown and hitherto unimagined tribes. Later in life we
merely see interesting strangers, and that is not at all the same
thing: the mystery, the magic, the sense and promise of unex-
plored bright worlds, no longer haunt us. And I remembered
now how I was haunted during those first months in Bruddersford. From Brigg Terrace the straightest way in or out of the city
was along the rather dreary Wabley Road, where the tall trams
went swaying and groaning. There I went too; still, in spite of
my uncle and aunt and their friends, a stranger and lonely, and
choked up with that daft mixture of pride and humility which
we know best in our later teens. And there I noticed, going into
town and coming out of it, a group that varied in size, rang-
ing from three people to eight or nine, but that always had the
same group identity in my mind, and that always suggested the
mysterious and fascinating unknown tribe and hinted at a life

infinitely richer than my own. On the tram-top, on which they often rode, I would move as near them as possible; and if I saw them walking I would if necessary cross the road to share the same pavement. If they all disappeared for several days, I already began to feel that some sentence of exile, monstrous in its injustice, had been passed, and passed not against them but against me.

I was certain that one family formed the nucleus of this group, but I was not able to decide who belonged to the family and who didn't. Several times a possible father took charge of the group: a brownish, tallish man who wore no hat, dressed in old tweeds, was rather bald in front but had thick greying hair and a long humorous face. Again, a handsome quiet woman, occasionally seen, suggested a possible mother. But exactly who were their children and who their children's friends, I could not decide. There was a youth, perhaps a year or two older than I was, all thick tweeds and flowing tie and wild hair and cherrywood pipe and bellows of laughter; and I would not admit to myself that I cared much for him, although secretly I was impressed and almost humiliated by the sight and sound of him. He was always carrying a messy armful of something —it might be books or music or even provisions—and he could occupy about a quarter of a tram-top within three seconds. The others who mattered were all girls, the queens and princesses of the mysterious brilliant tribe. There was a very young untidy one, sublimely careless of appearances, who was always excited about something and had blazing green eyes. There was a smiling, downy, golden one, who was sometimes attended by a big, black-haired chap whom I envied and half-hated. Then there was a rather older girl, who had a creamy-pale face, dark brows and huge grey eyes; and it was she who once caught my glance, when I was sitting near on the tram, and gave me an amused look half in recognition, the only sign of my existence that I received from the group. But then they were tremendously absorbed in themselves and their doings. Harried by the untidy youth and the green-eyed girl, they were always on their way to some exciting event or were returning to something still better at home. The talkative members never stopped talking, often disputing passionately, and even the quiet ones seemed to exist exclusively and intensely within the aura of the group. I stared at them from the outer darkness, enraptured, wistful and open-mouthed. I knew that they lived somewhere farther along Wabley Road than the turning I took up to Brigg Terrace; but that is all I did know. I would walk that way in the hope of seeing them. Deep in the daft recesses of my being I had some sort of belief that sooner or later an extraordinary series of events, not to be imagined in detail, would land me in their hidden enchanted garden, and their front door would open—on a hall full of girls all smiling and wide-eyed—never to be closed to me again. But in that wilderness of suburban Drives and Groves I merely lost myself without once finding them. They only appeared—and always suddenly, magically—on Wabley Road. Nor could I discover who they were. I never happened to see them when I was with my aunt or uncle, and my elaborately casual questions about them in Brigg Terrace brought no result. October came, and with it a sharper smell of smoke in the streets, and I wandered down those fading Drives and Groves kicking the piles of damp sycamore leaves, for now I no longer saw the group anywhere. They might have been blue butterflies and have vanished with the sun.

"Well, Greg lad," said Uncle Miles, on one of these October afternoons, "I think I've managed it for you. Of course you'll have to go and see 'em yourself—answer a few questions and so on—but it ought to be all right."

I knew without asking that this meant a job, for he had been making enquiries about one for me since the beginning of September. I asked about it, pretending to be rather more eager and excited than I really felt. Uncle Miles was beaming and triumphant.

"It's not my end o' the trade," said my uncle, who at times took himself very seriously as a business man. "It's the wool end, not manufacturing."

"Well, I'm very glad to hear it," said Aunt Hilda. "That's where the money's made, Gregory. You can't go wrong with the raw wool—you just buy it and sell it—without even *touching* it —and make a fortune."

"I don't know so much about that," said my uncle.

"Now don't be silly, Miles. We know dozens of 'em. Fortunes! And twenty years ago some of 'em were living in cottage houses and hadn't ten pounds to call their own. Look at Harriet's husband's cousin—the one whose wife took so poorly. I remember seeing that poor woman coming out of Dr. Fawcett's—"

"Never mind about Dr. Fawcett," cried Uncle Miles, winking at me. "Greg doesn't want to know about old Fawcett—he wants to know what his job is—don't you, lad? Well, if you get it, it's with Hawes and Co., Canal Street. They're different to most o' the wool firms, Hawes and Co. are—bit more la-di-dah, which ought to suit you all right, Greg. They're really a London firm, with a branch here in Bruddersford. Raw wool, both cross-breds and merinos—and some tops and noils, and they do both a home trade and an export trade. Joe Ackworth's with them," he told my aunt, who obviously knew Mr. Ackworth. "I happened to see him this morning in Tublin's—"

"What were you doing in Tublin's this morning?" she demanded. Tublin's was a well-known grill and bar in Market Street.

"Telling Joe Ackworth about our Gregory," my uncle replied hastily. "And he's to go down there tomorrow afternoon, for an interview. Joe said it wasn't really his business—he's the wool buyer—but he thought it would be all right. I told him you knew a bit o' French and German, Greg. And that what you really wanted was to learn the business. Joe said he'd do his best for you. He'll be there—but you'll have to ask for Mr. Alington— he's really the boss so far as you're concerned. I've heard of him, but I don't know him. He's not a local man. London put him in."

"Alington?" And my aunt began searching the vast vaults of her memory. "I fancy Mrs. Rankin knows them. They live somewhere the other side of the cemetery—Wabley Wood way. I remember Mrs. Rankin telling me that Mrs. Alington had had a terrible time with one of her children—appendicitis, I think it was. I believe it was touch-and-go." She turned to me. "You'd better wear your nice blue suit tomorrow, Gregory."

"He couldn't look worse than Joe Ackworth whatever he wore," said my uncle.

"Now Miles! He's not Joe Ackworth—and he ought to look neat and tidy and make a good first impression. It's half the battle," continued my aunt, who had never been inside a wool office in her life, "making a good first impression. And don't forget Mr. Alington doesn't come from round here—he's probably one of these fancy London chaps, all dressed up for show." For Aunt Hilda, like most Bruddersford folk in those days, still thought of men from London as fantastic debauched dandies.

So the following afternoon I took the tram along Wabley Road to town, dressed up for show myself, wearing my best blue suit, a painfully high stiff collar, and one of those black silk-knitted ties that were so popular then and now seem to have disappeared. From Smithson Square I walked along to Canal Street, which was a short street running between high stone warehouses like black fortresses, in a region I had never explored before, between the grimy bulk of the Midland Station and the fatty pea soup of the canal. Great bales of wool were being hoisted from carts or were swinging out from the upper floors of the warehouses, and shouts of warning echoed down the blackening canyons of those streets. The shoes of enormous cart-horses struck sparks from the cobbles. Men wearing cloth caps and those blue-check overall coats or aprons, known locally as "brats," kept appearing and disappearing. And it was very smelly down there, with a hide-and-skin establishment producing the most appalling reek.

I found the office of Hawes and Company on a dark first floor. After some hesitation I tapped on a little opaque window labelled "Enquiries," which was flung open, to frame the red hair and giant freckles of a boy about fifteen. I told him who I was and why I was there. Then a loud angry voice, speaking in a marked Yorkshire accent, bellowed from somewhere inside: "Tell 'im to come in 'ere an' see me."

The boy opened a door and showed me into a longish narrow room that had a counter on one side, near the windows, and on the other side, reaching the high ceiling, a wall of bins or racks filled with wool samples in blue paper. Leaning against the counter was a middle-aged man with a broad blunt face, who also wore a brat and an old cloth cap, which was too small for

him and made him look like a North Country comedian. He
was sucking an empty pipe, and making grunting noises, and
scowling heavily, and appeared to be in a towering rage.

"This is him, Mr. Ackworth," said the boy.

"Ah know," Mr. Ackworth shouted. "Now you get down to
that Conditionin' 'Ouse—an' sharp about it. Go on, lad, go on."
The boy, whose red hair and freckles were even more startling
in this light, did not seem at all intimidated by this bellow. He
nodded and grinned cheerfully, tore off his brat and threw it at a
hook near the door, and went off whistling.

Mr. Ackworth now took a good look at me, and I could
remember feeling a fool, standing there in my neat blue suit and
silly high collar.

"You're the lad Miles Lofthouse was tellin' me about yes-
terda', eh?" he shouted. "What's name? Ah forget."

"Gregory Dawson," I told him, trying desperately to appear
at ease.

"Ay, of course—of course. Silly of me." He had stopped
shouting now, and had taken to muttering. His hard stare had
softened. "Ah knew yer mother, lad. Ah was in Parkside Congregational choir wi' yer mother, ower twenty-five year ago, when
Ah wor young an' daft an' thowt Ah could sing. Ah wor worst
bloody tenor they ever 'ad. Ay—Gregory Dawson. She married
a chap called Dawson, didn't she, an' went to India—eh?" He
looked me over again now. "Bit of a toff—aren't yer?"

I risked a grin with him then. "Not really. But my aunt made
me put my best clothes on."

"Ay, an' Ah'll bet she did." He made a sound that might have
been a chuckle. "Ah know 'er. Very respectable family yer aunt
belongs to, lad. Too respectable to live, some of 'em. D'yer
know owt about this trade?"

I told him candidly that I didn't.

"Well, that'll do, so long as we know. Ah meet young chaps
now down at Exchange—wi' good jobs, some of 'em—an'
they know no more about wool than I know about my wife's
fancywork. Now—what's this?" And he banged on the counter,
making a great dust, one of his samples in blue paper, and then
opened it for me.

"It's raw wool, I suppose."

"Well, yer suppose wrong," he cried, spreading the stuff out. "It's camel 'air, that is—an' mucky stuff it is an' all." He pointed to the dust and bits of dried dung. "An' that's come from some desert, that 'as, so take a good look at it. I expect yer think we know nowt 'ere in Bruddersford, but let me tell yer, lad, we go out to the ends o' the earth, an' ends o' the earth come 'ere an' all. Just remember that, lad." And then he was called to a telephone that was hanging on the wall near the door. His telephone manner was even more brutally direct. "Well, you tell your Mr. Boothroyd from me not to talk daft," he shouted down the instrument. "That's our price an' he'll not get ha'penny more. . . . Ah've 'eard that tale from you afore. You always think cross-breds is goin' up when yer've got a bag or two to sell. . . . Well, tak' it or leave it, Ah don't care." And he banged down the earpiece on its hook, then turned to me and grinned. "Tryin' it on. Their Mr. Boothroyd! Yer'll see—they'll accept our offer before afternoon's done. Now—wrap that sample up."

I made a very poor job of it, partly because I wanted to keep my suit clean, and also because there seemed to be far too much hair and dust for that amount of paper. But this failure seemed to please him.

"Yer not framin' right, lad," he shouted, and pushed me out of the way. "Now—watch me. See—press it down, then tuck it in. An' yer might as well learn 'cos yer'll 'ave plenty o' this to do if yer come an' work 'ere wi' me. An' that's the idea. Mr. Alington could put yer in t'office an' fetch out young Ellis to 'elp me, but if yer've onny sense, lad, yer'll stay out 'ere wi' me an' learn summat worth knowing."

I said that that was what I wanted to do.

"Ay," he continued, not looking pleased at all, "Ah dare say. But don't forget yer 'aven't got job yet. It's not for me to say yer can start 'ere, though Ah've put a word in for yer. Mr. Alington does all that side o' the business, an' yer'll 'ave to see 'im."

"Yes, I know. Is he in?"

"Ay, but 'e's busy for a minute. We've summat else to do 'ere, y'know, lad, besides talk to you. Now—just wait, an' Ah'll see."

He went out, not the way I had entered but through a

doorway that apparently led into an office, for I could hear a typewriter clattering away and also somebody talking on the telephone. A minute later I could hear him roaring for me to go through there, and I went into the rather small general office, where several people were working and where there were high desks and those tall stools that seem to belong to the Dickens world. Feeling rather like Nicholas Nickleby I went through this office, and joined Mr. Ackworth in the doorway of Mr. Alington's private room.

"This is 'im," Mr. Ackworth announced. "Gregory Dawson. Ah know 'is uncle, an' Ah knew 'is mother. An' 'e seems a decent sensible lad." And off he went, leaving me to face Mr. Alington alone.

"Hello!" said Mr. Alington, smiling. "Sit down there and wait a moment, will you?" And he began signing some letters.

If he had looked at me a second or two longer, he might have concluded that I was half-witted. I was staring at him open-mouthed. I was—as they like to say in Bruddersford—flabbergasted. It was like opening an office door and finding King Priam or Merlin sitting at a desk. This Mr. Alington was the brownish, tallish man, the possible Father, I had seen several times with the magic group.

He looked up from his letters and his long and rather leathery face crinkled into a grin. "Seen me before?"

"Yes, sir," I stammered.

"You were looking as if you had." He grinned again, to show that this was merely a little joke between us. "Shan't be more than half a minute now."

He looked far more like a free-and-easy schoolmaster than a man in the wool business. His baldness in front, framed as it was by thick crisp hair rather like shavings of dark pewter, gave him an immense professorial forehead. He had thick eyebrows too, and rather sunken eyes of a greenish-brown colour, which lit up wonderfully. (I decided that he must be the father of the girl with the blazing green eyes.) He had not much of a nose, and what made his face long and humorous were his upper lip and a long narrow chin. There was a bit of the actor—the serious-Shakespearean-Benson kind—mixed with the schoolmaster in his appearance. Perhaps a dash of the poet too—or was it the painter? I could see that he was wearing an old Harris tweed jacket, a grey woollen shirt, and a faded green poplin tie. No neat blue suit and high collar here. I wanted to tell him that I did not always look like this.

"Where have we met?" he was asking. Apparently he had finished with his letters now.

I told him, hesitantly, that I had seen him on the Wabley Road tram.

"All talking our heads off, eh? My family's apt to behave as if it owned any tram it rides in, especially my boy and the youngest girl."

"Has she got green eyes and is she always excited?"

He laughed. "That's Bridget. You've been keeping your eyes open, Dawson."

"I couldn't help noticing those girls, sir. There are two others, both very pretty—one fair and the other dark."

"Well, for your information, the dark one's called Joan and the fair one Eva." Now he broke off, stopped smiling and pulled down his heavy brows, alarming me for a moment, until I realised that his scowl had a touch of burlesque about it. "Look here, young fella, I didn't ask you in to talk about my family. If you want to come and work for us, then you must answer *my* questions. That's right, isn't it? Though I suppose I ought to answer some of yours too—eh? Now—let's see."

So I spent the next few minutes telling him about myself. Once I had recovered from my first surprise and shyness, I found him very easy to talk to. He did not try to stand on his dignity and was not patronising and not self-conscious, and I liked him. He tested my arithmetic, and I translated some French and floundered through a little German for him; and it all went very well.

"All right, Dawson," he said, regarding me thoughtfully. "You can join us as soon as you like. We'll pay you a pound a week, which is as much as you can expect at first. Now you can either start in the office or you can go into the sample-room and help Mr. Ackworth. He needs somebody—and Ellis, I believe, would rather stay in the office. Now you've had some talk with Mr.

Ackworth, who's our wool buyer—and a very good one too. Do you think you could get along with him?"

I said that I thought I could, as indeed I did, because I had guessed from the first that Mr. Ackworth's loud voice and angry manner were merely part of his performance as a rich Bruddersford character.

"Then you're wiser than young Ellis," said Mr. Alington, smiling. "You'll learn far more with Mr. Ackworth—and find it more amusing too. But he'll make you work, y'know, Dawson —and what's your other name? Gregory?—and sometimes you'll have to work late for him on the samples. It's greasy work too—so don't forget to provide yourself with two or three over-alls—brats. Nine in the morning then—and your department is the sample-room, Gregory."

Then, just as I was going out, he said: "By the way, any special interests—hobbies—enthusiasms?"

"Well, sir, I try to write a little—"

"Verse or prose?"

"Well—both. And I read a lot. And walk. And I like music—"

His face lit up. "Good boy, good boy! I like all those things too, except that I don't try to write—dropped that years ago. I think we'll suit each other. The last youth, who left us a week or two ago, cared for nothing but collecting stamps—a silly, old man's game—and it always worried me. Off you go, Gregory —and you might tell Mr. Ackworth he's got a new assistant."

I do not know if I would have remembered what I said then to Ackworth or, what would certainly be more entertaining, what Ackworth said to me, but at that very moment when I was recalling how I went through the general office on my way back to the sampling-room, the telephone bell rang in my room at the Royal Ocean Hotel, to drop thirty-odd years on my back, and I was told there was a call from London. It was Brent of course.

"How's it going, Greg?" he began.

I told him I had just done a good day's work on the script and didn't see why I shouldn't have another good day tomorrow.

"Don't bet on it," he said drily. "Elizabeth arrived today, two weeks earlier than we expected." This was Elizabeth Earl,

whom we were bringing over from Hollywood, where she was
now among the top-ranking eight, to star in *The Lady Hits Back*.
"She wanted to talk to you tonight—she says you're old friends
—but I told her to get to bed—the air trip had shaken her up a
bit. But the point is this—she insists upon coming down to see
you tomorrow—says she wants to talk script and doesn't want
to be seen around town for a few days—and as I can't get away,
Adony, who's feeling restless, is coming down with her. And I'm
sending Jake along too." Jake West was Brent's publicity man.
"They'll be in about tea-time, and the office has fixed up about
their rooms with the hotel, so you've nothing to do. Except that
if you're the old sweetie she says you are, just keep her pleased
and contented. She seems a bit touchy—that may have been the
trip, of course; she's not supposed to be difficult. But I have a
grim idea that she and George Adony aren't going to like each
other."

"I don't think they will," I told him. "But I wish they wouldn't
come down here to start disliking each other. In fact, I wish they
weren't coming, any of 'em. But I suppose there's nothing to be
done about that now."

"Not a single dam' thing, Greg," he said. "What were you
doing when I called you? Drinking? Thinking? Or both?"

"Just thinking. About my past."

"Does Elizabeth come into it? She sounded as if she might."

"No, of course she doesn't. She was only just toddling at the
time that I was busy remembering. I was back before the first
war. 1912, to be exact. I'm getting on, y'know, Brent."

"You won't think so tomorrow night, Greg." He chuckled.
"Wait till you see Elizabeth again. Not my type of course—
but she really is something to look at. Well—keep everything
smooth and happy down there."

For a moment or two I experienced that feeling of loneliness
and sadness which comes immediately after a long-distance call
from somebody you know very well. Although it was fairly late,
I was tempted to pull on some clothes and go below for a drink
and a chat. I resisted the temptation by giving myself something
else to do, first cleaning a pipe and then opening a new tin of
tobacco—and opening a new tin of tobacco is one of the lasting

small pleasures of life. Then I returned to my big arm-chair, refused to give a single thought to Elizabeth Earl and George Adony and to what might happen the next day; and after a few minutes of confused recollections, I picked my way back across the years to Canal Street and Brigg Terrace.

THREE

Once you settle down deliberately to remember, it is surprising how much comes back, some of it in the sharpest detail. But of course not all of it comes back. For instance, I remembered that that red-haired and hugely freckled office-boy at Hawes's was called, most unsuitably, Bernard, but I could not bring back his surname. It was the same with the fair plump typist, who wore eyeglasses, often misty with tears, and was engaged in a dreary damp sort of way to an oldish science-master in Wakefield: I can only remember her as Bertha. The other people in the office there were Harold Ellis, only a year or two older than I was, and the cashier, Croxton. Ellis may have had a passionate life of his own outside the office—he was, I believe, attracting favourable notice in local photographic circles—but in the office he always seemed to me so dim that he was hardly real. Croxton was real, and was in fact the only person at Hawes's whom I disliked. He was a middle-aged bachelor, carefully dressed, who had a long nose and a pointed moustache, and who took so much trouble not to speak with the local accent that he achieved something quite elaborately false. He was quite an able man, being a good linguist and a very neat quick worker, but behind his elaborate false accent and pompous manner there was something rat-like and scurrying: he was the type that, thirty years later in other places, inevitably turned into collaborators and Quisling stooges. He disliked me from the first, chiefly because he had not been consulted when I had been given my job there. A born intriguer himself, he believed, I think, that I had been brought in by Joe Ackworth, of whom he was jealous, to act as a kind of spy.

Fortunately I had very little to do with the office, for I was out in the sample-room, working under Mr. Ackworth. When I was not in the sample-room or running round the town, collecting or delivering samples, I was upstairs in the warehouse, which

occupied the rest of the building. The head warehouseman
was a rum character always known as Old Sam. He had been
a sergeant in the army at one time, knew his Africa and India,
and had something wrong with one hand, on which he always
wore a glove. His eyes were odd, and represented the two sides
of his character, for one eye was fixed and glaring, a military eye,
while the other, which had quite an independent existence, was
restless and twinkling and friendly. According to his mood, you
seemed to see more of one eye than the other. He and that other
character, Joe Ackworth, frequently clashed, and then they
stood only about a yard from each other and bellowed at the top
of their formidable voices. About twice a month Old Sam got
very drunk, usually on a Friday night, and then the next morning he would be late, would have a black eye or a bruised cheek,
and would be very stiff and military and remote in manner. He
was an enthusiastic Free Thinker, and during his dinner-hour or
when there was nothing to do in the warehouse, he would sit
in his greasy cubbyhole at the back and slowly spell out, with
many a chuckle, his favourite passages from the rationalist
classics. Sometimes when I was up there, waiting with him for
some load to be delivered, we had friendly but unsatisfactory
arguments about God and the churches and the parsons. He
talked a lot of rot, but then, I imagine, so did I. His favourite
and over-worked phrase was: "Stands to reason," and the wilder
his statements were, the more they stood to reason. He shared
my dislike of Croxton, who was always trying to interfere in
warehouse matters; and although he sometimes argued with
and shouted at Joe Ackworth, I soon discovered that, like me,
Old Sam thoroughly enjoyed him.

The secret of Joe Ackworth, whom I soon came to like enormously, was that he played for all it was worth, day and night, a
character part. This character performance, almost always on
identical lines, was common then among a certain class of Bruddersford wool men. Often they were men whose work took
them away a good deal, for Bruddersford men went all over the
world then; and they must have decided that if they could not be
cosmopolitan then they would be as aggressively provincial as
possible, and would deliberately exaggerate every West Riding

trait, broadening their accent, often assuming a brutal insensi-
tiveness and pugnacity, and pretending they cared about nothing but money and eating and drinking and fat cigars. (W. H.
Hudson somewhere describes meeting one of them, who, he
discovered to his surprise, came every year to a certain place to
listen to the nightingales.) Joe Ackworth was this type. Behind
his bellowing and blustering, he was far more sensitive, far more
aware of other people's feelings, than the genteel and mincing
Croxton. He had a passion, among other things, for roses,
which flourished in the heavy clay soil of Bruddersford; and he
spent a great deal of his spare time and money growing roses,
and experimenting with new varieties, and every year he sent
a selection of them to the famous Saltaire Rose Show. He was
also, as I found out soon to my astonishment, a knowledgeable
reader, especially of history and solid fiction; and it was he who
lent me Mrs. Garnett's translations of the great Russian novel-
ists. "Summat to get yer teeth into 'ere, lad," he said of them.
"They wrote about life, them chaps did—an' no bloody fairy
tales for schoolkids. Ah went to Russia one time—just the once,
that's all—an' if ever they get properly started an' get rid o' their
Grand Dukes an' suchlike—they'll mak' some of us sit up, Rus-
sians will. You mark my words, lad." And I did, and remembered
his prophecy afterwards.

Mr. Alington understood and appreciated Joe Ackworth, and
although now and again they disagreed violently—and once
or twice I caught sight of Mr. Alington white with temper and
Joe purple with genuine fury—they made a good team, each
realising that there were things better left to the other man.
Ackworth, who was not only our buyer but a salesman too,
would have nothing to do with our foreign customers and some
of the grander ones at home: he left them to the easier and
more graceful methods of Mr. Alington, who for his part acted
on the sensible theory that Joe could handle most of the local
men better than he could. Mr. Alington of course was often in
and out of the sample-room and the warehouse—though he
frequently went to London to the head office, and sometimes
made a hasty short visit to the Continent—but although I saw
him often, and he was always easy and friendly, I was for some

time disappointed and secretly rather miserable because I felt I had made no real progress with him, and none towards that enchanted group of his, since the first wonderful afternoon. I never saw him outside Canal Street, and during those early weeks he never said another word about his family. All this was reasonable enough, but it was an anti-climax after that first miraculous encounter, which promised more than what was reasonable. And now that I saw him every day, on pleasant but rather disenchanting terms, solidly stuffed with wool samples, somehow I never caught sight of the group or any individual members of it. I felt obscurely that this was Mr. Alington's fault, as if he had made the promised magic stop working, and I was now inclined to think less of him than I did of Mr. Ackworth, who incidentally had a high opinion of Mr. Alington, a very high opinion indeed when one remembers that Mr. Alington was not a Bruddersford man but came from the flimsy and treacherous South.

But in this slightly disappointed and vaguely disenchanted fashion, I was beginning to settle down in Bruddersford. I called at the Central Free Library, which was not far away from Canal Street, and brought away volumes of Wells and Bennett, Chesterton and Shaw, Yeats and George Moore, all in the same dark thick binding. I hunted for cheap secondhand books in the covered Market. I ate rather meagre and fancy meals in vaguely oriental cafés, all beads and bamboo, and enjoyed much cheaper and larger meals in the Market and elsewhere, sitting in wooden pews and polishing off vast helpings of meat-and-potato pie or fried hake or cod. I attended readings by the Bruddersford Playgoers' Society, where I made a few friends and felt the faint stirrings of passion for a good-looking schoolteacher, ten years my senior and hardly aware of my existence. I bought tickets for the monthly concerts of the Musical Society in the enormous Gladstone Hall, where the Halle Orchestra thundered Beethoven and Brahms at us; and also patronised—and the word is carefully chosen—the occasional Saturday night concerts of the Bruddersford Symphony Orchestra, which had two of the chanciest French horns I have ever listened to, so uncertain, so mournfully dubious and fearing, that the whole audience

would breathe a loud sigh of relief when they reached the end
of any solo passage. And sometimes in company with my Uncle
Miles, given a night off by Aunt Hilda, I would go to the second
"house" of the Imperial Music-Hall, where in our worn plush
seats in the dress circle, price one-and-sixpence, we would listen
to Little Tich and George Robey, Vesta Tilley and Maidie Scott
(a deliciously saucy comedienne), Jack and Evelyn (and he was
a superb improvising droll), and a glorious comic with a round
face and an impossible moustache and an indescribably ridiculous manner, one of the best comics I ever saw, who drank hard
and died young, called Jimmy Learmouth. We used to read of
what seemed to us the fantastic salaries paid to these variety
stars—a hundred pounds a week!—and little did I realise then,
or even wildly dream, that the time would come when I would
work for and be thoroughly acquainted with players who would
receive more than ten times those salaries and yet not possess
one-tenth of the talent. Thus we progress. Looking back soberly
at those music-hall shows, and making every allowance for my
youth and for the infectious enjoyment of Uncle Miles, I see now
that in those noisy smoky halls, with their brassy orchestras,
their plush and tarnished gilt, their crudely coloured spotlights
raying down from the gallery, we were basking in the brilliant
Indian Summer of a popular art, a unique folk art that sprang
out of the gusto and irony, the sense of pathos and the illimitable humour of the English industrial people, braving it out in
their mills and foundries and dingy crowded towns; an art that
flourished, withered and decayed well within a man's lifetime,
but that, before it lost all vitality, scattered its seeds, its precious
seeds of rich warm humanity, all over the darkening world, and
sent an obscure droll called Chaplin as far as California so that
his flickering image could go out to conquer the earth.

With work to do, a home to go back to, and so much that was
new to enjoy, I ought to have been more than content during
those first months in Bruddersford. But I wanted then—as I
suppose I have always wanted since—that little more which is
everything, that touch of the miraculous and the magical which
enables us to lose sight of, to forget and ignore, the machinery
of living, the ledgers of pleasure and boredom. (All of which

means, I take it, that I am essentially a romantic.) Where was the group and the mysterious bright world it promised? The still, misty-smoky mornings of autumn vanished with the damp dead leaves, and now it was winter and black rain fell on Wabley Road and in Canal Street and Smithson Square, where I often ran with my bundles of samples to the Post Office, and on clear mornings the distant hills were powdered with snow. In Brigg Terrace the whist-drive season had set in, and there was a great buying of little cards with pencils attached, of First Prizes and Booby Prizes, and Aunt Hilda and her friends were baking rich pound cakes and pouring sherry into the trifle. The chapels were advertising their performances, earlier each year, of Handel's *Messiah*. Cotton-wool snowflakes and imitation holly in the shop windows were already hinting at Christmas. "Mr. Puff" of the *Bruddersford Evening Express*, in his theatrical column, was beginning to mention possible famous Principal Boys and comics for the Annual Grand Pantomime of the Theatre Royal. And then, as suddenly and unexpectedly as if an invisible demi-god had pulled a string, my real Bruddersford history began.

It started, I remembered, with a modest little prologue. Rather late one afternoon, when Bernard the office-boy was out and I was attending to the door, I heard somebody come in, and I went out at once because we were waiting for some samples. It was a girl, and I recognised her immediately as the girl who had glanced at me once, half in recognition, on the tram-top, the one with the pale face, dark brows and large grey eyes, and therefore the Alington daughter called Joan.

"Is my father in—Mr. Alington?" she asked, rather hesitantly and not really looking at me.

"Well—no—he isn't just now," I told her, very apologetically as if it might almost be my fault. "But I don't think he'll be long," I continued, although actually I didn't know where he was or how long he would be. "Wouldn't you like to wait in his room?"

She hesitated a moment and then said she would wait, and though she must have known the way as well as a did, I insisted upon taking her through into Mr. Alington's private office. In there she had a good look at me—she had a grave level candid glance that was infinitely more impressive than her speech—

and I could distinctly remember that I felt myself blushing in front of it.

"Are you Gregory Dawson?" she asked.

There came to me then, like a great blue diamond, one of those moments of pure happiness. I really existed; and the magic group knew that I really existed. Nevertheless, when I admitted that I was Gregory Dawson, I did it in a stumbling and shame-faced fashion.

"I'm Joan Alington," she told me, all calm and clear and huge dark-fringed grey eyes. "I've seen you once or twice on the tram, haven't I?"

"Yes." I hesitated a moment, then took courage. "I used to wonder who you all were. I expect I stared a bit."

"Yes, you did." And she smiled. "I don't blame you. We make such a row, don't we?"

"It wasn't that," I said. "It was because you looked—interesting." And I trotted out that miserable word rather apologetically.

"I'm not," she said, sincerely and seriously and with no mock modesty about it, "at least—not very. But some of the others are." Together and in silence we contemplated the superb interestingness of these others for half a minute or so. Then she took my breath away by remarking: "My father says you want to be a writer. What are you writing?"

The fact that Mr. Alington had actually told his family that I wanted to be a writer was wonderful. But the question she had tacked on to that statement was a desperate one. At eighteen, unless you are a prodigy, you are writing everything—and nothing. Just round the corner, waiting until you have a little spare time, are epic poems (the Fall of Atlantis was my favourite theme), five-act dramas in blank verse, huge satirical prose works; but it is hard to explain how near they are and how certain you are of them, when all you have to show, if called upon to offer evidence, are a few notes and disgustingly unsuccessful beginnings. So I felt—and no doubt looked—embarrassed, and muttered something about writing poems and essays.

Noticing my embarrassment, she changed the subject and said she had heard I liked music. Did I attend the Musical Society's concerts? They all did, but for one reason and another they had missed the last two. "But we're all going to the one next Friday," she continued. "Are you going? Well, we shall see you there. We all sit in the front row of the West Gallery. Dad says that's the very best place for hearing."

If Mr. Alington didn't arrive at that very moment, he came in soon afterwards; and I went back to my samples. It was now merely a matter of existing somehow or other until the following Friday. I knew then, I think that this was the real beginning; or at any rate I realised that Friday night would decide whether I joined the magic group or remained for ever outside it. For the next few days, I squeezed the wool into its blue paper, wrote quantities and prices on the slippery little sample tickets, jumped on and off trams and walked the wet streets, all in a vague dream.

Gladstone Hall was nothing to look at—it was a square ugly building seating about four thousand people—but it made a fine concert hall, and its acoustics, especially in the great gallery, were magnificent. My ticket, which worked out at ninepence a concert, was for one of the Side Galleries, the North Gallery. Unlike the superior people in the West Gallery, we had no reserved and numbered seats, so I took care to be one of the first to charge up the long gaslit flights of stone steps, and I found a place on the front row towards the centre, and therefore with a good view of the front row of the West Gallery. It was a Halle Orchestra concert, and I could remember the very programme: Prelude to the Third Act of the *Meistersingers;* Strauss's *Don Quixote* tone poem; and Brahms's *Fourth Symphony.* In those days Gladstone Hall had electric lighting round the walls and in the corridors but still kept its enormous gas chandelier, which was like a vast swarming of luminous and twinkling bees above our heads, and brought to the great auditorium that cosy golden mistiness, that October glow, which vanished from our stages with gas lighting. Before the oboe, far below, had plaintively signalled its tuning note to the other instruments, I was staring across a few yards of this golden mistiness at the Alington group, which was assembled in full force, so full indeed that I was not quite sure where the group began or ended. Mr. Alington was there, and the handsome woman who might be Mrs.

Alington. There was a bright cluster of girls—Joan, Bridget
(bouncing with excitement) and the smiling sleepy Eva, and two
other girls I did not know. Mr. Alington's son, the tweedy untidy
youth, was there, also the big black-haired chap I did not like,
and another man, whom I had seen at the Playgoers' Society,
a tall, bony but powerful man with greying hair and a brown
face, a man who always looked cool and amused. Yes, it was the
group most formidably arrayed, with a hundred orchestral players below tuning up, and Brahms, Wagner and Richard Strauss
waiting in the wings, so to speak, to heighten the magic. Joan
saw and recognised me, smiled and waved, and then obviously
mentioned me to her father, who also smiled and waved; and
several of the others looked my way. I experienced that feeling
—common in childhood, rarer in youth and almost unknown
later in life, at least among men—of cosy enchantment, that
sense of having snugly to hand, under the same protecting roof,
almost all this earth's most precious persons and things; which is
the secret of a child's Christmas.

The themes of the *Meistersingers* majestically entwined
themselves. The huge glittering orchestra of Strauss brought
us the windmills and the sheep and the bewildered comments
of Sancho, if not the soul of Don Quixote; although I have an
idea that I was too busy watching and wondering about the man
with the wind machine, on that occasion, to take in much of
the music. The interval came, and as no smoking was allowed
in the auditorium, the smokers departed, with the orchestra, to
light their pipes in the corridors. Through the blue haze behind
the West Gallery I saw the long dramatic face of Mr. Alington
grinning at me.

"Hello, Gregory. Enjoying yourself? Oliver, this is Gregory
Dawson, who works with me. Oliver's just come home from
Cambridge." This was of course the untidy tweedy youth, now
puffing away at an immense cherrywood pipe. Cambridge too.
I was deeply impressed and rather shy. Fortunately he was glow-
ing with enthusiasm and full of loud undergraduate talk.

"I heard Nikisch do the Strauss," he shouted at us. "Much
better. More guts. More tangle and tingle. More *diablerie*.
Nikisch is full of *diablerie*. But what I'm waiting for now, souls,

is the Brahms. That scherzo! Tum-tum-tum-tum-tah-da. That's the stuff. Shlumpumpitter!"

He fairly bellowed this last mysterious word. "What?" I cried, bewildered and startled.

"The whole thing," he bellowed. "Shlumpumpitter!"

"Don't worry, Gregory," said his father. "That doesn't mean anything. It's just a noise he makes at these times. You haven't to mind him. Now then—this is Ben Kerry—and this is Jock Barniston."

Ben Kerry was the big black-haired chap, and now I noticed that he had those sulky smouldering good looks that most women like and that I didn't like then and have never liked since. Jock Barniston was the powerful, bony, cool and amused man. He said nothing but twinkled at me in a friendly fashion. Kerry was not unfriendly but somehow gave me the impression that I didn't amount to much. He brought me down to earth with a rush.

But Mr. Alington took me into the blue again. "Let's see, Gregory—don't you live in our part of the world? Well then, come and have some coffee and cake with us after the concert. It won't be late, and we always like to simmer down in company."

"The cake's not bad," said Oliver. "In fact, it's jolly good. But the coffee's muck, I warn you. They simply don't know how to make it. Too much water."

"That's because we don't want to be awake all night," said his father. "At least I don't, even if you do. This isn't Cambridge. And we've got work to do tomorrow morning, haven't we, Gregory?"

"The orchestra's in," Kerry told us, moving off.

"I'll meet you at the tram, Mr. Alington," I said eagerly.

"I'll look out for you," shouted Oliver. "Shlumpumpitter!"

I had just time to hurry back to my seat before the strings went swaying into the first movement of the Brahms, calling and answering each other with those beautiful short phrases, like exquisite voices heard suddenly in a strange house. But I doubt if I did that noble work even the barest justice that night, for I was impatient to be travelling on the tram with the group, no longer staring at them from the outside but now one of them.

Actually it was not late when the concert was over, for in those days our concerts began early, and at half-past nine we were all in Smithson Square waiting for our tram. By this time I had been introduced to Bridget and Eva and had discovered that the handsome quiet woman was indeed their mother, Mrs. Alington. The other two girls and Kerry and Barniston were still with us, and I shared a seat on the tram-top, several seats away from any of the others, with Jock Barniston. Within a minute or two, while the tram was still groaning on its way up to Wabley Road, I had realised that his look of cool amusement did not mean that he was supercilious or patronising. It was indeed a fortunate chance that landed me next to Jock Barniston on the way out to the Alingtons', that first time. He was years older than I was —he must have been about forty—but he talked to me as if he were the same age and weight; and he asked me some friendly questions and tried to put me at my ease at once, guessing that I was feeling both shy and excited. As the journey lasted nearly half an hour there was time for him to answer some of my questions too; and I learned from him, among other things, that the green-eyed Bridget was seriously studying the violin and that the other two girls were musical friends of hers, and that Ben Kerry, who was the brightest young man on the *Bruddersford* Evening Express and ready for Fleet Street, was half engaged to Eva Alington. He also told me that I was not to be afraid of Mrs. Alington, who often gave strangers a wrong impression, simply because she was shy and reserved, in sharp contrast to most of her family, and often withdrew herself, possibly suggesting that she was cold and unfriendly, because she was not robust and could not squander her energy as the others did.

Here at this point, though it broke the thread of my recollection, I could not help stopping to think about Jock Barniston. He was one of those very rare persons—and we probably do not meet more than three or four in a lifetime—who do little or nothing of any consequence, make no effort to attract attention, seem content with the commonplace, and yet leave with everybody who knows them an enduring impression of integrity and strength, of vast unused powers, of carelessly veiled greatness. In India Jock Barniston would probably have been regarded as an adept of *Karma-Yoga*, perhaps as one who rested easily between two strenuous and glorious lives, merely going through a routine of living for one incarnation. There was nothing eccentric about his way of life: he had a partnership in a small estate agency, was looked after by an elder sister, and lived frugally in a bachelor fashion; he had many women friends but no love affairs, yet showed no sign of any emotional attachment to the men he knew. Once, roused by a strike—a year or two before I went to Bruddersford—he had made the finest speech the town ever remembered hearing. And several letters he sent to the local press suggested that he could have been a first-class journalist. He had refused constituencies, important jobs, all manner of tempting offers; what he never refused were the appeals instinctively made to him by all kinds of people in deep trouble; and if you knew him at all then he was the man you turned to at once. Through it all he remained cool and amused yet friendly, like a well-wisher sent to us from some other and nobler planet. On any commonsense view of this life he was not to be explained at all, and to this day, though I, like many others, remember him with affection, he remains to me a mystery. In August, 1914, he joined a local territorial battalion, was made a corporal and insisted upon staying a corporal, moved about the trenches as if they were a mere extension of Market Street, and was killed on the Somme in 1916. He was awarded a posthumous V.C., and even this seemed to his battalion, who felt lost without him, the merest slight token of a recognition. And perhaps he knew already, when he was talking to me on the tram in December of 1912, that before the next four years were out, that body which he had put on like an overcoat to wear among us would be so much bleeding meat in a sandbag; and this knowledge may have made him look even more cool and amused. He was an enigma, this heroic emperor in disguise; I think he came from a long way off, to drink beer and coffee with us, to smoke a pipe and hear our troubles, to vanish in the slaughter-house of the First World War, and then perhaps to make some cool and amused report on us to some authority outside the solar system. Here I told myself not to be fanciful; but what solidly remained of Jock Barniston, agreed upon by all who knew him—his strange detachment, his flashes of power, his sense of stature and majesty behind the veil—was mystery enough. And this was the man who paid my first tramfare to the Alingtons'.

Dark as it was when we arrived, I recognised the house, a square detached villa, as one I had passed several times during my earlier wanderings down there in search of the group. This made me feel that although I had clearly gained something, I had also lost something: it was the self of two or three months before, completely bewitched, who ought to have been turning in through that stone gateway. Still, I was sufficiently excited and happy. The house was of course considerably larger than ours in Brigg Terrace; and its whole atmosphere was different. It was far less tidy, by no means speckless, and you knew at once that a lot of careless busy people, mostly young, lived in it, and that still more people were always coming and going there; and that the details of comfort and convenience might not be attended to, but they did not much matter there; you realised at once that it was a home and not merely a house, and a home of a kind too for more people than the ones who lived in it. I didn't know what would happen to me there; I might have been made miserable within the next hour; yet somehow I knew at once that I would be going there often, as those two girls and Ben Kerry and Jock Barniston obviously did. Behind the feeling that all this was new and strange was a mysterious conviction that I had at last arrived where I belonged.

We found our way into a large room on the left of the hall, a room with a grand piano, some crowded open bookshelves, and well-used odds and ends of furniture. Sitting over a book near the fire was a boy about fourteen. This was the youngest of the Alingtons, David; and he had hair like his father's and wide and rather luminous grey eyes like his mother's. There was nothing of the embarrassed schoolboy about him. He had a direct and rather precise manner, as if he had already made up his mind about most things; which suggests that he was an insufferable kid, whereas he was nothing of the sort. In fact, I liked him, although I could not have explained why I did.

"Have you been to the concert too?" he asked me.

"Yes. You weren't there, were you?"

"No. I could have gone, but I don't like those concerts—too big and noisy—too much row. The band banging away, and then everybody clapping like mad, just to make a row too. I've been reading about astronomy. Do you know anything about astronomy?"

"No, not much. I've started reading books about astronomy with great enthusiasm, but as soon as they go into details I get bored."

He nodded. "This man says there can't be life anywhere but on the Earth. That seems silly to me. I don't see why there shouldn't be creatures on other planets arguing that there can't be life here. Do you like H. G. Wells?"

I replied truthfully that I did. For that matter, I still do.

"So do I," he said. "Not the ones about love and politics and stuff—but the others. Bridget says he's too frightening. She says she always feels that he's really on the side of the other creatures and would rather have monsters from Mars and the moon than ordinary people—but I think she's wrong there. He's just rather bad-tempered, that's all. I think it would be better if he was a bit calmer and not so impatient." And he looked at me like a little mandarin. "What do you do?"

I told him I worked for his father at Hawes and Company, and that I hadn't been there very long.

"He thinks I ought to go into that business. He's not desperately keen, y'know, like fathers in novels, but he thinks it might be a good idea, specially as Oliver refuses to have anything to do with it. Oliver hates regular hours. He likes to work like mad, day and night, and then not do anything for weeks, just hang about, and that's no good for business—is it? I'm not like that, but I don't want just to buy things and then sell them—that seems to me a silly way of spending your time." Now he lowered his voice a little. "Dad thinks so too, though sometimes he pretends he doesn't."

"Have some cake, you two?" This was Joan Alington, who smiled at me as if we were old friends now. "You ought to be going to bed now, y'know, David."

"Yes," said David calmly. "I'll go when I've eaten this." He looked at me. "You ought to go and talk to some of the others now. I must warn you that both those girls Bridget has brought in are rather idiotic, especially the fat dark one."

The one he meant was called Dorothy Sawley, and, a few minutes later, after having exchanged some remarks with her, I was ready to agree with David about her. She was not fat but she was plump, with a round flushed face and lips that were too thick and too wet. Bridget brought her in because she was rather a good 'cellist. There are some people who always seem to remain staring and guffawing foreign peasants, and Dorothy Sawley was always to me one of these people. Something about me—and I never discovered what it was—made her giggle; and to the end she giggled, and to this day may be giggling somewhere at the last faint memory of me. The other girl, whose name was Wilson, was small, foxy and serious; and she played the piano, I gathered, although she did not have much chance of playing at the Alington's because Mr. Alington himself also played the piano in an enthusiastic sketchy fashion. I talked to both these girls for a few minutes until the coffee arrived with Mrs. Alington and Eva and Bridget.

If Jock Barniston had not warned me about Mrs. Alington, I would certainly have felt I was unwelcome there and would probably have gone early, never to return. Her handsome clear-eyed fairness was faintly frosted over; she had a tiny impersonal smile that did not help at all; and a rather cold and precise way of speaking, not unlike David's but far more intimidating just because she was a woman and the hostess.

"My husband told us about you," she said, after handing me my coffee. "He's interested in everybody in the office. And the children are always asking him questions too. Do you like being in Bruddersford?"

I said that I did, although I didn't know many people yet. No doubt my manner hinted that it would be a great treat for everybody once I did know more people. At any rate her smile suggested something of the kind.

"I didn't like it here at first," she said. "It seemed so cold and harsh, and I thought people were unfriendly. But now it seems different. You haven't any sugar. Eva—you have the sugar."

So now I was faced with Eva, who brought the sugar and with it the colossal candied plum of her own looks. Here at home she was still the same golden, downy, smiling creature I had gaped at on the tram. Background made no difference to Eva, as it did most emphatically to Bridget Alington, who could look plain in one place and almost radiantly beautiful in another. Eva seemed to exist in a transparent envelope, protecting her against all outside weather and influences, and through which you peered at her in her unbroken, sunny, sleepy afternoon. It was not, however, an indestructible envelope, as we were to discover; and even then, right at the first, dazzled and beglamoured as I was by her shining looks, I believe I felt in a vague and melancholy fashion that behind that untroubled blue gaze, that smooth wide forehead and smiling mouth, that languid voice, was a spirit too weak, too passive, what we should now call defeatist, a spirit very different from that of the younger and harder Bridget, who now joined us.

"Do you play or sing?" Eva was asking me.

"No, not really," I told her, convinced that nothing I could ever hope to do for years would ever interest her in me. "Do you?" I asked. And if she had turned away without troubling to answer me, I should not have been much surprised.

But she did answer me. "Well, I sing a little, but I'm not very much good. Am I, Bridget?"

"No, you're not," said Bridget, quite seriously. Then she looked hard at me. Her eyes really were greenish, even when seen so close. She was a little younger than I was, perhaps only a few months, but definitely younger in manner, still with something of the fierce sincerity of the child about her; and obviously if you were her kind of person then she challenged you at once to be completely honest, with no grown-up shuffling and faking. This I sensed at once, so that I was as impressed by her, and as much reduced in my own estimation of myself, as I had been a minute or two before by Eva. Between them, I think, they turned me into a stammering midget.

"You write things, don't you?" said Bridget, taking me in. "Do you read them to people then?"

"No, I don't," I mumbled. "At least, I haven't done so far."

Probably chaps were always reading their stuff here: Ben Kerry
might start at any moment. So I was apologetic.

"A jolly good job too," said Bridget.

Eva laughed, a slow lazy laugh that didn't really seem to have
much to do with us: it came from her distant land of ripe corn
and winding rivers and sunlight. Bridget ignored it.

"You may say that's unfair," Bridget continued, still staring at
me, "because I'm always wanting to play my fiddle. But that's
different."

"It isn't, you know, darling," said Eva.

"Yes, it is. Music isn't *embarrassing* in the same way," Bridget
went on, chiefly to me. "I don't mind reading poetry and stuff
that people have done—and even trying to tell them afterwards
what I think of it—but I don't want it *read* to me. The person
looks and sounds silly—and then I'm sorry and then I'm furious
—and—oh!—it's all a mess. So I warn you, Gregory Dawson."

I said I didn't need to be warned. "And anyhow," I said, feeling
more confident now that she had mentioned my name, "I don't
ask anybody to bother about me as a writer. I've hardly started.
Your father happened to ask me what I was interested in, so I
told him. But you needn't worry about me, I'm not going to
read anything to you." I must have sounded almost indignant;
and at that moment I had forgotten that I had thought it wonderful, when Joan mentioned it, that Mr. Alington had told his
family I wanted to be a writer.

"All right, keep cool," said Bridget.

"Well, you started it, Bridget," said Eva.

"Don't be ancient," said Bridget, turning to her. "The fact is,
Eva, you're getting jolly patronising these days." She nodded to
me. "Don't let her do it on you. She's only started just lately.
Let's have some more cake." She looked round and shouted for
it.

Oliver, who had been talking to Kerry and Jock Barniston,
came across to offer us a fine thick sandwich cake. "The cake's
the best thing round here. They think the Hallé's better than
the London Symphony, but it isn't. It's the cake—*r-r-rich da-amp
cake*," he shouted, and waved his other hand, which was holding
his ridiculous cherrywood pipe, and spilt a lot of ash.

"Look, you idiot!" cried Bridget. "And what about those songs?"

"I knew there was *something*," said Oliver, deeply interested. "I thought it was laundry, and when we came back I went to my bedroom and poked about a bit, wondering why I was there. And all the time it wasn't laundry, it was the songs—the *so-o-o-ongs*," he sang.

"*Dodderite*," said Bridget severely.

"*Mumboady*," he cried mournfully, and closed his eyes and bowed his head. Then he presented me with the rest of his cake, grinning widely, flourished that dangerous pipe of his again, and cried: "Yes, the songs. *Shlumpumpitter!*" And went striding out.

"I didn't understand that last part," I said.

Eva smiled. "You tell him," she said to Joan, who was just joining us. And Eva went smoothly and smilingly to Ben Kerry, whose dark face lit up at once.

"Oliver and Bridget have a special language of their own," Joan explained, while Bridget wolfed a vast lump of cake. "Bits of ritual too, though they've dropped most of that. What were they doing?"

"He forgot to bring those songs down," said Bridget.

"Then it must have been *Dodderite* and *Mumboady*," said Joan. "That's one of their more sensible ones—and sometimes I use it myself."

"You're not supposed to," Bridget told her, through the cake.

"Don't be disgusting, Bridget. Look—crumbs!" She turned to me. "We're not really mad, y'know, Gregory."

"I didn't think you were."

"I'd better talk to the girls," Bridget muttered, and left us.

"You came along with Jock Barniston, didn't you?" said Joan, looking at me with those grave fine eyes. She had a habit, which was part of her and not merely a social trick, of making such questions sound deeply interesting and important, as if the most momentous confidences might soon be exchanged between you.

"Yes, I did. He asked me some questions and then I asked him some. I like him."

"Everybody does. He was one of the first friends my father

made here in Bruddersford." She glanced round the room. "Where is Dad?"

And then I realised that I hadn't seen him since we came into the house. "He hasn't gone to bed, has he?" I enquired anxiously.

Joan laughed. "No fear. He's always one of the last. Besides it isn't late. Perhaps he suddenly remembered a letter he had to write—that sometimes happens. Does he forget things at the office?"

"Well, honestly," I confessed, "I don't know. I'm not important enough to know—really. I just wrap up bits of wool in blue paper and put tickets and labels on them."

"Is that all? Why, I could do that."

"Of course you could. But I wouldn't if I were you," I said. "You could find something much more interesting to do."

"Well, I have." She might have gone on to tell me what it was, but at that moment Mr. Alington came in. I was still holding the cake, and he came over to take a piece.

"I had two or three letters to write," he explained. "What's happening here?"

"Eating and drinking and talking," said Joan. "And Oliver's gone to find those songs he was talking about."

"They'll probably have desperately difficult accompaniments," he said. "I'd better keep in the background." He turned to me. "Have you read any of Ben Kerry's things? He's had some in the *Yorkshire Post* as well as the *Evening Express*. He can write."

I remembered then that I had seen some of them—little carefully written essays about books and walking in the Dales. Newspapers still published such things in those days. "Yes, I have read some of his articles," I replied cautiously.

Joan gave me a curious quick glance. "You sound as if you don't like them."

Even at eighteen I was not shy when it came to airing my literary opinions. "Bit too much Conrad about them, isn't there?"

"Well," said Mr. Alington mildly, "Ben happens to have a passion for Conrad just now. And why not, Gregory?"

Joan gave me another look, as if to tell me to speak up and say what I thought. And I did. "It's all right Conrad writing like that. But I don't think anybody ought to imitate him. It isn't really

an English style, Mr. Alington. It's as if it was being translated
out of another language. And it didn't seem to me—though of
course I haven't read many of Kerry's things—to fit the subjects
he was writing about. At least, that's what I felt," I concluded
rather lamely.

"And I agree," said Joan, to my relief.

"Well, well," said Mr. Alington, amused but not patronising.
"I still think it's a pleasure to come on one of them, and that
Ben's a clever chap who'll very soon make a name for himself.
You'll see. And I doubt if he'll be here very much longer. So we
must make the most of him."

"We can leave that to Eva," said Joan. She didn't sound spite-
ful but there was a flick of malice in the remark. And I was certain then that she didn't like Ben Kerry very much.

"Poor pussy, poor pussy," cried Mr. Alington, as if he was
playing the parlour game.

"No, Dad," she protested, "I wasn't being catty. But really I
do think Eva—" And there she stopped, probably because she
suddenly realised that I was listening too. This made me feel
rather uncomfortable. She must have noticed this, for she gave
me a most warm friendly smile. "Oh—poor you! Still holding
the cake. Here, let me take it."

"Now look who's here," said Mr. Alington.

An apologetic and rather untidy little woman, with a rosy
dimpling face, had just arrived, followed by a short thick-set man
who had an aggressive nose and shrewd little eyes, and spoke in
a loud harsh voice. This was Councillor Knott and his wife. I had
never seen Councillor Knott before but I had heard a good deal
about him, both from my Uncle Miles, who regarded him with
amused admiration, and from local gossip. He was always being
mentioned, though never with approval, in the local papers. He
was indeed a Bruddersford personality of some importance,
for he was the most tireless and pugnacious of the Socialists on
the Council. He would come to no terms with the purple and
outraged Tories or even with the mild and deprecating Liberals.
When royal favours were to be bestowed upon the city, it was
Councillor Knott who would jump up and in his loudest, harsh-
est tones denounce all such flummery and demand a revolution

and a republic. He hurried to support any and every strike, no matter how small, and told wealthy employers that they were feeding their fat carcasses with the children of the poor. It was impossible to intimidate him, to suppress him, or even to shout him down. Very few Bruddersford folk agreed with him, but having an appreciative eye for a character, most of them found it hard to dislike him. And now it appeared that the Knotts were neighbours of the Alingtons, and frequent callers.

"Oh, Mrs. Alington," little Mrs. Knott was saying, "I said to Fred you wouldn't want to see us at this time of night, but he insisted—you know what he is."

"Quite right too," cried Mr. Alington, smiling. "It's early yet. We'll have some music soon. What's been happening, Fred?"

"We gave 'em hell tonight, John," said Knott. "At least I did. I thought old Colonel Tupworth 'ud 'ave a stroke. He shook his fist at me. I says: 'Look, you're not in the militia now, Colonel. Keep them 'ands down. Use your reason—if you've got any.' Feeding of necessitous school children, that's what we were debating. We'll get it through all right."

"Good for you," cried Mr. Alington. And Joan and one or two of the others said something of the same kind.

"No, nothing to eat, thanks, love," said Knott, as one of the girls offered him something. "I 'ad a bite coming along—"

"D'you know what he did?" said Mrs. Knott, dimpling away. "He bought some fish and chips and walked along Wabley Road eating them out of the paper bag. Really, Fred—you are awful." She regarded him with that delighted satisfaction of a wife to whom her husband is devoted but who cannot control his independent and assertive masculinity, which remains therefore a mysterious and fascinating force.

"Well, you 'ad some as well," he retorted, making the others laugh and his wife blush.

"If you were going to disgrace us both, then I didn't see why I should go hungry."

"Certainly not, Susie," said Jock Barniston, who was a friend of theirs. "And she's won this round, Fred. Now tell us what happened tonight in the Council meeting."

"Oh well, we'll get it through all right," said Knott, lighting a blackened stubby pipe that just suited him. "Liberals 'ave all come round, of course. Colonel Tupworth an' silly old Brogton an' that lot groaned an' moaned away, as usual. Said we were encouraging parents to dodge their responsibilities, at the tax-payers' expense too. Y'know, the usual stuff. One chap—that wholesale grocer chap who came into his uncle's business and 'as never done anything with it an' talks to us all the time about enterprise—well, he said we wanted to discourage enterprise an' initiative. I says: 'Look 'ere—some days the kids who are 'ungry get buns an' milk an' some days they'll get stew an' rice pudding. Is it the buns an' milk or the stew an' rice pudding that's going to take away enterprise an' initiative? I know that if I was a 'ungry schoolkid,' I says, 'they'd put enterprise an' initi-ative into me.' He says: 'I'm not thinking about the children.' I 'ad 'im then, John. I says, like a flash: 'No, I know you're not. But we are. An' so would you if you'd ever gone to school with your belly-button knockin' against your backbone—' "

"Fred!" cried his wife. "You're hopeless. Now just be quiet for a bit now and let somebody else get a word in."

"Certainly," said Knott, winking at me, just because I hap-pened to be standing near him. "I've talked enough tonight, I can tell you. But what about a bit o' music?"

"It's here," cried Oliver, who had arrived with his usual messy armful. "Some songs I want to hear."

"And suppose we don't want to hear them?" said his father.

"You said you did—all of you," cried Oliver indignantly.

"We do, Oliver," said Mrs. Alington, smiling at him. He was obviously somebody special for her. I saw him return her smile, and noticed then that behind his clowning and loud undergrad-uate manner there was a quick charm, probably irresistible to his mother.

"Two or three of these songs," Oliver shouted across to the girls, "have trio accompaniments—and I've all the parts here. Better leave this to the girls, Dad. Come on, girlies."

"An' let's all sit down an' shut up," Councillor Knott bel-lowed, promptly sitting on the floor, where I joined him. "I've 'eard nothin' but gassin' for 'ours an' 'ours an' I want a bit o' music. An' I'd turn a light or two off, John, if I was you."

"Whose house is this, Fred?" demanded his wife. "And who told you to run it?"

"He's right, though," said Mr. Alington, switching off the light near the fire. "He often is, though I hate to admit it."

While Bridget with her violin, and Dorothy Sawley, who had produced a 'cello from somewhere, were tuning up near the piano, and the Wilson girl and Oliver were fussing with the music, Councillor Knott re-lit his black little pipe, which reeked atrociously, and talked quietly to me, sitting beside him. "Workin' for John Alington at Hawes's, aren't you, lad? Thought I 'eard somebody say so. Well, John's all right. I wouldn't call 'im a fighter—he's not—an' perhaps a bit too much of the Liberal about 'im—but he's a grand chap, John is, an' there's not many better. He runs his business an' doesn't let it run 'im, as some of 'em do. Knows 'ow to enjoy life the right way. An' that's all we ask—just for a chance for workin' folk to enjoy life the right way—to see their families growin' up, fine and strong—to meet their friends and 'ave a talk and a laugh together—to walk over the moors at the week-end—to read some books worth reading —to go to a theatre or to listen to some music. Like John and 'is family do 'ere—'cos they 'appen to be some o' the lucky ones. Yes, that's all we ask—just for a decent chance for the folk that do most o' the work, so that they don't 'ave to spend all their lives goin' in and out o' mills an' mucky back streets an' pubs. It isn't a lot to ask. Every ruling class there's ever been asked for a hundred times as much for doin' a dam' sight less. And social-ism's coming, lad. You mark my words. There's no stoppin' it, though some o' the Tories 'ud go to any length to try and stop it—you'll see—an' if they're not careful, just bein' obstructive, they'll land themselves in a 'ell of a mess. It's one road or the other, from now on, lad. You just take notice o' what I'm saying and remember it. 'Yes, that's what Fred Knott told me,' you'll say. And I'll tell you another thing. Some folk'll tell you I'm a 'ard man, a bitter man, a chap who's against everything, who thinks about nowt but hours an' wages. Well, they're all wrong. I'm a fighter, that's all—an' what I fight for, an' what I'll go on fighting for till I drop, is more good life for the people, especially the poor muckers that don't know where they are and can't talk for themselves. I want them to 'ave everything I've got, enjoy everything I've enjoyed—yes, an' better. An' if John Alington and his family give me a bit o' good music, then I take it—same as I do the great works o' the poets, Shelley an' Whitman an' William Morris—an' try and make it 'elp me in the good fight. And I'd advise you to do the same, lad, soon as you can."

I never took his advice, if only because I chose another way, but I never forgot it. Fred Knott represented, I suppose, that earlier and more innocent phase of the Labour Movement, when it was still uncorrupted by power, not yet embittered by the thought of lost leaders, still lit by the sunrise of simple and noble aspirations. He was a limited man, not without a childish vanity, but I think he had something I have rarely found in later and more important Labour politicians, who knew more than he did but also seemed to me to have forgotten some essential things that he always remembered.

While Knott was talking to me, the others had settled down in their dim firelit places, and the musicians, beneath a big standard lamp near the piano, were ready to begin. The songs were mostly contemporary work, heard by Oliver in Cambridge, and they were all unfamiliar to me. Only two were English, the rest being Russian, French and German. They had for me that richly evocative quality which belongs to art when it is as strange as it is beautiful, when it can be enjoyed but not yet understood. As they played and sang I had glimpses of incomprehensible lives. . . . I wandered through remote forests, dark and melancholy, towards decaying towers . . . a little window would open on an orchard bright with unknown blossom . . . lovers met at midnight in Prague or Budapest . . . the anemones were crimson with the blood of the dying hussar . . . poets in black cloaks trailed along the grey salt-crusted dunes . . . under the high blue noon a mysterious procession went past the fields of corn . . . girls waited in shuttered rooms, looked in the glass and saw that they were old women . . . in search of the Chinese princess with the lute and the emerald birds, we died in the desert . . . witches muttered to executioners . . . we lived, gathered roses and drank wine, laughed and died, and lived again, waking in woods without a name, staring at the pine-needles and the rusting dagger. . . .

But all the time too I could see across the room the grave pale face of Joan, darkly mysterious in that shadowy corner, and once or twice I thought she smiled at me, signalling from a hidden land. I could see Bridget, sharply illuminated above her violin, her eyes veiled, her features strongly and nobly sculptured by the light, her face taking on a kind of stern beauty I had never suspected in her. And on the other side of the piano, full in the light, was Eva, sometimes singing in a high clear voice, the golden smiling girl, the sleepy princess of the enchanted trams, still an incredible figure though here so close. And thus seeing them, mistily through the music, I think I fell in love with all three at once. This is possible at eighteen, when love is magic rather than revealed desire, when it rises in us like a tide on which the mind can float, when it can be exquisite and poignant and yet entirely unfocussed, arched above a whole company like a rainbow. It seemed to me the most wonderful thing that could ever happen that I should simply be there. The evening ought to go on and on, I felt, for ever.

"Come and see us again soon, Gregory," said Mr. Alington at the front door, as I left with Jock Barniston and the Wilson girl.

"Yes, thank you very much, Mr. Alington." But when can I, when can I? And I could hear the girls laughing inside, half-lost already, with magic briars and thorns growing between them and me. Giving a final glance at Mr. Alington's long, dark, dramatic face, smiling now, I made up my mind in a flash that there could be no better life anywhere than his, that here was the perfect example, that I never need leave Bruddersford or Hawes and Company to have everything I wanted.

At that point, leaving that old self wild with hope outside the Alingtons' front door on a December night in 1912, I deliberately stopped remembering. It was late, and I got up to prepare for bed. I had not thought of myself as I was when I first knew the Alingtons for a long time, and now remembering so clearly what I felt outside the door, that I had only to do what Alington had done and then life would be wonderful, I asked myself, over the washstand in my bedroom, if that daft conviction had gone down so deep that I could never disturb it again but that it could for ever disturb me. Did that explain, or help to explain, why I

had never settled anywhere for long, why I had always refused
safe and regular jobs, why no place and position ever seem to me
my place and position, why I had spent so much money casually
and half in a dream, and why I was here, in this ridiculous vast
bedroom, still with the two old suitcases and the typewriter
and nothing else, nobody else? I had thought that the war—the
First World War, in which I fought—had been responsible for
all my subsequent restlessness. But now I wondered if the root
cause were not to be found in what happened before, buried in
the Alington business; and as I climbed into bed I decided that
here was yet another reason, and perhaps the most important
reason, why I should return and explore the past as thoroughly
as my memory would allow me to do.

"All right, Dawson," I said aloud—for it was time that bedroom heard a voice—"but no more tonight. You've too much to
do tomorrow. You've broken the thread, so now let it wait while
you sleep." And, oddly enough, I did sleep.

FOUR

The next morning I awoke with that heavy confused feeling which comes at the beginning of a hard day. I realised it would be a hard day before I could remember what the programme was. Then I sorted it out. I had to put in a long morning on the script. Why? Then I remembered that Elizabeth, George Adony and Jake West would be at the hotel by tea-time, which meant that there would be talk about the script but no more work on it that day. And then I was determined to get back to myself in Bruddersford again as soon as possible, and I decided that if the afternoon should be fine I would sit on the cliff and give myself some air while I did my remembering. I don't know what had gone on in my unconscious during the night, but something had happened down there, for I woke up feeling that the recovery of my Bruddersford memories was just as much an essential task as finishing the script. The past had not lost but had gained importance during the night. And it was a nuisance that Elizabeth (although I was fond of Elizabeth), Adony and Jake West were descending upon me. I didn't want to talk to them, or to anybody else, until I had remembered exactly what happened after the Nixeys came to Bruddersford.

The work went well all morning, and it was half-past one when I knocked off for lunch. For once there was no wind to rattle the dining-room windows, and the afternoon was warm and clear. Between the hotel and the next cove was a winding path along the high cliff, and I found a little hollow just off this path, and there I settled down with a couple of pipes. The strong sunlight seemed to crush fragrance out of the gorse and the grass; I could hear the sea-birds screaming in the blue air and the tide sucking at the pebbles far below; and at no time was I oblivious of the huge gold procession of the afternoon; and yet within a few minutes of lighting my first pipe I was back in Bruddersford again, back in the sleet and dark of that far-off

December. I was a middle-aged man lolling on a sunlit Cornish cliff; I was also a youth in a West Riding town in 1912 once again; and I had a feeling too that I was neither of them, that both were character parts in their appropriate sets, and that both adventures—to continue the jargon of my trade—were sequences in a film to be shown God-knows-where.

After that first visit to the Alingtons' nothing came back to me, before Christmas, except a rather vague recollection of a row at the office. Croxton, the cashier, was very ambitious and liked to think of himself as an all-round wool-man and not merely a cashier, with the result that if he was given the slightest opportunity he would come into the sample-room and give me orders. Mr. Ackworth, who was my boss, had told me to take no notice of Croxton. This was awkward for me, and the fact that Croxton had disliked me from the first did not make it any better. On this occasion Mr. Ackworth, who had a cold, had gone home early, and just as I was clearing up for the evening, Croxton darted into the sample-room and, in his pompous fussy manner, told me that we should have to make up and send off some samples to our German agent that very night.

"Now come on, stir yourself," he cried, bursting with self-importance. "No use standing there looking sulky, Dawson. Got to be done, that's all."

"Yes, but look here—" I began.

"There's no *look here* about it," he said angrily, throwing a lot of sample tags on the counter. "Just do what you're told, and try to look pleasant while you're doing it."

"Mr. Ackworth told me—"

Croxton's long nose seemed to quiver with fury. "I don't want to know what Mr. Ackworth told you. Mr. Ackworth's not here and I am. These samples have to go tonight, and we've only just time to catch the post. Get those cross-breds down, and hurry up."

I went up the ladder, but grumbled as I went.

"What are you muttering about?"

"I'm not muttering," I told him. "I'm only saying that Mr. Ackworth told me that no samples were to go out—"

"Don't be a blockhead," shouted Croxton. "He only meant that he has to do it if he's here. But he's gone home, hasn't he? So I'll have to see to it. Come on—don't stand there like a monkey-up-a-stick. Hand down those cross-breds."

As luck would have it I reached up carelessly, probably with a trembling hand, and down went a heavy and greasy parcel of raw wool that hit Croxton on the shoulder. It did not hurt him but it shattered his dignity. In his fury he shook the ladder, and after I had jumped down he tried to shake me too. But although I was twenty years younger than he was, I was heavier and stronger, and I pushed him off. His anger now hardened into a cold white calm.

"All right, Dawson. That's quite enough. You can put your hat and coat on and go home. I'll talk to Mr. Alington about you in the morning." He turned his back on me and shouted to Harold Ellis in the office to come out and help him. If Mr. Alington had been in his room I would have gone to him there and then, but he had gone to London and was not returning until late that night.

Next morning we had a message from Mr. Ackworth to say that he was taking the day off to nurse his cold. Mr. Alington was rather late, and most of the morning had gone before he sent for me. He did not give me his usual smile.

"Mr. Croxton has just made a very serious complaint about you, Gregory," he began, looking sad rather than severe. "He tells me that when he asked you to work a little later than usual, last night, first you were sulky, and then you lost your temper and threw some wool at him. I was away and so was Mr. Ackworth. Mr. Croxton was in charge here. Why didn't you do what he told you to do?"

"I didn't lose my temper and throw anything at him," I said. "That's not true. It was an accident. He lost his temper with me—"

"Never mind about all that," he said sharply. "I want to know first why you refused to do a little extra work when it was necessary."

When we are young, hopeful but uncertain, we feel that injustice comes clanging down like an iron curtain, and so at once we begin to struggle and to shout. "I didn't, Mr. Alington," I cried. "It wasn't like that at all. He doesn't like me—"

"Stop bellowing nonsense at me. If you've got anything to say, then say it properly."

I found it impossible to say anything for a few moments, and no doubt I looked a sullen young lout, capable of throwing all the wool in the sample-room at anybody.

Mr. Alington sighed and threw an impatient glance at the letters on his desk. "Well?"

"All I did, Mr. Alington," I began carefully, "was to try to explain to Mr. Croxton, when he told me to help him with the samples, that Mr. Ackworth had told me that no samples were to go out unless he saw them—or you, of course. He said I hadn't to take orders from Mr. Croxton."

"Did you tell Mr. Croxton that?"

"No, he never gave me a chance to tell him. He lost his temper as soon as I began trying to tell him."

He raised his fascinating thick eyebrows, which always seemed to have a life of their own, like two hairy little pets. And his long face twitched slightly, as if he wanted to smile but thought that he had better not. "And you kept your temper?"

"Yes, sir, until he began shaking the ladder and then tried to shake me. I wasn't going to have that—he shouldn't have done it. And he ought to have listened to me. I was only trying to tell him what Mr. Ackworth had told me. And you said I had to work under Mr. Ackworth."

"Not if he's at home with a cold. Somebody has to run this office." He was quite sharp again. "The next time Mr. Croxton is in charge, just do what he tells you to do, Gregory. That's all."

"But what can I do if—"

He cut me short. "That's enough. Just go back and get on with your work now. And I can quite understand Mr. Croxton resenting that surly argumentative manner of yours, Gregory. I don't like it myself. Try to improve it."

Youth has its sudden flashes of insight as well as its moments of blundering and bewilderment. As I turned at the door, staring at him and feeling that this was not the Mr. Alington I knew but a peevish and unreasonable stranger, I realised that he had come back from London anxious and worried about something and that there was in him a strain of weakness that would not allow him to settle the issue between Ackworth and Croxton. He was putting me in the wrong, and speaking out of his usual character, to hide even from himself this weakness of his. Because I realised this, there was only one thing I could do now. "Yes, Mr. Alington," I replied meekly.

Ackworth was back the next morning, and angrier than ever because of his cold. As soon as he glanced at the outgoing sample book, he began bellowing.

"Now what the 'ell's this? Come 'ere lad, come 'ere. There's a list o' cross-breds 'ere gone to Germany, day afore yesterday, an' it's as long as me arm. Look for yerself, lad. Bit o' Croxton's doin', this is, Ah can tell by 'is writing. Just as soon as me back's turned!" He banged down the book, and glared at me. "Now what's use o' talkin' to yer, lad—eh? Ah just might as well talk to them weight-scales. Didn't Ah tell you right at first that you're working wi' me 'ere in this sample-room and wi' nobody else, an' if Ah'm not 'ere, then it's your job to see there's no damned 'anky-panky! Ah did, didn't Ah? Yer ought to 'ave your backside kicked, an' Ah've 'alf a mind to do it—big as y'are."

"I've had enough of this," I shouted, glaring back at him. "I get into a row with Croxton because I try to tell him what you said. Then I get into a row with Mr. Alington, who says I ought to do what Croxton tells me to do. And now *you* start. It isn't my fault if you can't decide who's running this place—"

"Now look, lad, any more cheek an' bloody impudence from you—"

"Oh rats!" I tore off the brat I was wearing and flung it on the counter. "I've had enough. I told you, it isn't my fault—"

"No, it's mine."

Mr. Alington was standing in the doorway, smiling at me. I felt a fool.

"Yes, my fault," he continued. "But what were you going to do, Gregory?"

"I'm not sure," I mumbled. "I think I was going home."

He raised his eyebrows. "Do you want to leave us then?"

"No, I don't, Mr. Alington," I replied earnestly. "But after Mr. Ackworth had started on me too—all for something that wasn't my fault—"

"Now, lad, just shut up," said Ackworth, "an' put that brat on an' get on wi' a bit o' work. Look—Ah've a list 'ere for yer to get on wi'—an' they've all to go right sharp."

"Just a minute though, Gregory," said Mr. Alington, not smiling now. "I'm sorry. And I admit you're really not at fault—"

"No, he's not," Ackworth confessed. "But for all that, Ah'd just as soon he 'adn't so much to say for 'imself."

"We'll try to organise things so that you know where you are in future," Mr. Alington told me, smiling again. "And now make up your sample list at the other end there. I want to talk to Mr. Ackworth."

While I was busy at the other end of the room, they leaned over the counter, close together, and talked quietly. I caught only a few words here and there, but I overheard enough to make me realise they were not discussing our little quarrel but something to do with our London office, about which I knew nothing. I did gather, however, that Old Somebody had decided to retire, that most of Old Somebody's shares were being taken over by a man called Buckner, and that Mr. Alington was worried and that, in Ackworth's opinion, he had every reason to be. Then I had to go to their end of the counter for the sample book, and I heard Mr. Alington say: ". . . Yes, a young nephew of Buckner's called Nixey. I met him for a few minutes. He seemed pleasant enough . . . And that was the first time I heard Nixey's name.

It had of course no interest for me then. I cared nothing for Buckner or for any nephew of his. So far I had heard very little about the London Office and had never met anybody from there. What was important to me then was that Mr. Alington, by apologising at the right moment and treating me as if I were an equal and not merely a loud angry boy, had put everything right between us again. The only difference—and it was a serious difference to me—was that I felt self-conscious about him now, as I had done when I had first gone there, and I knew that it would probably be days and days, perhaps whole weeks, before I would be able to visit the Alingtons again. He had told me to go and see them again soon, but now if I did go I felt he might think I was taking advantage of this morning's scene. That is how I saw the situation, and it never occurred to me then that

Mr. Alington might not see it in the same solemn light. Nobody had ever told me that it is the middle-aged who are free-and-easy in their social relations and that it is youth that is so punctilious and anxious.

It would be Christmas too in a few days. And I had counted on wonderful Christmas visits to the Alingtons. I had seen myself feasting in the magic circle, not on Christmas Day itself of course, but possibly on Christmas Eve or Boxing Day. And afterwards too, for in Bruddersford in those days they celebrated the season in a huge, rich, leisurely style. Since then, in other places, I had begun to think that Christmas, starting in early November, was something largely invented by the Advertising and Gift departments of the stores, a commercial racket to boost the mid-winter trade in profitable lines. In those days before 1914, certainly in Yorkshire, there was far less of this standardised *Merrie Yuletide* salesmanship, but a great deal more hearty and widespread enjoyment of the season itself. Christmas arrived at the proper time, late on the twenty-fourth of December, but once it did arrive then it really was Christmas —and often with snow too. Brass bands played and choirs sang in the streets; you went not to one friend's house but to a dozen; acres of rich pound cake and mince pies were washed down by cataracts of old beer and port, whisky and rum; the air was fragrant and thick with cigar smoke, as if the very mill chimneys had taken to puffing them; whole warehouses of presents were exchanged; every interior looked like a vast Flemish still life of turkeys, geese, hams, puddings, candied fruit, dark purple bottles, figs, dates, chocolates, holly, and coloured or gilded paper hats; it was Cockaigne and "the lost traveller's dream under the hill"; and there has been nothing like it since and perhaps there never will be anything like it again.

Although, I believe, there was a law against it, cases of liquor and boxes of cigars and other gifts arrived in the office, from firms to which we gave business, and Joe Ackworth, now recovered from his cold and already smelling of whisky and Havana, turned himself into a kind of stocky, shaven and angry Santa Claus. Croxton paid us double money and at the same time faintly sketched, in a gentlemanly fashion, his idea of a cashier about to enjoy a Merry Christmas. Mr. Alington rushed in and out, laden with parcels. Up in the warehouse Old Sam, who had mysteriously contrived to get drunk during his dinner-hour, spent the last afternoon arguing about religion with three wool-sorters, who were not pious nor keen theologians but liked to disagree with Old Sam. "Come 'ere, Greg lad," he shouted at me when I appeared up there. His military eye had a terrific fixed glare now, while the other one, the civilian and independent eye, alternately twinkled and watered. "Nah this is a sensible young feller," he told the wool-sorters, "an' Ah'll bet yer owt yer like 'e agrees wi' me. An' why? 'Cos it stands to bloody reason. Peace an' Goodwill? Certainly—certainly! Ah'm all for it—Christmas an' all. But don't try to tell me abaht gods 'aving sons born i' cowsheds, 'cos it's all me eye an' Betty Martin. Ah use me 'ead, not like some of yer."

"Well, you didn't use yer 'ead," said Joe Ackworth, suddenly appearing from nowhere, "when you put them bales 'ere. Look at 'em. An' Ah told you."

"Yes, Ah did use me 'ead an' all," shouted Old Sam, who always shouted back at Ackworth even when sober. "It's best place for 'em 'cos they're goin' out afore them merinos. Yer've forgotten that, 'aven't yer, eh? Ay, well Ah didn't. So it stands to reason."

"Go on," Ackworth shouted at him. "Ah can't be bothered arguing wi' you. But could you do wi' a cigar or two?"

"Ay, Ah could an' all," replied Old Sam aggressively. "An' so could these chaps. So don't be so dam' stingy, Mr. Ackworth—an' get on wi' t'job."

Still looking angry, and muttering all manner of insults, Ackworth promptly distributed a handful or two of cigars among them. "Partagas, some of these are—and you wouldn't know the difference if they were bloody cabbages."

One or two of them lit their cigars there and then, and somehow Christmas seemed suddenly to have arrived.

Ackworth took me back to the sample-room with him. "Nah look, lad," he began, as if to find fault with me. "You don't know where Ah live—do you? Well it's called *Rosebank*, and it's last 'ouse but one on the right as you go towards Wabley Glen. Tak' tram to Wabley terminus, then it's quarter of an hour's walk up the 'ill. An' Ah'm tellin' you 'cos we give a bit of a party on Boxing Day night. Nah don't come if you don't want to," he shouted angrily. "Please your bloody self. But if you do come, you'll be welcome."

I thanked him but said something about not knowing what my uncle and aunt might want me to do on that evening. Actually I knew they had no plans for Boxing Day, but I was still hoping to receive an invitation from the Alingtons. Joe Ackworth and his *Rosebank* were all very well, but it was still the Alingtons who possessed all the magic, and unfortunately this magic had a nasty trick of draining all the colour and life out of any expectations elsewhere. I had promised to spend Christmas Eve and Christmas Day with my uncle and aunt and their friends, which was the least I could do; but there was no magic in that and I was only being dutiful. And as Mr. Alington, to my great disappointment, never even dropped a hint about my going to visit his family, I left the office for the Christmas holidays feeling that I had not much to look forward to. I went home almost sullenly.

Now all my life I have found that whenever I have expected a great deal I have been disappointed, but that on the other hand when I have looked forward to nothing but a mere routine of existence, I have been agreeably surprised by what I have been given. So it was with this particular Christmas. It was—as they used to say in Bruddersford—"better ner like." Instead of so much middle-aged dreariness, to be endured for the sake of my aunt and my uncle (who deserved much more from me than that), actually it was fun.

Christmas Eve, as was the pleasant custom then, was devoted to visiting friends. These were chiefly members of my aunt and uncle's whist-drive circle, and among them were some very rum characters. (And I asked myself, on that Cornish cliff edge, if such characters still existed. If so, I never met them.) There was Mr. Peckel, who was enormously stout, had a high whinnying voice, could perform astonishingly good conjuring tricks, and was terrified of his wife, who was tiny but very fierce. There was Mr. Warkwood, who looked rather like Abraham Lincoln, read Herbert Spencer over and over again, and was such a determined individualist that he fought an unending battle with all tax-collectors. His wife was plump and jolly, never understood what her husband was talking about, and was famous for her pastry. There was Mr. Dunster, a massive growling man, notorious for his rough tongue at the mill, but renowned too for his passion for and knowledge of wild flowers, which often took him for a thirty-mile walk over the moors. And if he had had a few whiskies, Mr. Dunster solemnly rose to sing *Asleep in the Deep* in a terrifying bass voice. Another man, whose name now I couldn't remember, was the chief foreign correspondent at one of the big manufacturer's, and was fluent in half a dozen languages. His wife, a fluttery woman hung about with exotic ornaments, was not Yorkshire but came from the South somewhere, and somehow one felt that her husband had acquired her along with the languages as the apotheosis of the foreign. I was always rather surprised when the pair of them didn't talk in broken English, and I had a notion that they were breaking it somewhere at the back of their minds. Then there was Mr. Blackshaw, who was a waste merchant, a large solemn man, very kind and generous but without the tiniest glimmer of any sense of humour, so that my Uncle Miles and other wags were always playing tricks on him. My uncle's chief accomplice, and my own favourite in this group, was a lighthearted wholesale tobacconist called Johnny Luckett, who had thick curly hair, a tremendous black moustache, and very dashing clothes, and always seemed to be slightly tight. Johnny Luckett had two sisters who were on the stage, and he and Mrs. Luckett, who was a big careless woman with a big careless voice who occasionally sang at concerts, seemed to be more than half on the stage themselves. They went to all the shows in the neighbourhood, knew all the theatrical gossip, and were often invited to mysterious parties at the Crown Hotel. Johnny could strum on the piano for hours and knew the words of hundreds of comic songs. After he had sung a few of these, and Mrs. Luckett had obliged with *In Old Madrid* and *I Was Dreaming*, they would sing, with superb point and assurance, *Tell Me, Pretty Maiden* from *Floradora*. They fascinated me, these Lucketts, and I was always sorry I didn't

know them better. Finally—and I remembered that they were
our last host and hostess that Christmas Eve—there were the
Puckrups, a kind little couple, different and rather frightened,
who had unexpectedly inherited a great deal of money, and now
lived, uneasily, in a gloomy oldish mansion, among servants
who terrified them, and timidly offered the most lavish hospitality. After all those years I could still see little Mr. Puckrup apologetically pouring out fine old brandy as if it were stale beer, and
Mrs. Puckrup nervously extending a hand to the bell-pull.

But to describe these people in this brief and cold-blooded
fashion, as if they were caged in a zoo, is all wrong. They existed
in their own atmosphere, and it was an atmosphere of friend-
liness, affection, easy hospitality and comfortable old jokes.
No doubt they had troubles unknown to me then as a youth.
Their world didn't seem as secure, rich and warm to them as
it has since appeared to me. Nevertheless, when all allowance
has been made for my youth and ignorance, I am certain these
people lived in a world, in an atmosphere, that I have never
discovered again since 1914, when the guns began to roar and
the corpses piled up. The gaiety, at Christmas Eve or any other
time, has always seemed forced and feverish since then. My
Uncle Miles and his friends weren't trying to forget anything.
The haunting hadn't begun. The cruelty was still unrevealed;
the huge heartbreak wasn't there. No irony in the bells and the
carols. You could still have a Merry Christmas.

So we did. Perhaps Christmas Day itself wasn't quite as
merry as Christmas Eve. Ancient relatives, many of them strange
to me, arrived in Brigg Terrace for dinner at half-past one.
Some of them seemed as fantastic to me as dinosaurs. There
were bewhiskered great-uncles and creaking great-aunts, who
bellowed genealogy across the table and afterwards, in the vast
somnolence of the afternoon, heavy with plum pudding and
flavoured still with rum, loosened their incredible sets of false
teeth and muttered and snored. In the evening, yawning and
rather bilious after so much rich cake and mince pie, we played
Newmarket for shells and coloured counters, and one terrible
old great-aunt persisted in cheating. Throughout the day these
ancients talked about me as if I were not there or could not

understand English (and indeed their Yorkshire accent was sometimes so broad that I could hardly understand *them*), and after giving me another hard stare would cry: "Nay, Miles, he's just like his mother. Same nose an' eyes. Tak's me right back, he does. Ah'm just sayin', 'Ilda, lad's image of 'is mother." One of the great-uncles, who didn't look as if he were worth fourpence, put five sovereigns into my hand just before he left, and when I stammered something about its being too much, stared angrily at me and cried: "Don't talk so daft, lad. Yer can spend it on some bit o' lad's silliness, an' Ah can't. Tak' it an' shut up." Even my aunt and uncle were young in such a company, and I was hardly born. I was fascinated by some of the talk, which reached back to the grimmest period of West Riding industrialism, when the comics in the singing-rooms made jokes about coughing turning to spitting, and there was a kind of *Wuthering Heights* atmosphere even in the weaving-sheds; but before the day was done I longed to see a young face and meet a pair of eyes that belonged to my own generation. I was weary of the mustiness of old age; besides, I had eaten far too much.

On Boxing Day afternoon, when all Bruddersford seemed to be shut up in a huge cold cupboard, into which an occasional flurry of snow found its way, I went a long walk with my uncle, who needed one as much as I did. My uncle and aunt were going that night to the Dunsters', and when my uncle heard that Mr. Ackworth had given me an invitation to a Boxing Day party, he advised me to go. I couldn't sit at home and do nothing on Boxing Night, he said, and they would probably settle down to play whist at the Dunsters'. So I put on my best suit, muffled myself up, and took the tram to the Wabley terminus. From there I climbed, through a whirl of snowflakes, up towards the edge of the Glen. I felt as if I were looking for Mr. Ackworth and his party in the Antarctic.

"Good lad! Glad to see you," roared Mr. Ackworth in the hall, helping me off with my heavy overcoat. "Got a bit o' good stuff i' this overcoat an' all. Ah'll bet your Uncle Miles chose that for you, didn't he? Well, you know one or two of 'em 'ere, but not so many. Mostly neighbours. Introduce yourself, lad. Ah can't be bothered. 'Ere's the wife, though. Better be introduced to 'er or

there'll be ructions. Annie, this is young Gregory Dawson who
'elps me in t'sample-room."

"How do you do?" said Mrs. Ackworth in a very deep voice.
She was a stately, rather handsome woman, who seemed to
think that it was her duty to have dignity enough for both of
them, with the result that she was not unlike a duchess in a
George Edwardes musical comedy. "Seasonable weather, isn't
it?"

"Ay, an' what this lad needs is a drop o' summat to warm 'im
up an' get 'im started," said Mr. Ackworth, winking at me.

He took me into a little room full of books, told me to look
around it, and then after a minute or two came back with a
steaming glass of a very generous size. "Mulled old ale. Warm
you up in a jiffy, lad. Now get it down."

It was the strongest stuff I had ever tasted up to that time, and
it was hot and I drank it quickly. Then I found I had a great desire
to giggle. Mr. Ackworth, Mrs. Ackworth, and their party that
I had not yet seen, they all seemed to me exquisitely droll. Mr.
Ackworth led me across the hall into a drawing-room packed
with people, most of them very hot and many of them very
fat. The Bruddersford agent of the Canal Company, whom I
recognised although at that moment he was blindfolded, was
trying to pin a paper tail on to an outline of a donkey. And then
I saw that the three Alington girls were there, Joan and Eva and
Bridget. They smiled, and I made my way, through a solid but
almost steaming ton or so of wool merchants and wives, to join
them in their corner. I was one of the magic circle. And this, I
realised at once, was a wonderful party.

"You look peculiar tonight," said Eva, smiling her rich sleepy
smile.

"I think it's mulled old ale," I told her.

"Anyhow," said Bridget, with emphasis, "it's a peculiar
party."

"Are the others here?" I asked.

"No, only us," replied Joan. "All the rest of the family's gone
somewhere else. But won't we do?"

"Yes, it's marvellous," I said. "I never expected to see you all
here. I'd given you up for this Christmas. I was disappointed."

Bridget stared at me, widening her green eyes. "I don't understand you. And I've argued about you a bit. Which one of us is it you're so keen on knowing."

"It's all three," I said earnestly. "No, really it is. I mean—well—" and then I stopped, not knowing how to go on. But I looked from one to the other of them. Bridget still stared; Joan wore a little puzzled frown; and Eva smiled lazily out of her mysterious golden afternoon.

A massive woman, purple-faced and upholstered, had now been blindfolded.

"Nay, steady, Sally," Mr. Ackworth shouted above the din, "or you'll bust something. Don't turn 'er round, Arthur. She doesn't know where she is now, an' God knows where she'll be pinnin' that tail."

"I love Mr. Ackworth," said Eva dreamily.

"He's all right," said Bridget guardedly, "but I'll bet they'll be playing filthy kissing games soon. You'll see. And—gosh!—isn't it hot?"

"Yes, and I'm very thirsty," said Joan.

"I'll get you something," I told her, and scrambled my way to the other end of the room, where I found some claret cup, and returned precariously with three glasses of it.

"Bless you, Gregory!" cried Joan, her fine grey eyes warm and friendly.

"Chuck it, Joan," said Bridget.

"Chuck what?"

"You know what," replied Bridget darkly.

Joan looked at me and raised her eyebrows, so I raised mine too. I didn't know what they were talking about, but I was desperately anxious not to be left out of anything. But I didn't please Bridget. "Don't be a chump, Gregory," she said.

"I didn't know I was one."

"I believe you are." Bridget turned her attention to the party. "Now what's going to happen?"

Mr. Ackworth was shouting that it was time the young ones had a chance. "An' when Ah say that, Ah include meself."

"Here it comes," Bridget muttered.

And it did, the kissing game. For the first few minutes our

corner was left alone, but then Mr. Ackworth had his chance and chose Joan, and then she chose me, and out I went to her in the hall. I was very shy, for not only was she a few years older than I was but she was also still more than a girl, still a piece of magic, and I was afraid not merely of offending her but also of breaking a spell.

"Not like that," she whispered. "Like this, Gregory."

It was a light kiss but firm and very sweet. And sitting there, a middle-aged man, on that Cornish cliff edge, thirty-odd years afterwards, I remembered it as if it had happened only a few minutes before. So much had gone, and yet the memory of that sudden quick pressure of a girl's lips remained. And then a weight of sadness fell on that fragrant hollow in the cliff, and I felt as if I had been dead for years and years and had not known it until then. With an effort I wrenched myself out of this blue-and-gold afternoon, which no longer had any more life in it for me than a vast painted curtain, and returned to the hall in Joe Ackworth's house.

"Now who is your choice?" asked Joan. "Mrs. Ackworth?"

"Never. I think—" and I remembered Bridget's disgust—"it had better be Eva."

"I knew it would be," said Joan, not without a touch of scorn. "You're all the same."

Eva came out smiling. She was, I remembered then, wearing a long pale-blue dress that night, a modest kind of evening dress that girls wore then. She moved smoothly into my arms, and I kissed her several times. It was very pleasant of course, yet curiously unsatisfying, as if there, so close, was that country of golden afternoons, with its meadows and shining rivers, and yet one had not advanced a yard into it.

When I got back to her, Bridget was eating candied fruit, licking her fingers, and looking grumpy. "I think you're all disgusting," she announced, "and it's rather a disgusting party. I don't think I'd play here, even if I was begged to. Eating's the thing to do here, and I'm jolly well going to eat myself sick."

At that moment a man called Leaton, whom I had seen at the office, where he used to do our insurance business for goods in transit, came up to us. He was a tall, bony fellow with a harsh

Bruddersford voice, a sardonic type. "Aren't you Mr. Alington's daughters?" he asked.

After I'd introduced him, he went on: "Your father told me one of you was studying the violin. Which one is it?"

"It's me," said Bridget, not regarding him with any interest.

"Well, later on, if you've brought your fiddle, we might 'ave a go," said Leaton, rubbing his huge bony hands together. "Joe Ackworth's got a good piano 'ere—Steinway."

"Can you play?" asked Bridget, still without much interest.

"Ay, a bit. Organ an' piano. 'Obby o' mine, you might say," said Leaton. "Got owt with you?"

Bridget replied that, at Mr. Ackworth's very special request, she had brought her fiddle and a few odds and ends of music, but that she didn't feel much like playing.

"'Appen you will later," said Leaton, grinning and looking more uncouth than ever. "If crowd goes in t'other room, we might 'ave a go." And off he went.

"And happen not," muttered Bridget. "You know him—what does he do?"

"Wool insurance," I told her.

"Pooh! He'll be awful."

"You don't know," said Joan. "And don't be so jolly conceited, Bridget."

"I don't like you tonight, Joan. Nor you," she added, turning to me. "In fact I don't like being here at all, and I wish I hadn't come. It's all too fat and frowsty and wool-merchanty."

Some game that involved the billiards-table was now proposed, and most of the guests went to play this game, but our little group stayed on in the drawing-room. After a few minutes Mr. Ackworth himself, carrying more food and drink, joined us. "If that lot stays out," he said, "Ah'll get 'Erbert Leaton to play a bit for us."

"Can that man really play?" asked Bridget, rather loftily.

But you couldn't take that line with Mr. Ackworth. "Nah then, young Bridget," he said, grinning at her. "That'll do from you. Ah suppose you think 'cos 'Erbert's a slammocky-lookin' sort o' chap an' earns 'is livin' in t'insurance, he amounts to nowt. Well, that's where you're wrong. 'Erbert could 'ave easy earned 'is livin' by music, but bein' an independent sort o'chap he'd rather keep it as a 'obby. An' tak' that grin off your face, young woman," he added sternly.

"All right, Mr. Ackworth." Bridget was demure now. "I'd love to hear him play."

"An' what 'ave you brought with you? Summat good, Ah 'ope. None o' this caffy music. We like solid stuff up 'ere on t'Glen. Go an' fetch it, lass."

Bridget trotted off obediently.

Eva said: "That's the way to treat Bridget. Mr. Ackworth, you ought to come and live with us."

"Ah wouldn't be paid to. Ah like peace an' quiet," he said seriously.

Joan laughed. "I don't associate you with peace and quiet, Mr. Ackworth."

"Neither do I," and I grinned at him, "but I have an idea we all imagine we like peace and quiet. And perhaps we do—in our own way."

"Ah'll tell you what it is," said Mr. Ackworth to the two girls, "Gregory 'ere's a bit of a Clever Dick. An' either he'll 'ave to mak' summat special out of 'imself or he'll be one o' them that nobody wants to talk to or listen to."

I stared at him, for this matched exactly my secret thoughts about myself. He gave me a knowing wink. I glanced at the girls. Eva was looking faintly puzzled, but Joan was nodding wisely. It was a queer moment, and I never forgot it.

Herbert Leaton came up again, still rubbing his huge hands and pulling his long bony fingers and making them crack. He was followed by Bridget, carrying her violin and music-case.

"Nah, sitha, 'Erbert lad," said Mr. Ackworth, in an even broader accent than his usual one, "Ah'm goin' to give thee a glass o' right good whisky—special stuff, lad—an' then tha's goin' to play t'piano for us. An' Ah want thee to show these clever bairns just 'ow to do it, 'cos they think they knaw summat an' they knaw nowt yet. Nah, 'ere's thy whisky—an' Ah'll fix t'piano up for thee."

Leaton guffawed, and looked like a lanky North Country

comedian in a pantomime. "Thanks, Joe. An' 'ere's to me an' my wife's 'usband." And down went the whisky.

Bridget made a face at us. By this time Mr. Ackworth had cleared some plates and ash-trays off the top of the grand piano and had opened it. Leaton went shambling across, cracking his fingers harder than ever. "What's it to be, Joe?" he asked as he sat down.

"Please thysen, lad," replied Mr. Ackworth, lighting a cigar. "But a bit o' Bach 'ud do me."

"Me an' all," said Leaton, hunching himself up over the keyboard and spreading those long bony fingers.

Bridget looked surprised. Then she stopped fidgeting with her own music and settled down to listen.

With one clean stroke, as clean as his opening phrases, Leaton cut straight through the insurance business, the wool trade, Bruddersford, and the Twentieth Century, straight through to the Eighteenth Century and Johann Sebastian Bach. These huge hands of his brought out every note, unfaltering and crystal clear. He had too, what many Bach pianists never quite achieve, a singing tone, a warmth and flush, as of sunlight on the marble. Preludes and fugues sang and climbed, and went thundering by. Joe Ackworth's piano became a whole world of changing tone and colour.

"No, no, no, please!" cried Bridget, running over to him when he stopped, and almost embracing him. "You can't stop now, you can't—you mustn't. Go on. Go on—*please*, Mr. Leaton." There was a break in her voice, and her eyes were very bright.

"Ah told you—didn't Ah—that you knew nowt," observed Mr. Ackworth complacently. "'Ave another drop o' whisky, 'Erbert?"

"Never mind whisky," cried Bridget. "And I admit we know *nowt*. But tell him he must keep on playing. He's wonderful. And I couldn't possibly play now."

Leaton wheeled round on his stool. "'Ow d'yer mean?"

"Not after you I couldn't—"

"Nah stop that." And Leaton held out one hand for the whisky, and held out the other for Bridget's music. "What you got there? Let's 'ave a look. Nah 'ere's a bit o' Bach—"

"I couldn't, I couldn't—not after you." Bridget danced about in her apprehension. "It would sound frightful. Joan—Gregory—back me up—wouldn't it sound frightful?"

"What about the César Franck?" asked Joan.

"Well—I might try—" said Bridget, hesitating.

"Me an' 'Erbert thinks that's thinnish stuff," said Mr. Ackworth, once again surprising me.

"It'll do, Joe, it'll do," said Leaton.

"Do you know it?" asked Bridget.

"Ay, Ah've played it—"

"Didn't you play it that time at Gladstone 'All when Thingumbob's accompanist didn't turn up?" began Mr. Ackworth.

"Never mind about that, Joe."

"Yes, all right, Mr. Leaton," said Bridget. "But who was Thingumbob?"

Herbert Leaton grinned and winked, looking more grotesque than ever. "Ysaye."

"Ysaye!" Bridget almost screamed. Then she sat down, her face scarlet. "Golly! Golly, golly, golly! Look—I'll never understand anything round here—never, never. I'll have to go away and live somewhere else. You go to one place and meet one lot of people, all very nice and natty. And they don't know anything about anything. Hopeless. So you think: 'Well, nobody knows anything about anything—and that's that.' Then you go to another place—and meet another lot of people—and they jolly well look as if they don't know anything about anything—and then somebody like you"—and she pointed an accusing finger at Leaton—"turns up who plays Bach like an angel, though you pretend to be in the insurance business or some silliness, and then you say you'll play the César Franck with me and it turns out that you've played it with Ysaye. And you're as bad, Mr. Ackworth, because I never knew you bothered about music at all—"

"Ah tell you, young Bridget. You know nowt—yet. Give yourself a bit o' time, lass."

"It's all right saying that," Bridget grumbled. "And I know you think I'm very young and silly. I expect I am—really, though I don't feel like that inside. But it *is* puzzling here. Isn't it, Gregory? You must have found that out."

"Yes, it is. Bridget's quite right. You never know what anybody's going to say and do next. If you think they know something, as Bridget says, then they don't know anything. And if
you think they don't know anything, then they know all kinds of
things that surprise you. I can't get used to it either."

"Nah, stop natterin', you kids," said Mr. Ackworth. "An' if
you two are goin' to play, then get on with it."

So they played the César Franck sonata, and I could see
and hear them still, two world wars away, as I closed my eyes
to the Cornish sunlight and shut out of my mind the whole
fretting and half-ruined planet of this later year. I could still
hear Bridget's brave if rather uncertain tone, with its growing tenderness and grave passion, and Leaton's easy and fluid
piano tone; and with an effort I could still catch a glimpse of
his ungainly hunched figure and Bridget's frowning little face
and her tumbling hair. We had, I remembered, more Bach after
that, then food and drink with the rest of the party, and more
games and nonsense, with Bridget now in tearing high spirits. I
could recall too walking down to the Alingtons' with the three
girls, through the thickening snow and the blanket of the night,
and after that the trudging and slipping, slipping and trudging,
from the Alingtons' to Brigg Terrace, alone but aglow with the
immense vague dreams of youth. For wasn't my world, in the
snow and the darkness, opening like a flower?

I had a sharp disappointment, however, a day or two later,
when I was back at work in Canal Street. Although the holiday
was over, the Christmas season itself was by no means ended
and there were still plenty of mince pies and almonds and
raisins left to eat. I decided I would call on the Alingtons that
night, and after the late high tea we always had at Brigg Terrace,
I put on my best suit and caught the tram down at the corner of
Wabley Road. (And there was no escape, I reflected, from the
tram in this Bruddersford narrative. Our days began and ended
with trams. And I myself must have known greater heights
and depths of emotion in those trams than in all the assorted
vehicles, the buses, trains, steamships, cars, aeroplanes, I have
travelled in since then.) When I found myself once again outside that square detached villa, this time unaccompanied and

uninvited, my blood went leaping. I hesitated a moment, then marched up the tiny drive. Courage and enterprise, I felt, would be amply rewarded. This would be the best night yet. At the end of it I would find myself still further inside the magic circle, securely established within it. I rang the bell, and seemed to hear my heart thump.

The door opened to show me most of the Alington family standing in the hall, and all wrapped up in heavy coats and scarves. "Is it the cab?" I heard someone shout. Somebody else was saying that she didn't think so. I felt like running a mile without stopping. But there I was, half inside the hall, blushing and stammering.

"Why, it's you, Gregory," said Mr. Alington, coming forward. "Nothing wrong, is there?"

I remembered then that he had been out of the office during the later part of the afternoon, and I would have given a good deal to have been able to tell him that the place had been burned down, that Mr. Ackworth had gone mad, that fantastic urgent telegrams had arrived from London, anything, anything. "N-no, Mr. Alington. I—er—just happened to be passing—and—er— thought I'd just—"

"Oh what a pity!" said Mrs. Alington, in her calm clear way, which at that moment I detested. "I'm afraid we're all going out tonight. A dance at the Forests'."

Joan and Eva—I didn't see Bridget—smiled vaguely, very vaguely, as if I wasn't really there or they didn't quite know me, as if in spirit they were already dancing like mad with these mysterious and magnificent Forests.

"Yes, sorry about that, Gregory," said Mr. Alington. And he sounded vague too. "Better close the door. Won't you—er— come in a minute?"

"No, thanks. Just looked in—happened to be passing, that's all," I replied, hastily and gruffly, and hurried out before anybody could say another word, a dwarf rejected and despised. But on my way back home I became a giant, lonely and implacable, before whom the Forest family, whoever they were, knelt almost in tears to offer, in vain, innumerable invitations to dances. "Just this once, Mr. Dawson," they pleaded. "All the Alingtons will be there." Bah! And back in Brigg Terrace I went straight up to my bedroom and wrote exactly three-hundred-and-forty-five words of a short story, so bitter, so aloof, so deeply ironical, that even I, a day or two later, found it unreadable.

For the next few days a cold calm intellectual, beyond the reach of easy enchantment, found his way into the sample-room of Messrs. Hawes and Co. Ltd., Canal Street, Brudders-ford. Mr. Ackworth, who was insensitive to these fine shades of mood, told me several times that I must be sickening for a cold, and advised ammoniated tincture of quinine and some of my uncle's whisky, hot with sugar and lemon. I was very cool and aloof with Mr. Alington, and if he did not notice this, as apparently he didn't, I put it down to the fact that we were having more trouble with our German agent. Neither Mr. Alington nor Mr. Ackworth approved of our German agent, who had been appointed, against their advice, by our London office. In my new role as the austere student, the intellectual hermit, I shut myself in my bedroom at Brigg Terrace, lit my noisy little gas-fire, and read *Sartor Resartus* and Thoreau's *Walden*, two masterpieces that might have been specially designed for youth in its sulks.

Then Mr. Alington decided that he must go to Germany himself and Mr. Ackworth and I were busy sending a new range of samples to our chief German customers. We had to work late, and Mr. Alington was there too, writing letters. When I was ready to leave, he called me.

"Oh, Gregory—look—there's something—yes, I know what it is. We have seats for the pantomime tomorrow night—the whole family—and now I can't go. I'd be glad if you'd take my seat. Um?"

This was the moment to make it plain to the Alingtons that they were dealing now with the solitary student who had lost all interest in them. But that flimsy character fled the scene at once. I heard myself replying: "Yes, thanks very much, Mr. Alington. Shall I meet them at the theatre?"

"Yes, and you probably won't have time to go home first. So you must join the family at supper afterwards. I'll tell them you're coming along. Oliver will have the tickets."

Very good seats they were too, bang in the middle of the front row of the dress circle. There were eight of us altogether: Mrs. Alington, and the three girls, Oliver and the young boy, David, and that black-haired young journalist, Ben Kerry, who seemed much more friendly this time than he had done after the concert. I sat between Bridget and Joan, with Oliver on the other side of Joan. Oliver was in great form, and kept on startling his neighbours by shouting "Shlumpumpitter!," and he and Bridget played an elaborate game in which they recognised various imaginary characters in the audience, leaning across Joan and me to exchange fantastic information in clear loud tones. I had arrived at an age and a mental attitude that encouraged me to despise pantomime. (But pantomime was far better then, when the great days of the Music-Hall were still with us, than it has ever been since.) However, I enjoyed that pantomime, which was *Cinderella*. The seedy Baron was played by an excellent comic whose name I have long forgotten, but I could still remember his trick of whirling his little cane, wiggling his rump, and repeating his remarks—"It's been a terrible day. I say it's been a terrible day"—all of which Oliver and I worked to death for weeks afterwards. The Ugly Sisters were two knock-about drolls, who had one glorious scene in which they smashed a lot of kitchen stuff, to the special delight of Bridget. Cinderella herself had saucy black curls. There was one of those tongue-twisting chorus songs that we were all encouraged to sing. It was a good pantomime. I might have enjoyed it even if I had been alone. Secure and snug with the Alingtons, to whose magic, still potent, a certain friendly cosiness had been added, I loved that pantomime, and was half inside its fairy tale. Its three hours or so had the timeless generosity of a happy dream. It seemed to offer not a mere addition to ordinary life but another kind of life, which had always been waiting for me behind some corner. Here, not in the pantomime, but in the Alingtons plus the pantomime, the corner was turned, the secret door opened. And I felt myself, as one always does at such times, stimulated and enriched on every different level of my being, so that while I listened and stared at the stage, and exchanged quick smiling glances with Bridget and Joan and Oliver, I felt sure that great

stories and dreams were now waiting for me to write them, and
that existence was fruitful, good, and for ever to be trusted.

When we crowded into the tram, telling each other the best
bits of the pantomime, still held in intimacy by our laughter, I
felt I really knew the Alingtons at last, and was almost one of
them. Even Mrs. Alington, whom I had suspected before (quite
wrongly) of rather disliking me, was now easy and friendly and
almost maternal. And Ben Kerry, who had seemed to me before
to be stiff and conceited, now turned out to be a quick-witted
and amusing chap, with lots of good stories about his newspaper jobs. We kept up the fun all through supper, the first of
those large but rather sketchy meals, so different from my Aunt
Hilda's careful hospitality, that I came to know so well at the
Alingtons'. Now that I was more at ease with them I discovered I
had a vein of clowning that matched Oliver's and Bridget's, and I
worked it hard. The solemn young David would turn brick-red,
suddenly splutter and then cry with laughter. Eva and Ben Kerry
kept smiling at each other, and then vanished after supper. Mrs.
Alington then took charge of David, who was a delicate boy, and
marched him upstairs. Bridget and Oliver, who could not come
down to earth, dashed off to play some music they suddenly
remembered. So I insisted upon helping Joan to do the washing-
up. The Alingtons had one maid but this had been her night off
and she had gone early to bed.

"It's very nice of you, Gregory," said Joan, as she washed and
I dried. "But really you needn't bother—and it's a beastly night
and I should hate it if you had to walk home."

"That doesn't matter." And I felt it didn't, although she was
right about the night, which had turned to sleet. "And it isn't
particularly nice of me. First, because I like being in here with
you—"

"What—in this messy old kitchen?" And she laughed.

"Yes. And the other thing is—well, I don't want tonight to
stop, I don't want to let go of it. You see, I've enjoyed it so much.
And when it stops, then it might stop for ever. Like losing your
way—never finding the way back to some wonderful place
where you've been happy."

"You're a queer boy, Gregory," she said, startling me. It had

never occurred to me that one of them would see me as anything but ordinary, they being the extraordinary people. I tried
not too successfully to explain this to Joan.

"No," she said slowly, "as far as I'm concerned, it's just the
other way round. Tell me a bit more about yourself. There's
only you, isn't there?"

I told her briefly about my father and mother and how I came
to be living with Uncle Miles and Aunt Hilda. But when I had
done, we had finished the washing-up, and Joan was drying her
hands. Staring at her pale face, framed in the dark of her hair
and the surrounding gloom of the kitchen, which was large and
badly lit, I thought how strange it was that she, who was the
oldest of them and therefore, though perhaps only four years or
so older than I was, further removed from me than Eva, Oliver
and Bridget, should be the one who always seemed most interested in me. And I said as much, rather shyly.

"Oh, that's easy to explain," she replied lightly. "You see,
you hardly know Oliver yet, and he's really rather shy. Then all
the real interest Eva has in other people, outside the family, is
concentrated upon Ben, as you must have noticed. And Bridget
—well, she's not really interested in people yet—she's full of
herself and her music and various wild ideas. So that leaves only
me, not counting Father and Mother—and they both like you,
by the way—and David, who's still at the inhuman stage. So
just now, Gregory, you'll have to put up with me." She smiled,
then came closer, her eyes fixed on mine and looking vast and
mournful and ready to fill with tears. "Gregory, there's something I want to say to you. Something you can do for me, if you
will. Listen, this is very serious. I'm worried about Father."

"Why?" I was surprised. "There's nothing wrong with him,
is there?"

"No, not really," she whispered hastily. "But I'm worried
because sometimes he seems so worried. Only just lately. And
I think it must be something to do with the business. It can't
be anything else. And you're there in the office with him, and
you must know a lot of things that we don't know, so will you
please tell me if you should find out what's worrying him. No,
don't bother talking about it now—besides, there isn't time—

Mother'll be down in a minute—but just remember, will you, please, Gregory?" And she looked at me solemnly, rather as if we had just discovered together that life is really a dangerous affair, not at all like a pantomime, and then held out her hand, which I grasped for a moment. "Here's Mother—don't say anything to her."

"Yes, we've finished," I said to Mrs. Alington. "And I must go now or I'll miss the last tram. I've had a wonderful evening—I'll never forget it, never—and thank you very much." She seemed surprised by my earnestness, but she told me to come and see them again soon. And the last tram had gone, but not the sleet and the slush, of which there were two long black miles. But secure within that inner world, in which we have our real being, the lights still glowed and glittered, the band played, the dancers twirled, the supper table was laid, and the faces that promised eternal friendship, immortal love, smiled out of one enchantment at another.

Then came a gap, not in my life but in my remembrance. Try as I might I could not recall in any detail a single event of the three or four months that followed my visit to the pantomime. Certainly I saw a good deal of the Alingtons, calling at the house or going with some of them, and Ben Kerry and Jock Barniston, to concerts and once or twice to the Theatre Royal and the Imperial Music-Hall. It must have been during that time that, through Ben Kerry's influence, I had several semi-humorous little sketches of Bruddersford life accepted by the *Evening Express,* copies of which were carried about, and proudly shown to the whole whist-drive circle, by my Uncle Miles; and this arrival in print gave me a certain modest standing among the intelligentsia and coming men of the town, and even impressed Bridget Alington. I seemed to remember too that we were not very busy in Canal Street during that time, that Mr. Alington was away a good deal, and that I had nothing of much importance to report about him to Joan. And I went once or twice to the Bruddersford Arts Club, and acquired, in time for spring, and following the fashion for the more creative spirits of the period, a pair of massive brogue shoes and a suit of violent and shaggy Harris tweed. And spring came at last, as welcome to us

among the sleety Pennines as it had been to the medieval poets
freed from the long darkness of their winters. April opened vast
casements for Bruddersford. The moors waited at the tram
terminus. Where the last mill chimney dipped below the grey
stone walls, the larks rose from the smooth grass and the ling
—and sang. When May arrived the salty upland air was kind, the
rocks were warming, the moorland tracks were springy or dry
and glittering, newly washed as if by some invisible tides; and if
you were lucky in your day, blue summer was up there on the
roof long before it found its way down into the streets.

In those days there were well-built stone cottages, within
sight of Broadstone Moor, to be rented for a shilling or
eighteenpence a week, and all manner of folk in Bruddersford,
cheerfully doing without all conveniences, did rent them. The
Alingtons had two adjoining cottages, stout as little fortresses
and with hardly more window space, in a village called Bulsden,
on the edge of Broadstone Moor. There they spent their week-
ends as soon as the fine weather came, and there they invited
their friends, usually for the day. On a fine Sunday morning, late
in May that year, Jock Barniston and I set out to walk to Bulsden and the Alingtons, taking some extra provisions to them in
a haversack. Jock and I met, by previous arrangement, on the
Wabley Road, just before the church bells began ringing, and
turning our faces towards the moors we strode out manfully.
And, after more than thirty years, I could remember the very
feel and smell of that glorious Sunday morning, could see again
the fresh green of the trees in the Park on our left and the golden
hazy vacancy of the streets running down to our right, could
catch the steady pounding of our heavy shoes on the pavement.
Jock wore his old faded greenish tweed coat and a dark blue
shirt, and looked bigger and browner than ever, and, as usual,
as if he had just arrived from some mysterious and far distant
place. It was curious: one was always running into Jock, meeting
him here, going with him there, and actually he rarely left Bruddersford for long, and yet he always gave one the impression
that he had just returned after a long and probably very strange
journey, from Patagonia, from the moon, from some other solar
system. Yet he made no attempt to appear mysterious or even

detached; he was always cheerful, companionable, ready to go anywhere or do anything in reason, a kind of youngish uncle; but because of some odd quality of the spirit, some inner aloofness, some part of him that was turned away from us, he always seemed the long-distance traveller halted for a brief space.

We pounded along—for Jock was a tremendous walker, and though I was fairly tall I had to keep going hard to maintain the pace he set, and was always rather breathless—and talked as we went. It was, I declared enthusiastically, a glorious morning, and added that I looked forward to a grand day. We were all to stay out at Bulsden until we had had a late tea, and then we were coming back to the Alingtons' house in Bruddersford for some Sunday music—a perfect arrangement.

Jock didn't reply for a minute or two. Then he said, rather hesitantly for him: "My sister was gloomy about it at breakfast."

"About what—today?"

"Yes, but not the weather. She said it would end badly for us all."

I knew vaguely there was something peculiar about Jock's sister, whom I had never met and nobody seemed to know. And he had never talked about her to me before. I felt I had to go carefully. "What did she mean, Jock?"

"Sometimes when she's had a bad night—and she's rather an invalid and sleeps badly—she tells me things in the morning. It's a kind of second sight, y'know. I thought you knew about her, Gregory."

"No, not a thing," I said, puffing away, for Jock was still going at full speed. This seemed a queer topic for a sunny morning and the deserted Sunday road. Unbelievable stuff. Yet one had to believe Jock. "Is she always right?"

"Not always, but usually she is. She was very definite about it this morning. However, there it is, and it's no use worrying about it."

"But what does she say is going to happen?"

"She didn't know," said Jock. "Or at least, if she did know, she didn't tell me. Something unexpected—and no good'll come of it."

I stared ahead at the brightening day and wondered behind which patch of blue radiance the dark shape was forming. Or was it all nonsense? I knew Jock didn't want to talk any more about it, so I kept quiet.

"Don't say anything to the Alingtons, Gregory," he said, after a long pause. "Just forget what I said. And give me the haversack now—my turn. How are Hawes and Company?"

"Bit boring. A new chap's coming up soon from the London office—to learn the business. He's the nephew of some rich old boy who's more or less taking over in London. I believe Joe Ackworth and Mr. Alington don't like the idea. I hear them whispering in corners sometimes, but of course they don't say anything to me. Both of them, I think, have an idea I shan't stay much longer in the wool business—and they're right. I shan't. I want to write, y'know, Jock."

"Yes, and so you ought," said Jock, who was always encouraging, just as he was always ready to read his friends' manuscripts, listen to their music, look at their pictures, and listen to all their troubles. But he had a cautious, sensible side to him. He was never of this world, but he knew how it behaved, rather like a wise priest. "But you can write and be in a wool office too, Gregory. Don't be in a hurry to run away. I know you could probably get a job on a newspaper—Ben Kerry said as much the other day—but if you take my advice you won't. It's easier to write what you want in a wool office than it is while you're working on a newspaper. I'm not too sure about Ben, who's talking now about going up to Fleet Street."

I felt a sudden pang of envy. Ben had too much: cleverness, confidence, tremendous energy, good looks, and the adoring Eva Alington. I suppose I was always rather jealous of Ben.

"I don't know what Mr. Alington could have done," I said rather idly. "Lots of things, I suppose. But do you think he was right to stay in the wool business?"

Jock considered this carefully. "I don't know what John Alington would have done. Unless he could have been some kind of teacher or lecturer. Ever heard him give a lecture or take a class? He's first-rate. Went to a Fabian Summer School with him once. He had some offers then, but with that family of his I suppose he felt he couldn't risk it. Pity, in some ways. Because I doubt if he is right where he is in the wool business."

This surprised me. "He seems good at it. Why do you say that?"

"He was lucky being with a firm like Hawes," Jock replied. "Up to now they're different from most of the others here. But if it comes to a pinch—and it easily might—then I doubt if John's tough enough to take the strain."

I remembered then what I had thought about Mr. Alington sometimes. "You may be right. Joe Ackworth's more the type. He's as tough as old leather. But for all that, I have an idea that Alington's more use to the firm than Old Joe is. He's got more ideas and dash, yet knows just when to be energetic and when not to bother. Toughness isn't everything."

"I never said it was. But sooner or later, in the wool business, you've got to have it. I've seen a lot more of it than you have, Gregory—even though I've never been in it—and it all looks deceptively easy and casual but somewhere behind all that pipe-smoking and coffee-drinking and domino-playing there's a battlefield. That's one reason I kept away from it. I don't like battlefields," Jock concluded with a grin. His sister hadn't told him he was soon to see plenty of battlefields and on the last of them win the Victoria Cross and meet his death. Or had she? There was no telling what Jock knew. He moved forward powerfully and smoothly, his long brown face impassive again, like a chief of some mysterious noble tribe of Indians.

We were out of Bruddersford now and our faces were turned towards the hills. Larks were singing and lambs were calling. The grey stone walls, which would go on and on to climb and bind the highest moor, were now on each side of us. The last touch of haze vanished, the blue lifted and deepened, and the gold light seemed to have weight as well as warmth. I wanted to go on talking about the Alingtons but didn't know where to begin again.

As if he knew what I was thinking, Jock said: "You mustn't care too much about the Alingtons."

"Why—why, Jock," I stammered, taken by surprise, "what makes you say that? Look here—tell me candidly—I haven't been making a fool of myself, have I?" For at that age we care passionately about not making fools of ourselves and yet never know when we might be doing it.

"Not at all," said Jock. "Nobody's been laughing at you, if that's what you mean. The girls used to giggle sometimes, but that's nothing. You know what girls are."

I didn't, but promptly replied that I did. "But what exactly did you mean, then, when you said I mustn't care too much about the Alingtons?"

"Well, I didn't mean that we haven't to be fond of other people," said Jock, "that we haven't to enjoy and be devoted to our friends."

"I didn't think you did mean that," I told him. "But what exactly did you mean?"

But before he answered that, he made me explain to him what I had felt about them when I first noticed them on the tram. And I was fairly honest in my reply, explaining about the little magic circle. "And I suppose that if the three girls hadn't been so good-looking," I concluded, "I wouldn't have felt all that. But that doesn't explain it all, not by a long chalk. It was the sort of total effect that did it—a whole mysterious rich intimate life going on, with me outside it. And I had to be inside it."

"That's rather clever of you, Gregory. You're a rum lad. Sometimes you're as wise as an owl and sometimes as simple as an egg. But the point is, of course, that you came here feeling lonely and rather miserable, with no family of your own —because I don't think your uncle and aunt really count—and then you saw the Alingtons. Well, that's all right. I'm devoted to them myself, as you know. But you mustn't make them stand for more than they ought to stand for, you mustn't turn them into symbols, which is, I believe, what men do, for instance, when they're infatuated with most unsuitable young women. Magic shouldn't come in with people."

"It's got to come in somewhere," I told him. For I believed that then, and believe it still. Life without magic soon begins to wither.

"All right. But I think it belongs to our relation with what isn't human, and there I think our ancestors were wiser than we are, because in their universe they left plenty of room for the magical but warned everybody to be careful of it. We pretend it doesn't exist, and then smuggle it in through the wrong doors. Which I believe you're doing."

"Just because I was attracted to the Alingtons? And was a bit fanciful about them? Jock, I think that's rot."

"All right, it's rot. But just let me talk a little more, and then I'll shut up, Greg. The Alingtons are an amusing, rather clever, very charming family, and I'm fond of 'em all. But don't try to make them add up to anything more than that. Don't turn them, somewhere at the back of your mind, into something they aren't and wouldn't pretend to be. Don't make everything stand or fall by them. Switch off the magic, which comes from you and not from them. Don't cast a spell over yourself and imagine that they're doing it. Take them in your stride, and don't fix anything. See what I mean?"

"No, not quite," I said rather sulkily. "I know I'm being warned about something, that's all."

"Not warned against *them*," he declared emphatically. "You know that. Warned against yourself in relation to them. You can go a long way—and give us something good—if you travel easily and lightly, seeing people as they are, just as people and not as symbolic figures, and not leaving parts of yourself behind, frozen in some enchantment."

I think I understood him even then, though I pretended not to. I understand him now all right, now that I am years older than he was then—hard though that is to believe. I fancy that I sulked a little, feeling that he had deliberately cast a shadow on so glorious a day.

"Look—there's the *White Horse*—and it's open. Let's have some beer," said Jock.

The *White Horse* was a nice old pub, at the Bruddersford end of the straggling village of Bulsden. Among the sensations I seem to have missed for years and years, sensations that appear to have vanished never to return, was the one I experienced then, that of plunging from the sunlight into the deliciously dark cool interior, smelling of beer and fresh sawdust and fried ham and eggs. And the last time I was up there the old *White Horse* had gone and in its place was a large road house, offering a dance band and bogus Martinis, and not until I arrive among the smiling hills of Paradise shall I see the original old *White Horse* again.

An odd-looking chap, with a long fattish body and a small head crowned by a mop of white hair, was standing at the bar, downing a pint. He had a painter's box and a light easel with him. "Nah Jock," he cried, grinning so that his weatherbeaten face seemed to crack all over, "have a pint wi' me."

Jock introduced us. He was Stanley Mervin, an artist, who chiefly painted landscapes in water-colour, and lived somewhere the other side of Bulsden. I knew him by repute, and had seen several of his drawings and sketches of the moors and Dale villages at the Alingtons'. They were very good, with much of the breadth and ease and masterly rapid statement of light and colour of the grand old tradition of English water-colour.

"We're going to the Alingtons'," Jock explained.

"So am I, lad, so am I," cried Mervin. "The missis'll be there this minute, wondering what the heck's become o' me. Well, we'll ha' this pint an' then be off. Ah've been out since early on 'aving a go at that little bridge at Broadstone Beck End. An' if Ah've had one try at that little beggar Ah've had a dozen. Never could get bloody tone right. But Ah think Ah've got it this time. 'Ere, you can have a look for yourselves, lads."

He took us to the deep-set little window and showed us what he had done. There on the rough thick paper, reduced to their simplest possible terms, were the stream, glinting and dimpling, the stone arch of the bridge flushed in morning sunlight, the moor and the hills. It was the morning caught for ever. It was the time, the place, and a sensitive man's feeling about that time and that place, stated once and for all: It was art and a little miracle. I cried out my admiration, and wished I could buy the lovely thing then and there; and Jock solemnly added his approval.

Mervin nodded and grinned with some complacency. "It's 'it or miss with this sort o' caper, an' Ah fancy this time Ah've rung the bloody bell. Gregory Dawson, eh?" He stared at me ruminatively out of small bloodshot eyes. "'Aven't Ah seen some little pieces o' yours in the *Bruddersford Evening Express* lately? Ay, well, they're not bad, not bad at all. Are they, Jock? Only—look, lad—don't try to be clever. Keep it straight an' simple. That's trouble wi' Ben Kerry, in my opinion. He's a bit of a Clever Dick, Ben is. Nah in a year or two, if you'll just keep it all straight an' simple an' don't try to show 'ow clever y'are, you'll be knocking spots off Ben an' a good many more. You're only a young lad yet, you've plenty o' time. Ah wish Ah 'ad—Ah'd show 'em summat—but Ah started late an' Ah'm gettin' on."

"Not you, Stanley," said Jock. "You'll be climbing these moors and daubing away for the next thirty years."

(But Jock was wrong for once. Stanley Mervin had a stroke in the autumn of 1914, and two years later, when I was out in France, I read of his death in a Bruddersford paper somebody sent out.)

Chuckling away, Mervin collected his apparatus, and the three of us went out into the dazzling village street. Mervin seemed to know all the men who were hanging about there, waiting for their roast beef and Yorkshire pudding, and exchanged greetings with most of them at the top of his loud hoarse voice. He was not at all my idea of an artist and, in my ignorance, I found it hard to associate this odd rough-spoken chap with those water-colours, at once so delicate and precise.

"Ah 'ope you've got summat to eat in that knapsack," he said. "Ah told the wife to tak' a few things down. Ah like John Alington an' his wife but they're apt to be a bit fancy an' sketchy wi' their meals, an' Ah like summat solid, specially after gettin' up so early. Ay, Ah'm right peckish."

Jock and I were too. But we assured him that there was a solid contribution in the haversack.

Mervin turned to me, grinning, as we came to the top of the village street. "An' which o' them three lasses of his are you gone on, lad?"

"I've been wondering that," said Jock.

"All three, I think," I said, grinning too. "But Joan's older than I am, and I'm afraid Eva's already out of my reach—"

"Well, that leaves young Bridget," said Mervin. "And she's best o' the three, to my mind, though Ah'm sayin' nowt against the other two. But Bridget's got most in her, you'll see. Ah'll back 'er against lot of 'em. Ah'm right fond o' young Bridget. Knows nowt about paintin' naturally, but for all that she knows what's what—an' picks out the good uns every time. She'll like this Ah've just done—you'll see."

"She can't like it any better than I do," I told him. "I want to stare at it again."

"An' so you shall, lad."

"This may sound silly, but it isn't. I feel a lot better—more ready to try to do something good myself—now that I've seen that drawing of yours, Mr. Mervin."

He gave me a nudge in the ribs with the elbow of the arm that was carrying the paintbox. "If that's silly, lad—it's sort o' silliness Ah like. An' there's nowt silly about it. Don't let nobody persuade you it is, neither. What is dam' silly—an' Ah get sick to death of it—is all this bloody daft solemn talk round 'ere about merinos going up tuppence a pound an' cross-breds coming down tuppence a pound—an' so forth an' so on. Ah'd twenty years of it, doin' my paintin' at week-ends, an' then one fine Monday morning Ah says to the wife 'Ah'm just wastin' my time.' She says 'Ah know you are, an' you'll be rare an' late for the office if you don't hurry up.' Ah says 'Nah look, Alice, Ah'm not going to any office. That's what Ah'm tellin' you. Ah'm wastin' no more o' my time in offices. If Ah go on much longer, Ah'll be dead an' buried afore Ah can turn round.' She says 'Well, tell 'em you're poorly an' tak' a few days off.' Ah says 'Ah'm goin' to tell 'em Ah never felt better in my life an' Ah'm goin' to tak' rest of it off.' She says 'Nay, Stanley, we can't afford it, lad.' Ah says 'We can't afford not to do it, lass.' She says 'We can't keep this house goin' on what you'll make sellin' your pictures.' Ah says 'Ah knows we can't, but what the hamlet do we want to keep this house goin' for? Let somebody else keep it goin',', Ah says to her. 'Why, you're always tellin' me it's more than you can manage. Well, stop tryin' to manage it then,' Ah says, 'an' we'll tak' a cottage out Broadstone Moor way.' An' so we did, an' Ah never went back, an' the first year or two it was 'ard goin', we must 'ave lived on a pound a week, but if Ah wanted to go out an' paint, Ah went out an' painted, an' if Ah wanted to stop in, then Ah stopped in—an' if you ask me, Ah've just about been 'appiest bloody man in Yorkshire ever since. Merinos can go up an' cross-breds come down till they're both out o' sight, for all Ah care. But Ah will say that for John Alington—he may be still in the business, but he talks about summat sensible, like a chap

with his eyes an' ears open an' not like a talking white mouse in
a cage, same as some of 'em."

The Alington cottages were the middle ones of a row of six
in a little hollow between Bulsden and the moor. They looked
out on to a smooth green, beyond which the rocky moorland
rose sharply. We descended from the road to this green, waving
to several familiar figures we saw down there. Oliver was away
at Cambridge, but all the other Alingtons were there; and Mrs.
Mervin, a plump little woman who laughed a great deal. Ben
Kerry wasn't there, as he had some newspaper job to do and
would not be joining us until the evening, back at Bruddersford.
The downstairs rooms of the cottages had been knocked into
one, brightly painted and colour-washed and with additional
window space in it; and there we had a crowded, uproarious
lunch, with a noble selection of cold meats and an enormous
salad, huge helpings of fruit tart and cream, and Wensleydale
cheese, a delectable cheese that, so far as I am concerned, vanished from the earth when it also lost its peace and goodwill.

There was, I remembered, much argument at the table about
what was going to happen to the world. Mr. Alington, who
was in very high spirits all that day, was even more optimistic
than usual, and declared that war among the great powers was
very unlikely indeed. Too much attention was being paid to
the antics of a comparatively small war-mongering group in
Germany, whereas the rest of us there, who did not visit Germany regularly as he did, were apt to forget how strong German
socialism and liberalism were becoming. Men weren't foolish
enough to hurl millions of troops, thousands of great guns, and
vast battleships by the score, into the furnace of war. We were
already too civilised for that. And Mrs. Alington, who spoke out
for once, warmly agreed with him.

"What are they for then?" demanded Mervin. "Ah mean, all
these cannons an' machine-guns an' battleships an' what not—
aeroplanes an' all, Ah dare say. What are they for?"

"To frighten the nations into keeping peace," said Mr. Alington.

"Don't tell me that," cried Mervin. "Stands to reason, with
all that stuff ready to go off, somebody'll pull the trigger one

o' these fine days. Ah think you're kiddin' yourself, John. As for bein' civilised, Ah can't see we're any more civilised than what our great-great-grandfathers were—an' 'appen a bit less in some things."

"You don't know anything about it, Stanley," said Mr. Alington.

"That's a fact," said the painter bluntly. "An' neither do you, John. But Ah do know this—the more you lump folk together, an' let 'em read dam' silly newspapers, an' give 'em big guns to play about with, then the bigger the bang'll be when it comes."

"You don't trust human nature," said Mrs. Alington.

"Ah trust it up to a point when Ah've just got a few bits of it to deal wi'," replied Mervin, "but when you go an' lump it all together, way we do now, then it's nowt but childish. What do you say, Jock?"

Jock took out his pipe, for although we were still sitting round the table we had finished eating, and looked hard at the stem as if there might be something wrong with it. "Wars from now on will be lunacy, of course—"

"Just what I'm saying," cried Mr. Alington.

"But collectively people don't mind lunacy. They often find it easier than sanity, and more of a relief."

"I think that's silly, Jock," said Mrs. Alington.

"No, it isn't," said Joan, rather sharply. "Go on, Jock."

"Why, no," said Jock, with an air of mild surprise, "I've finished. We've all finished. We're wasting a grand afternoon. What about clearing away and then walking over the moor?"

"Cricket first," said young David, who might be an odd, detached and studious boy but had a few enthusiasms in common with the average West Riding lad. "Father and I choose. And bags I Gregory."

"Bags you helping to clear away," said his mother, rising from the table. We all assisted, and during the washing and drying of the plates and cutlery David and his father chose their sides. After that, while the rest of them put away the things, David and Jock and I went out on to the green and got the pitch ready. We played with a fairly heavy red rubber ball. Our side was David and I, Bridget (wild but useful), and Mrs. Alington and Mrs.

Mervin, who were passengers. On the other side, Mr. Alington was quite good, an artful slow bowler, Mervin was a slogging bat and a fast but inaccurate bowler, Joan and Jock were active but not skilful, and Eva was exquisite, dreamy and useless. We were watched by three small boys and two stout men in Sunday suits too tight for them, who were as solemn as if Hirst and Rhodes were performing. Our side won by twenty-seven runs, in spite of the fact that Mrs. Alington and Mrs. Mervin soon tended to lose all interest in the game, and that Bridget left us to talk earnestly to her 'cello-playing friend, the plump flushed giggling girl, Dorothy Sawley, who arrived in the middle of the game, 'cello and all. I was the star performer of the afternoon, but was told by Bridget—on our own side too—not to be "so jolly cocky about it" and was giggled at by Dorothy Sawley, in her capacity as a staring and guffawing foreign peasant. And one of the stout spectators took me aside, solemnly and mysteriously, to say that he had a "bit of a pull" with the Bulsden Cricket Club and might get me a trial with the Second Eleven.

Then we filled two baskets with tea things and Jock and I, Mervin and Mr. Alington, took turns carrying them a mile or two across the moor, shimmering in the full blaze of the afternoon, towards a secret dingle, a bright green cleft in the moorside, where that beck whose bridge below Mervin had painted went flashing between mossy stones and high banks of bracken. Looking back, so long afterwards, I found I could not remember what we said and did there, only the hour and the place and the golden mood. Perhaps my memory deliberately failed me. Perhaps the artist buried in my unconscious, plumping for the boldest Impressionism, decided to offer my conscious mind nothing but a blur of sunlight and green leaves and shining water, of laughing girls and long-vanished friendly faces, of bread and jam and happy nonsense in a lost Arcadia. Sitting on the edge of that hollow in the Cornish cliff—for by this time I had got tired of sprawling inside the hollow itself—I could no more believe that by taking a train or two and then walking a few miles I could find that dingle on Broadstone Moor again than I could believe that it would be possible to hire a car and go in search of Rosalind and Touchstone in the Forest of Arden. I admit that I didn't try hard to remember. Perhaps I even retreated, wincing, from an area where a nerve was lying uncovered, only waiting for a touch to ache and scream. So I drew a curtain over the sun-flecked faces, the gold and the green gloom, the water sliding over the moss, the echoing shouts of laughter, the wise foolishness, the lost glory. . . .

But I remembered clearly enough how we said good-bye to the Mervins and then trooped back, in the vast fragrant cool of the evening, to the inevitable tram and Bruddersford. Except for Dorothy Sawley, clutching her 'cello, we were now enormously at ease with each other, a little drunk with air and sunlight, each one of us almost a caricature of himself or herself, and often deliberately heightening ourselves. Even Jock, the coolest and most self-contained of us, let himself go, and as he went a little way ahead with Joan, from the tram to the Alingtons' house, I noticed how often she laughed.

"Joan's happy now," Eva said to me, in her easy lazy fashion.

"Why specially now?" I asked.

"She has Jock all to herself."

I was surprised. "Why, does she want Jock all to herself?"

"Of course. She adores him. Didn't you know?"

I said that I didn't, truthfully enough. "Are you sure?" I asked.

"Don't be silly. Of course I am. Ask Bridget."

I didn't particularly want to ask Bridget, and anyhow Bridget was now demanding that we should have some music as soon as we arrived indoors. "No nonsense about writing letters," she told her father. "Or reading. I've dragged poor Dorothy all round the place with her 'cello, and so you've jolly well got to make up the trio."

"All right," said Mr. Alington. "We'll do the Schubert—if the others don't mind."

"The others," said Bridget severely, "will love it. Won't you, Gregory?"

I said that I was all for it. "In fact," I added, "I was just about to suggest we had some music—to round off the day. Perfect."

"Sometimes, Gregory, you're rather awful," said Bridget, with a flash of her green eyes. "But at other times you're nicer than any of the chaps who come here."

"When am I awful?" I demanded, curious at once.

"When you're rather pompous and think you're being clever and pretending to know a lot. After all, you're only about a year older than I am—if that—and I can't see that you know very much really. Do you remember when you used to stare at us in the tram? I was furious, and Eva used to laugh at you, and only Joan stood up for you. But that's because Joan does stand up for people. I believe she does it chiefly to please Jock Barniston, who has such a good word for everybody that I could murder him sometimes. And I don't think he understands music really. He just listens patiently—like Joan—but it doesn't excite him. Now you do care about it. I know, because I've watched you."

"I've never seen you watching me, Bridget."

"Oh, I've had my eye on you. Did you know that I might go to Leipzig next year? Daddy's almost persuaded. Perhaps after we've played the Schubert tonight, I'll ask him again—and then if he says Yes—that'll make the day perfect."

"Then I hope he does. It's been a wonderful day for me."

"You haven't finished it yet. Oh!" And she stopped. We had just turned into their little drive. Joan and Jock Barniston and Eva were standing outside the front door talking to Ben Kerry, who had evidently been waiting for us to return. Bridget had put a hand—she had small square hands, now rather grubby—on my arm, and was staring at me. She shook back her reddish-brown hair. Her nose had several more freckles on it.

"What's the matter?" I asked. I thought she must have forgotten something, left her fiddle or music somewhere.

"Why can't we hold on? Why can't we all agree and say 'This is what we want, and we'll hold on to it and won't have it changed by anybody.' Why can't we, Gregory? Tell me." She was very urgent, tugging at my arm now as if the answer might be pulled out of me that way.

I was bewildered and probably stared at her with my mouth wide open. I didn't understand what she was getting at. But what I saw, as I stared in my bewilderment, was Bridget herself as I had never seen her before. It was as if I saw her not only as she was that moment but as she soon would be, with the woman added to the girl; and the rather square face, with its absurd

pert nose and wide mouth, was touched and transformed by
an unexpected delicacy and fragility; and I had a sudden vision
of somebody rare, beautiful and terribly vulnerable. There was
tragic helplessness in the great eyes, now dark hollows.

"Why, Bridget," I stammered, more deeply confused by what
I had seen than by what she had said, "I don't know what you
mean. What do you want me to do?"

"Nothing, nothing," she answered, impatient with herself as
well as with me. "I'm just talking rot." And she swung away and
hurried towards the house.

With the lights on but with no curtains drawn, we were all
in the long drawing-room again. Bridget and Dorothy Sawley
were tuning their instruments. Mr. Alington was smoking his
pipe and lowering those fascinating eyebrows of his at the piano
part of the Schubert *B Flat Major Trio*. Ben Kerry and Eva, dark
head and golden head, were sitting close together, not looking at
each other but secure in their own tiny world. Joan was smiling
at nothing, her eyes deeply shadowed; and Jock was smoking
placidly, the voyager at rest. Young David, flushed and yawning,
was leaning against his mother's knee, while she darted quick
smiling maternal glances at them all. And I was where I had so
often wanted to be, magically encircled, green fathoms deep in
contentment. The doors and windows were open to the dark
tenderness of the night.

Mr. Alington turned himself into a bowing foreign musical
celebrity. "Lad-eess an' Shentlements," he announced porten-
tously. "By spec-iale reek-vest—Schubert *Trio*—*B Flat Ma-jorr*.
Violin—Mees Bridgeet Alington. 'Cello—Mees Dorot'y Sawlee.
At piano—mineself—Johann—Alington. Your attention—pleess!"

So the trio began, and soon they came to the slow movement
I had just heard in the lounge of the Royal Ocean Hotel, the
music that had brought back my youth so sharply; and first
the 'cello crooned and rocked and then went sliding away to
murmur its regret while the violin with its piercing sweetness
curved and rocked in the same little tune. And then there were
two strangers standing in the doorway, among the splinters of
the Schubert.

"Look, Mr. Alington, I'm most frightfully sorry," the man was saying. "We did ring several times, but couldn't make anybody hear. And I thought you'd like to know we'd arrived at last."

There were introductions. Malcolm Nixey, who'd come from the London office to work with us for a time in Canal Street. His wife, Eleanor. No, they were all right for rooms—staying at the Midland for a day or two—but thought they ought to look in and let the Alingtons know they'd arrived. Yes, they'd had some food. And wouldn't we like to go on with our music? And Bridget, scowling, said No it didn't matter, thanks.

They both looked about thirty to me, and seemed rather alike. Not that they closely resembled each other—she was darkly handsome and sparkling, whereas he was merely smooth and dapper—but they clearly suggested the same background, the same style of life, the same outlook. They were people from a large rich city descending upon a much smaller place, well away from the centre of things. There was no obvious conde-scension, no patronage. They were polite and, realising that the music should not have been interrupted, anxious now to please. They talked quickly, in crisp—almost brittle—tones. They were clearly used to meeting lots of people. Nixey knew that I worked at Hawes and Company, and told me we'd be meeting the next morning, sketching a sort of comradeship of the wool trade. Mrs. Nixey exerted herself, in a quick easy fashion, with Mrs. Alington and Joan and Eva, who were all rather shy. (Bridget was now muttering darkly in a corner to Dorothy Sawley.) She made one or two little jokes about journalism to Ben Kerry, who seemed rather dazzled. And indeed she was very handsome, with those fine eyes, creamy skin, and a superb proud neck; a dark swan queen, a lady from a far country.

And at this very moment when I was busy holding the image of Eleanor Nixey, as she appeared that first night, in my mind's eye, I was disturbed by the sound of somebody approaching along the cliff path that came near where I was sitting. I turned round and saw an elderly lady, fairly erect but moving slowly and using a stick. It was Lady Harndean: it was Eleanor Nixey with thirty-odd more years on her back. And as she came nearer, looked at me with those same eyes, recognised me and smiled, I experienced a sensation so profoundly disturbing that it seemed as if my spine contracted and shivered. What I perceived then, in a blinding flash of revelation, was that the real Eleanor Nixey was neither the handsome young woman I had been remembering nor the elderly woman I saw before me, both of whom were nothing but distorted fleeting reflections in time, that the real Eleanor Nixey was somewhere behind all these appearances and fragmentary distortions, existing outside change and time; and that what was true of her was of course true of us all. It is easy enough to say this, but at that moment I *felt* it too, felt it in all my being, and was left shaken by it, half terrified, half in ecstasy.

"Why, Mr. Dawson," she said, stopping as I scrambled to my feet, "I seem to have startled you. You were thinking hard about something—your work, probably—and now I've interrupted you. Sorry! Are you walking back to the hotel?"

"Yes, it must be tea-time." And we walked on together, slowly. "As a matter of fact I was thinking about you. I was deep in the past—and have been all afternoon. And I'd just arrived at the evening—it was a Sunday late in May in 1913—when you and your husband suddenly arrived at the Alingtons' and burst in on us during a Schubert trio."

"Oh—the Alingtons—yes. Let me think. I've forgotten about the music—I don't pretend to be musical, and Malcolm isn't either—but I do seem to remember our calling on them just after we'd arrived in Bruddersford." She said nothing more for a few moments, then added lightly: "But it's all so long ago, isn't it? Everybody in the hotel is very excited about your film people coming here. Tell me about them."

"Elizabeth Earl and George Adony. You must have seen her—she's a great star now in Hollywood, though she's English—and she's come over to play the leading part in this film I'm busy writing. George Adony is to direct the picture. He's a Hungarian." But while I was talking I was telling myself that there had been something false, a suggestion of strain, in the way in which she had dismissed that arrival long ago in Bruddersford. She was a bit too light and easy, and in too much of a hurry to get rid of the subject. I hadn't expected her to be deeply interested. And now, just because she pretended she wasn't, I knew that she was. I wasn't the only one who remembered.

And then, just as we came to the little gate on the cliff side of the hotel grounds, she stopped me by touching my arm, looked at me and smiled. "What was I wearing that night?"

She took me by surprise. "What night? Do you mean when you first arrived at the Alingtons'?"

"Yes. You said you were busy remembering it. What was I wearing?"

"Good God!—I've no idea."

She looked through me now, over the graves and ruins of two world wars. "One of those absurd picture hats," she said dreamily, "and a black *crêpe de Chine* hobble skirt and a cream georgette jabot. Very grand and smart then—particularly for Bruddersford."

"Yes," I said. "I'll bet it was."

FIVE

As soon as we reached the hotel I discovered that Elizabeth and the other two had not yet arrived, so I had a quick cup of tea and then went up to my room. There were a few small corrections I wanted to make in the first two sequences before Elizabeth saw the script. After I attended to these corrections I read on and made several more. I must have been working nearly an hour when I heard the knock.

"Come in," I shouted, thinking it was one of the maids.

There was Elizabeth, the famous Elizabeth Earl, wearing a grey travelling outfit and a pale yellow scarf. She looked very beautiful, and in glorious technicolour.

"Darling!" she cried; held the scene for a moment; and then came hurrying in and kissed me.

I was surprised. After twenty years in the theatrical and film worlds I am thoroughly acquainted with this *Darling* and kissing business, even though I don't indulge in it myself. But this was different. Elizabeth's "Darling!" sounded as if she meant it. The kiss was real too. As if we were lovers; and we weren't and never had been. We had been great friends—and in Hollywood too, where solid friendship isn't easy to find; we hadn't seen each other for several years and had exchanged longish letters fairly regularly; and Liz was an affectionate girl, determined not to be spoilt by all the film-star nonsense. But even when I remembered all this, the warmth of her entrance still surprised me.

She looked me over, and then sat down. "You're thinner, Greg."

"It's the rations. And not drinking as much as I used to do on the Coast."

"You're a bit greyer too. But it suits you. What about me?"

"You forget, Liz, that I've had hours of you on the screen since I left Hollywood. In fact, when we were wondering if we could get you over for this film, George Brent and I had miles of you run off for us. My dear girl, you've got one of the dozen best-known faces in the world."

She smiled, but I knew it wasn't because of the best-known faces. "Nobody's called me *my dear girl* since I saw you off at Glendale. Nice. But you still haven't told me how I look. Pictures don't count. I'm here now."

I took a good searching look at her. She looked more like her film self now—that famous, mysterious, enigmatically smiling woman with the broad low forehead, the unusual width between the eyes, the slightly oblique set of the eyes, the perky little nose—than she had done when I had said good-bye to her on the Coast, perhaps because they had kept her working hard, with less time off to be her ordinary self. How old was she now? Thirty-five? Well, she looked it. But that was all right to me. But there was something I'd forgotten about her, and I told her so.

"What is it?" she asked, deeply interested, rather anxious.

"Something the camera men don't get, not even in technicolour," I said. "Your eyes are grey, but they're a sort of warm velvety grey—very unusual, Liz. And that doesn't quite come through on the screen, not even in the best close-ups."

"What about the rest of me?" she demanded.

"All right. A shade more mature, but better than ever. A bit more like these characters you play, but I don't mind that—I've always had a weakness, as you know, for those exquisite mysterious creatures, even when they have stolen necklaces in their handbags."

She pulled a face. "I thought you'd be downstairs waiting for me."

"I meant to be, and then I thought you might have been held up, and there were one or two things I wanted to do to the script —all for your sake."

"I'm longing to read it. It sounds exciting, but I wouldn't let Brent tell me the whole story." She smiled now, and gave me one of her wide-eyed solemn looks. "It's lovely to be back, Greg. But sad too. Last night I cried."

"Why?"

"I don't know." Liz could never bother analysing and explaining her feelings, which was one reason why she was never boring, unlike all those actresses who do nothing but analyse and explain themselves.

"Brent told me on the telephone that the plane had shaken you up, so you'd gone to bed."

"I told him that to get rid of him," she said. "Not that I dislike him but he's the kind who wants to throw parties. And I just didn't feel like talking to people—except you. I wanted to call you up last night, but Brent was against it, and then I decided to come down here today instead—much better. A nice silly English sort of hotel too." She glanced around in a cosy intimate sort of way, as if we'd just taken over the place together. "Your room's just like mine. It has a tower bit too. I'm just underneath you. And we have a special little staircase—did you notice?"

"If you're directly below, you'll probably hear me pacing the floor. I keep late hours too. You'd better change."

"No, I don't mind. If I'm asleep it won't waken me—nothing does. And if I'm awake, then I'll like hearing it. And if it gets bad, then I'll come up and talk to you."

"I ought to warn you, Liz," I told her, "that although these gigantic rooms are big enough to be drawing-rooms, studies and dining-rooms combined, officially they're bedrooms—so you be careful."

"Rubbish! The manageress told me she was sorry there weren't any sitting-rooms to be had, but that these turret rooms —I think that's what she called them—were really sitting-rooms as well as bedrooms. So shut up about being careful. And have you been careful?"

I laughed. "I haven't even had to think about it. I came down here to work."

"Yes, I know. Brent explained about that." She waited a moment. "How are you, Greg darling?"

"All right, Liz, thank you. Just a sour old hack, toiling away at a script."

"You're different somehow. I don't mean to look at. But different inside, I suspect. You're not in love with somebody, are you—and have been keeping it dark?"

"Hell, no! I'm a thousand years old. When I'm not working on the script, I spend my time thinking of my distant past—

about the time when you were just toddling. And that's all there is to say about me—"

"I'm not sure," she said darkly. "I'm not at all sure. But go on—change the subject if you want to."

"How are you getting on with George Adony?"

"So far I don't like him very much. Tell me about him."

"Well, I wrote to you—remember—"

"Yes, about what a good director he was—but I knew that. And it isn't what I mean. You know what I mean."

I lit a pipe, which gave me time to think. This was tricky. We had all to work together on the picture, yet I had to be honest with Liz. "To begin with," I said slowly, "George Adony has a genuine passion for films—and not just because he makes money and gains kudos out of 'em—but because when he's discussing a story or a set or casting and when he's working on the floor, he's arranging life to look as he wants it to look and he's giving it some particular meaning of his own. He's a Central European, partly Jewish—and he's intelligent, lecherous, pessimistic. He has that bottomless pessimism so many of them have. He's as fixed in disillusion as an old headwaiter. He thinks we're all as naïve as children, although in many ways he's as naïve himself."

"He's got those bright little sad eyes that some monkeys have," said Liz thoughtfully. "Go on about him before he comes bursting in."

"I haven't much more to say. I don't know him really well. I always feel he's unhappy here in England, in spite of his success. I think he despises us because we aren't more intelligent, and then dislikes us—and is a bit afraid—because we seem able to get on very well without his kind of intelligence. Although he'd have been one of the first to suffer, because he was definitely anti-Nazi and only got out one jump ahead of the Gestapo, I sometimes suspect that he was secretly disappointed that we didn't lose the war—and can't quite understand yet why we didn't. He could see our stupidity but he couldn't see that the Nazis were a dam' sight stupider—really dense. The fact is, there's a devil of a lot here he misses seeing and understanding, clever as he is. In that —though in nothing else—he's like some Americans I know."

"Well, don't look at me like that, Greg darling. I'm not an American, and I've argued for hours and hours with them, trying to make them understand. You remember what you wrote to me—about so many Americans simply not wanting to see Britain as it really is and always insisting on that fake old Hollywood Britain—my God—I ought to know it, the number of times they've made me play the lady of the manor—well, honestly, Greg, I've argued and argued about that—and still they wouldn't understand. Well, if I'm appearing downstairs for dinner, I suppose I'd better have a bath and change. Can I take the first two sequences with me?"

She was standing now. I went across and put the script into her hands. Then we stood still, silent, staring at each other. I suddenly felt a great affection for her.

"What, Greg?"

"I'm glad you're here, Liz. It suddenly came over me how glad I was you were here."

"You didn't much care before, did you?" she said very quietly. "I knew. And I was terribly disappointed—and hurt."

"I'm sorry. But it's hard to explain. When I come to a place like this to work, I don't talk to anybody, don't bother with other people, and sink deep down inside myself. And it takes me some time to come up again, that's all." It wasn't, but it was near enough.

"You needn't explain," she said. "It's all right now. I must go." She put her cheek to mine for a moment, contrived to kiss me lightly somewhere in the neighbourhood of my left ear, and then made a quick but graceful exit. I felt confused and restless. I knew I couldn't work and I didn't want to sit and think, so I changed into the only decent suit I had with me and went downstairs to find Adony and Jake West. They were in the far corner of the bar drinking whisky: an odd pair—George Adony, short, slight, dapper, with his disproportionate head and long pale face; and Jake West, almost bloated, with a swollen purple face, boisterous and hoarse-voiced, never quite tight and never quite sober, with all the automatic and indestructible bonhomie of the publicity and advertising world. They had that corner of the bar to themselves, for it was too early yet for the people who wanted a cocktail before dinner.

"George wants to know," said Jake grinning, "what you've got that he hasn't got."

"I can tell him that," I said, grinning too, "but why is it worrying him?"

"You explain, George," said Jake. "I'll order another round. Whisky for you, Gregory? Okay—don't move. Tell him, George."

Adony looked at me mournfully and reproachfully, and I saw at once that whatever was coming was something more than a mere idle gag of Jake's. "I think I am rather angry with you, Gregory," he began, in his precise way. "Not of course about what you have got and I have got—that is Jake—but because we must think about our film. And you should have told us—or if you did tell Brent, then he should have told me."

"Told you what? What *is* this?"

"I should have been told—because it is important and may make difficulties—that Elizabeth Earl is in love with you."

"And that's why he wants to know what you've got that he hasn't got." Jake was back, with the drinks.

"Be quiet, Jake. This is serious," and Adony looked sharply at me, "and must be settled quickly."

"There isn't anything to settle," I said, annoyed now. "You weren't told anything because there isn't anything to tell you. There's nothing of that sort between Elizabeth and me. We're old and very good friends, that's all. And you knew that."

"You realise that it is important for me to know," Adony went on, in the same sharp tone. "I have to direct this picture. It is Brent's biggest commitment. Elizabeth Earl is a great star. You write the script. If you and she—"

"Yes, yes," I cut in impatiently, "you needn't draw a map, George. But I tell you we aren't like that. And never have been. Just get that into your head."

Adony looked bewildered. "Everything she has said and done so far suggests to me that she is in love with you. And Jake agrees with me."

"No, George, I said it might easily be like that," said Jake, who liked to keep in with everybody and not take sides. "But I did point out that Gregory'd been over here since—when was it?

—1940—and that I knew he'd turned down a lot of good offers to go back to Hollywood."

"But we agreed that they could have had a serious quarrel, which they had now made up." And Adony looked at me suspiciously.

"Oh for God's sake—stop romancing," I cried. "You sound like a pair of dotty schoolgirls."

"When five hundred thousand pounds are at stake," said Adony, "to say nothing of my reputation as a director, I do not talk or act like a schoolgirl. In fact, though I have been compared to many things, I have never before been compared to a schoolgirl. It is not a comparison that impresses me. But I should like the truth about you two—and quickly, please, Gregory." He swallowed his whisky but kept his eyes fixed on mine.

"All right then, keep quiet and listen," I told him, struggling free of my annoyance. "There's nothing very odd and mysterious about my relationship with Elizabeth, once you know a little about her history and character. Back in '36, she was playing her first part in the West End, after year's of weekly Rep. and tours. It wasn't an important part and she didn't make any noise in it, I gather, but it happened that Melfoy, the Hollywood agent, was over here and saw her. He was probably tight at the time—"

"He was stinking the whole time he was over here," said Jake, grinning reminiscently. "That was the time he signed two waiters from the Grill, and chased one of Drew's parlourmaids out into Avenue Road. Poor ol' Melfoy! He was good too."

"Well, he persuaded Mertz to give Elizabeth a contract," I continued, "and she was shipped off to the Coast—and there was quite a bit of publicity on this side. You probably remember it, Jake? Well, out there they gave her a test and a couple of bit parts and then they didn't want her."

"They must have been stupid," said Adony, who was always glad to take a crack at Hollywood. "She must have had something even then."

"Not so much as you'd think," I told him. "She wasn't making the best of her looks. And she was just a second-rate English actress, with too much of the wrong kind of stage experience. Anyhow they didn't want her—and when they don't want you out there, you know it. After a time you begin to wonder if you've got leprosy or something. I was under contract to Mertz at that time, so I saw what was happening. She was English, and a quiet sensible sort of girl, and she knew people and places I'd known, so I took hold of her, gave her a lot of advice, introduced her to some useful people, persuaded her to change her appearance and style, and when I left Mertz and went over to Sam Gruman, I argued Sam into taking up her contract from Mertz. I wrote in a part for her in a script I'd taken over from two of Sam's boys, and though it was a small part, she stole that picture. So Sam tore up the old contract and gave her a better one, groomed her, and then starred her with Terry Bleck in *Yellow Roses*."

"You did not write that, I think," said Adony.

"No. I'd nothing to do with it," I replied.

"I am glad," said Adony. "It was dam' awful bad—that film."

"I didn't care for it myself," I told him. "But it grossed about three million dollars. And it put Elizabeth right at the top."

I drank my whisky. A feeling of utter staleness, weariness, exhaustion, had suddenly descended upon me, and I didn't know why or where it came from. I didn't want to be there, talking to those two, but didn't particularly want to be anywhere else or doing anything else, for that matter.

"But that is not the end of the story," said Adony.

"No, not quite. As you may remember, she married Terry Bleck—she for the first time, he for the fourth, as the gossip columns used to say. I didn't see much of her for some months after that, chiefly because Bleck and I disliked each other. The marriage didn't work of course, and she left him. I did what I could to help her through a rather bad time, and finally packed her off with old Ethel Ferryman to a ranch out on the Mohave Desert. Sometimes I'd go out and stay with them there, and I arranged with Sam Gruman, who was getting very worried about her, to write a story specially for her. That was *The Lonely Huntress*, which Sam let me co-produce, so I saw a lot of Elizabeth about then both on and off the floor. That brought her an Oscar, and of course a terrific rating. Then the war came, and as soon as I'd worked out my contract, I came back here and didn't see Elizabeth again until this evening. But we used to write and give each other the news. We were friends. And if you try hard enough you can have friends—even in the motion picture business."

Adony was thoughtful. "Yes, all this is very possible, even though it is not what I expected."

"It's what I've always heard," said Jake, who couldn't afford not to appear in the know. "And I remember now she's said one or two very nice things about you helping her, Greg, in interviews I've read. And that's since you left Hollywood, so they wouldn't have been studio hand-outs."

"There's only one thing more I want to say," I said. "And that's about Elizabeth herself. It'll help us with the film too." I waited a moment because I had to make an effort to break through that sense of staleness and weariness. And the bar was filling up now and I had to talk quietly, but I was anxious to fix what I had to say in their minds. "Now I needn't tell you two that stars who are bang at the top, as she is, are in a ridiculous position. They can't possibly live up to their own apparent importance. They're sitting on mushrooms a mile high. It's as if you took that barman and suddenly gave him half China. So some of them drive themselves—and a lot of other people—nearly dotty, trying to discover what they have that's so wonderful. Some of the others really think they *have* something that fully justifies their importance—and try to behave like Nero or Cleopatra—you know—"

They knew, and muttered names to prove it.

"But a few," I continued, "a very few, I'll admit, just stay the same people they always were—"

"Never," said Adony sharply, "never, never. It is not possible. They may act that part—nice, simple, modest—kind to old friends—but inside they must be different. It is impossible for them to be otherwise. You are going to tell us that Elizabeth Earl is one of these rare ones?"

"Yes, I am. And I think I can explain why. The crack-pots belong to two classes. Either they're artists or would-be artists —or they're simply born garage-hands or chambermaids who happen to have been given Aladdin's lamp. But you'll find that the few big stars who stay the same people never belong to either of these groups. Like Elizabeth. She began as a nice sensible girl who was a reasonably hard-working but by no means brilliant actress—the kind it's useful to have in a second-rate stock company. But she happens to have the kind of looks that, with some careful grooming, are now dead right for the screen, and also one or two tricks of voice and manner that a good script-writer and a clever director know just what to do with—so here she is at the top. But she doesn't think she's Duse or Bernhardt, and at the same time, being a sensible woman who's been acting for eighteen years or so, she's no mere chambermaid rubbing Aladdin's lamp. She's a conscientious hard-working pro who knows she's had a mountain of luck, and that's that. And that's the way to treat her. So don't worry, George. You'll find her easy to work with."

"She has that reputation," said Jake. "Though from what Brent said, I think he found her a bit edgy last night. But that may have been the trip."

"We shall see," said George Adony dubiously, plucking at his fleshy lower lip, "we shall see. I am not sure you are the best judge of this, Gregory my friend. And I apologise for being so curious about your private life, but it was the film I was worried about, you understand."

I said that I understand that but I didn't understand why I shouldn't be the best judge of the character and outlook of a woman I knew so well.

He was ready for me. "Because obviously with her you are in a special class—and quite right too. You are the one who was sorry for her when she was a nobody, who gave her good advice, who found work for her, who wrote fine parts for her, who was never merely infatuated as so many other men must have been, who was the solid cool Englishman, the missing father, the big brother, the stern confessor, the maestro who gave the early lessons and for whom they never lose their respect—"

"Oh, drop it, George. And there's the dinner-gong. By the way, Elizabeth's coming down to dinner."

"I know," said Jake. "I've fixed a table. But we've still time for a quick one."

I shook my head, and Adony said mournfully: "No, thank you, Jake. I think I am a little tight already. Too much whisky and not enough to eat all day. Let us get out of here. I hate all these people."

Jake grinned. "They're customers, George."

"Do you think I do not know it?"

We were just in time to see Liz come sailing into the lounge. She was wearing a long black dress, and looked vivid and happy, as if everything was a great treat. As she approached us, I noticed Adony staring at her with a cold camera eye, probably working out a long shot for the first sequence.

"You three have been drinking," said Liz. "What have you been talking about?"

"About you of course, Miss Earl," said Adony.

Liz glanced at me, with a slight lift of her eyebrows.

"It's all right," I said to her. "I did most of the talking. It was shop really. Let's go in and eat. And don't expect much. We live a sparse life down here, far away from the Black Market."

The dining-room of the Royal Ocean Hotel did its best to preserve the gentlemanly tradition of not paying too much attention to a fellow-guest. But most of the diners could have done better if we had brought in with us a bright emerald elephant with an illuminated trunk. They took their eyes away from the radiant Elizabeth so carefully that you could almost hear the sockets creaking. And I was amused to notice how much more conversation there was than usual, most of it in a breathy undertone: it was rather like dining at a conspirators' conference. The younger waitresses, who just stared and stared with their mouths wide open, had the best time.

George Adony, after trying a spoonful of gravy soup and then pushing his plate away, had glanced around and shrewdly estimated the sensation Elizabeth's appearance had caused. "Observe the ladies and gentlemen," he told us. "I think their hands are shaking. They are spilling their dreadful soup. All because of you, Miss Earl."

"Why, I was just thinking the opposite," cried Liz, who was genuinely astonished. "I was thinking how nice it is when there's no fuss."

"This is England and not America," said Adony. "You are forgetting. There is a terrible fuss here tonight. The arrival of five cabinet ministers would have less effect. Gregory will agree with me, and he knows, having been here for weeks."

"It's true. They're all excited. The temperature's up several degrees."

"Movies," said Adony, slowly and mournfully, "the power of movies. It is frightening. We talk of it as an industry. We talk of it as entertainment. It is more—much, much more. What we are doing is filling a horrible vacuum, where once there were gods and goddesses and then afterwards saints and guardian angels. We are mythologists. We are the only licensed necromancers and wizards, shamans and medicine men. It is not the conscious mind, which we merely tickle, but the deep unconscious that is our territory. You imagine, Gregory my friend, that Miss Earl is simply a good actress, with a beautiful face and figure, easy to photograph. It is not so. She is now a magical image in the world's dream life. That is why even the hands of the English ladies and gentlemen here are shaking—and in many countries we would have to call the police in to protect her—because into this dining-room there has come a figure, exquisite, smiling but demoniac, from the mythical and magical darkness. Movies! Box office entertainment! The film industry! Bah! The scientists experiment with the atom, and they are regarded with terror and awe—eh? But we experiment with the world's unconscious, we play tricks with its psyche, we produce shining symbolic images in the living darkness, we move into the vacant hells and empty paradises. Is there another piece of this chicken for me?" he demanded of the headwaiter, who was standing at his elbow, fascinated.

"No, sir. I'm afraid there isn't."

"Then please go away. Unless you know of something good for us to drink. What have you done about that, Jake?"

Liz winked at me. The conference over the wine list left us temporarily alone together. She had the wide shining look of a little girl at a long-awaited party. I couldn't imagine what made her so happy.

"Liz, you look as if you're having a wonderful time," I told her.

"But I am, darling, I am. The script's grand. And it's such fun being here. I'll tell you a secret." She leaned forward. "I've never stayed in this kind of hotel before in England. Couldn't afford to on the kind of salary I used to get."

"On the kind of salary you get now, you could buy the dam' place." I was a bit surly because I thought she was putting on an act, which wasn't like her.

She looked disappointed, and then I saw that I was wrong. "That's not the same thing. *Do* understand. I've been away for years and years."

"Sorry, Liz," I muttered. The other two had now come out of their huddle over the wine list.

"One or two people here I know," said Jake, hoarsely confidential. "City types. Had money in films during the big gold rush. Chap called Horncastle over there. And another one somewhere—got a title from the Chamberlain Government."

Adony made a contemptuous noise, but I was interested. "Was his name Nixey? Now Lord Harndean?"

"That's the bloke. Didn't think you'd have known him. Dry dullish chap. Met him here, I suppose, eh?"

"I have met him here," I replied rather carefully. "But as a matter of fact I knew him—and his wife—years and years ago, before the 1914 war, up in Bruddersford. We worked in the same wool office for a time."

Liz pounced on this at once. "Is that why you've been thinking about your past? You remember what you said? Is it because you met these people again?"

"Yes, I suppose so." I made it as casual as I could. But I ought to have remembered that Liz was quick and perceptive about me, probably because we'd been close friends and had spent a lot of time together without being lovers and lost in the coloured fogs and electric storms of passion. I was deliberately casual because I didn't want to talk about the Nixeys and the past, and I think she guessed this too, just as she had guessed that this encounter with them was important to me. But she couldn't quite restrain her curiosity.

"Which are they?" she asked Jake.

"Oh, you can't see them from here," he told her. "And anyhow they're a couple of dry sticks. But I'll tell you what, Miss Earl," he continued, on the job now. "I've been thinking that—if you don't mind—you might just spend half an hour—no more, just half an hour—in the lounge after dinner, and then I'll introduce one or two of these people. Then you won't seem too cheap and easy, and not too snooty either. These people don't matter much, but they're influential in their own way, and may be going back to town in a day or two—y'know."

"I don't mind," she said. "I'll do whatever you think I ought to do."

"Jake is right," said Adony. "Half an hour—then vanish. It will leave just the right impression."

Liz glanced at me enquiringly, but I said nothing.

"I'll fix it," said Jake. "We'll take our time and let them get out first. And I'll order our coffee to be served out there—brandy too if they've got any decent brandy."

"They have," I said. "But Elizabeth doesn't drink—I don't want any—and George here has had enough."

"That was before dinner," said Adony gloomily. "Now I need more. There are some types here I could use—much better than the character actors they send us, for each one adds his or her bit of theatre to the film so that in the end there is a terrible falseness. It is the curse of British movies—this atmosphere of theatre that creeps in with the small-part character actors. In Hollywood they are more fortunate, being so far from theatres —eh, Miss Earl?"

That took us comfortably through the rest of dinner. I said very little, although Liz appealed to me several times. I was back again, among the old bones in that desert, where I had been before dinner, feeling stale, weary and exhausted. My life seemed about as nourishing as the tins of celluloid they were discussing. I stared at Elizabeth as an old churchyard ghost might stare at a bride. She made me feel old and done for. What was she so happy and radiant about anyhow? Or was it simply that she was still in her middle thirties and had been regularly obtaining her fair share of vitamins? (Or was it more than her fair share?) I had felt better before these people came charging into my quiet life, when I was just working on the script and then spending my afternoons and late evenings re-discovering my past. Yet I didn't like to think that; simply because I was fond of Elizabeth and she was so obviously delighted to be here. But it was a fact, and one that I didn't enjoy, that I had felt ten times more alive that afternoon on the cliff, when I was really back in Bruddersford with the Alingtons, than I did now, listening drearily to Elizabeth and George Adony talking about films.

When we went into the lounge Liz and I had a minute to ourselves. "What's the matter, Greg?" she asked softly.

"Nothing really. I'm feeling a bit stale. Perhaps I'm tired. Or it may be spring. When I was a kid they used to pour all sorts of stuff into us about this time of year. Nobody bothers now, and perhaps that's where we're wrong."

"I'm not staying long down here."

"Neither am I, Liz. I never do." At the other end of the lounge the trio was slogging away at a selection from *Tosca*. "By the way, you must meet that trio—not tonight but when it's quieter. The pianist is a Czech and he's the brother of little Zenek who's an assistant director at Paramount. And the two girls are filling in from the Royal College and are nice youngsters—especially the violinist, Susan. I chaff them sometimes about the stuff they have to play, and now and then they trot out the masters for the good of my ear and their own souls. You'll like them, Liz. And now here we go."

I said that because Jake West, now bursting with booze and professional bonhomie, was bringing up the first of the fortunate few to be presented at the Court of the Silver Screen. The man Horncastle, who looked a smoother darker version of Jake himself, only pickled and bottled in the City instead of in Fleet Street and the studios. Then a grim beaky pair called Lincing, the kind of rich who always seem to be in self-inflicted quarantine, and who appeared to be for ever arriving and departing mournfully in a mammoth Rolls. And then came Lord and Lady Harndean—my old friends, as they instantly declared themselves to be, Malcolm and Eleanor Nixey. After a few minutes Jake was deep in hoarse guffawing boozy talk with the man Horncastle, and Adony was addressing himself fluently and malevolently to the Lincings, who stared at the white-faced little demon with horror; and I stood by and watched the Nixeys blink and smirk and politely grimace, as oldish folk of their sort always do when they are feeling rather shy and removed from their own background, in the warmth and radiance, the Californian sunshine, of Elizabeth's glamour and fame and two-hundred-thousand-dollar contracts.

It was very odd, very confusing, this unexpected overlapping of two worlds, with Time playing tricks in both of them. Somewhere at the back of my mind, waiting for the lights to go on in the theatre of memory, the Nixeys, young and smart and smiling confidently, were still standing in the doorway of the Alingtons' drawing-room. And now here they were talking to Elizabeth. Jake had casually dismissed them as "a couple of dry sticks," and I saw what he meant. Yes, they were dry now, brittle, with no juice, no ripeness; thin, papery, sterile. And it was not age alone that had done it. They had always lacked something essential and vital; perhaps a whole dimension was missing, so that although they had succeeded in everything they had attempted, it was only in Flatland, among triumphs cut out of the thinnest cardboard. And then as I leaned against the back of Elizabeth's chair, looking but not listening properly, withdrawn into myself, I understood what it was that was so worrying, after all these years, about the Nixeys. It was the fact that now they seemed so ordinary, were merely the kind of people you met in this kind of hotel. It was only because of what I remembered about them in Bruddersford so long ago that I could single them out and pay them any special attention. Yet there had been a time when they had seemed to me quite extraordinary. And it was not, I decided, because I had changed and we had all grown much older, than now they seemed commonplace. No, it was because what had once been a tiny fifth column was now a settled and familiar army of occupation.

All right, there were now far more rootless, parasitic and acquisitive people about. But that discovery, even if it could be called one, didn't explain what suddenly happened to me then. For at that moment the feeling of flatness and staleness and exhaustion vanished, and in its place I felt a bewildering but painful sense of loss, like a man bereaved and desolate. It came from nowhere, took me by surprise, and couldn't be explained.

But I knew I couldn't stay another minute in the huge glaring idiocy of that lounge. I hurried out, making for the entrance hall and the front door. But there was no going out, for the threatened rainstorm had arrived, and I stood for a few minutes at the door staring at the jiggling rods of rain, the dark torrents of spring.

Then I went up to my room and turned on one small light near the door, leaving the turret end lost in shadow. That absurd room took on a new character: it seemed a thousand miles from the lounge below; it was a corner of some forgotten castle high in the blinding storm; it was a refuge for lost travellers; and there, as the spring night drummed unceasingly, I returned again to my youth, and made myself remember. . . .

SIX

During his first few months with us, at Hawes and Company, Malcolm Nixey mostly worked in the office with Croxton, and we didn't see much of him out in the sample-room. I had to confess to myself that I hadn't disliked him at first. I think that on the whole I rather liked him then. He was a thinnish, dapper fellow of thirty or so in those days: a narrow face, with hair brushed glossily back after the prevailing fashion, a small clipped moustache, restless eyes. He smiled a great deal, and often laughed in a staccato mechanical manner, as men do who carry about and distribute tiny jokes like small change but who have no real sense of humour. He was very dressy, very neat and quick—the kind of man who enters an engagement at once, with a flick or two of a gold pencil, into an exquisite little diary. There was a metropolitan air about him. At last I had met a man-about-town. Even in Bruddersford, it seemed to me, he led a West End life, popping in and out of everywhere, spending money trying and tasting everything. I couldn't help being rather fascinated by this new and dashing type.

He was polite and pleasant to everybody, including Joe Ackworth, who plainly didn't like him. The office staff—the damp Bertha, the dim Harold Ellis, and Bernard the boy—were captivated by him. To me, small fry though I was, he was more than polite and pleasant, he was determinedly friendly. "Look, old man," he would say, after he had ventured into the sample-room and Ackworth had muttered some advice and then marched out, "I didn't quite get the hang of that. Tell me—what is it all about? D'you mind?" Because I was fairly new too, and was not a Bruddersfordian, his manner always hinted that we were in the same boat. And because I was in the sample-room he probably imagined that I knew more about the business than I actually did, although on this point Croxton could have put him right. (But no doubt he didn't believe everything Croxton told him.)

His attitude towards Mr. Alington, during those first months, was very carefully adjusted and balanced. There was a deference towards an older and more experienced man, the head of this Bruddersford branch, but along with it, modifying it, was a constant suggestion that he was at least Alington's social equal and that behind him were the London office and formidable if mysterious powers. All this kept Mr. Alington uneasy, so that he never seemed to me his ordinary genial self when Nixey was about. This meant a change in the whole atmosphere of the place. We had a stranger with us.

When Nixey did come out of the office, to give us a hand in the sample-room—and I overheard Mr. Alington telling Ackworth that the London office had suggested this—he was quick and intelligent, never pretending to know more than he did know, and almost prostrated himself before Joe Ackworth's vast experience. But we always felt he was not really with us. The old ease and intimacy vanished. And one afternoon—it must have been late that summer—Ackworth watched him go out, to pay his first call on a Bruddersford firm, and for once spoke his mind to me.

"You knaw, lad," said Ackworth, staring at the place where Nixey had been standing a minute before, and blowing hard down his empty pipe, "yon's a crafty beggar."

"Nixey?"

"Ay. If he's up to any bloody good 'ere, then Ah'm a ring-tailed monkey. An' if Ah wor John Alington," he continued, talking more to himself than to me, "Ah'd tell 'em in London that no matter whose nephew he is, either Ah go or he does. John's too soft." Then he realised he had said too much. "What yer standin' there for, lad, wi' your mouth wide open? Get them merinos down, an' let's get on, if yer don't want to be 'ere all night."

A few days later we finished work about half-past six, and I went off to have an evening in town, for my uncle and aunt were away. After going along to the General Post Office with Bernard the office-boy, for there was a particularly big load of samples to be posted that night, I suddenly remembered that I had left a book I had borrowed from Jock Barniston in my desk in the sample-room, and as I thought I might want to read it in bed and

I had nothing to do at the moment anyhow, I decided to go back to Canal Street. I let myself in, found the book where I had left it, and then heard voices, a quick mutter, in the office. I opened the door between the sample-room and the office—and there were Nixey and Croxton, their heads together in a conspiratorial haze of smoke.

Croxton was startled, then furious. "What the devil do you want, Dawson?" he shouted.

"I only came back for something I'd forgotten. Then I heard voices."

Croxton's outburst had taken my attention away from Nixey, so I didn't notice if he had been startled and angry too. But now he came forward, cool and smiling.

"I'm at a loose end, so I was telling Mr. Croxton a thing or two about the City."

"And I must go," Croxton muttered, clearing his desk, and doing it with just that extra touch of deliberation which gave his action a false and theatrical air.

"What are you doing this evening?" Nixey asked me.

"Nothing very much. Hadn't decided yet."

"Same here. What about your having a bite of dinner with me, old man—and then we might think of going somewhere afterwards, eh?" He must have noticed my hesitation and instantly guessed one of the reasons for it, because he added casually: "My treat. I'm rather flush at the moment. Let's go along to the Market Grill." He turned to Croxton. "Don't forget what I told you about that South African stuff. It's worth knowing. I had it from my uncle, who's always in the know—a very clever old boy. Come on, Dawson. 'Night, Croxton, old man."

The Market Grill was a place where solid and substantial Bruddersford men went for meals as solid and substantial as themselves, and was famous for its steaks and chump chops. (I haven't seen such lumps of meat for years and I doubt if I would know what to do with one of them now.) I had often heard about it but had never been there before: I couldn't afford the Market Grill prices. Nixey obviously could afford them, and seemed to be well known there. After we had given our order, he asked me if I would like to go with him to the nine o'clock show, the

"Second House" as we called it, at the Imperial Music-Hall, and when I said that I would, he coolly told the waiter to telephone for two stalls; which seemed to me a grand man-about-town way of doing things.

Nixey was a careful host, especially for a lad of my age, but I noticed even then, grateful and impressed though I was, that somehow he was an unsatisfactory companion. You didn't have as good a time as you expected to have, or as he assumed you were having; he was never completely with you; and his companionship had a thin, flat and temporary quality. Thus, while we were at the Market Grill, although he ordered a tremendous meal he only trifled with it, pushing the food about with his fork and then pecking here and there; and his restless little eyes were always throwing glances round the place, and he would recognise somebody he knew, nod and smile and perhaps wave a hand; and he would ask me questions about myself, with a flattering eagerness, but would lose interest in my replies. It is a type I know only too well now, but then it was new and puzzling. He had heard already that I occasionally wrote little things for the local papers, and he told me that he knew one or two journalists in London and also a man who wrote revue sketches and made a "damned nice thing" out of them. With the intuition of youth I realised that it would be impossible for me to explain to him what I felt about writing, so I didn't try. Now and then, however, casually, he brought the talk round to Hawes and Company. And there was the usual suggestion that he and I were the two outsiders, temporary and amused visitors to Bruddersford.

"Ackworth now," he said. "You've been working with him all the time. He's the sort of chap who'd never have a chance in a London firm of any importance. Eh? But I suppose it's all right here, where they go in for that type. Probably quite popular, eh, old man?"

"Somebody told me he's one of the best-known men in the wool trade," I replied. "And he knows all about it. That roughness of his is just put on. It's part of a game he plays—being a character. A lot of them here do it."

"Can't stand me," said Nixey. "Don't know why. I haven't done him any harm."

"It's just his manner," I said, though I knew very well that in this instance it wasn't. "He's all right when you get to know him."

"Croxton's been working with him for years now, and they don't get on. What about that?"

As he and Croxton seemed to be so thick, I didn't want to say too much about Croxton, so I merely muttered that they just didn't like each other.

"Any particular reason, old man?" (And this "old man" of his had a peculiar light glancing tone of its own. It didn't suggest, wasn't meant to suggest, that he was fond of you, that you were old friends, but hinted at a smooth and easy and metropolitan comradeship, turning you into a man-about-town too.)

"Well," I replied deliberately. "Ackworth thinks that Croxton should stick to his job as cashier and not interfere with the wool end of the business. We've had rows sometimes because Croxton has come out and given me orders about samples. There was a big row—and I nearly left the firm—just before last Christmas." Nixey was interested, as I saw at once from his eyes. For once he was really with me. "What happened? Between ourselves of course, naturally."

I didn't want to tell him, but he was older than I was, and was standing me a good dinner and then a stall at the Imperial, so I felt he was entitled to the story, such as it was. And for once I couldn't complain that he didn't listen properly.

"So Mr. Alington apologised to you," he said when I had finished. "He must like you."

"I think he does," I replied. "I often go and spend an evening there. You remember, I was there when you and Mrs. Nixey first turned up. But I don't think that's why he apologised. It was simply because he'd lost his temper with me about something that wasn't my fault. He'd have done the same to anybody in the same circumstances. He's like that."

This didn't interest Nixey. "But did he really settle it between Ackworth and Croxton? Has there been any trouble since?"

"Once or twice we've been on the edge of it," I answered, rather reluctantly. "Like the other day, you remember. But anyhow that's the chief reason why Ackworth and Croxton don't get on. And I'm for Ackworth. I don't like Croxton much myself." And when I said that I wasn't forgetting that Nixey and Croxton were very thick. I didn't care if Croxton was told I didn't like him.

"Croxton's a pretty smart chap," said Nixey. "And if you ask me—between ourselves, old man—I don't think it's fair he should be kept out of the sample-room and not given more of the real business to do. But that's just my opinion. Though I wouldn't hesitate to mention it to Alington, if the subject came up." He gave a quick glance round that had something very characteristic about it, then smiled at me. "I've an idea that competition's getting keener in this business, especially on the exporting side, and it needs fellows who are keen to run it. Alington's all right—decent chap—clever in some ways—but is he keen enough? I doubt it. Between ourselves, I very much doubt it. He may be off-colour or something—it may be all just temporary—but just now I don't get the impression that he's really pushing the business on. In fact, quite the opposite. Very much, of course, between ourselves, old man. Time we went."

And he didn't give me time to answer him, and once we were on our way to the Imperial I felt it would be all wrong to re-open the subject. I would have told him that he was mistaken about Mr. Alington, but as we walked along Market Street I wondered rather miserably if there was not something in what he said, particularly from the London office point of view. To put an end to that, I asked him about Mrs. Nixey. He replied airily that she was flourishing and gay and off somewhere, he didn't know where.

"We don't hang round each other's necks as they do here, y'know," he said. "Sometimes we go out together, sometimes we don't—it depends what's happening. I believe tonight she's gone to the theatre with that newspaper chap you know—Kerry."

"Ben Kerry." I was surprised.

"Yes. Why not?"

"Oh—I don't know. Only he's practically engaged to one of the Alington girls—Eva, the very pretty fair one."

"Is he?" That sharper note came into Nixey's voice again.

Then it disappeared. "Well, I don't blame him. She looked rather a knock-out, that one. However I only said that Eleanor had gone to the theatre with him—at least I think that was the arrangement. She likes the theatre, and I don't care for it—unless it's a good Gaiety show. Let's hope the Alington kid won't be jealous. That might put Eleanor's back up." He laughed. And afterwards I remembered that laugh.

I went so often to the Imperial and had so many rich but confused memories of it that I could not recall any details of that night's show, though I was certain it was a good one. I was certain of that because I remembered clearly feeling a widening gulf between Nixey and myself. That was due to the fact that, as it was a good show, I became absorbed in it, whereas he merely stared at it and idly half-listened to it. I like giving any form of entertainment my full attention, getting everything possible out of it, meeting the performers squarely halfway; and if the show is not worth this small amount of trouble, then I want to walk out and try something else. (And if I still feel like that, you may be sure I very much felt like that in those days.) But Nixey didn't seem able to lose himself and really make one of the audience. He would make remarks, stare about him, or want to slip out to the bar. This detachment of his irritated me, for though I became absorbed in the show I couldn't help being conscious of my host by my side and couldn't very well ignore him. I decided that I never wanted to see anything with him again: we just didn't fit as companions for a night out.

The last turn was as usual the old flickering Bioscope—and how astonished I would have been if somebody had told me then I would spend years writing stories for the thing—and Nixey said: "Come on, let's get out. Not worth staying for, and we can escape the rush." And as we came out of the smoky hall into the immense calm and sweetness of the summer night, he said: "Not a bad show. Seen better, but seen a lot worse too. Like to come up to my place for a drink? We're only five minutes away, y'know. Got rooms now, quite comfortable, in one of those biggish old houses in Leggett Lane." I thanked him, said I must hurry for my tram, thanked him for the whole evening, and went off at a smart pace. Actually I walked home, to get some air and exercise, and all the way there, through streets turning solemn and tender with the night, the half of my mind that was not yet invaded and possessed by the darkness and the mystery was busy with queries and conclusions about Nixey. There was nothing about him, I decided, that you could lay a finger on and declare to be wrong, yet what he offered you, in his dapper and pleasant fashion, never added up to anything satisfying and right. He was never quite there on the spot with you. If he was enjoying anything, then it was not something he was sharing with you. He seemed to turn to you just a thin edge of himself. His eyes looked at you but told you nothing. And if most of him was somewhere else, where was it and what was happening there?

Here I pulled myself back to the Royal Ocean Hotel, to, remind myself that in the lounge below, probably playing bridge if not still making inane remarks to Elizabeth, there was a certain elderly gentleman called Lord Harndean who was none other than this same Malcolm Nixey who stood me a dinner at the Market Grill and a show at the Imperial Music-Hall, Bruddersford. I felt a strong desire to rush down and hurry him out of that lounge, to bring him up here or take him out into the wild wet night, and to say to him: "It's the late summer of 1913, and we've just come out of the Imperial and I've refused an invitation, very flattering in itself to a lad my age, to have a final drink in your rooms in Leggett Lane. So now you're going home alone—thinking what, feeling what? Give me a glimpse of you, the real you, just during those five minutes, and I'll not ask a single other question. Now, Nixey!" But of course I didn't do anything of the kind. I lit another pipe, walked up and down the room for a minute or two, and then settled down again to find my way back to Bruddersford and that late summer of 1913, the last late summer of a whole age.

What about the Alingtons just then? I had to poke about and sort out my recollections to find them. But then I remembered that there had been the holidays. Most of them had been away, and Oliver, who had gone off with some Cambridge friends, Bridget, who had vanished with her musical chums, and Eva, who had not been well during the summer, I had hardly seen

at all. I had had a fortnight away myself, joining my uncle and
aunt at Silverdale, where they had taken a furnished house,
overlooking the wide estuary and the illimitable ribbed sand,
with the large solemn Mr. Blackshaw and his family. There was
Mrs. Blackshaw, a rather fierce untidy little woman, red-haired
and freckled; there was a Blackshaw youth about my age,
reluctantly freed from the Technical College to which he carried his passion for electrical engineering (and to the despair of
his mother and my Aunt Hilda, he and I detested each other at
sight); and, to complete the unattractiveness of the party, there
was a little Blackshaw girl of about nine, most inappropriately
called Laura, who combined her father's solemnity with her
mother's reddish fierceness and had an unladylike habit of following me about and of trying to bribe me with sticky sweets.
(On wet afternoons she made me play two-handed Ludo.) No
doubt it was a healthy holiday, and did me all the good that my
Aunt Hilda swore it did, but the Blackshaws were no substitute
for the Alingtons, and all the magic was elsewhere. But now,
about the middle of September, the wandering Alingtons were
returning.

Just after my evening with Nixey, I remembered, I hurried
down the dark stairs on my way to the Conditioning House, and
arrived at the bottom of them, blinking at the huge golden
afternoon, to bump into Bridget Alington, looking like a green-
eyed gipsy.

"Hello!" I cried, grinning with delight. "You're back, then.
But your father isn't in."

"I know he isn't," she replied with dignity, as if she had been
doing a lot of growing-up while she had been away and was
determined to prove it. "As a matter of fact I haven't come to see
him. It's you."

"Oh—me. Well, here I am, Bridget." And very fatuous I must
have sounded.

"What's the matter with you?" she enquired severely. "What's
so funny about this? I don't see anything to grin at. Unless it's me."

I assured her that it wasn't, that coming out of the dingy
office into the bright afternoon and suddenly seeing her there
had made me gape and grin.

"All right. You remember that queer man we met at Mr. Ackworth's last Christmas—the one who played the piano so marvellously—Mr. Leaton? Well, Oliver and I are going to his house tonight—I'm going to play—and we thought you might like to come too. You needn't if you don't want," she added haughtily. "But Mr. Leaton said you could—and Oliver thought it might be a good idea. About half-past eight—and here's the address."

I glanced at the bit of paper she had thrust into my hand, and when I looked up again she was hurrying down Canal Street in what might be described as a haughty and dignified rush. There was something different about her, and then I realised what it was—her skirts were longer and her hair was up and she was now supposed to be a young lady. I stared after her, through the smoky gold of Canal Street, with delight and tenderness.

Herbert Leaton lived in what had once been a farm-house, on the edge of the Glen, not very far from Joe Ackworth. Bridget and Oliver were already there when I arrived, and were being nervously entertained by Mrs. Leaton, an anxious little woman who looked as if she had never recovered from the shock of marrying such a strange fellow as Herbert. (But like most women tied to wilful, intractable and mysterious males, she was clearly devoted to him.) He had had to go out, but would be back any minute. The four of us were huddled together in a tiny front room, crammed with genteel knick-knacks, a beastly little place. Mrs. Leaton talked dreary commonplaces, smiling nervously all the time, while bewilderment and despair alternately peeped out of her eyes. Oliver, who was a nice lad, did his best to help, with some small assistance from me; but Bridget began to look puzzled and rather depressed, and I felt she was wondering if this was not all a mistake and asking herself if the Leaton she remembered at Ackworth's party really existed. Finally she muttered to Oliver "*Dodderite!*" and added a contrite "*Mumboady!*"

"Beg pardon," cried little Mrs. Leaton, staring at her.

Bridget went scarlet, and Oliver had to come to the rescue. "It's all this music that does it," he told Mrs. Leaton. "Don't you find that with Mr. Leaton? They can go on muttering queerly for hours and hours, with their *Allegro* and *Rubato*. Why can't they say it in English?"

Mrs. Leaton was relieved, and nodded brightly. "I don't understand it, and don't pretend to. But I like to hear Herbert play some of his pieces, when they've a nice tune. He laughs at me, but I don't mind. We can't all be musical, can we? But it makes a nice hobby for him."

Bridget stared at her in terror. But Mrs. Leaton continued, more cheerful and confident now: "Shall I make you a cup of coffee now or would you rather wait? Herbert said it would be better later on, but you know what he is. All right—later on then. Yes, his music gives him a nice hobby, and it wouldn't be the same if he had to earn his living by it, as I told him when he asked me. Yes, he asked me. He said: 'Now I leave it to you, Annie—you've more sense than I have.' And I said: 'Whatever they say, Herbert, you stick to the Insurance.' So he did."

"Oh, that's why he isn't a professional, eh?" said Bridget, in a rather unfriendly tone. "You persuaded him not to be."

"Yes, I did," replied Mrs. Leaton stoutly. "And I'd do the same again tomorrow. I don't know much about music, but I do know Herbert. And I know how independent he is. So I said to him: 'You be independent with your music, which is what you care about, and stick to the Insurance, which will give us enough to live on.' Of course his music brings us in a good bit extra—you'd be surprised—but he hasn't to depend on it. And that's how it ought to be, at least with somebody like him." And she nodded at Bridget, as if these last remarks disposed of her.

"Ah'm back, Annie. Are they 'ere?" Leaton had arrived, and was bellowing away, in his harsh West Riding voice, from the very front door. He burst in on us, looking longer and bonier than ever in that tiny room. "Sorry Ah'm late but Ah'd to go and 'ave a word wi' Joe Ackroyd. 'Ow do? 'Ow do? Pleased to meet yer, young man." This to Oliver. Then he turned to Bridget. "'Ope you're in fine fettle, young woman, 'cos Ah feel like givin' yer a doin' tonight. An' what are we all sittin' in 'ere for, this is no good to us—it's Annie's little tea-an'-bun 'ole this is. We want summat better nor this. Come on—come on." And he marched us out, clapping and rubbing his huge hands, and the three of us who had been so grand and patronising before he arrived, now followed him like trained mice.

"Nah this is my place—an' it's summat like," he announced, and showed us into a long bare room at the back of the house. It contained a fine Steinway concert grand, a few chairs and music-stands, some shelves of music and books, and that was all. Bridget lit up at once. "It's just right," she declared, looking round.

"Course it is," Leaton shouted. "Course it is. Ah took a bit o' trouble wi' this room. Nah, lads, sit down—an' if yer want to smoke there's cigarettes an' a tin o' good tobacco there, so 'elp yerselves. An' 'ave a look on them shelves—second lot down—an' see if there's owt yer fancy for us to play. Ah've got a bit o' new stuff. Chap brought me a parcel from Leipzig t'other day." He went lumbering over to the piano, pulling and cracking his fingers, while Bridget was eagerly exploring among the shelves and Oliver and I settled down, in the manner of our kind, to sprawl and smoke. "Ah'm like footballers that 'ave to kick ball about afore they start," he told us across the shining length of the Steinway. "Ah've got 'ands that feel like ducks' feet 'alf the time. Must give 'em a run an' warm up." Then he went straight into the Brahms *Paganini Variations*, taken at full speed, hurling us into torrents and cascades of sound.

Oliver sat up. "Crikey!" he cried, making wide eyes at me and then across at Bridget, who nodded triumphantly, as if to say: "What did I tell you?" Mrs. Leaton crept in and sat bolt upright on a little chair, suggesting the demure but confident proprietor of performing elephants. Sometimes grimacing in his concentration, at others looking up to nod and wink at us, Leaton went whizzing round the curves and down the glittering ice slopes of Brahms-Paganini.

"Show-off stuff," he announced at the end, "but it's given me a warm-up, and nah we'll get goin' wi' some solid tack. Get fiddle out, young Bridget."

It was after midnight when we left, full of coffee and beer, cake and Yorkshire parkin, and dizzy with music. And what came back to me, far clearer than any memory of the evening's music, was our walk home, down from the edge of the Glen. We had the road to ourselves. (Motor-cars rarely ventured out at night in those days.) We seemed to expand in a gaseous fashion to take up most of the road. We were very young and no doubt very silly, but you could afford to be young and silly then. The mid-September night, the last of its kind we would ever spend together, for this was already 1913, was deep blue against the black cup of the Pennines, and it was windless and gentle. There were white constellations above, and yellow ones below, made by the distant patterns of street lamps on the hills. Oliver carried Bridget's violin, and I took her music-case, and she marched and capered between us, arm-in-arm. When we were not clowning, breathlessly we sketched gigantic plans, broad and vague as the night. Bridget became expansive because she felt released from the tension, as well as fresh from the triumph, of playing with Leaton, who had praised her. Oliver and I expanded because we had spent the evening listening, though in the heady and self-haunted fashion of youth, and felt it was our turn now. Bridget was to have a year here, a year there, Leipzig, Odessa, Brussels, and then emerge to shake the world. I was to write everything that could be written, better than anybody had ever written it before. (Nothing said about narrowing it all down to film scripts for Sam Gruman and Brent.) Oliver, who was one of those enthusiastic cleverish lads who skate along the edge of all the arts but have no creative drive in them, had recently lent a hand in bringing out the latest undergraduate periodical, the usual affair of pompous satire, indignant leading articles about nothing, and uneasy verses on prostitutes seen at a distance; and he was now seeing himself as an editor and a publisher, doing audacious things with *format*, giving a gay and impudent twist to idealism, bringing together, between cover after cover, each a brighter orange than the last, a dozen choice spirits of his acquaintance (including me), all ready at any time now to set a match to the dusty old globe.

"*Shlumpumpitter!*" cried Oliver. "I tell you, souls, Forbes and Eric Seed and I worked out the whole thing—planned it to the last dot—one night at the end of last term. As a matter of fact, it was in May Week, and we'd all gone to the Corpus Ball, and drunk some champagne, and then Forbes barged up and said: 'Look here, Alington, this is pretty tedious—what about getting hold of Eric and drinking some beer in my rooms and really *talk-*

ing?' And we did, till five—or was it six?—and worked out the whole thing, Eric to do the designing, and Forbes and I to edit. Everything brand-new, down to the advertising. I tell you, we had some *wonderful* ideas—and Forbes has some money—not enough perhaps but he says he can easily raise some more—and Eric knows just the place for an office—in fact, we're going to look at it some time this term. Remind me sometime, Gregory, to give you the details of the scheme—you too, Bridget, if you're interested. First, this monthly, and a few little books—and then the whole thing in terrific full swing." He made singing noises then for a minute or two, stopped to take breath, then said, lifting his face to the starlight: "Life, souls, life! You either take it or reject it. Plenty of people reject it—yes, turn it down flat. We know dozens of 'em. But I take it, I accept it, the whole dam' tangling tingling business. I tell you," he shouted to the planets, the twinkle of suns, the hollows where lurked the unknown universes, "you're bloody wonderful. *Shlumpumpitter!*"

Yes, it was Oliver and not Bridget who took possession of my memory of that night. Perhaps because I never saw him like that again. But then there wasn't much time. Things went wrong too soon for the Alingtons; and then, only a year later, he and I were both in the army and miles apart. He was killed near Givenchy towards the end of May, 1915; and a one-legged captain, whom I met in a military hospital late in '16, had been in the same battalion and told me about him. "Our old bastard of a C.O. didn't like young Alington, thought he was a bit barmy and unreliable, but the rest of us knew he was all right," said the captain. "He had some dam' pretty sisters, I saw their photographs. We didn't tell 'em there wasn't enough of him left to fill a sandbag." And that was the last I heard of Oliver Alington for some time, and I doubt if I mentioned his name again myself until that night with Joan, early in '19. But while I sat there in the Royal Ocean Hotel, so long afterwards, holding him in my memory, there Oliver still was, raising his excited young face to the starlight and crying: "*Shlumpumpitter!*"

It couldn't have been long after that visit to the Leatons, I reflected, when we had a surprise in Canal Street that had some important consequences. One morning, Bernard the office-boy being out, I had to attend to the door. There arrived a youngish foreigner in a light grey suit a bit too tight for him. He looked at me as if I was hardly there, and announced himself haughtily as Mr. Albert Harfner. I knew then that he must be connected with a big German firm that was about our best foreign customer; and as I had often heard Mr. Alington and Ackworth talking about in old Julius Harfner, who was the managing-director of this firm and quite a friend of Mr. Alington's, I guessed, rightly as it turned out, that this Albert was old Harfner's son. He was fairly tall, with sloping shoulders, and not fat as yet, but he had that shining, featureless, pink-eggy look so many Germans have, and though he wore rimless eyeglasses there was something indecently naked about his face, as if he had just decided to expose it. I took a dislike to him even while I was explaining that Mr. Alington was out but would be back shortly. And then the fun began.

Malcolm Nixey came hurrying out of the office, and at the same time Ackworth came puffing and blowing out of the sample-room. Both of them spoke at once, but it was to Nixey that Harfner turned, greeting him with about as much enthusiasm as that kind of German can pump up. It appeared that they had met in London, and were almost chums already. And while Ackworth, completely ignored, was for once merely dithering, Nixey took charge, and, talking at full speed, swept Harfner into Mr. Alington's room and closed the door behind them.

Ackworth went stamping and snorting back to the sample-room, the very hairs on his neck bristling. I followed him, saying nothing. Then he turned on me: "What the hangment did you let that chap get 'old of 'im for, yer young donkey?"

"How could I stop him?" I demanded. "Don't start blaming me. He talked to Nixey because he knew him and didn't know you."

"Ah dare say, but yer should 'ave nipped in 'ere an' told me first."

"There wasn't time. Before I could move, you and Nixey dashed out—"

"Ah knaw, Ah knaw," he rumbled. "An' shut up, Ah want to think." He sucked his pipe, thinking hard. When he spoke again he did it quietly, with a conspiratorial air. "Just prop that door open"—and he pointed to the door that led from the sample-room to the little vestibule place where we had just had our scene with Harfner—"'cos Ah want to catch Mr. Alington as soon as he comes in, afore he goes in to 'is own room an' sees them two. There's a bit o' bloody monkey business goin' on 'ere, lad."

Ten minutes later Mr. Alington came in, and was duly intercepted, Ackworth taking him into the far corner of the sample-room, while I carefully closed the door that had been propped open. I didn't overhear all they said, but I heard enough to explain what was worrying Ackworth. I gathered that Mr. Alington didn't like this young Albert Harfner, who was very different from his old father, and found it difficult to do business with him. But Mr. Alington didn't attach much importance to the fact that Albert had come instead of his father, because he knew that the old man had not been well for the last year or so. It would, he said, make business tougher to handle, far less of a friendly affair, but that was all. But Joe Ackworth, whose hoarse whisper was easily overheard, was far more disturbed. What worried him was the arrival of Albert Harfner so soon after Nixey had been planted on us, and also the fact that these two had met before and were obviously friendly. Ackworth saw some deep plotting in all this.

"Now, Joe," I heard Mr. Alington say, "as I've told you before, just because you object to Nixey being here, you mustn't begin imagining elaborate conspiracies. I knew Albert Harfner had visited the London office; they told me at the time—it must have been just before Nixey came here."

"Ay, an' Ah'll bet it wor," said Ackworth suspiciously.

Mr. Alington had to laugh. "What about it? Why shouldn't they be friendly? Probably Nixey took him about a bit in London —they're just about the same age and probably have the same tastes, just as old Julius and I had. There's nothing in that, though I admit I don't like the way Nixey seems to have behaved —taking him straight into my room like that—"

"Ah should think not," cried Ackworth, not troubling now to lower his voice. "Ah never knew such bloody cheek an' impudence. A chap that's 'ardly been 'ere long enough to turn around, knaws as much abaht wool as Ah knaw about making toffee, an' goes an' marches one o' the firm's best customers into your room as if he owned the place. But 'appen he does," he added gloomily, "or thinks he will soon—"

"Joe, I've told you before—"

But Ackworth, speaking more earnestly than I had ever known him do before, cut in sharply: "Nah, John, just listen a minute, an' let me 'ave my say an' then Ah'll shut up, once an' for all. You an' me's worked together 'ere a good long time, an' you knaw me an' Ah knaw you. Often Ah lose me temper, an' then Ah say things Ah don't mean. But this is diff'rent, an' mak' no mistake abaht it, John. Nah Ah'm givin' you fair warnin'. This Nixey chap should never 'ave been sent 'ere, way he was. An' Ah say that neither 'im nor them that's sent 'im is up to any good. Ah told yer that at first, an' nah Ah knaw 'im Ah'm sure of it. An' this Harfner job's just part of it—you'll see, John. Afore we knaw where we are we'll find we can't get an order from them unless Nixey's summat to do with it. An' if we keep Nixey aht of it, we'll get no order—an' then London'll be askin' us what we think we're doin' losin' best foreign customer we've got—an' then afore so long—"

But there he had to stop because I had to warn them, for I heard Nixey and Harfner coming out of Mr. Alington's room. Mr. Alington hurried out to meet Harfner, and Nixey returned to the office. But he was not allowed to stay there because Ackworth, still purple and bristling, shouted at him to come out to the sample-room. This time there was no pretence of whispering or keeping anything from me: Ackworth had either forgotten I was there or simply didn't care what I heard. Nixey came in smiling, though I noticed something set and wary in his manner.

"Nah, look 'ere, Mr. Nixey," Ackworth began, ponderous in an attempt to keep his temper, "Ah don't knaw who or what you are in London—an' Ah don't much care—but 'ere you're just a chap startin' to learn the business who knaws abaht as much as the office-lad."

"Well, I'm doing my best," said Nixey coolly. "Any harm in that?"

Ackworth exploded, and probably Nixey meant him to. "There's plenty o' bloody 'arm in you marchin' Mr. Harfner off like that, into Mr. Alington's room an' all. Who the 'ell d'you think you are, eh? When we want you to run this business an' talk to one of our best customers, we'll ask you, but it'll be some time yet, let me tell you."

Nixey went white, and his eyes narrowed. "My uncle, Mr. Buckner, happens to have acquired a large interest in this firm, Mr. Ackworth, and it was he who arranged for me to come here and learn something about the business. And I happen to know Mr. Harfner—and he wanted to talk to me—so I took him into Mr. Alington's room because I knew it was empty. If Mr. Alington objects, then he can tell me so, but don't forget—it's his room and not yours. Anything else?"

"Ay, there is," said Ackworth angrily. "Just keep out o' my way —an' remember you're 'ere to learn, not to interfere." And he turned his back on Nixey, who had now recovered himself and gave me a slight little smile as he went out.

Harfner came back that afternoon and looked at samples with Mr. Alington and Ackworth and talked a little business with them. But nothing was settled. I could see that his manner, which was rather arrogant and condescending, made Ackworth angry and Mr. Alington uneasy. He was only staying in Bruddersford until the following Monday, and of course had other calls to pay. Mr. Alington, trying hard to be genial, invited him to dine, but Harfner rather stiffly excused himself, saying that he was too busy. He didn't look the type who would work at night and refuse to enjoy himself, and I guessed then that he and Nixey had arranged to do the town together.

After Harfner had gone, and I was putting the samples away, Mr. Alington lingered at the far end of the room, frowning and rubbing his long chin. Ackworth busied himself with a list of samples to go out that night, and said nothing. The place had a melancholy, half-defeated look. I heard Mr. Alington toss a few low-voiced remarks along the counter, as he leaned more heavily upon it; and then he raised his voice.

"I always liked old Julius Harfner, Joe," he said slowly. "He could be a hard old codger, and he'd beat you down if you'd let him. But he always kept his word, and once you'd done with business he could be delightful. We've had some grand evenings —music or at the theatre or just talking, politics, philosophy, anything. We'd a good deal in common. I don't know why I said we *had*—he's not dead, though he's not strong—growing old, of course—"

"Ah'm beginnin' to think he's dead as far as we're concerned," said Ackworth grimly.

"I hope not. I'm fond of the old man—and I liked his Germany, the old Liberal Germany—often narrow, bit stuffy, but cultivated, honourable, kind. But this one—Albert—he's the new Germany, Joe—the one people are beginning to be frightened of, and perhaps they're quite right. Old Julius and I understood each other, and found plenty in our minds that could be understood. But this one—and there are a lot of 'em now, Joe—he can't see anything in me, and I can't see anything in him, except a hard ego rattling about in his empty inside. I was annoyed, but I was also rather relieved," he added, with a laugh that had a touch of the apologetic in it, "when he told me he'd no evenings free for me. I wouldn't have known what to do with him. There's a kind of—what is it?—arrogant *blankness* about these younger Germans, a tinny hollowness, a sort of sleep-walker's rigidity, a lunatic stiffness, as if they had only one thought and it had mesmerised them. Of course they aren't the majority, and they're usually either in the army or are well-to-do members of the reserve of officers, like Albert Harfner. D'you understand what I feel about him, Joe?"

"More or less," said Ackworth. "But don't think yon chap 'as no pals. There's one 'ere—ay, Nixey. An' Ah'll bet he'll not be too busy to see a bit o' Nixey's company, an' all that goes with it, next few nights. You mark my words."

Mr. Alington was doubtful. But Ackworth and I were right in our guesses: Nixey had taken charge of Harfner, and they were seen together, in various places round the town, on several evenings that followed. Late on Saturday morning, after Mr. Alington and Ackworth had gone and I was tidying up the sample-room counter, Nixey came casually into the sample-room, looking as if he was just about to go. He asked me several

questions about some cross-bred tops that we had been sampling, and though I wondered why he should ask I saw no reason
why I shouldn't answer him, so I told him all I knew.

"Thanks, old man. Like to keep in touch with what's happening, and Ackworth won't give me more than a dirty look these
days. By the way, you remember that chap Harfner? Well, I'm
giving a little party for him tomorrow night at my place, just a
free-and-easy affair with a few drinks, to try to forget it's Sunday
night in Bruddersford, eh? Why don't you come along? Any
time after eight. Address is Fourteen, Leggett Lane—we have
the first floor. My wife'll be glad to see you again, old man."

I didn't notice any particular signs of joy in Eleanor Nixey
when I met her at the top of the stairs, about quarter to nine the
next night. She greeted me brightly enough, but I thought I saw
disappointment cloud her face for a moment when she could
see who it was, as if she had come out to welcome somebody
else. She was looking very handsome indeed, red and white and
black, smart and sparkling. She waved me gaily into the party,
which consisted of about twenty people, eating and drinking
and jabbering, and a fat man at the piano rattling out ragtime.
Nixey was moving round, nodding and smiling and offering
drinks; his eyes as restless as usual; busy but not really absorbed,
not enjoying anything. Harfner was there of course, naked-
faced but pinker than when he arrived at the office, and obviously he had already had a few drinks. I kept away from him.
"*Fiddle-up, Yiddle-up, on your violin,*" the fat man sang, the dyed
curls on his neck shiny with sweat. A massive upholstered sort
of woman near me suddenly moved, to reveal our Mr. Croxton,
immensely genteel but already a trifle swimmy about the eyes.
Two girls, who looked like shorter and coarser versions of Eleanor Nixey, moved across to the piano and joined the fat man:
"*Dog-gone, yew'd better begin—an' play a leetle tune upon your vi-o-
lin.*" Croxton now recognised the youth standing modestly with
his glass of beer as young Gregory Dawson of the sample-room,
and gave me two unwelcome nods. A man with a check tweed
coat and a blue-black moustache, who looked surprisingly like
the incredible villains of the films of that period, came up, stared
fiercely at me, and said: "You're young Jimmy Murchison, aren't

you?" When I assured him I wasn't, he surprised me again by giving me a slow wink, as if the secrets of the Murchisons were safe with him. Two men just behind me talked rapidly in low voices: "... I offered him fifty-three ... that's brought you in a pretty penny, old boy. ... I told him it was a firm offer. ... Take it or leave it, old boy. ... So I said: 'Make it seventy-eight,' I said. ... So that's let our old Jimmy out. ..." A woman like an over-ripe peach asked me to bring her a glass of champagne, and when I did she put a plump white be-diamonded hand to my cheek and told me archly I was a nice boy. *"Honey, looka here, looka here, looka here,"* sang the fat man, and the two girls at his side sang in reply: *"What is it, dee-ar, what is it, dee-ar?"* The man with the check tweed coat and the blue-black moustache caught my eye and then gave me another slow wink. It was at that point that I discovered what I have known only too well ever since, namely, that at a party of this kind you must penetrate to its core at once, get right inside and identify yourself with it, or it all seems a dreary lunacy. I was outside this party of Nixey's in the spirit, so it seemed both daft and depressing. Early as it still was, I thought about going home.

But the fat man and the girls paused to refresh themselves, there was a sudden quiet spell, and then there came a little peal of laughter from the door. It came from Eleanor Nixey, as I knew at once, and yet somehow it was not like her; clean out of character, it seemed to me. Too gay, unforced, self-forgetting; not belonging to this party at all. She was standing near the doorway with somebody who had just arrived. It was Ben Kerry; and now he was laughing too. What was the joke? And then I knew that really there wasn't one. They were just excited about something, perhaps excited about each other. I made for the door, without saying good-bye to Nixey, who was busy with Harfner and two girls.

"Hello, Kerry!" I stood squarely in front of him. Mrs. Nixey had gone in search of drinks for them both.

He was as surprised to see me as I had been to see him. A bit embarrassed too, I thought. "Hello, Dawson! Didn't expect to see you here."

I reminded him that Nixey was in our office. Then I said,

trying to make it as casual as possible: "Seen the Alingtons
lately?"

"No. They've mostly been away, haven't they? I know Eva
has. You been out there at all?" But he didn't wait for my reply.
"By the way, I liked that little thing of yours we printed last week
—your best yet, I think." He turned to Mrs. Nixey, who had
arrived with two whiskies. "You know that Gregory Dawson
here writes some very good stuff for us. You keep an eye on him.
That is, if you're fond of reading, which you aren't."

"I am," she said. "I never stop."

They both laughed—a little one this time but a small cousin
of the one I heard before. They looked at each other as they
laughed. Both darkly handsome: Kerry was a few years younger
but big, ruddy, weak somewhere inside perhaps but powerful
enough from the outside; and Eleanor Nixey, vivacious, wiry
but graceful, a Catherine wheel with coloured sparks at the
whirling edge and a hard smouldering centre; a badly balanced
pair, and not the kind of people to be looking at each other like
that and laughing. I said good night to them, but I doubted if
they heard me.

It was hard to space out properly the times I remembered
best. Probably there were whole weeks lost without one surviv-
ing memory, lost in the smoke and rain of that Bruddersford
autumn. Was it just after Nixey's party that I spent an evening
with Jock Barniston and his sister? I couldn't remember. But
there, not to be ignored, now dominating the flickering little
inner stage of memory, was that tremendous leading lady,
making her single appearance—Jock Barniston's sister. I must
have been seeing Jock once or twice a week at this time—he was
always popping up even if one didn't have a definite appoint-
ment with him—and some time not long after that Sunday
evening at the Nixeys' Jock astonished me, as he would have
astonished any of his acquaintance, by suggesting in his easy
offhand fashion that I should go to his place and have supper
with him and his sister. He said that something I had written had
interested her, and for once she had asked him to bring home
one of his new friends. Now nobody I knew—not one of the
Alingtons, for instance—had ever been taken by Jock to meet his

sister. It was understood that there was something queer about
her, and that while she looked after Jock, keeping house for him,
he had to look after her too and couldn't, in fact, leave her very
long. She never went anywhere, or if she did then nobody knew
about it. Jock never discussed her, never even mentioned all that
side of his life. (But that proved nothing, because Jock always
went his own way, was kind and compassionate but always
detached, a being from some other planet, older and wiser than
ours.) And now I was asked to meet her. I was astonished; I felt
flattered; I was burningly curious.

They lived in a gloomy little house in one of those squares,
too near the centre of the growing city, that had gone sliding
down the social scale, leaving the manufacturers and merchants
and now hobnobbing with the cheaper dentists, agents for cor-
sets, and touring actors. The hall and the ground-floor rooms
were badly lit and were filled with furniture too big for them, so
that vast sideboards menaced you and giant bookcases threatened to knock you flat. I felt at once that all this had nothing to
do with Jock himself, that this was the sister, who had known
better days, clinging to family treasures. She didn't make an
appearance at once, and I imagined that she was in the kitchen
helping to cook supper; though when we did go into the dining-
room and she came in a minute or two later, I found it impossible to imagine her in any kitchen.

"Dorothy," said Jock, still as calm and easy as ever, "this is
Gregory Dawson. You remember——you liked his thing in the
Evening Express?"

"Yes of course," she said, taking my outstretched hand and
holding it a moment or two while she stared at me, "there were
one or two sentences you wrote there that interested me . . . yes,
that I liked . . . very much." She said this without a smile, in a
deep murmuring tone like that of a distant 'cello, and stared at
me with strange deep-violet eyes.

She seemed to me a terrifying woman. If we had met anywhere else, I would have bolted. The idea that she could be anybody's sister (even Jock's) and be called Dorothy was fantastic.
She was immensely tall and very thin, and she was dressed, as if
for some impossible Victorian picnic, in yards and yards of pale

yellow stuff. In those days women seemed to have a lot of hair; but she didn't even make a pretence, and had only some fading ropy curls, like faint scrollwork at the top of a high column. I felt at once that not only had this woman not come from any kitchen but that it was equally impossible to imagine her coming out of any other room in the house: she had come from Somewhere Else, slipped through a crack in ordinary reality. What was so frightening about her was that in spite of all the individual and unusual features of her appearance, including those extraordinary deep-violet eyes, she looked like Jock, only an elongated Jock, outside sex and age, stalking around in a bad dream. There is a door at the back of our minds that opens slowly in the dusk there to admit creatures like this, creatures who are strange, out of proportion, who come from the other side of the moon to stare and mutter at us, but who yet have some devilish likeness to people we know. Jock's sister seemed one of them, and at once the whole evening—the house, the furniture, everything that was said and done—was illuminated and shadowed round with the light and dark of a dream, was incredible, waiting to vanish with the night, and yet memorably real.

We sat down to supper, but what sort of supper I couldn't remember, and doubted if I noticed at the time. Jock talked in his usual style, and I did my best to keep going with him, but I couldn't help feeling embarrassed and intimidated, with this terrific Miss Barniston towering over me. But for some time she kept silent, just pecking away at her food and occasionally staring at me with eyes that were like tropical midnights.

Finally she murmured: "Your mother ... she died, didn't she?"

"Yes, she did," I stammered. "In India—two years ago. My father too."

She nodded very slowly. "I think I saw her.... I knew her ... years ago."

There was no reason why she shouldn't have known my mother; nevertheless, I was startled. And what did she mean when she said she had seen my mother? Seen her where, when, how?

"You were writing for her, you know," Miss Barniston continued, in her slow deep voice that seemed to come a long way. "I recognised her . . . you remember, Jock? . . . before I knew who you were." She paused, to stare at me again. "When you are writing . . . do you feel suddenly inspired at times . . . as if a new force had come to aid you?"

Even in those days, when I was still the young amateur, I didn't like this approach to the business of writing; and found myself constantly irritated by the hard-headed types, who asked me how I went about "getting copy," as they always called it, and by the soulful types who asked me how long I had to "wait for inspiration." Miss Barniston was a soulful type—but with a difference. "Well, I don't know," I told her. "I don't pretend to know a lot about it yet. But of course sometimes you find everything coming easily—and at other times—well, you don't," I ended lamely.

"It's all . . . quite different . . . from what you imagine," she murmured. "Like the dead and the living . . . some people you think are alive are really dead . . . and others you think are dead are really alive. . . ."

"Now, Dorothy," said Jock, not sharply but in an easy affectionate tone, and not suggesting that she might frighten me but that soon she might begin to bore me. Meanwhile I was still struggling with a vision of Bruddersford filled with bustling automata who were really dead and, moving invisibly among them, slipping through on strange errands, the smiling dead who were really alive. And because the thought of my mother was mixed up in this, it was something more than an idle fancy, and cut deeper.

"Yes, dear," she said, with unexpected meekness, and left the talk to Jock and me until we went into the other room. There, while Jock and I smoked and chatted, sprawling at each side of the fire, she sat immensely upright at a little table and played Patience. And in that stuffy room, badly lit and over-crowded with furniture and shadowy in the corners, I had the feeling that we were a long way from anywhere. Bruddersford and its trams and pubs and newspaper-boys had retreated and dwindled to a faint twinkle. An old clock ticked relentlessly, like the stroke of an engine carrying us somewhere. It was very peculiar in there, and, though I put up a fair pretence of easy chat, I didn't like it.

Miss Barniston gave an exclamation of dismay, and I turned and saw that now she was staring at the cards, as if reading them instead of playing with them. She looked at her brother, with a suggestion of apology. "I think . . . I must look at the cards for Gregory Dawson," she announced.

"I don't suppose he wants you to, Dorothy," said Jock.

She looked at me, and I said that of course I didn't mind and would be delighted. I did some shuffling and cutting business for her and she laid out the cards, while Jock, who seemed to have withdrawn himself from us, smoked in silence. This wasn't the first time I had had my fortune told with cards, and I was fairly familiar with the rigmarole about dark men and fair women and journeys and strange beds and money coming to me, and thought it all a tedious parlour trick.

But here, with no giggling girls present and none of the usual jokes, it was different. This wasn't a party but a session with the vast sibylline Miss Barniston. She might be a bit cracked; she might be a creature staring and murmuring at us out of some other world; but whatever she was, she was formidable and no joke. And I kept glancing at her with secret apprehension as she peered at the cards, foreshortening her immensely long bony face and appearing to elongate her long thin hands. The old clock in the far corner behind her now thudded rather than ticked, full speed ahead for somewhere.

"Always the same," said Miss Barniston, suddenly dropping her vague murmur, "always the same. Every time I look for anybody. Change and an ending . . . everything changing . . . ending and beginning again . . . with rivers of blood flowing towards us . . . great rivers of blood. . . ."

Jock felt compelled to speak, probably because there was now a sharp edge to her voice. "Don't bother about it, Dorothy. You've told me before. And Gregory doesn't really want to know."

"Yes, he does," she said, without looking at me, still staring at the cards. "And he ought to know . . . to prepare himself . . . though he won't be prepared . . . not for all these changes . . .

something of him will be caught, fastened, left behind while he goes on.... Yes, he goes on ... unlike so many others ... but not the same as he is now ... changed ... sad, not believing ... something left behind. ..."

I found my voice. "Can you tell me what's going to happen to me? Am I going to stay in Bruddersford? And if not, where am I going and what am I going to do?"

"No, you're not staying here," she announced with surprising decision. "You'll go in less than a year ... go for ever ... and be in danger ... often and often in danger. But before that everything will have changed for you ... and the place where your heart is now will be all broken and trampled on ... death coming ... and the end of love and of trust." She looked solemnly at Jock. "I see here what I saw for you the other night, Jock ... only it's worse for him ... of course. ..."

I had to ask: "Why do you say *of course*?"

She smiled, and it was the first and the last time I ever saw her smile. "Because nothing that can happen can be really bad for Jock. You know that, don't you?"

And because I did, or at least had somehow always imagined that about him, I stared at her open-mouthed.

"Though there'll be danger," she said, almost briskly now as if concluding the mere routine of the job, "you'll live a long time. Yes, and you'll write many things, though not what you think you will write now, and you'll go to the other side of the world and write there for a long time and be paid a great deal of money. But you won't care about the money. You'll be busy but not very happy. Something missing, lost, gone. But in the end, after a long time, you may be happy ... rounded ... fulfilled." She rose to her great height, and as I got up too, for it was plain that she was leaving us, she came forward and put her hands on my shoulders. She looked exhausted, suddenly frail, a woman now, and to my astonishment I saw there were tears in her eyes. "I'll tell your mother, Gregory," she said gently. "I'm glad to have seen you. Be a good boy. We shall never meet again—here." And then she walked straight out, and she was right, for we never met again and I never even learned how or when she died.

I sat down in a huge wondering silence, waiting for Jock to

say something. When he didn't, I burst out with: "I hate that beastly clock in the corner."

Jock grinned. "I'm sorry. I rather like it. What's wrong with it, lad?"

"I dunno. I feel it's just ticking us away."

"We can't be ticked away." He smoked away in his slow contented fashion, which always made you feel that his tobacco must be much better than yours, though actually he didn't care what he smoked. "I didn't want to explain about Dorothy before you met her," he began carefully, "because it might have made you self-conscious and she'd have noticed it. She's—well, peculiar, as you've seen, and sometimes she's worse—in fact, much worse—than she's been tonight. She had a bad shock, about fifteen years ago, and it sort of turned her sideways to the world, if you see what I mean. She depends upon me, and in a lot of ways I depend upon her."

"Does that mean you could never leave her?" I asked.

"I couldn't leave her here long," he replied, "but if I had to go, she could live with an old friend of hers up in Wharfedale. It may come to that soon."

I was surprised. "Why, where are you going, Jock? Or are you thinking of getting married?"

He laughed. "No, I'll never marry, lad. But I know there'll be a war soon—yes, I know what they all say, John Alington and the rest of 'em—but I know it's coming."

This was new to me, not the possibility of war but his belief that it was bound to come. "But even if there should be a war, Jock, where do you come in?"

"We'll all be in it. I'll be in it. You'll be in it. That's what Dorothy was meaning. I don't know if she gets it from my mind, or I get it from hers, or we both get it from somewhere else. But there it is. Perhaps in a year or so," he added quietly, not talking for effect—Jock never did that—but calmly stating a fact.

I was hastily remembering what his sister had told me. "So that was what she meant. Jock—I'm sorry but I don't believe it."

"All right, Gregory." He grinned. "Doesn't matter. What's on at the Imperial this week?"

Bruddersford, waiting to receive me in the square outside,

didn't believe it either, and every gas-mantle in the street lamps suggested that I had been spending the evening with a pair of eccentrics. But one half of me, the one that looked towards the shadows, waiting for dreams to be lighted there, had none of this certainty. "But that woman's barmy," I told this half. "And so am I," it whispered.

The very next night—and this I remembered clearly—I went along to the Alingtons, although I didn't know who would be in there and it was a gusty wettish night. But I felt I must talk to somebody, and preferably to one of them. Joan let me in, and she said that only she and young David were downstairs. Eva had gone to bed with a headache; Bridget was practising with a trio somewhere; and Mr. and Mrs. Alington were upstairs packing his bags for his Continental trip, for he was off in the morning. (Oliver was at Cambridge, of course.) We went into the long room, where David raised his head from a book for four seconds, to greet me in his usual calm and clear manner. We sat down, but Joan seemed restless and a bit worried.

"What's it like out?" she asked.

"Dark, windy and rather wet," I told her.

She jumped up. "Let's go for a walk. I'm dying for some air. Come on—you've got a good mac and so have I."

After all those years I could still see us setting out for that walk, Joan buttoned up in her mackintosh and wearing a floppy Donegal tweed hat that gave her pale good looks an attractive rakish air; the blurred street lamps along the deserted avenues; the occasional glitter of privet and laurel leaves; distant trams creeping along like golden insects; and I could feel again the little pull of Joan's hand on my arm as we turned the gusty corners, and the wind that came from the black hills stinging my cheeks.

"You wish it were Bridget or Eva," Joan cried, with a kind of forced gaiety that wasn't like her, "but don't forget I'm the one among the Alingtons who really takes trouble over you, Gregory."

"Of course you are," I said, thinking that there was something in what she said, even though she wasn't serious. "And I came to your house tonight, dying to talk hard to one of you, and I think you're really the best."

"As a matter of fact I am," and she was more than half serious now. "And I've been wanting to talk to you for several days—no, weeks really." The wind came tearing at us. "But let's wait until it's quieter," she shouted.

"Which way shall we go?" I bellowed.

"Wabley Wood, eh?" And again she had to shout as the wind tore down at us and the whole street set up a defiant rattle. "Let's hurry." And saying no more, we went battling on, arm-in-arm.

As we dropped down towards Wabley Wood the wind quietened but its blown drops turned into steady rain. "This is a bit too much," she said, "unless there's somewhere to shelter down here. And trees are hopeless at this time of year."

"There's half a hut just off the road at the bottom," I told her, "and if nobody's bagged it, we can shelter there nicely—and talk too. Come on now—run." And I took her hand and we raced through the rain down into the dark hollow, where I led her off the road and, after a minute's search, found the shelter I had remembered. Nobody was there. We were out of the rain, with black dripping night all around us, and shoulder to shoulder we leaned against the dry corrugated iron wall of the workmen's hut, triumphant and out of breath. After a minute or so I lit my pipe, and had time to catch the friendly gleam of her grey eyes before the match went out. The rain drummed and spat, and we felt small and cosy in a huge darkness, warmed by a new intimacy, ready for secrets.

"Gregory," she began, as soon as my pipe demanded no more attention, "you remember you promised to tell me about things at the office—when I said I was worried about my father? You did promise, didn't you? Well, I'm far more worried about him now, and you're not telling me things. No—just a minute. I heard him say to Mother that he didn't want to dash off to Germany again but that he just had to go. What's happening? And who is this man Nixey—and somebody called Harfner—this new one, not the old man, he was sweet—and what's the matter?"

"All right," I said. "I'll tell you. I know I promised, and I've been meaning to talk to you for some weeks now."

"Well, why haven't you then? I know we haven't been alone

much, but that could easily have been managed. I do think you're the limit, Gregory."

"I'm sorry, Joan, but the trouble is—things have been piling up so much at the office lately that I've kept feeling I ought to wait so that I could tell you a bit more—you know what I mean? Well, first, about Nixey—"

"I don't like him," she cried at once. "We all dislike him. I hope you do." She gave me a nudge, as if voices weren't enough in that darkness. "Say you do, and then tell me about him."

"Well, I don't," I said. "Though I must admit he's done nothing to me. As a matter of fact he's always quite friendly—if you can call anything friendly that he does. He was sent up here, to learn the business, by a rich uncle who now has a large share in the firm. We've never seen this uncle, but I suppose your father has. But I think—and so does Ackworth—that Malcolm Nixey isn't just here to learn the business, so that he can go back to the London office. Now he wants to run our office—or at least to have a big say in running it. I've come to the conclusion that he's out for everything he can get, and that he's plotting and intriguing like mad—and he's that type, I'm sure, never forgetting himself and always wondering what he can make out of every situation—"

"I'll bet he is," cried Joan, with an echo of Bridget in her tone, as if they had already discussed Nixey.

"I've overheard Ackworth warning your father several times against him—"

"And I don't suppose Dad listened to him—"

"No, I don't think he did. Though he's worried now—you're quite right. And this is where Harfner comes in. Instead of the old man, who's ill, this young Harfner, Albert, came over a few weeks ago, and he and Nixey, who'd met before, spent all their evenings together. Then Harfner went back without giving us an order—and his firm are about our biggest customers—and your father thought that was because he wanted to talk things over with old Julius, who's still the boss. Then your father wrote to them, and we sent a fresh batch of samples—"

"Wait, Gregory," she cried. "Don't go on now about samples and prices and cross-breds and things, because anyhow it's boring and I get all mixed up."

"I'm not going to. The point is this—that yesterday we had a letter from Harfner's firm, saying they didn't intend to buy any-thing from us this season. Well, that was a terrific blow, because your father and Joe Ackworth were counting on this order of theirs. And Ackworth said at once that there was something fishy about it—'bloody 'anky-panky' he actually called it. But that's not all. Nixey came into the sample-room when they were talking about this letter, and I saw his face, Joan, and just for a second—that's all, a second—but I couldn't mistake it—there was a sort of flicker of satisfaction went across it. He knew jolly well that letter was coming, that's my belief."

"Yes, I see, Gregory," said Joan, in a small meek voice. "Is that all? I don't mean it isn't enough—but—oh, you know what I mean."

"No, it isn't all. This morning your father said he'd have to dash off to Germany—to look into all this—and he told Croxton the cashier, who's a pal of Nixey's, to make some arrangements about money for him. Well then, Nixey came into the sample-room, because that's where your father was all morning, and said that he ought to go to Germany too and that Albert Harfner had told him it would be better for the firm if he did. Then there was a terrific row. Ackworth lost his temper of course, but then he always does with Nixey. But for once your father did too, and was really angry—I've never seen him so angry—"

"Was he quite white—suddenly?" Joan demanded.

"Yes, he was. And I've never seen him like that before."

"That's what happens when he's really angry. And it doesn't often happen. Poor Dad! Was Nixey angry too?"

"No, that's where he's so clever," I told her. "He keeps his temper—and is quite cool and if he doesn't keep on smiling then merely looks rather pained—and that tends to put other people in the wrong. He said he'd have to tell his uncle and the other directors in London, and your father said he didn't care who he told, that he was in charge of this Bruddersford branch of the firm, didn't take orders from Nixey, and told him to get back into the office or leave the place and go back to London. Nixey stared at him for a minute—not really a minute, I suppose, but it seemed a very long silent stare, then nodded without saying a word and went back into the office. And when I came away tonight, he and Croxton were still in the office, when everybody else had gone, and I'm certain they weren't working."

"Never mind them," said Joan. "How was my father—I mean, after the row was over?"

"Well"—and I hesitated—"I thought he looked pretty sick about it. Ackworth suggested he should go home—and leave us to finish the sampling for him—but he wouldn't."

"So that's it," she said slowly. "I knew something had happened. So did Mother. Well—it's horrible—"

"Now, wait a minute, Joan—"

"No, it isn't what you've told me—though that's bad enough, I suppose—especially if you think it is—but I feel it's horrible because—because—of something creeping up on us, changing and spoiling everything—what's the matter?"

She asked that because I had given a little exclamation, suddenly remembering what Jock Barniston's sister had said the evening before. Out in the night again, with darkness so close, that queer session with Jock Barniston's sister, that immense and terrifying Dorothy, acquired a depth of reality and a host of wild meanings that it had lost during the bustle of daylight. But I couldn't begin explaining all that, so I merely replied: "Nothing, nothing. I only thought of something. Go on."

"No, that's all," she said, and was silent.

She had slipped a hand under my arm, and I could feel her fingers picking at my sleeve. The wind had come back and was blowing the rain away, and the dark wood creaked and muttered. It was no longer all a blackness, we could see a little now, but what we saw, from grey distance to ebony branch, was sodden, bleak and homeless. I felt Joan shiver.

"We can go now, if you like," she said in a toneless voice. "The rain's almost stopped."

"No, we'd better wait a bit," I told her, "unless you're feeling cold."

"I wasn't shivering because I was cold. Oh, Gregory—" and her voice trailed off.

"What, Joan?"

"I don't know," she whispered. "I don't know."

"Well, then," I said stoutly, "don't worry about it. You know I went to a party that Nixey gave for Eggy Harfner—really to do a bit of spying—and a fat man with sweaty curls played ragtime and sang. He sang: *Fiddle-up, Yiddle-up, On your vi-o-lin.*" And I tried to remember the rest of it.

She laughed and squeezed my arm. "You're very sweet, Gregory—and if you were only four years older—no, five—perhaps six—I think I'd fall in love with you. But as it is, you're quite safe. Who was at the beastly party? At least, I hope it was beastly."

"It was." And I told her a little about it, but I didn't say anything about Ben Kerry and Mrs. Nixey. Poor Eva apparently had one headache already.

"And now," she said, to my surprise and dismay (for I didn't know then that they rarely let you off), "you can tell me why you cried out when I talked about something creeping up on us, changing and spoiling everything. Go on. Don't be mean."

"I met Jock Barniston's sister last night," I began.

"Good Lord! What's she like? Tell me quick. We've all been wondering about her for years."

"Well, she's peculiar," I said carefully.

"Mad, isn't she?" she whispered, so near that I felt her breath on my cheek.

Almost in a whisper too, very close to her there in the dark, I described my evening at the Barnistons', the fantastic Dorothy, the fortune-telling, and I ended by telling her most of what Jock had said to me after his sister had left us. And when I had done I realised that now her shoulder was pressing into my arm and that the dim oval of her face had vanished. She had turned her head away from me. She was crying. And I knew it was because she was in love with Jock, and that what I had told her, perhaps together with all those hints of menace and gathering disaster, had now taken from her the last glimmer of hope of ever having Jock for herself.

"Joan, I'm sorry, I oughtn't to have told you," I said, wheeling away from the wall to face her. And because I really was sorry and I wanted to comfort her, I put my arms round her and drew her close to me. In a choked miserable voice she muttered something I couldn't catch, and the only reply I could make was to tell her not to cry and not to care. I tightened one arm round her and removed the other arm to take her hands from her face and to lift it nearer mine. I kissed her damp salty cheeks and then her lips. In another minute her arms were round my neck, her body was pressing against mine, and her warm smooth lips, which seemed to have some strange flavour of the sea in them, flickered and then leapt into a wild exciting life of their own, which I had to share, like a flame in all that darkness. And this, I told myself as I strained exultantly, was what it was all about: I knew at last. But did I? For *I* think I knew too, lost as I was in that double mystery of surging blood and the huge enveloping night that deliberately drew us so close, that by this time I wasn't kissing her, Joan Alington, but any girl's warm salt-sweet face, and that she wasn't really kissing me but an image of somebody else.

And as if she suddenly became aware of this fatal knowledge, she turned her face away, so that I found myself tasting wet Donegal tweed, jerked her body back, and gave me a violent push with both hands. "Don't be so stupid," she cried angrily, as if we had been wrestling and not been embracing for the last five minutes. "No, stop it—silly young fool! I want to go home."

"All right," I muttered, almost as angry as she was now, and understanding for the first time in my life why women often received such rough treatment, for there was in me a tide of energy still roaring to be released somehow. But I dropped back, and dug my hands into my raincoat pockets. I could hear her breathing hard. "Let's go. I'm not stopping you."

Sullenly we picked our way over the sodden ground and among the black dripping trees until we came to the road. Actually it couldn't have been very late, but it felt very late; and the night was now high and clear, with a cold glitter of stars in it. We trudged away for some time in silence.

"If you ever tell anybody about this," she said finally, "I'll never speak to you again."

"Why should I want to tell anybody about it?" I demanded in a loud contemptuous tone.

"You're furious now, aren't you?"

"Yes, I am. I don't like being told I'm stupid and a silly young fool, especially when it comes from a girl who's been kissing me hard a minute before—"

"Oh shut up about it," she cried.

"Certainly," I said, with the immense pomp and grandeur of the very young, "certainly." And I remained shut for the next mile.

Then when we were within five minutes of the Alingtons' house, she surprised me by suddenly becoming almost apologetic. "I was angry with myself really, Gregory, not with you. And I didn't really know what I was saying, I just wanted to stop myself from behaving so ridiculously. I don't think you're a silly young fool. And you've been very sweet to me before that—too nice perhaps."

"All right," I said gruffly, not sulking but unable to change my part in the scene as quickly as she could. It is one of the handicaps of being a young male; afterwards you learn some of the dodges.

She stopped under the lamp at their corner, tilting her face in the greenish light to smile at me wistfully. She looked pale and sweet and spiritual, not quite the usual Joan Alington but nearly back to her. I felt fairly friendly again, though somewhere deep in my blood a spark of anger burned that was not quenched until a night more than five years later.

"We'll forget it all, won't we?" she said softly.

"All right," I said, not liking her any better but with no desire to quarrel. I was, in fact, longing to go home and to write for an hour.

"We're friends again, aren't we, Gregory?"

"Yes, of course, Joan," I replied patiently, a bit too patiently, for she gave me a sharp look.

"Well, don't come any further," she said briskly, "and thank you for the walk. Good night."

It was late when I reached home—and even Uncle Miles, who liked to stay up for a final crack with me, was in bed—and I was tired after all that walking and weather and excitement, but nevertheless—and after all those years I could sit there in the Royal Ocean Hotel and clearly remember myself doing it —I did clamp myself down and write for an hour, and write too as well as I knew how. "And that, Dawson my lad," I told myself, getting out of my chair to ease a touch of cramp, after sitting and remembering so long, "is where you had the advantage over poor Joan."

I paced my room for a minute or two, and the Bruddersford of late 1913 retreated and faded. If you keep still immediately after waking from a dream, you can generally recall most of the dream, but if you move too soon you tear the whole delicate fabric into faintly coloured tantalising threads. Now I found myself in much the same situation. When I returned to my chair, after lighting another pipe, I knew I had done an hour's good writing after leaving Joan that night but I couldn't remember where to go from there. Canal Street on darkening afternoons ... Mr. Alington away ... Ackworth worried ... Nixey vaguely triumphant. Dodging Joan, for her sake more than mine, and then finding when I did meet her, with the others there too, that she showed not a flicker of embarrassment, as if Wabley Wood didn't exist. A quarrel with Bridget . . . ? When was that and how did it happen? Memory, for the first time, returned a complete blank. Instead, I remembered a party, and without wanting to recall it. Queer, but although I have never liked parties, at any age or in any place, not only have I persisted in attending them but I have also persisted in remembering them, even when far more important events—that quarrel with Bridget, for instance —refuse to come back. This party must have taken place not long after I went walking with Joan, and only a week or two before Christmas.

It was a theatrical party, on a Sunday night in an upstairs private room at the *Crown*, a large and gaudy pub across the way from the Imperial Music-Hall, and much frequented by touring actors and variety people. Oddly enough, my entry into this dashing and bohemian gathering came by way of my uncle's whist-drive circle. Among these sober Blackshaws, Warkwoods, Dunsters, were, as I have already mentioned, Johnny Luckett and his wife; and Johnny had two sisters on the stage, and Mrs. Luckett still sang semi-professionally, and they were always going to theatres and music-halls, in Bradford, Leeds, anywhere, and running round with actors and singers, talking theatrical gossip, getting rather tight and missing last trains. (I thought then that they had a wonderful time, and even now I am not so certain that they didn't or that we could show them anything they wouldn't dismiss with contempt. It is true that Johnny, who was a wholesale tobacconist in a careless sort of way, went bankrupt during the first year of World War One and shortly afterwards was found dead in Merton Park; but then, unlike most of us now, he had had his roaring good time first.) On this particular Sunday afternoon in December, an unusually mild day, I was out for a solitary walk and ran into Johnny Luckett, also alone and looking as if he were trying to walk off the effect of a huge lunch and eight large whiskies. With his tremendous black moustache, loud check suit and masterful eye he looked something between a rather tight conjuror and a ringmaster off duty. He hailed me as if we were both on barges in a fog.

"Well, well, well!" he cried. "Young Gregory Dawson—and looking like one of the ker-nuts, one of the ber-boys—eh? I hear you're writing for the papers these days."

I said I was, and left it at that, because it was no use trying to explain the difference between my lofty literary ambitions and his writing for the papers. They were all one to him.

"That's the idea," he said, and produced a long black cigar, companion to the one he was smoking. "Try one of these."

"Thank you, Mr. Luckett. Good, are they?"

"Samples from South America. And bloody awful." He roared with laughter. "Left on my only-only today. Wife's had to dash over to Leeds to substitute at the last minute for an oratorio. God!—I hate oratorios—they'll be the ruin of this district yet. Now then, Gregory boy"—and he looked at me solemnly, tightened my tie, and enveloped me in a rich reek of cigar, whisky and Hungarian pomade—"if you're writing for the papers, then you ought to see a bit of Life—eh? Well, what are you doing tonight?"

I muttered something about seeing friends, but one sweep of his hand instantly brushed them aside.

"See your friends any time—if they are your friends," he said. "Now if it's *one* friend—in skirts—that's different. It isn't, eh? Then you come with me tonight, my boy. Some pros I know

are giving a party at the *Crown*—private room upstairs—all
very select and plenty of everything and the very best. Nice
mixture. Some of this year's pantomime crowd, just arrived to
start rehearsals—some of last week's lot from the Royal—some
of the variety turns from the Imperial—and so on and so forth.
And any pal of mine heartily welcome, especially if he writes
for the papers. Now then—where do we meet? Just inside the
Crown private bar—eight o'clock. Wear that suit—couldn't be
better—but that tie's damned dull and it keeps slipping—I'd try
another. And don't smoke that cigar. Tell your uncle to give it to
Blackshaw. Going home now to have a snooze. Toodle-oo—till
eight o'clock."

Johnny may or may not have had his snooze but he had
certainly contrived to down a good many more drinks before
I met him in the *Crown*. He couldn't be said to be drunk—he
never was drunk—but he was even further away than usual
from being sober. He introduced me to a droll little man called
Tubby Fuller, and said in a loud whisper: "Gets a steady eighty a
week and earns it—make you laugh yourself sick"; after which
I overheard him saying to Tubby: "Cleverest lad in the town
—writes for all the papers in the North—big influence." This
astonishing statement, which I couldn't contradict as I was not
supposed to have heard it, put me in a false position for the rest
of the evening, for when we went upstairs to the party Tubby
must have told everybody in the profession there that they had
only to talk to me to obtain the widest publicity, with the result
that I never had a moment to myself. "Look, old boy," the men
would say, "you know me and I know you. Both at the top in
our own lines, eh? Right. Well, believe me when I say they went
down on their knees—right down on their knees, old boy—to
beg me to play Idle Jack at Sheffield this season—and that's
after three consecutive panto seasons there, old boy—but I said
'Sorry, but they want me in Bruddersford this year, and I've a
lot o' friends there——'—my very words, old boy—'so it's dear
old Bruddersford for me this time.' An' you can print that, old
boy." Or vast blonde Fairy Queens would almost impale me on
their perfumed and glittering bosoms as they whispered in their
cooing contralto: "You're musical, I know, Mr. Lawson, because

I read everything you write. So I don't need to tell you, my dear, that to attempt an *aria*—Italian, proper classical music—in a panto, as I'm goin' to do this year, is something more than a mere novelty, although of course it *is* a novelty—and you can say so. When I told dear old Tommy Sprake—and what would we do without him, eh?—he said 'Well, dear, it's a novelty, so we'll risk it.' And you know what they're like in Hull as a rule—very sticky, as you know very well, Mr. Lawson—well, they *raved* last year—encores even at matinées. And just drop me a line if you want photos, dear." Thanks to Johnny, I became one of the main attractions of the evening, and felt both a cheat and a fool.

In those days, days that were already numbered, touring actors and variety *artistes* didn't make any pretence of being ordinary citizens and taxpayers. To begin with, they looked quite different. Their clothes, judged by the standards of the respectable bourgeoisie (not Johnny Luckett and his kind), were outrageous, with everything wildly overdone: tweeds too thick and patterns too loud; waistcoat openings cut too low and ties too bright; overcoats too thick, too long, too loose; and all topped with impossible hats. Even the men never seemed to clean off all their make-up: they had blue-black smudges round their eyes and their cheeks were pink and shining not with health but with a mixture of grease-paint and cocoa-butter. Longish curling hair, very thick just above the ears, was still the fashion among the men. The ladies wore enough make-up to announce at once that they were actresses. Nowadays probably I wouldn't notice that amount of make-up, but in those days it was at once fascinating and repelling, condemning me to stare at them in wonder but making me feel at the same time that I didn't want to come too close to these gaudy and bedaubed creatures. The manners of both sexes alternated between a solemn professional dignity, impossible in a wool merchant, and the uproarious free-and-easy, which brought out the most shocking language and the most dubious stories in mixed company, but was saved from being disgusting by something naïve and childlike in the performers. In spite of their strangeness, but not because of it, I liked the players better then than I do now, after working with them for years; and not because I was young

and foolish then and am now middle-aged and perhaps not quite
so foolish, but because I think they were healthier in spirit when
they exaggerated outwardly the difference between themselves
and their audiences and played at being actors all the time. Now
when so many of them have carefully suppressed these signs
and badges of their profession, and go about looking like law-
yers and dentists and the wives and daughters of deacons, what
cannot come out has turned and worked its way inward, often
subtly corrupting the mind and heart.

So I felt that night at the *Crown* that I was not among my own
sort but surrounded by fantastic foreigners and eighty-pounds-
a-week gipsies. And of course I couldn't help feeling a fraud as
they came up and poured out publicity material for my imaginary columns. But I was happier among them, spiritually more
at ease, than I would be now—or at any time during these last
fifteen years—attending a similar party. And having decided this,
then instead of trying to recall exactly what happened at that
party at the *Crown*, I began to remember parties in Hollywood,
and wondered if I could persuade Elizabeth for once to analyse
her feelings, to see how they would compare with mine.

But this wouldn't do. The thread, such as it was, would escape
me altogether soon, if I wasn't careful. I asked myself why I had
remembered that party at the *Crown* at all, in view of the fact
that I wasn't sitting there to think about actors but to remember
my early life in Bruddersford and my relations with the Alingtons. I worked my way back into that smoky, noisy room, over-
charged with the organised vitality of the theatre, surrounded
myself again with the grimacing comedians and the smiling
soubrettes of 1913, listened again, a solemn young clown, to the
publicity stories that would never be written, ate veal-and-ham
pie and drank claret cup, and waited to see what turned up, to
explain why I should remember it at all at that moment.

And then they were there: Eleanor Nixey, smart and gay,
ready to enjoy herself but somehow making it plain that she
was *at* but not *of* the party; and Ben Kerry, big and flushed
and a bit tight. Clearly he had brought her, for Ben did theatrical notices and occasional gossip stuff and would certainly
be asked to a party of this kind. There was no reason why he

shouldn't bring Mrs. Nixey, who might be amused by it. But I knew at once that this proved they were spending a lot of time together, that this was merely one evening out of many, and that no matter what they imagined they were up to, Eva's adored Ben and this handsome restless woman from London, as their manner plainly showed, couldn't help thinking of themselves now as a *pair*, bound by something that also separated them from everybody else. They didn't notice me, and after a minute or two I crossed the room to face them. But when I arrived, Ben Kerry had been grabbed by two actresses and was listening with obvious impatience to the kind of stuff I had had all the evening, while Eleanor Nixey stood by, making no attempt to listen but looking on with a cool scorn.

"Hello, Mrs. Nixey!" I cried, grinning at her. I had had several glasses of claret cup and was full of bounce.

"Oh—hello!" she said, smiling. "You do pop up, don't you? Is this the kind of party you like?"

"Up to a point," I said, suggesting the old party hand. "The professional touch is a bit overdone, isn't it?"

She nodded. "What a mob! I can't bear these second-rate theatrical people, but Ben said he ought to look in and that I might be amused." And inexperienced though I was, I guessed then that she had to bring him into the talk as soon as possible because it was glorious just to mention his name. And I could think what I liked, she didn't care.

But Ben was different. At that moment he turned and saw me. His instantaneous reaction gave him away. His face darkened at once, and he flashed me a furious glance. I was all wrong and oughtn't to have been there. Then as he turned sharply away, as if the two actresses were now saying something extremely interesting, I thought I saw him give a tiny involuntary shrug. I looked at Mrs. Nixey, and she was cool and amused.

"I hear that Eva Alington isn't very well," I said to her.

She raised her fine eyebrows. "Really! That's the fair one, isn't it? She's probably anæmic. She looks anæmic. I'm afraid I haven't seen those girls for some time." She gave me a wicked little smile. "They don't interest me, you know, as they probably do you."

I did my best to return the ball. "No, but I used to see Ben there a lot."

"Yes, he's quite a friend of the family, he tells me. The father's charming, I think, though Malcolm says he's not the world's brightest business man. But that doesn't worry me," she continued, still smiling, "because I don't care about business—or business men. All rather dull—um?"

There wasn't time for any more—we had to leave the game at thirty-all—because now Ben joined us, glaring at me like a red-and-black bull. "Excuse me a minute, Eleanor," he said; and then he had me in a quiet space near the door, and I thought for a moment, secretly terrified, that he was going to knock me down.

"I heard what you were saying to Mrs. Nixey," he began, still glaring at me. "What's the matter with you, Dawson? I'd like to punch you on the nose. Can't you mind your own damned business?"

I said that I didn't see that I wasn't minding my own business. "And anyhow," I went on, "I first met you at the Alingtons', and I first met Mrs. Nixey there too, so naturally I mentioned them to her—"

"Dragged them in, you mean," he growled. "I heard you. It's nothing to do with you whether I've been seeing Eva lately or not."

"I never said it was," I retorted. "And in fact I don't know whether you have been seeing her lately or not—"

"All right then—keep out of it, that's all."

I could still see him, though not distinctly, across the years, glaring at me, his usual smouldering sulky good looks now fiery with drink, embarrassment and anger; and I could still catch a twinge of the fear I felt—for he was much bigger and heavier than I was—before he finally swung away. He belonged to a category I have never liked, that of the dark, beefy, handsome males who when young are spoilt by all their women and later take to drink and a high blood pressure; and there must have always been something about me, perhaps what seemed to him just cool cheek, that from the very first had put him off me. But even while I re-lived that scene with him, held him there in front of me at the *Crown*, an indistinct, wavering but still menacing figure, I found myself thinking about him with compassion. There he was, torn between the pale, exquisite, adoring Eva, who no doubt could be dull enough, and this tricky, experienced, exciting woman from London, who was another man's wife; and as well as battling with his conscience and his desires, and feeling guilty one night and defiant again the next night, he had work he wanted to do, a style to find (a difficult time in a writer's life), and he was ambitious. And perhaps he was greedy for experience, with his conscious mind in a turmoil from bewildering and conflicting urges, just because in the dark of his unconscious there was already a whisper that time was running out fast. For Ben Kerry hadn't long to go. One morning in '16, on the Somme, the two Bruddersford "Pals' Battalions" were smashed into the chalk, and Ben was one of the subalterns. And then some people, politicians and editors, influential employers and the like, were surprised and pained afterwards to discover that places like Bruddersford appeared to be short of clever, lively young men. They ought to have looked in the chalk and among the sandbags.

But this was not clearing the fog between me and the Christmas of 1913. I couldn't even recall how and when and why Bridget and I had a quarrel, though I knew it was unexpected and bitter, arriving from her quarter, and that it didn't last long. And that, I felt sure, was before Christmas. And here I was, standing before the very last Christmas of that old world, with a fog of forgetfulness so thick that I couldn't even catch sight of a bit of tinsel in a shop window. Weeks of life, the rich and crowded weeks of youth, perhaps containing incidents that had determined or at least strongly influenced every important decision I had ever made since, had vanished, gone down and down, without a barrel or a spar to give me a clue. I didn't feel too tired to remember—it wasn't that—and looking at my watch I saw that it wasn't late, barely midnight. I knew very well that it is fatal to try to force one's memory, but in my impatience and annoyance I did attempt some forcing, and for several minutes I paced rather heavily up and down the room. Then somebody scratched at my door.

SEVEN

It was Elizabeth, as I knew very well it would be when I went to the door.

"Liz, I'm not sure about this," I said as I let her in. "Remember what I said. And you have to be careful."

"And I still say Rubbish," she cried. "We have this whole tower arrangement to ourselves, and I had only to come up our private little stairs. Do let's change the lighting, Greg. It looks so gloomy—like a mystery play. No, let me do it." And she messed about with the switches, finally achieving a subdued cosy effect round the two arm-chairs. "There, that's better. No wonder you were pacing about, with the room looking like that."

She sat down and smiled at me. She was wearing a turquoise velvet house-coat with a red-and-white corded sash, looked enchanting, and knew it. "Nice, isn't it? I got it just before I left, and hoped then you'd see me in it. Sit down and relax, darling, and don't go on frowning and whispering. Honestly there isn't anybody for miles. Not that it would matter if there was. And I warned you—remember?—that if I heard you pacing about, I'd pop up and see what was the matter. Isn't the story coming along?"

"No, that's all right, Liz," I told her. "It's all planned out to the end now, and it's only a matter of getting the stuff on paper, with perhaps just one or two tricky spots of dialogue in the last sequence. Look here, I hope I didn't wake you up."

"No, of course not. Actually I could only just hear you. But I thought it would be nice if we could talk. Especially," she added, looking at me reproachfully, "after you ran away so quickly downstairs."

"Well, I understood you were only going to be with those people about half an hour," I said, making it sound like a grumble. "That was Jake West's ration for you, I seem to remember."

"It lasted longer than that, of course. You know what it is.

And then, while I kept wondering where you were and if you were coming back, Adony took me into a corner and began explaining his idea of this part. He was quite helpful too, though I still don't like him much. What does he imagine about us, Greg?"

"He began by imagining all sorts of things," I replied, remembering my talk with him in the bar before dinner. "And I had to put him right. Also, while I was at it, I did my best to explain to him the sort of person you are."

Elizabeth looked solemn. "What did you say?"

It's the kind of question they always ask, and never in my life have I found myself willing and able to give a satisfactory reply. I suspect that there is here a fundamental sex difference. Most women are ready and even eager to answer that kind of question as well as to ask it, and most men just aren't. "I told him about you—briefly," I said. "What a film director ought to know about his star actress, that's all. I didn't particularly want to, but after all we have to work on this picture together."

She changed the subject. It was one of her many good qualities that she never nagged away at a topic. "I was a bit worried about you downstairs," she said. "You looked rather peculiar, I thought. I noticed it just before you dashed off, when I was talking to those people you used to know years ago in Yorkshire."

"I'd had enough of it—quite suddenly. It bores me to watch chaps like Jake doing their stuff. So I came up here."

"To work?"

"No, Liz, not to work. I can't work all the time. I've been smoking and thinking."

She nodded, rather as if what I had just said confirmed something she had thought about me. "Well, Greg, I think it's important I should talk to you. For your sake—and for mine too. I'll begin with me—that's not so important. You see, darling, it's not only that we're friends and haven't talked for ages—but here I am, all excited, coming back to England after all this time, all grand after trailing round for years just nobody, and you're the only person here I really can talk to, just because you're English and back from Hollywood too, and you understand the English part of it and the Hollywood part of it and—oh!—everything—"

"Yes, that's fair enough, Liz."

"You're very grumpy tonight," she said, making a face.

"Not really."

She considered me for a moment or two, then she smiled reminiscently. "Do you remember when you found me crying behind the writers' bungalow on the horrible Mertz lot? I felt that nobody wanted me and I wasn't any good."

"I know how you felt," I said. "That's one thing that's wrong with Hollywood—too many people crawling round the edge of that black pit."

But she didn't want to discuss Hollywood just then. "And then afterwards," she went on, "when I felt as if Terry had put me through a wringing machine and you made me go with Ethel Ferryman to that ranch on the Mohave Desert. I never told you how I hated that dam' phony ranch, with its buttermilk and cute salads from the magazines and the dust-storms every other day—and forsaken Hollywood wives sitting in rocking-chairs, all bitter as hell."

"No, you never told me," I said. "I didn't like the place myself. But it was the only thing to do with you, in the shape you were then, and it worked."

Her lovely face was alight. "What did work was you writing that marvellous story for me, and coming down to tell me about it. Do you remember how you'd get down there, late on Friday night, and I'd be waiting for you—and I used to have to fight like mad to keep enough decent food for us—and we'd sit up until all hours talking over the script and I knew it was going to be wonderful? And of course it was, but nothing that ever happened afterwards was as good as those nights. And sometimes if there was a moon and no dust-storm we'd go out—and just lean against a fence—and talk and talk. I could never persuade old Ethel, who was always wanting to know the details, that we weren't making love all that time. She always accused me of holding out on her—poor old Ethel! They were wonderful nights."

"They were," and meant it as I said it, captured for the moment by her mood. Yet I knew very well that they hadn't seemed particularly wonderful to me at the time. In fact I had often resented that long monotonous drive out to the ranch, and the equally long monotonous drive back to Beverly Hills on the Sunday; and it was only because Elizabeth had been such a wreck after her marriage to Terry Bleck, and because I had warned her against marrying him, and because I knew she depended on me and that I had to see her through, that I had dragged myself out there to the Mohave Desert, every dusty acre of which I thoroughly detested. "Yes, those were good times," I said, believing for the moment that they really were. The way we kid ourselves!

But Elizabeth wasn't deceived. "You don't really sound as if you meant it." She looked at me reproachfully again. Anybody listening to us would have thought we had been married for several years and that I had begun to neglect her. And anybody catching sight of her in that chair would probably have told me that I ought to be feeling deeply flattered. But I wasn't. In fact I felt rather annoyed. This wasn't like Liz, and it wasn't good enough, for after all there had never been anything between us to justify reproaches at midnight.

I suppose my face must have given me away, for now she swept across and kissed me, but fortunately for my good resolutions she didn't linger close to me but promptly returned to her chair. I filled a pipe, rather shakily, to keep myself rooted in my chair, and then made a great, grumpy middle-aged fuss about lighting it.

"You see, darling," she said earnestly, yet with a look that I remembered from so many films of hers that I began to feel we were playing a scene, "there's the second thing, the other reason why I must talk to you—yes, and at once—now. You, not me. What's the matter with you, Greg? There is something, isn't there? I felt it as soon as we met, this afternoon. Then after dinner you looked very odd—strained somehow—and suddenly dashed away. And now—well, it's just the same. It's as if —I'm attending to you, but you're not really attending to me. Yes, I know you're glad to see me—but still, it's as if most of you is busy somewhere else. And of course I know what it is to be like that, when you just can't bother with somebody although you like them well enough. But it's never been like that with us before—oh yes, when I was first married to Terry of course

—but you expected that—little fool that I was. But now we join up again—after all this time—and I was looking forward to it so much—and—and you're not really *here* with me—you're not, darling. What is it? You say you're not in love with anybody—though you behave just like a man who is."

"Well, I'm not, Liz," I said. "Put that right out of your head. I'm tired, probably. We've had quite a war here, y'know. This isn't America. You'll probably find us all a bit queer—"

"Oh stop it," she cried impatiently. "It isn't that at all. I understand about that. But this is something quite different. Something special to you, Greg. I *know*." She stared at me in a baffled but affectionate sort of way, which had something distinctly maternal about it and surprised me, because up to now I had been the big brother and had never noticed this streak in her, never suspected its existence in her. But now I might just have come back from college, changed and not saying anything, to be quite a worry to mother. I nearly said so.

"Yes, I'm worried about you," she continued, almost as if I had spoken. She leaned forward, resting her chin on her hands and her elbows on her knees; and affectionate bewilderment stared at me out of her wide grey eyes. It made me feel like a hero of Greek legend, sitting up to consult a goddess. Odd that behind all this, creating the situation, was a gawky lad trotting to and from a wool office in Canal Street, Bruddersford.

"You said that meeting those dreary people I talked to downstairs had started you off thinking about and remembering your past," she said, still staring speculatively at me. "They told me they remembered you too."

"They did, eh?" I sat up. "And what did they say?"

"Look at you now," she cried. "Yes, that must be it. I was right. What did they say? Oh—they just said—one or other of them, I forget which—that they knew you'd do something interesting later on—you were a clever sort of boy, a bit cheeky too, I gathered. They were as dull about you as they were about anything else—a pair of terrible dry old sticks. But that's it, isn't it? You've got caught up in something—and God knows why, because it must be ages ago—and it won't let you go." She challenged me to deny it.

I nodded. "It might be like that. I'm not saying it is, but it might be. And tonight, downstairs after dinner, I left in a hurry because I began thinking about those people—the Nixeys— Harndeans, they are now—and I felt I had to try to remember all that happened."

"Why is it so important?" she asked. "I've never heard you mention them—or even being in whatever it was—a wool office. Darling Greg, I don't understand."

"I don't—not yet. But I hope to, before I've finished."

"Are you sleepy?"

"No," I said, "but I think you ought to go to bed. You need plenty of sleep."

"I can sleep on in the morning. And I'm not sleepy yet. So tell me what it's all about."

"Not now, Liz," I said gently. "I'm still in the middle of it— like a story that's half worked out—and I need a bit more time."

"Will you tell me—when you've had your bit more time?" she pleaded.

"If you like," I said, "but it would probably bore you. It's only important to me, and I can't tell you even why I think it's important to me—not yet." I thought for a moment. "One mistake we're apt to make, though, is to assume that we are just ourselves as we are now, whereas that's only the thin top slice of us. And whatever has happened to us in the past is still there, perhaps still working away at us."

"That's psycho-analysis, isn't it?" she enquired solemnly. Outside her work Elizabeth has an innocent Book-of-the-Month mind.

"Not quite." And I grinned at her. "But let's leave it at that."

"Well, there's no need to laugh at me," she cried, sitting up and looking indignant. "I look forward to seeing you again— my very best friend—and now because you've met two dreary people from your distant past, when you were only a kid, there's a kind of damned wall between us. It's hateful—and I'm so miserably disappointed." And she sounded tearful, which was quite unusual for her.

"Why, Liz," I said penitently, getting up. "I didn't mean it to be a wall between us. And I've been eagerly waiting to see you too."

I sat on the arm of her chair and she pulled my face down and we kissed several times, as we had never done before. Up there in that little lighted space, deep in the night, we seemed a long way from other people, far away and on our own. I knew it was up to me to make the next move, one way or the other. And because I was so fond of her I didn't want us to start anything now that we had kept away from so far if we were not prepared to go straight on with it. I didn't know whether I was or not. I was too tangled up in the past to be clear about the present, and what I thought about Elizabeth or anybody or anything else. And this wasn't good enough. So I got up and walked away from that chair. There were some cigarettes on the table, and I took one and lit it as carefully as if it were a fifteen-shilling Havana cigar.

"Greg, will you admit one thing?" she said, getting up. "Then I'm going. You're all mixed up inside, aren't you? In a way you weren't before, when we were both on the Coast—eh?"

"A lot of things have happened since then—"

"You mean—war and all that stuff—?"

"Yes," I said, "war and all that stuff."

"But that's not what I mean," she said. "I'm allowing for that. It's you—inside yourself—that's mixed up—yes, all muddled and churned up. Aren't you?"

"I might be, Liz. It was all there before, of course, but the churning hadn't begun. That may make all the difference."

"I can only stay down here another day or two, Greg. Will you promise to tell me, to try to explain, before I go? I'm worried about you, and I don't want to be."

"I promise to tell you all I possibly can, even if it's necessary to take the whole day off to do it."

"The day after tomorrow perhaps—um?" she said, brightening, for Liz was a great day-out-and-picnic planner. "I'll see if we can hire a car." She nodded and smiled, and began walking slowly towards the door. I watched her with a sudden heartache. At the door she turned and looked at me; and I saw that she was tired now—for she had had a long day and been in the air, crossing the Atlantic, all the day before—and she seemed a little forlorn too; and her familiar bright beauty was touched with a softness and strangeness: she might have been some lost queen of legend. But even at that moment I began to wonder if I couldn't give her a scene in this new script in which she could look like that.

It came, the old wistful question: "What are you thinking?"

"I was thinking of giving you something new to do in the last sequence," I told her. "Something that would make you look just as you do now. Now pop off, my dear girl—and sleep well."

"Same to you. And no more of that pacing about, Greg. I'm damned if I'm going to be kept awake while you try to remember all the little girls you knew in Bruddersford. See you at lunch tomorrow—that sounds nice, doesn't it?"

"Yes, Liz, it does," I said. "Good night, my dear."

It looked a hellishly dull empty room when she had gone. I felt as cold and flat as a forgotten pancake. I could have done with some whisky, but there wasn't any. I still didn't feel sleepy, and when I am working hard I hate sleeping badly because my work usually suffers all the next day. As I undressed I chewed two tablets of medinal and then washed down the last bitter fragments with a glass of water. I knew that medinal acts slowly with me, but it was all I had there, and I thought that if I lay quietly in bed, not thinking about anything in particular, I might drop off fairly soon and then the medinal would begin to work. That would kill the night. We lords of the earth, I reflected as I climbed into bed, are always trying to kill time now—generally with a blunt instrument. The temperature of the sheets suggested cold storage, and I wondered then why the scientists, instead of fooling about with the atom, hadn't suggested to their bosses some way of putting about a third of the population of Europe into cold storage for a few months at a time, thus attempting to solve the food and transport problems. If the initial going-under were pleasant, and it was proved that no harm came to you while you were frozen and out, I decided that millions of people wouldn't wait to be selected for the experiment but would besiege the new department. (Human Cold Storage—*Hucolstor?*) And I played about with the idea as the basis of a story. The people who volunteered for *Hucolstor*, and who had had time for a good sleep and for several months hadn't

been badgered and hoodwinked and bullied, were thawed out
and wakened up, and then after a day or two's bewilderment
they began to roar with derisive laughter at all the nonsense of
our political, economic and social life, and promptly started a
revolution, popping thousands of Very Important Personages,
officials, prominent executives, into long-term *Hucolstor*. And as
so often happens with ideas that arrive late at night, I couldn't
decide whether I had something or was merely drivelling to
myself. Either way, the medinal whispered, it didn't matter now,
didn't matter . . . didn't . . . matter . . . I was off.

But I wasn't. That Bruddersford fog lifted, and there I was,
attending a party at the Alingtons' on the evening of the thirty-
first of December, 1913. It looked like being a good party, the
best there had been there since that evening when the Nixeys
first arrived. We had had, I remembered now, a sort of Christmas truce. Mr. Alington had returned from abroad determined
to make the best of Nixey's presence in the office, and Nixey
had shown no opposition; and even he and Joe Ackworth had
exchanged a few civil words. Oliver Alington was home of
course, which made things livelier. Ben Kerry had been seen
about with Eva again, and apparently wasn't meeting Eleanor
Nixey. I had had an article accepted by a London weekly, and
had bought myself a black velvet tie and an oversize curved
Peterson pipe. Just as there are short periods when the course of
a fatal disease is checked, and the patient sits up and smiles and
makes plans, so it is with a group or a community as it moves
towards dissolution: there is a halt, a truce, a breathing-space,
bringing cruel illusions of recovered health and well-being.
Well, we were in one of those, with all the rich paraphernalia of
a Bruddersford Christmas helping to sustain our illusions. And
now, to see the old year out and the new year in, we had this
party at Alingtons'. Joe Ackworth and his wife were going, and
Jock Barniston of course, but I didn't know who else would be
there. I arrived, however, with some of the old magic working
in me, as if it had only been a day or two since I had stared at this
fascinating family on top of the tram.

It was Eva, a smiling Corn Queen in silk, who let me in. I
had hardly had more than a glimpse of her for months, and was

delighted to see her looking so well and happy, even though it was clear that she had hoped it was Ben Kerry who was at the door and couldn't quite hide her disappointment. We couldn't say much, though, because Joe Ackworth and Councillor Knott, the fighting Socialist, were in the hall, puffing cigar smoke at each other and loudly arguing about politics.

"You an' your Liberals, Joe," Knott was shouting. "You're all just playin' at it, that's all. In ten years—nay, less—there won't be any Liberals, you'll see."

"Nah, talk sense, Fred," Ackworth bellowed at him. "Just talk a bit o' bloody sense for once, lad."

"I tell you—you'll 'ave to make your minds up whose side you're on, Joe. Are you for the workers or the boss class? Make up your mind, lad."

"Workers an' boss class! Aw dear, aw dear! Same old stuff."

"Yes, same old stuff," Knott shouted. "An' we'll go on repeatin' it, till we get it into some o' your thick skulls. Come down on one side or the other, Joe. Don't go on ditherin', lad, don't go on ditherin'."

"Who's ditherin'?" roared Ackworth. "When did Ah dither? That Ramsay Mac' o' yours, there's a ditherer if yer like. Ah 'eard 'im t'other week, an' it took 'im an hour to say nowt. Why, Lloyd George's worth a 'undred of 'im—"

"There you go, there you go," cried Knott, bristling like a terrier. "No principles, no policy—just personalities. Trouble wi' you, Joe Ackworth, is you're frivolous—just dam' frivolous."

This plunged Ackworth into noisy despair. "By gow, Ah've bin called all sorts i' my time—but *frivolous!* Nay, what the hangment, Fred lad—you're clean aht o' your mind—"

"Hey, you two!" This was Bridget, who had come darting out of the drawing-room. "Stop it. Standing there—shouting at each other!"

They grinned, a trifle sheepishly, and went forward into the drawing-room, while Bridget held the door open and gave them a stern look. Then when they had gone in, she turned to me.

"Hello, Gregory! Did Eva let you in?"

"Yes," I said. "Then she disappeared."

"She's waiting for Ben," Bridget whispered in a tone of deep disgust. "She's absolutely barmy on him. Really—it's frightful. She couldn't be worse if he was—was Kreisler—somebody really marvellous. And Joan's nearly as bad about Jock, though he's not really interested in her. And now Oliver has started raving about a red-haired girl at Girton. I don't know what's the matter with this family."

"Well, you needn't look at me like that, Bridget," I said, grinning. "I can't help it."

"I didn't say you could," she said, frowning a little. "It's something I wanted to tell you—oh, I remember. Will you and Oliver pick sides for charades? Get in a corner with him as soon as you go in. I'll be on your side," she added, rather loftily. "Oliver gets so silly."

We went in, and after going round and saying "How d'you do?" I followed my instructions and took Oliver into a corner. While we were there, Eva came in with Ben Kerry, looking as if she had just won a vast prize in a lottery. That made fourteen of us altogether. My charade team consisted of Bridget, Joan, Mrs. Alington, Joe Ackworth, Mrs. Knott, and young David, who was discovered sitting on a low stool behind the ample Mrs. Ackworth reading a work on astronomy. Oliver's side were to perform first, and he led out Eva and Ben Kerry, his father, Jock Barniston, Mrs. Ackworth and Councillor Knott. As usual with charades, those of us who were left, waiting to be entertained, were suddenly quiet, while the others who had gone out could be heard running up and down stairs, shouting at each other and laughing idiotically.

"Oh dear," said Mrs. Alington, "I hope they're not turning the whole place upside down."

"You have to—for charades," said young David calmly. "That's the point." And then he went back to his astronomy.

Joan and I had been clearing a space for them to act in, and when we sat down we found ourselves apart from the others. We munched almonds and raisins and over the dish of them that we shared I noticed her peeping at me from under her long dark lashes. She was looking very pretty in her pale demure way; but ever since that night in Wabley Wood I had felt that she was quite different from the girl I had first imagined her to

be, that she acted a part and that there were dubious hidden ele-
ments in her character, that what I originally took to be shyness
was more like slyness, and that there was a certain perversity in
her apparent reserve. There was something about her now that
made me feel lascivious. I stared at her surprisingly full white
neck: it had a necklace of three deep creases.

"Well, have you thought of a word, Gregory?" she asked,
with a faint air of mockery.

"No, what do you suggest, Joan? Two syllables or three?"

"Two are enough," she said. "Otherwise it's too long. Easier
to guess, of course. Unless we cheated a bit. For instance, we
might have *fatal* but make it *fat* and *all*."

"That's a bit thick," I said. "What about *nonsense?*"

"Too easy—and we've had it before. Come on, you're supposed to be a literary gent, aren't you, Gregory?"

"What about *good-bye*? Fairly easy, I know, but we might disguise it a little. And anyhow good is hard to spot, and then in the
next scene we can just have somebody saying *By the bye*. Yes, let's
have that, Joan."

I put my hand in the dish between us to take some more
almonds and raisins, and she put her hand in at the same time
and it seemed to me that she deliberately touched my hand with
hers, yet when I glanced at her she looked innocent and aloof.

"*Good-bye* it shall be, then," she said. "By the way, you know
there are still two more people to come. Your friends—the
Nixeys. Yes, they were invited and they accepted. Late, of
course, but then they would be, wouldn't they? I don't think Ben
knows they're coming," she added significantly, "though Eva
does."

"Oh—so you know about that, do you?"

"Yes, of course. And I'll bet you knew—and never said anything."

"Well, I've seen Ben with Mrs. Nixey several times and they
looked—well—"

"As if they were in love with each other?" she said.

"I don't know about that," I replied, rather cautiously. "I got
the impression they were very friendly—and excited about each
other—I must say. And the last time I saw them together, I had

rather a row with Ben." And I told her about the theatrical party at the *Crown*. I had just finished when some of Oliver's team came on to act the first syllable of their word.

The action seemed to be taking place in some lunatic shop. The stately Mrs. Ackworth, who still appeared to be her usual self although dressed outrageously, laboriously attended the mysterious wants of Messrs. Alington Senior, Barniston and Knott, who all wore other people's hats and coats, spoke all together or kept silent, and looked like nothing but three serious-minded men trying to play charades. It was not a very successful first act.

"I think," said young David solemnly, for having put down his book he now gave the game all his attention, "the first syllable is probably—"

"No, David darling," said Mrs. Alington, "don't tell us yet. We'll wait and then guess."

"Don't ask me," cried little Mrs. Knott, who had been laughing her head off, "'cos I've no idea. The sight of Fred in that hat was too much for me. Nay, nay!" And she began laughing all over again, being a jolly little woman and easily amused.

The next scene was more ambitious. It was Oriental. First we heard a gong, and then Oliver came in, wearing an assortment of dusters and tea-towels, and by elaborate kow-towing suggested a slave in some Eastern palace. The princess was Eva, who had ingeniously contrived an Oriental costume out of odds and ends and really looked a ravishing and voluptuous beauty. There were murmurs of admiration from our side.

"By gow, Eva lass," cried Joe Ackworth, who had had a whisky or two, "you're a sight for sore eyes. Nay this is summat like—better than a pantomime."

I happened then to give a quick glance at Joan by my side, and saw that instead of staring with smiling admiration, as the rest of us were, she was looking at Eva with narrowed eyes and her lips were compressed. But the next moment, as she realised I was glancing in her direction, her eyes were wide again and she was smiling.

Eva, a haughty and silent Turandot, sat erect on her throne while the salaaming Oliver went out, first to bang the gong

again, and then to admit Ben Kerry, who had got himself up
to look like some kind of wandering suitor, complete with
turban and a cloak made out of a green velvet table-cloth. The
costume, rough-and-ready though it was, suited his dark good
looks admirably, and he was a magnificent figure. He saluted the
haughty princess, who could not help lighting up at the sight of
him, knelt on one knee before her and began some long pseudo-
Oriental rigmarole, in which, no doubt, the second syllable had
been carefully planted. And as the princess graciously extended
a hand towards him, and he took the hand and kissed it, the
Nixeys walked in.

They began apologising and Mrs. Alington began welcoming
them, and the charade stopped for a few moments. After that
the scene was hastily concluded, without ever coming to life
again. Perhaps it was killed by the first flashing glance that Eleanor Nixey gave it, before she had time to compose herself. Ben
himself, I noticed, was unpleasantly surprised, and there was
something immediately tense about Eva.

"It looked very dramatic," said Mrs. Nixey, when Ben and
Eva had gone out. "I hope we didn't spoil it."

"No, of course not," said Mrs. Alington, the hostess now and
rather on her guard. "The children insisted on playing charades.
I hope you don't mind."

"You could play," said Bridget, with a very direct look at
Nixey. "It's not too late."

"No good at it," said Nixey, smiling.

"Have you ever tried?"

"Can't say I have—"

"Well, you can start tonight," said Ackworth. "Do you no 'arm."

"I should jolly well think not," cried Bridget, with a flashing
green glance at both Nixeys.

Mrs. Nixey smiled at her, not without a deliberate touch of
condescension. "And why would you jolly well think not?"

"Because I think it does people good to act the fool now and
again," Bridget retorted. There was more than a hint in her tone
that the Nixeys needed some good doing to them.

"Now Bridget!" cried Mrs. Alington, as if admitting that her
daughter had probably scored a point. "Come and sit here, Mrs.

Nixey. And somebody—Gregory, if you wouldn't mind—get Mr. Nixey a drink."

I led him to the table in the corner, and he helped himself to whisky. "You in on this, old man?" he whispered.

I told him my side went out next, and that he or his wife could join us if they wanted to.

"Not my style," he said. "Hate dressing up and acting the goat. Eleanor wouldn't mind dressing up—she's always doing it —but she wouldn't care for the performing part. But I must say, Dawson, that fair-haired Alington kid we just saw is something to look at twice, isn't she? I'd forgotten what a dazzler she is. Now where do I sit?"

"Over there," and I pointed to the place I had just left, next to Joan. And there he went, while I remained by the table at the back, curious to see how he and Joan would get along.

Bridget joined me, drank some lemonade, then muttered in my ear: "And I say *Blast 'em!* Yes, you know who. They'll spoil everything, you'll see. I'll be glad when it's our turn and we can get out." Then she shouted towards the door. "Hurry up, Oliver. Don't be all night."

The last scene was a messy romp, and I noticed that neither Ben nor Eva took part in it. Once or twice I looked at the Nixeys, for I had a good view of both of them from where I stood. Mrs. Nixey seemed to me to be well aware of the fact that Eva and Ben were still outside together, and she couldn't help glancing towards the door. As for Nixey, I saw him looking coolly and speculatively at Mr. Alington, who was trying, not very successfully, to play the fool in a coat turned inside-out and David's school cap.

Bridget, still standing close to me, startled me by whispering, as much to herself as to me: "Poor Dad! I'm sure he knows that man's staring at him and thinking he's a fool. Dad used to be awfully good at charades. I adored him when I was little. Oh —do get it over—hurry up!"

They got it over, and Oliver, mopping himself with one of the towels, demanded to know from us what the word was.

"Nay, lad, you got me beat," said Joe Ackworth, as if he were some visiting champion of charades.

"It's *Yuletide*," said David with calm disgust.

And so it was, and while the others noisily explained why they hadn't guessed it and David went straight back to astronomy, Eva and Ben Kerry came in, looking very self-conscious. Eva and Eleanor Nixey exchanged brief glances, very feminine, at once blankly impersonal and yet searching. Ben looked at neither of them but came across to my table for a drink. It was a very large whisky.

"Haven't taken to this stuff yet, I suppose, Dawson?"

"No, too strong for me," I said, young and humble.

"Too strong for you too," said Bridget sharply.

"My business, young Bridget," said Ben, grinning at her. "I don't criticise you for wolfing milk chocolate."

"I hate milk chocolate," she said, and left us.

"That kid's spoilt, in my opinion," said Ben. "Well—cheerio! I need this. So will you some day, you'll see. Especially if you take on Bridget—which, I imagine, is the idea, isn't it, Dawson?"

"I didn't know it was," I said, not liking his tone. "But she's certainly the one I like best. I hardly know Eva, though."

"She's a darling," he muttered. "Too good for any of us —except perhaps Jock. And he doesn't want any of 'em. Well, you'd better collect your lot and entertain us now."

We trooped off to the dining-room, which was still littered with the costumes and props of the other team, so that Mrs. Alington and Mrs. Knott did a lot of tut-tutting together. I explained about *Good-bye*, and it was agreed that it would do. While the rest of us discussed possible scenes, young David, now his own age and in a fine state of excitement, tore upstairs, to return, breathless and triumphant, with a large cardboard box full of whiskers, false noses and pink shiny masks. "I knew Dad and Oliver would forget these," he told us, bursting with glory and grandeur.

"Darling!" cried Mrs. Alington, looking at him as I had never seen her look before. And I had once thought her a cold reserved woman.

"Nah see 'ere," Joe Ackworth shouted. "Ah don't care what we supposed to do, but Ah must be a little lad. Ah've done it afore an' it allus goes with a big bang. Wife'll be in there expectin' it."

"I could be a master," said David eagerly, "and wear this nose and moustache."

"All right, then," I said, "the first scene's a school—and you can bring in the word *good*, David."

Bridget, busy wrecking her frock by stuffing it into a pair of her father's oldest flannel bags, insisted upon being in this scene, but Joan and the two older women said they would stay out of it and do some elaborate dressing up for scene two, which would be a small select tea-party. So David, transformed into a horrible little brute of a schoolmaster, the red-nosed, heavily ironic type, led the way to the drawing-room, followed by three monster pupils, played by G. Dawson, who looked an indeterminate sort of grotesque, Bridget, who suggested a lunatic ploughboy, and Joe Ackworth, whose red moon face shone beneath a tiny cricket cap. And thanks chiefly to David, to whom a bitter pedagogic manner seemed to come naturally, we did a bit of good clowning with something better than the usual scrambling charade style. (Even in those early days I liked a scene to *be* a scene.) And loudest of all were the peals of laughter from the stately Mrs. Ackworth.

"Let's do Fat People for the last bit," cried David, when we were back in the dining-room.

"What's Fat People?" asked Ackworth, who ought to have known, being one of them himself.

"We always used to do it," said Mrs. Alington, now a most fantastic matron. "The children used to adore it—everybody stuffing themselves with cushions and pretending to be enormous. Bridget, take Gregory with you—and find some of the things we used to use."

So while they went in to do their tea-party scene, Bridget took me upstairs, to rummage through attic wardrobes and old trunks. We could just hear the shouts of laughter from below. The two attics were crammed with things: the whole past of the family was up there.

"I've never been part of a family," I said. "Perhaps that's why you've all had such a fascination for me."

"Family life's peculiar," she said, working away. "Here—take this, Gregory. It usually seems pretty awful at the time—even holidays too. Yet when you look back, you feel it was wonderful."

"That's not just family life, that's everything."

"It's much more so with a family," she said. "Are you still fascinated by us?"

"Yes, in a way, though of course the strangeness has gone," I told her.

"Oh—has it? Well, don't you be too sure," she grunted, half inside a wardrobe. "Golly, I hate the stink of this moth stuff—I'd rather have moths. We're a lot stranger than you think, let me tell you."

"All right, go on telling me. I'm really curious. And I've never asked you before."

"Well, to begin with," she said, "the boys are the nicest. They really are."

"What about Eva, though?"

She made a snorting noise, then sneezed. "It's that beastly stuff. Look, grab these two. And Eva—well of course she's so pretty and sweet that everybody's always made a fuss of her —except Mother, who thinks she's rather silly. And she is, too— and awfully weak, yet obstinate in a kind of dim way. The thing to do really is just to *look* at Eva—and imagine things about her."

"And Joan?"

"Yes, I expected that. Here, this'll do now." She looked at me. "Joan's the oldest who's always been so *good*—so responsible and conscientious—and at school she was always held up to me as an example. But Joan's a sly boots really—and somewhere inside she's got a nasty temper. I say, this sounds rotten, doesn't it? And I'm fond of them really. But I thought I ought to tell you —you're so soft and sentimental, Gregory."

"Soft and sentimental!" I was outraged. Gregory Dawson, young but so cynical already, disillusioned, shrewd and hard behind that pleasant smiling youthful face. "Me!"

"Yes, you. The others don't see it, but I do. And you'll have to be careful or it'll slop over into all your writing. Ugh! I can see it coming."

I could hear shouts for us coming from below, but I didn't bother about them. I was really annoyed now. "Look here, Bridget, I must say that's a bit thick. You don't know—"

"I do know," she interrupted, mocking me. "And it isn't a bit thick. And they're shouting for us."

"I know they are. Let 'em shout. I want to know what you mean—"

"Poor old Gregory! Don't look so worried. You can't help it probably—"

"Oh—shut up, Bridget. And I'm no softer or more sentimental than you are."

"Of course you are. I'm not sentimental at all—and I'm hard—you'll see. But that doesn't mean I don't like you—you chump. Here!" And lightly she took my face between her hands and gave me a kiss. "Now then—we must go." And off she raced, leaving me to carry most of the old clothes.

"What have you two been doing?" said Joan.

"Getting these things—and talking about you," said Bridget. "Now come on—Fat People. *Good-bye to the Fats* is the title of this scene—isn't it, Gregory?"

Sometimes this sort of happy idiocy can be raised to such a height that it takes on a kind of poetic glory, and is never afterwards forgotten. This is what happened with our Fat People nonsense. Often in the trenches, shivering on the fire-step or crouched in little dug-outs that already smelt of the grave, I remembered with deep pleasure, with renewed hope, our Fat People, going back, as it were, to warm my hands at the roaring scene. As we stuffed and padded ourselves, the cheeks we blew out collapsed in laughter. David, Joan, Bridget and I were pretty good; Mrs. Alington, a vast dowager, and little Mrs. Knott, now five feet square and somehow sinister with it, were even better; and Ackworth, who started with some advantages and had found a huge false nose attached to cheeks like crimson hemispheres, was stupendous, a Falstaff of the wool trade. In a lumbering procession, bumping against each other all the way, we went swaying and wheezing into the drawing-room, which received us with a shout. We had arrived to take some mysterious cure. We were saying good-bye to our gigantic bellies and bottoms, to the four solid inches on our ribs, to fatness itself. We filled all the available space in that drawing-room; we were talking sea-cows and hippopotami, we were lard and suet in wistful conference; we were mountains of bosom and thigh exposed to a gale of laughter. And I remember noticing Mr. Alington, who was doubled up, purple and streaming with mirth, and remember thinking how queer he looked, how unlike his usual self: only a glimpse—and I was never to see him looking like that again.

"Good-bye, me old dumplings in stew," shouted Joe Ackworth, who was improvising wildly now, "me tripe an' trotters an' mashed, me plum puddings an' treacle puds an' currant duffs, me pork chops an' crackling an' Devonshire cream an' chocolate cake. Good-bye for ever—me old—"

"No, we must stop," cried Mrs. Alington, in her ordinary voice, which sounded strange at that moment. "I'm sorry, but we must stop. Look—it's five to twelve."

"Yes, of course," said Mr. Alington, jumping up. "Nearly midnight, and somebody must let the New Year in."

"Good-bye, good-bye, good-bye," Ackworth still went on.

"We know, Joe," his wife shouted. "That's the word. Now be quiet."

We Fats rushed back to the dining-room to shed our ridiculous clothes and cushions, and there was much talk about who was to let the New Year in. It had to be a dark man apparently; and Mr. Alington himself, who was dark enough, wouldn't do, because he had done it last year, and not, they thought, very successfully. In less than three minutes we were back in the drawing-room.

"Has anybody gone out?" asked Mrs. Alington. You had to go outside, wait for twelve o'clock to strike, and then be admitted, to let in the New Year properly.

"Yes," said Mr. Alington, "Mr. Nixey's gone."

"No," cried Bridget sharply, "that's all wrong. Somebody else must go."

Several people talked at once then, but Bridget could still be heard, saying it was all wrong.

"Ben, you're dark," cried Eva. "You go too. Hurry, hurry."

And she rushed him out of the room, and a moment later we heard the front door bang behind him. Oliver and his father and mother and Joan were now busy pouring and handing out drinks. The rest of us waited, some smiling, some uneasy, for the old year to die. Then came the distant chimes of midnight followed by the jangling and pealing, far and near, of church bells. There was a loud knocking at the front door.

"Eva's there already," said Mrs. Alington, smiling. "And you'd better go too, Mrs. Nixey, to let in your husband."

"Oh—should I?" said Eleanor Nixey, and sauntered out.

The Knotts were standing close to me, and now they looked at each other, forgetting the rest of us, these two battered little stalwarts, isolated for the moment by their mutual trust and tenderness.

"Well, Fred love," I heard her say softly, "a Happy New Year to you, lad."

He kissed her. "And to you, old lass. I hope it will be, I hope it will be." But his smile was dubious, his eyes solemn.

"A Happy New Year to everybody!" This was from Nixey and Ben Kerry, making their formal entrance, bringing us 1914. Eva and Eleanor Nixey followed them in, both silent and looking perturbed. It was—as I think more than one of us felt—an ill-omened beginning.

"Thank you, gentlemen," cried Mr. Alington, who had the forced geniality of a man stifling all doubts. "Now, have you all got something to drink? Right! We're going to drink a toast —a toast to the New Year—to 1914 and all that it will bring us —peace, prosperity and friendship."

As we drank after him somebody's glass fell, hit the fender, and smashed itself on the hearth.

"Eva, what's the matter?" young David screamed.

She had burst into wild sobbing, and now her mother was hurrying her out of the room. We tried to pretend that nothing had happened, but we couldn't manage it, and the party was in ruins. . . .

Again, as I lay there in bed, with the medinal already thickening and dulling the dark, there came, like the ache of a badly healed wound, that sense of loss and desolation and bereavement which I had felt downstairs. I fell asleep, but it was an uneasy sleep crowded with dreams, in which a self that was neither the lad in Bruddersford nor the middle-aged man of the Royal Ocean Hotel, but an ageless secret self, flitted through bewildering telescoped scenes that ran the chalk trenches of Picardy into Piccadilly Circus, and jammed Brigg Terrace and Canal Street into Hollywood and Beverly Hills; and everywhere that wandering secret self cried, "Lost, lost, lost!" searched and searched, and could never find what had to be found. . . .

EIGHT

Somebody was staring at me. I rubbed my eyes, and I stared back. It was George Adony, in a black silk dressing-gown and a crimson scarf, and he was looking yellow and puffy-eyed and small, a weary gnome. The curtains had been pulled back, and it was bright daylight.

"What's this about, George?" I said, struggling out of sleep.

"I am having breakfast with you, Gregory," he replied, and he waved a hand.

"Can't be done," I told him. "They won't serve breakfasts up in your room here."

"It has been done. I have fixed it. These things can always be fixed. I want to talk about the script, and if we do it here, while we have breakfast, it will save time. There is a train at eleven-thirty, and Jake and I are catching it. You are having for breakfast porridge, coffee and fish cakes."

"Good. I like fish cakes," I said, grinning.

"I knew you would. That's why I ordered them. For you, not for me. I hate porridge and fish cakes. And though it is a good script," he added, "as of course I knew it would be—I will tell you now that there are some porridge and fish cakes in it that must be removed."

I pulled myself out of bed to have a wash. "Well, we'll see about that, George. Get the breakfast and then we'll talk. It's a good idea, and I wouldn't have thought of it." But in the bathroom it didn't seem to me such a good idea. I had smoked too much and too late the night before, and must have spent the remaining hours battling with the medinal, and now I had a headache and felt depressed. As a rule I enjoy talking over the details of a script with a good director—and George Adony, I knew, was a good director—but he had picked the wrong morning or started too early. I put on my old thick dressing-gown and padded in to join him. The breakfast had arrived, and Adony was handing out two large tips.

"Just a couple of magicians, eh?" I grunted, as we faced one another across the table.

But he was in a serious mood this morning. "After you left us last night," be began, "I had some talk with Elizabeth Earl. I think you are right about her. She will be easy to work with, and will take direction nicely. She should give us an excellent performance. I shall tell Brent tonight that I am pleased." He was very much the dignified foreign maestro, just about to conduct *The Ring* at Salzburg. And he was making one of those pecking-smoking breakfasts, while I shovelled steadily away at the porridge and fish cakes.

"I still think, by the way, that she is in love with you," he said, after gulping down some coffee. "Not passionately—because she is not a passionate woman—but genuinely in love, in the Anglo-Saxon schoolgirl style."

"Don't let's bother about that, George," I told him. "We haven't much time—and I don't particularly want to discuss Elizabeth all over again this morning."

He nodded. "Story conference, then. It is of course a good story, as I said from the first."

"I'll tell you a secret," I whispered, "just between ourselves, George. I'm beginning to hate the dam' story."

He gave me a cold hard look. "Why is that? What is the matter with it?"

"Oh, I dunno. Perhaps because it's not like anything that happens or ever could happen. And it's beginning to bore me."

He turned the pages of the copy of the script I had given him the night before, arrived at the last sequence I had completed, and tapped it significantly with his forefinger. "It is here, that boredom. In the sequence where she runs away. You may have been sticking too close to it—down here, miles from anywhere —nothing to do, nobody to talk to. It is a good idea to work this way—I often do it myself—but it can easily be overdone. But we will come to that in a minute, Gregory. Just now I am wondering what you mean when you say you are beginning to hate this story because it is not like anything that happens or could happen. We are making a movie, aren't we? It is a good story for movies, full of nice twists and little surprises, never standing still, with plenty for the two stars and for me. In addition, Gregory, as you will remember we agreed when we discussed your original rough treatment, it has its own point of view."

"Well, perhaps I don't like its point of view any longer, George. Or I may be wondering why the hell we have to work so far away from ordinary life."

"Because that is what the customers want," he said. "Some kind of fairy tale."

"I sometimes wonder whether the customers—the people we all say we're trying to please—have any choice in the matter at all. Most of 'em just go to the movies, and chance their luck."

Obviously he didn't feel like arguing about this. He began looking at the script.

"Y'know, George, I'm older than you. I'm fifty. Sometimes I forget, and at other times I keep on remembering, and this is one of the mornings when I remember. Fifty."

He glanced up, smiling. "You don't look it," he said. "And what is wrong with being fifty? And what has fifty to do with our movie—*The Lady Hits Back?*"

"Perhaps it's the gentleman hitting back. Yes, yes—it's a good film story. It has all that you want and that they'll want. But what has it got that I want? That's what I'm beginning to ask myself, and, at fifty, questions like that take on a nasty awkward tone, George."

"Some other time I would like to argue all this," he said.

"All right, let's get to business." I pointed to the script. "You're worried about the running away sequence, aren't you? Hence the crack about porridge and fish cakes being in it. Well, what's wrong with it?"

"I never could shoot it," he said sharply. "And when I ask myself why and go back over the script, I see that you have not really worked out these scenes."

"You mean the hotel scenes, eh?"

"Yes, of course—all the hotel scenes. And very important, because now for the first time, after she has run away, we see her outside her own house. So everything must be very clear, and you have not made it clear, Gregory. You were feeling rather bored, no doubt—"

"No, I wasn't. Yes, I know that I said the story was beginning to bore me—but that's all happening at the back of my mind—I didn't say I'd begun to do bored scamped work."

George Adony had a curious hair-triggered temper. "But I say it," he shouted. "That is just what I do say. Yes, bored and scamped work—no bloody good at all."

"Either calm down or clear out, George. You're not on the floor now, and I'm not one of your technical boys. I was co-producing with Sam Gruman in Hollywood when you were still shouting through a megaphone at Denham telling the workmen to keep quiet. I could have been co-producing on this picture, but I told Brent I was tired of that studio of his. I'm tired of all their damned studios, as a matter of fact, and I want some new set-up or a long rest. But that doesn't mean I'm not seeing this film through. Brent's given me a good contract, and I'm chiefly responsible for Elizabeth coming over. Now you don't like those hotel scenes. Well, I do. And they're in that shape because that's how I wanted them to be."

"But nothing is clear, nothing is properly worked out," he protested, free of his tantrums now.

"That's the way it's meant to be. Look—she's marched off to an hotel, still in a fury, still quarrelling with him—and what happens? Nothing seems quite right and sensible there. The people seem peculiar. They do odd things. She overhears conversations that simply don't make sense. Everything's off the centre. Is it a bit sinister or is it all nonsense? She doesn't know, and we don't know—"

"We have to know," said Adony. "We are making a movie, not composing a highly subjective narrative. The audience must understand everything."

"For God's sake," I cried, "can't we credit them with a little imagination, just for ten minutes of the film?"

"No, because they have no imagination."

"If you ask me, we've gone on making everything so damned plain and simple, planting and motivating at every turn, that we've got half the audiences yawning their heads off. All right, we're working for nitwits. But don't let's make the fatal mistake of supposing they're even more nitwitted than they are. Let's have a little fun ourselves, now and again, and try catering for the brighter specimens. And don't tell me you can't shoot those scenes."

"No, no, if that is what you intended, I can shoot them very nicely," he muttered, not looking at me. "In fact I once planned a picture that was to be nearly all like that—very subjective. A man, a highly neurotic type, was tempted to commit murder, and it seemed to him that other crimes were being plotted and planned all round him, as if the world was full of murder. This was before the world was full of murder, you understand, and when I was young and innocent myself. In my own country too, not a comic refugee, away from home, on sufferance."

He looked small and melancholy, and I remembered what Liz had said about his having eyes like a monkey's. "George, last night I took some sleeping stuff that didn't quite work," I said, "and you know what that's like. So I'm not at my best this morning. If I was a bit heavy-handed in dealing with your little outburst, I'm sorry. And it wasn't good enough my telling you that I was beginning to feel bored with the story. Though, as I suggested, you misjudged me there. I was only telling you what was happening at the back of my mind, not apologising for anything in the script. I promise you that, with any luck, I'll be back in town next week with a completed script that you'll enjoy getting on to the floor. And if you're pleased with Elizabeth, well, she's pleased with you too, George. So you're all set."

Instead of disliking me, he was now staring at me, with bright sad eyes, as if I were the first friend he had seen for months. Like many men who achieve success the hard way and put on a tough front, he was at heart a lonely and forlorn little man. Coming over here, starting almost all over again in an alien atmosphere, God knows what snubs, what insults, he must have had to swallow on the way up. And he loved making films: they were his life.

"I will talk to Brent about this hotel sequence," he said softly. "Perhaps too you will explain it to Elizabeth, so that she understands before she sees Brent again. Come and eat with me one night soon at my house—I will have something special for us—and then we will talk properly and exchange ideas—about real movies. If this one is a success, perhaps they would let us make an experiment together." He picked up the script and rose from the table, delicately flicking ash from his dressing-gown. "I was married once. It was different then. I went home—and talked. Now I get into bed with this one and that—but there is no real talk. What do you do, Gregory?"

"Nothing these days," I replied. "Think about my past, that's all."

"It's a weakness of most Englishmen," he said. "Their inner faces—the real ones—are turned to the past. Their life is over at twenty-one. You should get married, my friend, while you are still attractive to women and can pick and choose. Elizabeth, for instance; though an actress—a star, too—is probably a mistake." He looked hopefully at me, as if a last-minute confidence would seal our friendship. He didn't get one, but we parted friends.

By the time I had dressed and had settled down to work, more than half the morning had gone. I still felt heavy and a bit drugged, but I slogged away at the script until just after one. I felt all the time that a good half of me was still tangled up with the Alingtons in Bruddersford, but I contrived, as a sound professional scribbler, to pay no attention to that half, and went doggedly on with the adventures of my glamorous, aggressive and unreal young woman, whose life in celluloid now seemed to me to belong to Brent, Elizabeth, George Adony, and not to me. It was awkward, but the fact remained, as I had confessed to Adony, that I had begun to take a dislike to this young beauty and her ridiculous antics.

I discovered Elizabeth waiting for me below. She was wearing enormous tortoise-shell spectacles, large enough for a Chinese philosopher, and peering through them, wide-eyed and delighted at *The Times*. "It's the advertisements, Greg," she explained. "I'd forgotten how fascinating they are—and how marvellously English. The only thing in America that's as good in its own way is *Variety*. Wouldn't it be heavenly if you could mix them up—the country-house ladies with their daffodil bulbs and prize Airedales, the retired majors with their small shoots, and the Show Biz boys and their hot femme canaries? Did you sleep well, darling?"

"Not very," I said, as we went into the dining-room. "I was too busy dreaming. Then George Adony came in and woke me up before I was ready for daylight."

"He told me you had breakfast together and talked script. He and Jake West have gone."

We ordered lunch, and I warned Liz that it always looked better on paper than it ever turned out to be on the table. The other women kept peeping at her to see how she looked in the daytime. I could almost hear them telling their husbands that she looked a bit older now than they had expected.

"By the way," she said, and I caught the note of apology at once, "we aren't to be left alone. Somebody else is on the way. I had a wire. Leo Blatt."

"Leo Blatt!" I stared at her angrily, as if this were her doing. "We don't want him here. At least, I don't."

"He's coming here to see you as well as to see me," she said. "And after all he's my agent, Greg."

"Well, he isn't mine," I grumbled.

"He was once, wasn't he? I seem to remember he was. In fact, it was you who put me on to him originally. You said he was the best agent in Hollywood. And I still believe he is."

"I didn't even know he was over here," I said, still grumbling.

"He left the Coast just before I did. And then missed me in London of course. So he's coming here, just for tonight."

"Why couldn't he wait a couple of days and see you in London?" I demanded, quite unreasonably, because I knew very well that Blatt hadn't asked her first but had simply told her he was on his way. "I suppose, though, that he has to pretend somehow to earn all the money he makes out of people like you, Elizabeth, and that a dash from London to Cornwall for an hour or two's talk is about all he can offer us, here in England, as evidence of spectacular service. Back home he can probably put searchlight signals on top of Radio City or use the battle fleet."

Elizabeth wasn't amused. She gave me a frosty glance. "He's leaving England in a day or two, and there are several things we have to talk over. If you don't want to see him, you needn't. But he still happens to be my agent."

"All right, Liz, all right," I said irritably. "I won't say another word. You give him a hearty welcome and have a nice talk with him."

"Why are you being so stuffily British all of a sudden? What's poor Leo done?"

"Nothing," I replied gloomily. "It just happens that the thought of him bouncing and barking round here tonight gives me no pleasure. I suppose there's no real harm in Leo Blatt— except that he's almost insufferable. He's the type that makes Americans so unpopular on this side of the Atlantic. There they are—energetic and helpful, generous and rich—and hardly any of us poor half-starved Europeans can stand 'em. It's too bad."

"And I don't believe it," she said emphatically. Then she gave me a curious look. "You wouldn't have said that a few years ago. Coming back here has changed you. You're beginning to talk about America as the Isolationists there talk about Britain."

She was serious, and the least I could do was to reply to her seriously. I thought for a moment. "I'm sorry to hear that, Liz," I began slowly. "Perhaps I have been piling up some prejudice. But some of us here in the film business can't help feeling rather bitter. Just look at it a minute. Our people here were up to the neck in the war, and half the time they lived like rats in holes, with anything that would explode or burn raining down on 'em. And if they found their way through the black-out to spend a shilling or two at the pictures—what did they see, only too often? The Sunset Boulevard notion of the war. The American Way of Life. Yanks winning the Battle for Democracy. The March of Time. And occasional films about London Taking It, a London full of dukes and toothless costermongers, films produced or directed often by Englishmen who'd hared across the Atlantic in '39 and seemed to have forgotten what England was like."

"You know I was in two of those," she said. "And I know they did a lot of good over there."

"All right, but they didn't do any good over here—and that's the point I'm making. Why should our people have had all that cheap muck dumped on 'em? They didn't want it."

"Well, why did they go and see it then?" she demanded.

"Look, Liz," I cried rather impatiently, "you're working from dark to dark in an aircraft factory, in a canteen, on the railway, and you have a night off—or you're a Tommy or an airman who's got a bit of leave and want to take out your wife or your girl friend—well, you just go to the pictures, to the nearest cinema you can find, and think yourself lucky to get in—and you don't know that people six thousand miles away, who don't care a damn about you and have never given you a thought, are just dumping their stuff on you. And at the same time you may be crowding out reasonably honest war pictures, made on the spot here by people who know what it's like. And another thing, Liz." But I stopped.

"All right, Greg," she said, with a tiny smile, half friendly, half ironic. She hadn't seen me so heated for a long time. "I can take a bit more."

"We come into this," I told her. "I came back here to write some film scripts if they wanted me to—it's the only thing I can really do. Well, they did want me to, and I wrote and sometimes co-produced some films. They weren't masterpieces—we had all kinds of difficulties, with raids and black-out, shortage of staff and studio space—but they were honest-to-God jobs. And you kept writing, asking me what I was doing. I had to tell you, from time to time. Why? Because out there you never saw any of those pictures I helped to make."

"I saw one—the one about the factory," she said quietly. "Sam Gruman had it run through for me at the studio. I sat there and cried, Greg."

"They happened to have a copy and so they ran it through for you as a favour. And that's all you saw of everything I'd done in the last five years. In other words, our pictures weren't being shown over there, while our people here had to take anything they decided to send over, no matter how unsuitable it might be or how much of a downright insult it might be sometimes. Now do you see?"

"Yes," she said doubtfully. "But I've talked to exhibitors over there and they saw they must have box office names—and—"

"And they must have this—and that—and the other, I know," I said angrily. "I've heard it. Every picture we send has to pass a competitive examination with one free place out of a hundred entries. All right, then, if that's the way it has to be—we'll have a similar one on this side, and stop most of this muck coming in. And I admit that all this hasn't much to do with Leo Blatt."

"Except that now you've decided he's insufferable. And he isn't. He talks a lot and does bounce round, as you say, but he's really generous and kind, as well as being full of energy and very amusing—and he's helped all sorts of people who've needed it."

"I know, I know," I groaned, "and that's what makes it all so damned difficult. If he was an out-and-out stinker, it would be simple enough. But he isn't. He isn't even conceited in himself —rather humble in some ways. But he has that awful collective conceit which seems to me the curse of America now, that feeling of inevitable national superiority—Victorian England had it badly—which makes decent people seem brash and insensitive."

"At least they're alive," she said sharply, "and half the people in this hotel are dead."

I couldn't deny it. I had said as much myself. But I had to make some sort of reply. "These aren't the English people. You're like the kind of American who moves between the Ritz, Berkeley Square and Claridges, and then writes articles about democracy in Britain."

"Let's have some coffee." She got up, and I followed her into the large lounge. It was one of those cruelly bright, windy afternoons, occasionally lashed by rain, that come with spring in South-West England. What I saw of it through the big windows didn't tempt me to go out. So before Liz, who seemed restless, could suggest a walk, I announced that I was going to rest for an hour, after which I would work through until nearly dinnertime. "By that time I may be strong enough to face Leo Blatt."

"You know, Greg," she said softly, "we're not really arguing about Leo or Hollywood or America and Britain—not really. We're just fighting. And the fight's going on somewhere behind the argument."

"That's very clever of you, Liz," I told her, and meant it too. She never used to have this kind of insight into a situation, and had never seemed to me very intuitive.

"Well, it's not like us. Why are we doing it?"

I ought to have replied, "Because of what happened between us last night," but I didn't. This wasn't the time for such talk.

But I knew we were antagonists now; no longer friends in the old easy fashion, and yet not lovers: we were out in No Man's Land. And I knew this couldn't last long, and that soon either we'd be coming closer or retreating, probably to avoid each other afterwards; and that whatever happened now, the old relationship was gone for good. Then I thought how queer it was that after years and years in which nothing much had happened to me, I now found myself compelled every few hours to face changes and to make decisions that might be of the gravest consequence. And I almost guessed then that within a week or so my life would be quite different. But I couldn't tell her any of this.

"It's my fault, my dear Liz," I said. "I had a poorish night, and then I had to talk to George Adony at a time when I like to be alone, so I'm still peevish. I'll be better tonight. At least I'll try to be. And I'll be down about half-past seven. But keep Blatt away from me before then—I must work."

I did work too, for nearly five hours. Just before half-past seven, when I was ready to go downstairs, a call came through from Brent in London. "I've just been talking to George Adony," he said. "And he tells me that you've taken a new line in the hotel sequence."

"Difference of atmosphere," I told him, "rather than a new line. I never liked what we had in that sequence—it was always one of those little bridge jobs, thin stuff—and it needed something to give it colour and life. This may not work, but it's worth trying."

"All right, go ahead, Gregory, and get on as fast as you can. When do you think you'll be through?"

"Four days' hard work will see it through, Brent."

"Oh—that's fine," cried the little voice in the telephone.

"Yes, but I've been sticking at it all today and I must have some time off tomorrow—or I'll feel stale. In other words, I can't promise the four days' hard work in four days—or even in five. Yes, of course, I'll do my best. I don't want to be down here much longer. I want to do some eating and drinking where the producers eat and drink."

"You shall. How's Elizabeth?"

"We were rather quarrelsome at lunch—but she's all right."

"George warns me that she's in love with you—"

"Oh, he's taken that to London with him, has he?" I said with some irritation. "I thought I'd finished with that." And to give him something else to think about, I added: "Leo Blatt's come down here for the night."

It worked. "So that's it, is it? I heard he'd been asking where Elizabeth had got to—"

"Well, he's her agent, y'know, Brent. Used to be mine too."

"Now listen, Gregory, don't let that fellow—and Elizabeth —talk you into walking out on us—"

"Don't worry, he's not going to talk me into anything. I never felt less like being persuaded. But I ought to go down now and have a look at him. So long, Brent!"

They weren't in the bar, which was crowded with colourless types, but in a corner of the big lounge, where Blatt was telling a terrified little waitress how to make the kind of rum cocktail he wanted. He looked just the same as he had done when I had last seen him in Hollywood. He still wore a suit of that peculiar brown shade, a cream shirt and a brilliant orange tie. He still looked, as so many Hollywood and New York theatrical agents look, as if he had been sitting up with a telephone every night for the past month and hadn't seen daylight, was heading for a nervous breakdown, and yet still had enough vitality left to run a small power plant. He spoke, as he always had done, as if he had a cold in his head. And while talking at full speed, he was as busy as ever, making notes, ringing bells, passing drinks, offering cigarettes, flicking on his lighter, jumping up and sitting down, like a one-man circus. Many a studio executive, weary and worn out, must have accepted his terms just to get rid of him.

"Well, well, well—Gregory Dawson," he cried in his thick hoarse voice, which was always about to give out and yet never did. "After all these years, eh? Came back to see the old country through the war. Just walked out on us. And, say—Greg—I respected you for it—yes, I was with you solid all the way on that. Never had a chance to tell you till now, but I'm going to tell you, here and now—and I said the same thing when I was talking about you to Elizabeth, didn't I, Elizabeth?—I'm going to tell you, Greg, I'd have done the same thing in your place. Gone straight back to the home folks in their time of trouble. And how are they?" He gazed at me earnestly.

"I haven't got any," I said drily.

Elizabeth giggled.

"You've been giving her drink," I said to him. "She only giggles like that when she's in liquor."

"I had one little Martini," she said.

"Little's right," cried Blatt. "And were they terrible! I've told 'em to shake us some good rum cocktails. Well, well—it's been a long time. But you're looking fine, Greg. And Elizabeth says you're turning out a dandy screen play for her. So the old hand hasn't lost its cunning." He surveyed me with mock admiration. "The only writer who ever made old Sam Gruman pay him a royalty on the gross. That was for *The Lonely Huntress*," he explained to Elizabeth, "the one he wrote for you—and did we go to town with it, I'll say we did. You must have pulled down close on a hundred thousand dollars on that picture, and we still get nice little cheques from Sam's office. What did you do with it all—to say nothing of what you'd stacked up before?"

"Declared it to the Treasury here," I told him. "Then they gave me sterling for it."

"So the pile's here instead of over there. What you got—a row of shops and one o' these dairy farms?"

"All I've got are two suitcases and an old steamer trunk. And a lot of receipts from the Inland Revenue. We pay it all out in taxes here, Leo."

The cocktails arrived, about eight of them. Blatt tasted one solemnly before Elizabeth and I were allowed to touch ours. "Okay," he said to the little waitress, giving her a tip, "and tell the barman from me it's not a bad first try. Not enough ice, though. Where do they keep the ice here in England? In safe deposit boxes? Well, Elizabeth, there's two for you—go on, two of 'em wouldn't make a real cocktail—and three each for Gregory an' me. Send 'em down, friends."

After we had begun to send them down, I said to him: "Well, Leo, what's the news?"

"The big news is that I talked to Sam Gruman last night—he's in New York right now, and the line they gave us was swell—I could hear Sam's dentures clicking, you know how they do—and Sam said—"

"No, Leo," said Elizabeth, cutting in quickly, "save that. We'll be going in to dinner in a minute."

"You bet! It'll keep."

I knew then that not only had Sam Gruman told him to get hold of me but that this offer of Sam's, whatever it was, had already been discussed by Elizabeth and Blatt. And I didn't feel very pleased.

"There's plenty of news, Greg," Blatt went on. "Technicolour's on the up an' up. So's television. And don't laugh—because this time it's true—the stereoscopic motion picture will be with us soon. Yep, the Coast's humming with new ideas."

"You're going to need 'em, Leo," I told him. "You've been making us all yawn lately. Talkies now are about where silent pictures were just before Warners threw Al Jolson at us. Either you've got to give us some really exciting technical improvements or put some new ideas into the pictures themselves."

"I guess we'll do both," he said, with a vague optimism that left me unconvinced. He began to talk then about the moves and countermoves of the financial interests behind the producing organisations and the circuits, but after a few minutes I stopped him.

"Don't bother, Leo. It's wasted on us. Elizabeth doesn't understand, and I just don't care." I swallowed my remaining cocktail, and discovered then, to my surprise, that I was feeling the effect of these mixtures. "I've come to the conclusion that all these fellows you're talking about, the bosses of the industry, are just a bunch of giant parasites, sucking the life out of films, ruining the best medium for communal entertainment that's been invented during the last two thousand years. They decide what films shall be made, yet they can't write films, can't direct 'em, can't act in 'em, can't design or make a set, wouldn't know how to start cutting—"

"Now, wait a minute, Greg," he cried. "These big executives can hire plenty o' fellas to do all that. And they organise and finance production and then market the product."

"So what? I didn't say we don't need a few managers and cashiers and salesmen. But they shouldn't employ the creative people, the men and women who really make the films. They should be employed by them. You've got it all the wrong way round. And except in a few instances, which resulted in some famous pictures," I continued, "it's always been the wrong way round. I'm tired of seeing a wonderful medium, with which you could do almost anything, bitched up by money-lenders and salesmen and second-rate solicitors on the make."

"Elizabeth," and he turned to her with a grin, "all these Reds over here have been getting at him."

She stood up. "Let's go in and eat. We need more food and less drink."

Until nearly the end of dinner she kept Blatt talking about people we knew in Hollywood, and we laughed a lot. Then, when the atmosphere was right for it, she must have given him a sign to go ahead, for suddenly he looked solemn.

"Listen, Greg," he began. "I was talking to Sam last night. And he wants you back. He's got big plans—he's got Benny Kohn and Schwartz in with him now—and you can be part of 'em. You can co-produce as well as script. Naturally he's got some ideas of his own—he's bought three Broadway successes and a couple of Books-of-the-Month—but he'll listen to you too, if you're all steamed up about anything. A three-year contract, and the terms surprised even me, though I didn't tell him so. He told me—"

"No, Leo, don't bother. You give old Sam my love, and tell him I hope to see him some time. But I'm not going back," I heard myself say, "I'm never going back."

"Greg!" This was Elizabeth, who was staring at me in dismay. For some reason or other I felt sad as I met and challenged that look on her face.

"Now I know just how you feel, Greg," said Blatt, bringing up all his reserves. "And I guess I'd feel the same way. You come back here because of the war. You see it through—and Brent and the rest of the boys here are durned nice to you—and you've produced some swell little motion pictures under difficulties—too bad they didn't have better releases on our side, but you know how it is."

"Yes, I know how it is," I said grimly.

He looked at me, his face hardening, and there was now a dramatic change in him. "I don't expect some of these fellas in London to face the facts, because they don't know 'em. They haven't been around long enough yet. But you have. You ought to know that over on our side we aren't playing at being in the motion picture business. It's one of our big industries, with a mountain of good American dollars behind it. And if we have to get tough, we can be plenty tough—and you ought to know that by this time, Gregory."

"Don't let's argue about that, Leo," I said quietly. "It's beside the point anyhow."

"No, it isn't," he cried. "I'm warning you not to put yourself out where it might be freezin' cold soon."

"All right, I'll have to take that chance. In the meantime, thank Sam, but tell him I'm not coming back—I'm staying here."

"What to do, Greg?" Elizabeth asked. "Just to go on working with Brent?"

"I wouldn't count on that," said Blatt, grinning. "You know what most of these boys are. Brent's already had one or two offers to go back to the Coast, and though he's refused so far, he might accept next time."

"I'm not counting on anything or anybody," I told them both. "And I don't know what I'm going to do. I only know what I'm not going to do."

Elizabeth was about to say something then, but Blatt stopped her. "I've some poker chips up in my bag. Suppose we collect a few people—you two ought to know a few who are almost human—and play a little poker upstairs. Then we'll all feel better and if we want to talk business before we go to bed, there'll still be time."

I remembered then that Elizabeth had always had a weakness for poker, which I had enjoyed at one time, but that was ten years ago and now it bored me. She nodded brightly and then looked enquiringly at me.

I shook my head. "Not for me, thanks, Leo. I've been off

poker for years. Besides, I've some work I want to do. But some of those people you met last night, Liz—try them—"

"Leo's already met one or two of them," she said. "He can ask them as soon as we go into the lounge. Are you sure you won't play, Greg?"

When we sat outside, and Blatt went off to muster his poker party, Elizabeth and I looked to each other over the coffee-cups. Then she asked: "Did you mean what you said to Leo?"

"Yes, Liz, I did."

She frowned. "But you never told me you'd made up your mind not to go to Hollywood again."

"I couldn't tell you, because I hadn't made up my mind. It was when he put it to me tonight that I knew definitely I never wanted to go back and work there again. So I said so."

She looked at me in despair. "I don't understand you any more, Greg. Something's happened. Will you come out with me tomorrow—I've hired a car—and tell me?"

"I'll tell you all I can, Liz."

She nodded and smiled, pretending hard that everything was all right now. We were silent. But my friends in the trio were throbbing and pounding away, and I began to hum along with them. Elizabeth gave them a look.

"The little girl who plays the violin is rather a duck," she said. "I talked to her for a minute at tea-time. She keeps looking across at you as if she's trying to attract your attention."

"She is," I said. "They're playing this Schubert trio specially for my benefit and so they want to be noticed. They first played it for me—two or three days ago." Was it only two or three days ago? "This is a repeat performance."

We were silent again, on an island with the music flowing all round us.

"What are you thinking about?" she asked, finally.

I looked up and noticed that Leo Blatt had collected his poker party and was now about to tell us he was ready. So I stood up. "I was thinking about death," I said. "And it would be more decent if I went and did it somewhere else. Good night, Liz—and have a good gamble."

NINE

As I went up to my room, after leaving Elizabeth, I continued to think about death. As soon as I had told her and Blatt that I didn't want to play poker I had decided that I must get back to my room and finish remembering about the Alingtons. And then while Elizabeth and I were sitting in silence and the trio were playing the Schubert, and even while I was humming, my memory had flashed back to that June afternoon in 1914 at Pikeley Scar, and I could even see little Laura Blackshaw silently staring, and I went scrambling over the rocks again with Jock Barniston to where Eva Alington was lying. So death arrived, but not just her death. Soon I was thinking about the death of a time, of a little world, of some part of myself. Not for years had I really given a thought to that early summer of 1914, but now, just because I had insisted on recalling so much of what happened before, had tried almost to re-live those two years or so in Bruddersford, it was as if in some huge lumber-room at the back of my mind I had come upon a lanky wondering lad, who had turned a startled face that was my own, while all around him the doors of cupboards and ward-robes were creaking open and the lids of old trunks were being raised, and there were eyes in the shadows and half-remembered voices called distantly. This was how it appeared while I was still down there in the lounge, and Elizabeth was asking about the trio and I could see Blatt collecting his poker party. But when I had settled down in my room, just as I had done the previous night, Elizabeth and Blatt and the lounge dwindled to a mere lighted point in my consciousness, while what had been the lumber-room dissolved into the houses and offices, streets and fields of Bruddersford and the West Riding just before the First World War.

The night before, try as I would, there had been gaps in my remembering, and some of them strange gaps that ought not to have been there. It was the same now, except that I felt that nothing important had failed to return to memory, only the weeks connecting the main events, all the details of my ordinary day-to-day life, had gone.

I could remember, clearly enough, the day that Joe Ackworth left us. It was somewhere between Easter and Whitsuntide. For two months or so Nixey had been in the sample-room with us. This move, which Ackworth disliked intensely, had been made after Mr. Alington had come back from a visit to our head office in London, where he must have been told that Nixey could not be kept out of the sample-room if he wished to work there. I had expected some terrific rows between Nixey and Ackworth, but to my surprise there had hardly been an angry word spoken between them. Nixey of course knew how to keep his temper; it was Ackworth who surprised me. I suppose I ought to have realised that Ackworth, now rather grim and silent, had passed the point where he merely flared up and shouted.

On this particular morning he came in rather late. "We'd better get them samples o' cross-bred tops off to Gothenburg and Breslau. Come on, lad. Where are they?"

"I don't know," I said. "I've been looking for them."

"We put 'em out last night," he said, marching along the counter.

"I know, but they're not here."

"Where's Mr. Nixey? 'Appen he knows."

"He might," I said. "But I haven't seen him this morning. I've only been here about quarter of an hour myself. You remember —you told me to call at Haley's this morning?"

"That's right, lad, Ah did. Well, where's Nixey? An' what's a dam' sight more important—where's them samples? Nay, they must be abaht somewhere. Let's 'ave another look, Gregory lad."

We were still looking when Croxton came out of his office. There was the ghost of a triumphant grin lurking somewhere about that unpleasant face of his, perhaps twitching his long nose and moustache. He gave an important little genteel cough.

"Well?" said Ackworth, staring hard at him.

"Nixey called in this morning," Croxton began.

"'Ow d'you mean—*called in?*" demanded Ackworth, at once showing signs of temper.

"He was catching the ten-thirty to London," said Croxton smoothly, enjoying himself. "And he looked in to collect some samples to take with him."

"Hellfire!" Ackworth bellowed. "D'you mean to tell me that Nixey's gone off wi' them samples without askin' me or Mr. Alington? Who told 'im to go to London? An' who told 'im to take samples?"

Croxton gave a little shrug and then fingered his moustache. "Probably the London office asked him to go. After all, he repre- sents them here, doesn't he?"

"It's news to me," said Ackworth, quietly now but staring very hard at Croxton. "But 'appen it isn't to you. Ah fancy you an' 'im's been thick as thieves right from the start. Nah just come in a minute an' shut that door, Croxton, 'cos Ah've summat Ah want to say to you."

"I'm rather busy," Croxton began.

"Shut that bloody door," said Ackworth fiercely, and Croxton did shut it, but he stayed close to it, defensively.

"Ay, Ah've summat to say to you," Ackworth continued, quietly now. "You an' me's never got on, an' Ah dare say that's been as much my fault as yours. But you could 'ave stood by Mr. Alington an' me an' this end o' the firm, an' you 'aven't. You've been well in wi' Nixey right from the start—ay an' Ah'll bet you've told 'im plenty an' all. You're one o' these Clever Dicks that 'aven't any real gumption, that's what you are. An' when Nixey come 'ere, you thought: 'That's the chap for me —smart London chap—an' Ah'll get in with 'im.' Well, Nixey's sharp enough—an' 'appen he'll be so sharp you'll not be so long afore you're cuttin' your fingers on 'im. You ought to 'ave sense enough to know that a chap like Nixey's not 'ere to learn any bloody wool trade—chaps like 'im don't learn trades—it's a mug's game to 'em—an' it wouldn't surprise me if when Ah've gone—an' Mr. Alington finds 'imself pushed out—an' you an' Nixey an' one or two more start runnin' this business, an' 'appen there's a boom in the wool trade—then Ah say it wouldn't sur- prise me if you come in one mornin' an' find Nixey an' his uncle an' that lot 'ave gone an' sold this business, an' all you've got is a month's notice. An' when that 'appens, don't come to me lookin' for a job, 'cos Ah wouldn't give you thirty bob a week workin' the 'oist—"

"When I want a job with you, Ackworth," Croxton began, white with temper, and nose and moustache quivering away.

"That's all, Croxton," said Ackworth, dominating him. "Ah've no more to say to you, except—if it's any satisfaction to you—to say that Ah fancy you've been busy 'elpin' to muck up one o' the best little firms i' the Bruddersford trade. An' no bloody good'll come of it to you or anybody else. Nah get back to your office."

After Croxton had gone, Ackworth blew hard down his empty pipe, leaned against the counter, and looked gloomily thoughtful. "Mr. Alington's not in yet, is he, lad?" he asked finally. "Wasn't he callin' at Wabley Combin' Mills this morning?"

I replied that I thought he was. Then I risked a question. "Is that true—what you said to Croxton—about what Nixey might do?"

"Well, Gregory lad," he said, deliberately broad, "Ah wasn't talkin' to thee. Tha's not supposed to be in on all this kind o' talk. Tha's still just a lad abaht place, even if tha does write pieces for *Evening Express* an' fancy thyself. Eh?"

"Yes, I know, Mr. Ackworth," I said. "And I'm not trying to interfere. But after all, I work here too—and so naturally I want to know what might happen."

"Fair enough, lad, fair enough. An' Ah 'elped to get you the job, 'cos Ah knew your mother." He was silent for a moment or two. "Ah'll give you a bit of advice, Gregory. An' just mark my words. If summat's done that you think isn't right, then start fightin' it like bloody 'ell bang off. Don't give in, an' then let yourself be pushed an' pushed, else you might find it's too late to start fightin' back—an' one more push an' you're over the edge."

(Many a time afterwards, in the army, in journalism and in film studios, I remembered what old Joe Ackworth said, when I saw good but weak men allowing themselves to be pushed nearer and nearer the edge just because they hadn't started fighting back early enough. A lot of people had thought that I was too touchy and unnecessarily aggressive, and probably I was; but I was remembering this piece of good advice. Twenty years after Joe Ackworth had talked to me, the Nazis began offering the world the finest large-scale example of these tactics, and we found a name for the victim's bewildered retreat towards the edge and called it *Appeasement*.)

I knew that Ackworth was thinking about Mr. Alington, who should have had a show-down with our London people as soon as it was proposed to dump Nixey on us; but I thought it better not to say anything. We began setting out another range of samples to be sent to Gothenburg and Breslau, and as we worked Ackworth began talking again.

"Ah'll tell you summat else, lad. If a chap learns a trade, he won't do so much 'arm. What Ah don't like are these Clever Dicks that don't learn a trade but want to mak' money fast an' easy, an' there's too many of 'em now an' there'll be a lot more afore we've finished. That's new London style—you know nowt abaht wool—you care nowt abaht it—but you see a chance o' gettin' quick profits aht o' wool—an' that's good enough—so it's wool today—an' summat else tomorrow. This Nixey an' his uncle Buckner—Ah'll bet owt you like that afore they've finished they've gone from wool to liver-pills, an' liver-pills to cotton, an' cotton to motor-cars—an' they don't care what the 'ell it is so long as they can grab a lump o' brass an' then be off. You've 'eard me argue wi' Fred Knott abaht socialism, but when it comes to this lot, who do nowt for the money they get, then Ah'm wi' Fred every time. A chap who learns a trade, whether it's wool or cotton or steel or timber or owt you like, comes to 'ave a respect for the stuff he 'andles an' wants to do his best for his customers. But these smart chaps who know nowt but 'ow to make money fast, they 'ave no customers, they're 'ere today an' gone tomorrow, an' only thing they've a respect for is money. An' Ah tell you, lad, they're no good to themselves nor nobody else. Nah mark my words."

I did, and experience proved them to be true. During the thirty years or so that followed this talk I never met a man who had an expert knowledge of things or the making of things who hadn't a decent and honest core to his character; and I never met a man who thought first of money and profits and cared nothing about the things he dealt in who seemed to me a satisfactory human being. In my own trade of making motion pictures, which attracted the easy-money boys almost from the first, the difference between these two types was most marked; and all that was rotten in the industry came from those who went into it not because they were fascinated by film-making but because they were first attracted by the possibility of huge quick profits. Of course the film-makers liked making money too—most of us do when we live in a society in which money opens so many doors and windows—but it was the films themselves that had started them off and had kept them hard at work; and there is the vital difference.

Not long after Ackworth had concluded this speech of his, Mr. Alington arrived in the office and came straight into the sample-room.

"The Wabley Combers were a bit difficult this morning, Joe," he announced. "Hello, what's the matter?"

"John," said Ackworth, going over to him and speaking in a low serious tone, "you an' me's got to 'ave a talk. Ah've stuck this as long as Ah could, chiefly for your sake, but nah Ah've 'ad enough. Not only 'as Nixey gone to London, withaht tellin' anybody, but he's also gone an' taken a range o' samples with 'im."

"Good God!" cried Mr. Alington. "What does he think he's doing?"

"What Ah've allus thought he was doin'," said Ackworth drily.

"Joe, come into my room," said Mr. Alington hurriedly.

And of course I heard no more, though now and again, during the next half-hour, I could just hear sounds that suggested that Ackworth was roaring his head off in there. Later I had to go on to the Conditioning House, and during the afternoon I did not see Ackworth at all, and Mr. Alington came out and worked with me in the sample-room. He looked worried, and twice he was called into the office to take a call from London. But late on Friday afternoon, when Ackworth and I were making up a range of samples, and were by ourselves, I heard the news.

"Well, Gregory lad," said Ackworth, "this is last lot o' samples you an' me'll make up 'ere. Ah'm leavin' you, lad."

I stared at him in dismay. "Do you mean—going for good, Mr. Ackworth?"

"Ay, for good. Sam Haley's been tellin' me for years he'd a nice job whenever Ah fancied it, so nah Ah'm off to work for Sam, who's an old friend o' mine an' doesn't 'ave no fancy chaps from London interferin' wi' his business. But Ah'm sorry to leave you, lad. You an' me's got on all right. At least Ah 'ope so, 'cos Ah knaw Ah've given you rough edge o' my tongue at times—but Ah didn't mean owt, Gregory lad."

"I know you didn't," I said, still staring at him. I couldn't imagine the sample-room without him. It would be a different place, smaller, colder, duller. "I wish you weren't going, Mr. Ackworth."

"So Ah do myself—in many ways," he muttered, glancing round. "Ah've been i' this little 'ole a good time—an' Ah'm goin' to miss it." Then he came closer and looked hard at me. He had shrewd and rather bloodshot little eyes, and whenever I think of him I see those eyes as I saw them at that moment. "Look, lad, what are you goin' to do wi' yourself? 'Ave you made up your mind, 'cos it's time you did—eh?"

I had made up my mind. "I don't want to stay in this business," I told him. "I want to write, Mr. Ackworth."

"Ay, Ah thought as much. It's chancy, lad, very chancy, though Ah don't say you've no talent for it. 'Appen you'll do well once you get really started."

"Well, I've thought a lot about it," I said, with the unfathomable gravity of youth. "I really have, Mr. Ackworth. And I've talked to one or two friends of mine. And as soon as I see a real chance of earning a living by writing, I shall take it. You know, I've had an article accepted by a London paper."

"Good lad! Well, if that's the idea, Ah've nowt to say. You're just markin' time like 'ere. If you 'adn't been," he went on, dropping his voice, "Ah'd 'ave told you to do what Ah'm doin' an' get out of 'ere. John Alington's as fine a chap in some ways as there is i' this business, but—but—well, there's summat up with 'im somewhere—he's just sort o' driftin' these days—as if he can't make up his mind—'appen he's not so well or summat—"

"I don't think he is," I said. "He doesn't look very well, does he? Quite different from what he did when I first came here. What's wrong, do you know?"

"Ah don't, lad. Ah wish Ah did. But Ah knaw this—that he's let that bloody little Nixey do it on 'im right an' left—and there'll be a lot o' trouble 'ere soon. But if you're not stayin' i' the wool trade, then it doesn't matter. In fact, you'd better stay 'ere, 'cos you might do John Alington a bit o' good. Well, Gregory lad, Ah expect Ah'll be seein' you, though not so often 'cos Ah'll be moving abaht country soon, goin' to the wool sales for Sam Haley."

So we said good-bye. I met him once again—it was at Eva Alington's funeral—and then the war came and I left Bruddersford. (I never went back there on leave because early in the war my uncle and aunt, who inherited a few thousands more, removed to Southport, and the few leaves I had were spent there.) But sometime in 1918 I sat up one night, at the officers' club in Boulogne, drinking those little bottles of Export Guinness with a Bruddersford fellow, and he told me that Sam Haley and Ackworth had made a lot of money and that early in '17 Joe Ackworth had had a stroke and six months later had died.

Nixey returned from London on the Monday following the Friday that Joe Ackworth left us, and he and Mr. Alington had a long talk in Mr. Alington's room, but I never knew what they said to each other. Nobody came to take Ackworth's place. Mr. Alington had to spend far more of his time with Nixey and me in the sample-room. I felt that he was now trying to make a great effort to pretend that everything was all right, and obviously it wasn't. Croxton came out now to give us a hand at times, and he and I had a few rows. Nixey was cool and quiet, and made himself as useful as possible. I couldn't remember very much about that time, except that I felt that somewhere behind the screen of routine and kept-up appearances everything was quietly going to pieces. And excited by one or two little successes, I was writing hard and not seeing many people.

Then came that Sunday, in June and not long after Whitsuntide. The invitation to spend the day with them came from Mr. Alington himself, who mentioned the expedition on Saturday morning. The family, with one or two friends like Jock Barniston, were going up the Dales as far as Pikeley Scar, which is a famous limestone cliff, not quite as wild and romantic as so many artists have pretended it is in their landscapes but a good place for a day's outing. Two kinds of country meet there, for you come down to the cliff edge on bare green slopes from the fell top, and feel you are among mountains, but the Scar marks the end of this country, and at its base are thick woods, pools and rocks and little cascades, and the river goes flashing among the leaves for miles. Above or below, Pikeley Scar is a good place for a picnic and for messing about throughout a long warm afternoon. I had been there two or three times, but never with the Alingtons.

Jock Barniston and I always felt that the Alingtons didn't want us with them all the time, so he and I arranged, as we had done before on these occasions, to meet fairly early on Sunday morning, take some food with us, and join the Alingtons not far from Pikeley Scar for a rather late picnic lunch. Then we would spend the rest of the day with them. But when I went home on Saturday afternoon and announced this programme, I found to my disgust that I was to be saddled with the little Blackshaw girl, Laura, the one who had followed me around, the previous summer, at Silverdale. My aunt was looking after this child for the week-end, the Blackshaw parents and the brother being away; and no sooner did I mention Sunday's picnic than this shameless ten-year-old, who was as solemnly obstinate as her father and as fierce as her little red-haired mother, instantly demanded to go with me, swearing that I had promised her some tremendous treat of this sort. I must have looked glum at the idea of taking her with me, because shortly afterwards my aunt took me on one side and said that it would be a great convenience to them if I took her, and that little Laura would enjoy it so much and would be no trouble to me. So I agreed to take her.

When I met Jock next morning at Wabley station, he was astonished to find me there with a freckled little girl with two stubby ginger plaits and a mysterious miniature haversack of her own. But Jock was fond of children and very good with them, and he told the round-eyed Laura that she was an excellent idea and would nicely complete the party. So off we went, in an almost empty little train, chuff-chuffing towards the Dales through the vacant and golden Sunday morning. (There don't seem to be any trains like that any more, empty and leisurely and chummy. All transport now seems to be fuss, crowds, rain and anger.) It was a dazzling June day, and the fields were thick with daisies and blazing with buttercups and dandelions. Determined to miss nothing, young Laura stared fiercely out of one window and then rushed across to the opposite window, telling us about everything she saw. Jock and I smoked and chatted. But he didn't seem as cheerful as usual. There was something worrying him, and finally, after I had challenged him, he admitted that he was feeling rather anxious about Eva Alington.

"Why do cows stare so much?" asked Laura, still glued to the window.

"They're not really staring," Jock told her. "They're just thinking things over quietly while they're chewing their dinners."

"What are they thinking about?"

"Nobody really knows," said Jock. "You watch 'em, Laura, and try to find out."

"What about Eva?" I asked him.

"I've got a letter for her that Ben asked me to give her," Jock replied quietly. "I don't know what's in it, but he isn't coming today—and she's expecting him—and I think this letter he's written does a bit more than explain why he isn't coming. I'm afraid poor Eva's going to have a bad day."

"Ben's got himself tangled up with Nixey's wife," I said. "I don't suppose he'll admit it, but that's the truth. And the sooner Eva realises it the better. She ought to forget about him. He's not worth bothering about."

"Yes, he is, even if you don't like him. There's no real harm in Ben. He's a fool at times, like the rest of us. But he's just right for Eva—and she knows it—and, well, I've got an idea we'd better do all we can for her today. I'm not feeling happy about it, Greg." And he regarded me sombrely, like some noble melancholy Red Indian chief.

We said no more. We sat in silence for several minutes. I doubt if I was really worried about Eva Alington or anybody else; yet there came to me then a curious feeling of helplessness and remote panic. I didn't know that anything would go badly wrong; yet I felt I had no control over events, which had their own pattern and colour, quite outside this green-and-gold day through which we were travelling, as if there was some other landscape, some country of the suffering heart and bewildered mind, behind these bright fields, these heights of bracken and ling.

Then we found that Laura had left the window, to stare at us accusingly. We weren't behaving properly. Here was the gold morning, the buttercups and cows, the picnic just round the corner, and there were Jock and I, silent, withdrawn, gloomy. "What's the matter?" she demanded. "Why are you two so miserable?"

Jock laughed and said: "I don't know, Laura. Something must have gone wrong with us."

"P'rhaps you're hungry," she said hopefully.

"Well, no," said Jock very slowly, "we're not hungry. But we think you are—a bit. We think you'd just like *something*."

Laura nodded. "You're very clever, Mr. Jock. I would like *something*. Shall I look in my haversack?"

So Laura started tucking in, and Jock and I felt better—at least I know that I did—and began talking again. The train went creeping up the dale, now a green trough between limestone ridges. It was after twelve when we arrived at the tiny Pikeley station. As soon as the train went on, the weighty silence of a hot Sunday noon descended upon us. Jock led the way across the fields to the place where we were to meet the Alingtons. Laura capered around us in ecstasy, like a puppy with dancing eyes. (I noticed then, for the first time, that she had very pretty eyes, a warm and glinting amber.) Jock and I trudged on, saying very little. We were climbing now, and although the limestone rocks still seemed to quiver in the hot sunlight, there was a coolish breeze.

Then we saw a couple of people whose backs seemed familiar. They were carrying a lot of gear and were moving slowly, and we soon overtook them. It was Stanley Mervin, the painter, and his wife. His face beneath its mop of white hair was brick-red and shining with sweat, and his plump little wife looked no cooler.

"Well, lads," cried Mervin. "We've been at it since six this morning on this caper, an' if Ah'd known how long it takes to get from Bulsden to Pikeley of a Sunday, John Alington could ha' whistled for all he'd ha' seen o' me. Look at missis—like a boiled puddin'. An' how are you, love?" he said solemnly to Laura, shaking her hand.

Realising at once that here was a nice funny man, Laura replied, with a broad grin, that she was very well.

"An' you look it," said Mervin, winking at her. "But as for me. Ah'm about dished."

"You shouldn't have brought so much stuff," said his wife. "You'll do no painting today, lad, yet you bring everything. Here, I'm sitting down." And down she went, with Laura by her side, among the daisies.

They had brought a substantial contribution to the picnic as well as Mervin's painting gear, and Jock and I took a look at their load and then began dividing it between us.

"Nay, lads, Ah'm no old man," Mervin protested.

"No, an' you're not a young one neither," said his wife, who was now helping Laura to make a daisy chain. "Eh, it's a grand day, though. Now, don't start smoking, Stanley, when you're so puffed."

"They've allus got a reason," said Mervin, regarding his wife quite amiably, "why you shouldn't do what you want to do. They must work it out in their spare time, an' mak' lists—you can't smoke 'cos you're puffed; you can't drink 'cos you're too 'ot; you mustn't work 'cos you're tired; you mustn't 'ave a nap 'cos you ought to be workin'. An' so forth, an' so forth."

"Nobody's listening to you," said his wife.

"I am," said Laura. "I think he's a funny man."

"That's right, love," said Mrs. Mervin. "He *is* a funny man."

"We ought to be moving on." And Jock began loading himself up, and I followed his example.

Mervin and I walked on together, a few yards behind the others. "The missis is quite right," he told me. "Ah've brought all this damn' stuff, but Ah'll do nowt today. Ah've 'ad a go at this country once or twice afore, but Ah can't mak' owt decent out of it. An' neither can them Academy chaps 'at comes up 'ere, with a cartload o' canvas an' paint, to do Pikeley Scar in a big way. Ah wouldn't give you a couple o' bob for the bloody lot." He squinted knowingly at the landscape. "You can tackle this limestone country best wi' a bit o' pencil an' nowt else. Greys an' greens—an' then when the sun's bang on it—pinks that nobody believes in an' you can't believe in yourself. You can't get tone right. An' no tone, no picture. Ah know," he continued, addressing the landscape itself now, "you're tryin' to get me to 'ave another do at you, but Ah'll be damned if Ah will." Then he hesitated. "Well, 'appen Ah might mak' a sketch or two."

I laughed. "I always remember you saying to me, the first time we met, that after you walked out of the wool trade and painted all the time, you'd been just about the happiest man in Yorkshire."

"That's right, lad. Only thing Ah regret is that Ah didn't do what I wanted to do sooner, instead o' wasting so much good time. Ah'm older than Ah look, and doctor says Ah've got to be careful 'cos my blood pressure's a lot too 'igh, so 'appen Ah'll not 'ave so much longer. An' Ah'll give you a bit of advice, Gregory, 'cos you're a clever lad wi' summat in you." But there he stopped.

"Go on," I said.

"If you've got summat in you that wants to be let out an' goes on natterin' at you day an' night, then you let go of everything else an' get it out. For that's your life, lad, an' don't let anybody tell you it isn't. An' if you don't get it out, it'll go bad in you. But if you do, even if you 'ave nowt for dinner but tea an' bread an' drippin', you're *alive*. An' that's a damn' sight more than 'alf these chaps stinkin' wi' brass can say. They 'ave to keep on makin' more an' spendin' more, buyin' this an' ownin' that, just to 'elp to mak' themselves believe they're alive. But they don't see owt, 'ear owt, feel owt. They've put themselves in jail, an' given themselves solitary confinement."

"You wouldn't say that about Mr. Alington," I said. I knew very well he wouldn't, but I was curious to know what he thought about Mr. Alington.

"No, of course not. Ah'm talkin' about some o' these big men i' the business, like my owd boss—now Sir Joseph Rabison,

Bart. Ah ran into 'im in Leeds, two or three year after Ah'd left 'im, an' he says: 'Ah, Mervin, what are you doing now?' An' Ah says: 'Ah'm paintin' an' livin' in a cottage on Broadstone Moor on about thirty bob a week.' An' he gives me a look an' says: 'You were doing a lot better than that with us.' Ah says: 'No, Ah wasn't, an' if you sold the whole business you couldn't buy what Ah'm 'aving.' That surprised 'im. But John Alington—well, he's different. Trouble about John is—he's one of our sort who's never gone an' done what he wanted to do, 'appen 'cos he didn't want hard enough. He's one o' them—an' Ah've known one or two more—who's doin' a kind o' tight-rope walkin', wi' business balancin' one side an' all the things he likes on the other—which is all right if you can keep goin' an' don't suddenly tumble off. But it's a strain. You 'aven't got your feet on the ground. An' if summat 'appens to give you a knock, then over you go. John's all right—Ah like John, an' all the family—but he's not chap he was when Ah first knew 'im—an' if business got 'arder, as it easily might, then Ah don't know 'ow long he'd last. Ah wouldn't aim at bein' a John Alington if Ah were you, lad."

We were now crossing a farm-yard—it was the last farm for several miles—and I knew that on the other side was the path that divided into two about a quarter of a mile farther on, the left-hand track then climbing to the top of the Scar and the right-hand one rapidly descending to the woods and the stream at the foot of the great cliff.

"An' Ah think Ah've told you this afore, Gregory lad," Mervin continued, as we left the farm-yard, "but Ah'll say it again. If you fancy them Alington girls—an' Ah don't blame you 'cos they're a bonny lot—then go for young Bridget. That's the one that's got the right stuff in 'er. Ah dare say she'd turn on you at times like a bloody little tiger, but some chap—an' ten to one it'll be some daft numbskull who doesn't deserve it—will get a wife in ten thousand there, who'll go with 'im to hell an' back. An' the missis says the same thing—an' she knows—one o' the same sort 'erself. Ah think that's them, isn't it?"

They were sitting in the shade of two stunted trees, a little to the right of where the path divided: Mr. and Mrs. Alington and Joan, Eva and Bridget. (Fortunately for him, as it turned out,

David, who suffered from hay-fever, had been kept at home.) The little scene, at which we seemed to stare between trembling gold bars of sunlight, looked charming; the girls wore wide summer dresses in pastel shades, Joan in blue, Eva in pink, Bridget in yellow; there were picnic things on the grass: it had the smiling domesticity, the lost leisure and ease, one felt, of the 60's, and one of the girls ought to have been reading from a new volume of Tennyson.

"Just try an' paint that, lad," I heard Mervin muttering. "It's all right doin' a bridge an' a beck an' a bit o' moor, but 'ave a go at that an' it'ud just break your bloody 'eart." Then he bellowed: "Well, 'ere we are. Got owt to sup, John?"

Eva and Bridget and Mr. Alington jumped up and came forward to meet us. Young Laura, suddenly shy again, dropped back to keep close to me, like a puppy uncertain of its reception. Then I saw Eva stop and turn away, bitterly disappointed because one of us wasn't Ben. After a moment or two, while the rest of us were chattering away, Jock went across to Eva and edged her farther away from us, presumably before giving her the letter. And I noticed that Joan, though now busy with the picnic things, glanced frequently in their direction. Bridget took charge of Laura, and the pair of them disappeared for several minutes. Then lunch was ready, and there was much shouting for everybody. But we had to wait a little time before Jock returned with Eva, who had obviously been crying.

Some things, like the sight of the Alington family waiting for us in the shade, stay in the memory, complete almost to the last detail; but other things, of equal if not greater importance, simply can't be recaptured. Try as I might, I couldn't remember anything that happened during our picnic lunch, not a word, not a look. It must have straggled on for rather a long time, for when we came to break up afterwards it was mid-afternoon, huge, somnolent, heavy with sunlight. Mr. and Mrs. Alington and the Mervins, who were tired, decided to stay for a while in the shade and told the rest of us to go where we pleased. Bridget offered Laura the delight of paddling in the stream below, and at Laura's request I went with them. As we rose to go I heard Eva asking Jock to accompany her to the top of the Scar; and when he agreed, and they got up to move off, I heard Joan sharply demanding to go with them. So those three took the left-hand track, to the top of the cliff, while Bridget and Laura and I went down the fairly steep path to the right, twisting among rocks, down to the woods and the glitter of water.

We paddled for half an hour or so, and then Bridget and I tired of it, and sat on a mossy rock and talked, while Laura wandered up the stream, nearer the foot of the cliff, and was soon out of sight. There was a sleepy enchantment about the place where Bridget and I lingered, with the stream gurgling and flashing at our feet, the green-and-gold pattern of leaves and sunlight above us, and the birds calling and twittering somewhere behind us. Bridget, who was often at her worst with me, mocking and arrogant, was now in one of her best moods, simple and sincere and wonderfully quick to understand. She talked about her music, I about my writing; and each of us seemed to know in a flash all that the other meant, magically bridging the gaps in our eager but stumbling young talk. There wasn't a word of sentiment but I felt that I loved her, as I would never love anybody else, and that soon she might easily love me too. But we weren't gay and excited, as youngsters falling in love so often are. And we didn't talk about ourselves in relation to each other, only about what we wanted to do and the kind of people we thought we were, as if looking at and examining life together. This may be an illusion, but I feel that behind the golden afternoon and the quick eager talk and the innumerable meetings of eyes, there was a shadow of sadness, as if we recognised remotely that we were really saying good-bye.

It was Jock who interrupted us. "I left Eva and Joan sitting on that little ledge just below the top of the Scar—you know the place? Warm up there. I thought I'd like to cool off."

Bridget looked at him. "What's the matter, Jock? Is it Eva?"

He nodded. "I brought her a letter from Ben, telling her he's in love with somebody else—"

"We know who that is," said Bridget scornfully. "And how could he? Think of Eva—and that silly scratchy woman—ugh!"

"She's taken a nasty knock," he continued, in a voice full of trouble, "and she hasn't taken it too well. And Joan's in a bad mood—"

"She's jealous because you were paying attention to Eva," cried Bridget, jumping up. "Joan can be beastly sometimes— really queer and horrible. You want me to go up there, don't you?"

She scrambled down from the rock, but then turned and looked at me. And she never looked at me like that again. "Thank you for our talk, Gregory. I liked it very much." And off she went—really, for ever.

Jock mopped his face, and then slowly filled his pipe. "Well, I didn't like it up there, and couldn't do anything. Probably made it worse. They need Bridget—or at least, Eva does. That's why I came down. Where's that child—Laura?"

"Farther up the stream, still paddling. She's all right, but I'll give her a shout to make sure." And after we heard her shout back, from somewhere just out of sight, we stayed where we were, smoking sleepily.

And then the day shivered and cracked. The scream we heard came from the direction of the Scar, a long sharp scream slicing through the whole afternoon and across half a dozen lives.

Jock and I exchanged a glance and then hurried along the bank, jumping from rocks and crashing through ferns. Round the corner, where the Scar towered two hundred feet and more, we passed little Laura, and I had just time to notice, as we cried to her to stay where she was, that her face seemed fixed in a blank stare, all eyes in a white mask. Here, where the trees ended and there was a great jumble of rocks at the base of the cliff, the afternoon seemed to glare down relentlessly. Everything was suddenly different, and hellish.

"My God!—look," Jock panted. "Over there—look."

The crumpled pink among those rocks looked as if strange flowers were growing there. I thought I saw a movement, but Eva was dead when we reached her. At first it was still Eva I saw, looking very young and frozen in rather foolish surprise. But after Jock and I had lifted the body on to a flat rock, it wasn't Eva but just a body. The golden smiling girl had gone. And now, as we stood looking down on what was left, it was too quiet there, and very warm and airless, and I felt as if I might soon be sick. Then we heard cries from the top of the Scar, and everything wakened up, and the next hour was screaming chaos.

It was little Laura who got me out of it. The child had had a nasty shock—she didn't cry but stayed quiet, white-faced and staring—and Mrs. Mervin told me I ought to take her home. So while it was all still a huddle of misery, with Mrs. Alington and Joan prostrate, and Bridget and her father looking drawn and tight-lipped and near the edge of a breakdown, Laura and I left them to trudge in silence across the fields to the station. We had some time to wait there, forlorn midgets in the vast rosy late afternoon, and suddenly the child burst into tearless sobs and clutched at me, and I held her tight. Then the little train arrived, and Laura and I sat close in a corner and I made her talk to me about what she did at school and at home. Once or twice, after gulping and hesitating, she gave me the impression of wanting to say something about what had happened that afternoon, but —wisely, as I thought then; unwisely, as I know now—I cut in and turned her attention to something else. The fields were as bright, the hawthorn as rich, as when we went chuff-chuffing up the dale that morning; and the grey limestone ridges were turning rosy in the late sunlight; but now Laura and I were glassed in by terror and grief. It seemed a long way back to Wabley Station. And then as we were drearily walking up to Brigg Terrace, poor Laura stopped, clutched at my arm, and turned up a face down which the tears were rolling at last. She had forgotten to bring back her little haversack.

I found myself refusing to recall in detail the inquest, at which, after much confused evidence, it was determined that Eva Alington met her death by accident, having fallen from the ledge near the top of Pikeley Scar; or the slow black horror of the funeral, which seemed to have nothing to do with the smiling golden Eva I remembered, for ever in her sunny sleepy afternoon. The day after the funeral we had a message at the office to say that Mr. Alington had collapsed. This left Nixey and Croxton in charge of the firm, and pleased with themselves if not openly triumphant. I thought of walking out on them—and discussed it with my Uncle Miles—and it was not because they

were both very amiable towards me, even giving me a rise of
ten shillings a week, that I stayed on, but chiefly because I felt
already that it wasn't worth making a move, that all things were
coming to an end. (An Austrian Archduke was assassinated at
Sarajevo, but I didn't know then that this remote event made the
great change a dead certainty.) So I lingered on, and fortunately
I hadn't too much to do, for business was quiet just then, and
there was indeed a curious emptiness about those bright days in
late June and early July.

I didn't call at the Alingtons', for I knew that Mrs. Alington
was busy nursing her husband and that Bridget, Joan and David,
together with Oliver, who had returned from Cambridge the
day after Eva was killed, had gone away. I saw Jock several times,
and exchanged news with him. I read a good deal, tried to write,
mouched about. Then I heard from Jock that Bridget and Oliver
had returned; and on a Sunday evening, when Mr. Alington had
been ill nearly a fortnight, I plucked up courage to go down to
the Alingtons'. Oliver let me in, told me his father wasn't much
better, and took me into the long room, where we talked in a
rather half-hearted fashion. After about ten minutes there was
a ring at the front door, and he came back with Eleanor and
Malcolm Nixey, who were telling him that they didn't mean
to stay but had merely called to enquire about his father. As if
fresh visitors should have fresh tidings—though I doubt if he
knew exactly what he was doing—Oliver told them he would
go upstairs and ask his mother. And he left the Nixeys, smart
and spruce and smiling, sitting on the couch opposite me, and
talking lightly about the weather and the news.

But it was Bridget, not Oliver, who entered a few minutes
later; Bridget with a face like paper and her green eyes blazing.
She acknowledged my presence there with a quick nod, and
then, not sitting down, turned on the Nixeys.

"You want to know how my father is," she began, looking
at them with loathing and speaking with the utmost bitterness.
"He's very ill. And that's because my sister died, and because,
before that, he'd been worried for some time. And you two have
done it, between you. Yes, you two, who came here and spoilt
everything—"

"Now, look here," said Nixey, making a slight move. "You don't know what you're saying—"

"I do," she told him, and then stood with her back to the door. "And you're not going until I've told you what I think about you. Grabbers—greedy selfish wicked grabbers—that's what you are, both of you." And now she blazed at Nixey. "You came here to sneak in and take my father's business away from him. He was happy there before you came—then you spoilt everything. And you probably don't even want it now you've got it. When he was very ill—and delirious—my father went on talking about it for hours and hours—my mother told me. All about you taking more and more—"

"This girl's hysterical," cried Eleanor Nixey, getting up. "We'd better go, Malcolm."

Bridget now turned on her. "In a minute you can go and never, never come back. But before you do, you're going to listen to what I have to say. You're another grabber. You took Ben Kerry away from Eva, just for a little amusement. And now Eva's dead—I don't think she wanted to live. You helped to kill her. Now get out, both of you, and don't ever come near us again."

She flung the door wide open for them, watched them go in silence, and not until we heard the front door close behind them did she make a move at all. But then she came forward and burst into tears. "I had to tell them," she sobbed. "I had to. Oh, I hate them, I hate them."

I took her in my arms, to comfort her, and told her that everything she said had been true. She leaned against me for a few moments, still shaken with sobs, while I muttered awkward little endearments. Then, almost angrily, she pulled herself away.

"No, no, that's all stupid," she cried, looking defiantly at me. "And I'm going away again. Good-bye."

And I remembered, as if it had happened only the day before, how she left me there gaping. I couldn't understand her change of mood. I wondered at the strange "Good-bye" she flung at me as she went. But her instinct to say it had been right. She went away, somewhere to the sea where her mother and father joined

her a few days afterwards, and before she returned to Bruddersford the war had arrived and I had disappeared into the army.
I wrote once, at some length, but receiving no reply I didn't
write again. I ran into all kinds of people I didn't particularly
want to meet, but I didn't see Bridget Alington again. And that,
I reflected dismally as I climbed into bed, was the end—apart
from the miserable little epilogue with Joan in '19; and I didn't
propose to recall *that* now—the very end of my Bruddersford
history, such as it was. And I was still puzzled as to what it was,
and what it might have done to me, and so found it difficult to
settle down and go to sleep.

TEN

Next morning as I was having breakfast downstairs, to my surprise—for I had clean forgotten that he was in the hotel—Leo Blatt came and sat at my table.

"You ought to come back to the Coast just to see what real coffee's like, Greg," he told me.

"We drink what we can, eat what we can, and try to forget about it, Leo," I said. "We're poor people just now. We threw all we'd got into the kitty. How was the poker game?"

"Peanuts. All I got was about twenty-five dollars an' a headache. I'm taking the train back this morning." He looked at me expectantly. I said nothing. "Look, Greg, I don't feel we got down to anything last night. What am I to tell Sam?"

"Give him my kindest regards, thank him for the offer, and say I can't accept it."

"Now listen, Greg, you don't want to worry about the tax end of it. We can fix it so that you can come out with some real dough—"

"It isn't that, Leo."

"Well, what is it, then? Sam's right on top now—and—"

"I'm sure he is," I said. "But I just don't want to go back, that's the point."

He regarded me earnestly. "Look, Greg, I don't want to knock your end of the industry here. You're making some nice pictures. But in Hollywood, however you play it, they're two or three jumps ahead of your boys, and it's going to stay that way. Don't count on anything here—"

"Leo, I'm not. You don't understand." I stopped, to wonder how much I could tell him.

"Okay, Greg. Go ahead and make me understand. Hell—I'm not just trying to sell you Sam's offer—I get all the business I want, you know that, Greg. You and I—we've been around together, haven't we? We're pals. Well, what's on your mind?"

"I don't exactly know, Leo. If I did, I'd tell you. But there comes a time when a man wants a change. I've come to that time. If I thought I could do anything but write film scripts, I think I would go and do it. I feel bored and dissatisfied. Going back to Hollywood wouldn't give me this change I want. It would be plunging deeper into the kind of work I'm tired of. Don't ask me what I want to do, because I don't know. All I know for certain is what I don't want to do. And if you offered me all M.G.M. on a plate, I wouldn't want it, just because I'd be going in the wrong direction. You've come at a bad time, Leo."

He nodded. "Believe it or not, Greg, but if you'd some glasses of orange-juice and some big steaks under your belt, you wouldn't be talking like this. You think it's something mental," he continued, with a profound air that didn't suit him, "but it isn't. It's physical—yes, sir—physical. Vitamin deficiency, that's what it is."

"It might be," I told him. "But that would be only part of the story."

"Elizabeth is disappointed," he said. "She was hoping you'd go back. You know that, don't you, Greg?"

"I believe she is, and I'm sorry." I stood up. "I'll be talking to her later today, but I must go and do an hour or two's work first. I'm down here working against time—you know how it is, Leo?"

"Sure. I ought to, after twenty years in the business. Any chance of you being back in London soon?"

"Depends when I finish this job, Leo."

"Then we can't make a date. But just remember, Greg, you've only to send me the good word and I'll fix you up on the Coast, even if Sam's offer doesn't stay open."

We made quite a little scene out of our good-bye, not only because Leo, with his sentimental streak, liked it that way, but also because I on my side suddenly felt—though I didn't say so—that I might never see him again, and I remembered that after all we'd had some good times together. It was, in a way, like saying good-bye to America itself.

I worked for an hour or so, and then had a message to say that Elizabeth was waiting below for me. I found her outside, talking to the driver of one of those colossal old Minervas that I hadn't seen for years. It looked as big as a landing-craft, and about half a ton heavier.

"He says there's a nice little place he knows, about thirty miles down the coast, where we can lunch," she explained, beaming at us both. Elizabeth adored an expedition of this sort, and always took the most optimistic view of its prospects. "Isn't it a lovely day, darling?"

It wasn't, for although the sun was out temporarily, there were obvious signs of rain blowing up from the West. But I hadn't the heart to tell her so, and neither had the driver, whose glance told me he knew even better than I did that rain was on its way. Who were we to tell the radiant lady that the sun now gilding her would shortly vanish?

"Fine!" I cried, with a look that included all the arrangements. We climbed into the interior of the old monster, where we found what was practically a sitting-room, complete with bunches of primroses and violets in metal vases, which Elizabeth eyed with delighted appreciation. "No fireplace or bookshelves," I said, "but otherwise a nice apartment."

"I've told him to drive slowly," said Elizabeth, as we lumbered off.

"He'll have to if he wants to guide this battleship down these Cornish lanes." The driver, who seemed remote now and was cut off from us by unusually thick glass partitions, would certainly not overhear our conversation. "But you couldn't have found a better car for a talking party, Liz."

"That's just what I thought. Perfect. By the way, I saw Leo Blatt for a minute before he went off this morning, and he told me you'd had some talk with him at breakfast. He says it's vitamins."

I grunted. "I heard him on the subject. Glasses of orange-juice and big steaks would make a man of me again."

"I know it sounds silly," she said earnestly, "but there might be something in it. He told me that one of the producers here told him that the men in the studio were much slower than they used to be, and that it was because they were under-fed."

"That's true. But it doesn't apply in the same way to a sedentary middle-aged writer who can afford to dine in good restaurants and supplement his rations. Forget about it, Liz. I told Leo why I didn't want to go back to Hollywood."

"Yes, he told me what you'd said—about feeling stale and wanting a change. I think you've been brooding too much down here. But you're going to explain about that, aren't you?"

"I'll do my best." I waited a little while before continuing. We were now rolling along a deep lane that was like a green tunnel, and we sat there in a kind of jungle gloom. It cut us off from the world and made us feel snug and intimate.

"But all I've been doing," I went on, "is remembering two years of my life that ended with the outbreak of the war in 1914. Seeing those people—the Harndeans, as they are now, the Nixeys as they were then—started me off. And not simply because I happened to know them while I was in Bruddersford. But it seemed to me then—and I've thought the same ever since —that when the Nixeys came, then they began to wreck and ruin nearly everything I cared about. Mind you, I hadn't given them —or my life in Bruddersford—a thought for years. But having forced myself to remember all I could of that time, I've begun to feel that by the summer of 1914 I'd lost a lot that I've never found again, and that perhaps I am what I am today because of what happened to me then. When you're my age, what you thought and felt at eighteen seems rather absurd and unimportant at first —you begin by being very condescending to your young and callow self—but I see now that that won't do, just because what happens to you when you're eighteen or so moulds and colours you as later things don't. And you carry that self forward into life, Liz. And another thing. I know that what happened to me then is very important, much more important than I imagined it would be, because I've tried to re-live that time and sometimes emotions have been released that I didn't think were there."

Liz was leaning back in her corner, half turned towards me, and now I glanced across to see that she was staring at me in a grave speculative fashion, her eyes wide and dark. "I see. Or I think I do. And that's why I felt you were different, as soon as we met. I thought something special—like falling in love—had happened to you just lately, but it's because of what happened years and years before we met. But—" and she hesitated a moment, frowning in concentration—"they could be the same thing, couldn't they, Greg? I mean, that you've just discovered more of yourself—important bits that might have been hidden away for ages. No, don't try to answer that. Just tell me what it was you remembered."

So, as we alternated between the green twilight of the lanes and the flashing stretches of coast road, I told her about going to Bruddersford, working at Hawes and Company, entering the enchanted circle of the Alingtons, and about everything of importance that happened right up to the evening when Bridget came down and told Malcolm and Eleanor Nixey what she thought of them. Before I had done, the sun had vanished and the car windows were streaming with rain.

"And there goes your lovely day, Liz," I told her.

"I know. It's a shame. But what happened after that?"

"Nothing really," I replied. "The war came and I joined up, and I never lived in Bruddersford again. Final fade-out on the Bruddersford-Alington story."

"Yes, but what became of everybody? You must have met some of them afterwards."

"Oliver Alington, Jock Barniston and Ben Kerry died in the war. An awful lot of chaps died in that war, Liz. People of my generation have been staring at gaps ever since. Alington himself died during the war. He never really recovered from that illness he had in the summer of '14."

"But what about the girls?" she asked, rather as if the men didn't matter. "I know Eva was killed—but what about the other two—Bridget and Joan? Didn't you ever meet or hear of them again?"

"Yes, once—just once," I told her. And then I stopped because the car had stopped. Apparently we had arrived at the nice little hotel the driver had promised us. We had just time, as we dashed through the rain, to see that it looked from the outside quite a nice little hotel, hanging above what would have been, on a fine day, an equally nice little cove. In the entrance lounge, where some people were hanging about waiting for lunch, Liz said: "You must tell me the rest over lunch, Greg. Go and get yourself a drink now. I don't want one, and I may be some little time because, among other things, I must telephone to our hotel." There was a little bar at the back, with nobody in it but an elderly purple-faced man behind the counter, and nothing to drink in it but bottled beer. "Last drop of spirits went the night before last," he explained. "Try two small bottles in a tankard —it tastes a bit better."

I did, and then took my tankard into a corner and lit a pipe. The rain was so heavy now that it was dark in there, dark and sad.

"Not turned out so nice, after all," said the purple-faced man. "Changeable at this time of year, very changeable." He sighed noisily. "Staying for lunch?"

I said I was and that there were two of us. He replied that he would "tell 'em in the dining-room," and went out, still making a sighing noise. Evidently he was the landlord. It might be a nice little hotel, but this was a most mournful little bar. I took a pull or two at my beer, smoked away, and stared at the racing raindrops on the window. And I wondered how I ought to answer Elizabeth's last question, if she repeated it at lunch; and then I began to remember that last encounter with Joan Alington.

It was the early spring of '19 and I had just arrived from France at Victoria Station. I was feeling very pleased with myself. Officially I had come home on leave but there was more than a fair chance that I would find that my demobilisation had gone through. So there was I, the old soldier, Captain G. Dawson, with a few drinks inside me already, to join all the drinks I had had the night before at Boulogne. It was the middle of the afternoon, and after dumping all my kit, except a small bag, in the cloak-room, I wandered towards the station entrance. I was beginning to plan my evening in London and was not looking where I was going, with the result that I bumped into a girl who was struggling along with a rather large suitcase. She gave an angry yelp and dropped the suitcase. I couldn't see her face because she was wearing one of those large floppy hats that were in the fashion then.

"I'm awfully sorry," I told her. "My fault entirely. Let me give you a hand with that suitcase—it's much too heavy for you."

"Gregory Dawson," she cried, staring up at me so that I could see her face now.

It was nearly five years since I had seen her last; a lot had happened to me during those years; and it took me a moment or two to recognise her as Joan Alington. And of course she had changed too. She was now in her late twenties, and looked thinner in the face. She had always been rather pale, but now she looked paler still, rather hollow-cheeked and drawn.

"You look quite different," she said. "It was really your voice I recognised. You always had a queer deep voice, Gregory." And she smiled, and suddenly looked much prettier.

"Well, Joan," I said, picking up her suitcase, "where do we go?"

She explained that she was teaching in a girls' boarding school somewhere in Sussex, that the school had just broken up for Easter, and that she was now on her way to spend a day or two in her cousin's flat in Earls Court.

"All right, that's where we go then," I said. "That is, if your cousin doesn't mind asking me to tea."

"Oh—she's away all this week," said Joan, with the secret little smile I remembered so well. "So we don't have to ask her. Will you really come and have tea, Gregory? I wish you would. It's lovely seeing you again."

I told her, with a kind of military masculine insolence that I had picked up during the last few years, that she couldn't get rid of me. We found a taxi at last, and then drove off to a rather decayed region, somewhere between West Kensington and Earls Court, where I carried our two bags up four tall flights of stairs to the cousin's flat. On the way there Joan had told me all about her life in this girls' school, which she detested. She didn't say anything about her family, and as I knew her father had died and that Oliver had been killed, I felt that she didn't want to say anything about her family yet, so I asked no questions.

The flat had quite a large sitting-room, done in a metallic green and with reproductions of the Impressionist masterpieces round the walls. I sprawled on a hefty divan and smoked while Joan went into the bedroom to unpack. She came out looking demure in a cream silk blouse and a dark blue skirt, of that awkward length, neither one thing nor the other, that they still wore then. She looked like one of the younger mistresses at a nice girls' school; that is, until you carefully examined her face, which had something, obviously there but not easily defined, that they wouldn't want at a nice girls' school. After looking in a little cubbyhole of a kitchen, she said there wouldn't be much for tea and asked if I would rather go out for it, but I told her that a cup of tea would do me and that we could go out later. So we had some tea, and stared together at an enormous half-ruined gas-fire. It was cosy but melancholy, and a long way removed from anything I had planned when I bumped into her in Victoria Station.

Finally, it came out. "You realise, don't you," she began, almost accusingly, "that you're about the only one still alive? Oliver. Jock. Ben Kerry. I suppose you knew about them?"

"Yes, Joan," I said gently. "I heard about all three of them. I'm sorry."

"I always knew Jock would be killed," she said, in a queer toneless voice. "I knew it from the first. I believe he knew too. He didn't care, you know, Gregory—I mean, about being killed. I don't think his life mattered to him as it does to most of us. Do you know what I mean about him?"

"Yes, I always felt something like that about Jock."

"Give me a cigarette, please, Gregory." And then she puffed away at it in a defiant and inexpert manner, not saying anything for a minute or two.

"I heard about your father too," I told her, thinking it would be better to end the casualty list while we were at it.

She nodded but didn't speak. As she leaned forward and stared at the gas-fire, I caught the glitter of tears in her eyes, but she wasn't actually crying.

"What about the rest of the family? Where are they?"

"Mother went down to Dorset to live with my aunt—her sister. And of course that's where David goes. He's at Cambridge now and is supposed to be very brilliant."

"What at?" Though I wasn't surprised at David's brilliance.

"Oh—maths and physics—and things. And as he isn't very strong he wasn't called up."

I waited a moment. "What about Bridget?"

She gave me a sidelong look and a crooked little smile. "I thought it's about time we got round to her. Well, Bridget kept on with her music, and then did one or two bits of war work, and now she's married. Last autumn—to an Irishman called Connally—Michael Connally—one of those dark Irishmen with blue eyes—very fascinating."

"I've met them."

"Bridget adores him. Perhaps that comes of being called Bridget."

"Why don't you like him?" I asked.

"I gave it away, did I? Well, I think he's one of those men who do it all on charm. I believe he's weak and selfish really, and won't be any good. He appeals to the silly side of Bridget. She has a silly side, you know, Gregory."

"We all have. Where are they living?"

"In Ireland—just outside Dublin. Bridget still thinks it's all wonderful. But it won't work—you'll see."

"I don't suppose I shall see," I said.

She looked at me. "You wrote to her once, didn't you?"

"Yes, and never got a reply."

"Bridget said something to me about it. She had to talk to somebody, and there wasn't Eva any more—and Oliver was away. She thought that if she replied and then you went on writing to each other, then it might mean more to you than it meant to her—or than she thought it would mean, not being sure about what she felt about you—and that that wouldn't be fair. When Michael came along," she added, not without relish, "it was very different. She just fell flat—and adored him."

"I'm not surprised," I said, determined not to show the jealousy she wanted me to feel. "Black hair and blue eyes and Irish charm, they're a strong combination. And after all, Joan, *I* never pretended to be very fascinating."

"Well, Gregory," and she took a good long look at me, "I always liked you—though you were a funny awkward sort of boy when we first met you—and now, I must say, you look even better than I thought you would. Uniform suits you, Gregory."

There was a bit more of this, but I wasn't listening very

carefully. In fact I was feeling very impatient, and I was telling myself that I didn't really like Joan very much, that she'd given me all the news I wanted, that I hated the look of that flat, and that if I'd any sense I'd clear out and start enjoying my leave.

She must have guessed what I was thinking, or at least guessed some of it—perhaps I made a slight but obviously impatient movement, for now she jumped up, put a hand on my shoulder, and made her fine grey eyes look very appealing. "I've told you what a dreary existence I'm having," she began, drooping a little. "And you know how horribly different life is now, with nearly everybody gone. I was nice to you when you were just a lonely boy, dying to know us. Wasn't I? Well, it's your turn now, Gregory. Oh—I know—this is the wrong way to talk to a man—all stupid—"

I thought it was too. But there were tears in her eyes and the hand on my shoulder was twisting and clutching. "All right, Joan. I'm glad it's my turn. What do you want me to do?"

"Take me out tonight," she cried. "To the kind of places you'd go to. I want some fun. And I can't bear it if you go away now and leave me here. You don't know what it's like for a girl when there seems hardly anybody or anything left. Just for tonight, Gregory."

I took her hand off my shoulder—and her hot little fingers were still twisting and clutching—and stood up. "I was going to suggest we went out, Joan. Let's dine somewhere, go to a show, and then dance."

Her eyes shone. They announced that I was Prince Charming and the Fairy Godmother rolled into one. "That would be perfect. You are a darling, Gregory." And she kissed me in an enthusiastic but inexperienced sort of way, rather like her way of smoking. "I wish I had a drink to give you, but I'm afraid there's nothing here."

"Don't worry about that. I've a bottle of whisky in my bag, and I'll give myself a drink and do some telephoning—for theatre seats and so on—while you start changing. I'd like a bath, though, when you've finished."

"I'll have mine now," she cried, all flutter and excitement, and looking much prettier. After I had done my telephoning and had poured out a drink for myself, she popped her head round the door, looking almost rosy now, to tell me that a bath was running for me. I took my time in the bath, and thought about Joan and how she seemed to be younger than I was now that we'd met on this side of the gulf of war, and that while I'd been growing she seemed to have been dwindling. And I told myself there wasn't much of the old Alington enchantment left here with poor Joan. But I felt that anyhow I had only the mildest interest in the Alingtons and in my life before the war. I was the wrong age, much too near, to take my eighteen-year-old self seriously.

Joan came into the sitting-room, all dressed up, a few minutes after I went back there. Still defying the girls' school, she insisted upon trying my whisky, and took a swig that left her gasping. She was very gay in a rather feverish manner, which I found a trifle embarrassing. We dined at a little French place I knew in Greek Street, and had a bottle of powerful Burgundy, which had had so much of its "chill taken off" that it was almost mulled. The food wasn't bad, but it was a very hot and noisy little place, where you didn't want to talk much but sweated away at your eating and drinking. I kept grinning across at Joan, and she gave me a lot of queenly little smiles. She looked very different from what she had done at Victoria Station that afternoon: her eyes were bright, and she had a spot of colour, and that drawn look had vanished.

"Thank you, Gregory," she said, as I waited for my change, "that was lovely. Just what I needed. What happens now?"

"You'll see. But my guess is—comedians and legs and coloured lights and smoke and noise."

"Like the dear old Imperial at Bruddersford—do you remember?"

"Yes. Only this will be more so. We must hurry."

It was one of those big rowdy revues popular at that time, with the chorus girls swarming over gangways into the auditorium, and half-tight fat profiteers in the stalls waving rattles. The whole thing was devised to prevent a single thought entering the head of anyone there: no wit, no real fun, no art. I was a bit tight, on leave again and out with a girl, but I hated the show, and hated the red-faced guffawing middle-aged men and their brassy women who were sitting all round us. This muck and this greedy rabble didn't seem worth the life of one stammering lance-corporal. We'd thrown away the best, only to keep and to fatten the worst. And this was our famous After The War, was it?

But I hadn't been teaching in a girls' boarding school in Sussex, living on shepherds' pie and prunes and setting an example in decorum to naughty Betty and spoilt little Doris, with my family broken up and dead men I loved far away in their graves; and so when I glanced at Joan and saw that her eyes were shining with excitement, that here was the fun she wanted, I didn't blame her, and did my best to smile back at her and look as if I were enjoying it. But once or twice, even though I thought that pre-war Bruddersford life of ours didn't matter very much, I couldn't help remembering us all—Bridget, Eva, Oliver, Mr. Alington and Jock—in the golden gaslit radiance of that gallery in the Gladstone Hall, with Wagner and Brahms thundering below, and with more music to come when we all gathered in that long room at the Alingtons'.

"I know it was all silly," said Joan, clinging to my arm in the packed foyer, as we went out, "but I loved it. I know you didn't, though. I could tell. You were just pretending to—for me, weren't you?"

"Well, I saw several shows like that the last time I was on leave," I told her. "And I suppose I'm a bit tired of them. But I'm glad you enjoyed it."

"Well, I did. Where can we go and dance?"

"Night club."

"I've never been to one. You are wonderful, Gregory, doing just what I wanted us to do." And she squeezed my arm.

I had to force myself to remember that this was one of the magical girls I used to stare at in the Wabley Road tram, the very one who came to the office that afternoon and told me they were all going to the concert on the following Friday, the Joan Alington I had walked and talked with at Bulsden and on Broadstone Moor, in a sunlight that seemed to have vanished from this earth. Now she seemed just a girl, any girl, I'd picked up for a night out. One of us—or was it both of us?—must have changed a lot during the last five years. And I found this bewildering and rather sad.

The night club was one of the smaller places I'd been to several times during my previous leave; not too swanky and expensive and not too tough, although there were usually some rather rum characters at large in there. It was packed, of course; but I managed to grab a table about quarto size, where I ordered sandwiches, a gin fizz for Joan, and some of their terrible whisky for myself. On one side of us, elbow to elbow, were a couple of women wearing stiff collars and black bow ties and with thickly powdered faces, so white and hard they looked like embittered clowns; and on the other side was a great grunting fellow of about eighteen stone with a peaky blonde girl of about eighteen years. All six of us rose together to dance to a band that apparently consisted of four life-sized marionettes operated by somebody who had delirium tremens. Consumptive waiters from the slums of Naples and Salonica brought in champagne to young tarts who had arrived with sozzled escorts, and then retired to yawn and sneer at us all. The war was over, democracy saved, and here was Merrie England.

Joan wasn't much of a dancer, and neither was I, but it didn't matter on that crowded little floor, and we shuffled round amorously with the rest of them, the sweat on our palms mingling. By the time I had had three or four doubles of that terrible whisky, genuine fire-water, the night's programme seemed simple enough, for Joan, large-eyed and soft-lipped now, pliant and yielding, appeared both desirous and desirable, and there was the flat waiting for us. And I suddenly remembered that rainy night when we sheltered in Wabley Wood and she pushed me away and called me a silly young fool.

"Where are you staying tonight, Gregory?" She asked this when we were back at our table after a long spell of holding and shuffling.

I grinned at her. "I forget the exact address, but it's a flat out Earls Court way—four floors up—green sitting-room—Impressionist masterpieces round the walls. Know it?"

She gave me her little sideways look and tiny smile. "I think so. Well, you can if you like. There's that divan. I slept on it the last time I stayed there."

"Very comfortable. I tried it, you remember. Like to go home now?"

"Not just yet, please, Gregory. The people here are so fascinating—awful, most of them, but fascinating. And could I have another drink, please? I seem to be frightfully thirsty—it's so hot in here."

If we'd left when I suggested we should, the story would have been different. But we stayed on long enough for me to have at least two more helpings of fire-water, while she finished her last drink, which was just the one more she shouldn't have had. The result was that while her present mood was only heightened, mine suddenly changed, as I had known it do before when I had drunk too much. I was still fairly clear-headed, and indeed saw and heard everything sharply, but I stopped being gay and amorous; shadows from the old unconscious now crept up; and I began to brood and be sullen. To hell with it all! I didn't want Joan. There might be somebody I did want, but I couldn't think who it might be; and it certainly wasn't Joan.

Down below, screaming through the drizzle for a taxi, were a tight major of Marines and a woman who looked like a mad white horse. Finally, after doing the old comrade with the major, we all shared a taxi, but the Horse Marines were dropped somewhere in Knightsbridge. Between there and Earls Court, Joan snuggled up to me and seemed more than half asleep, and we said nothing. I was still broody and sullen, and when we staggered into the flat, I insisted upon making up my bed on the divan, telling Joan that I was an old soldier and knew how these things should be done. So she left me to it, and when she came back, looking oddly small in bedroom slippers and some kind of wrap, and pale again now, tired but still bright-eyed and excited, I was sitting on the edge of my newly made bed, darkly ruminating.

"Gregory," she cried, "darling Gregory—you took me out, didn't you?—and gave me just what I wanted. It was perfect —really it was—and you were so sweet to me all the evening. And—you must understand this—it wasn't like being with somebody I'd just got to know—because you belonged to the happy time—the only boy left—and that's what made it so specially wonderful. Oh, Gregory—love me."

And she flung her arms round my neck and began kissing me in an impassioned but messy sort of way that I didn't enjoy. I got up, kissed her firmly but dispassionately, and then took her by the elbows and put her into the large chair opposite, where she waited, half laughing and half crying and wondering what was coming next, while I returned to the divan and lit a cigarette.

"What is it, Gregory? Why are you looking like that? Don't you—don't you—like me?"

"Yes of course I do, Joan. Now take it easy." I had been up late the night before and had had a long day, and though I wasn't particularly sleepy I felt exhausted and depressed. The evening hadn't given me anything, not a real lift anywhere, nothing but bad drink, noise, smoke and a stale sexiness. But I had to say something. "What you said, though, set me thinking and wondering."

"What about?" And she sounded rather anxious.

"About the time before the war—Bruddersford—and your father—and Jock—and Eva."

She didn't say anything but just stared at me from the depths of the large basket chair. She was all eyes, and quite still except for a hand that picked at the arm of the chair.

"I never really understood about Eva—I mean, what really happened. I heard your evidence read out at the inquest—I was there, you know, and I remember you weren't—the doctor said you weren't fit—but I knew that ledge on Pikeley Scar—and what you said about Eva slipping didn't seem to me to make much sense."

She was sitting up now. "What are you saying?"

"I'm only asking—what really happened, Joan. I've often wondered, and I didn't like saying anything at the time."

"You were like all the others," she cried, with an hysterical vehemence. "Yes—even Jock. You thought Eva was wonderful, just because she was so pretty. She was awfully stupid really. She wouldn't believe for ages that Ben Kerry was in love with that woman, just went on pretending and pretending, and then when he told her outright, in that letter Jock brought, that he'd finished with her, then she just hadn't anything left. I kept telling her not to be a fool, that he wasn't worth it. And there was Jock making a fuss of her—and you'd have done the same if you'd had a chance—I remember the way you looked at her—"

"All right, Joan," I said wearily. "Don't go on and on. The point is, then, that she didn't care what happened—and so she slipped off that perfectly safe ledge."

"No, she didn't." And Joan sprang out of the chair, and then stood there, glaring at me and biting her lips. She looked more than half insane, and she screamed at me. "If you must know, she threw herself off. I couldn't stop her. She just rushed to the edge—and went. She did, Gregory. She did—she did—she did—"

"For God's sake," I cried.

She hurried out, sobbing as she went, and slammed two doors between us. After a minute or two, I undressed, switched off the light, and wrapped the blankets round me on the divan. I tried not to think about Eva and Joan; I wanted to go to sleep; but of course it was hopeless. And the bad whisky, which seemed to keep flaring up in various parts of my inside, was making me feel sickish. After an hour or so of this misery, I heard a noise, and then, as I happened to be facing that way, I saw a gradually widening sliver of light from the doorway. I pretended to be asleep but I risked one narrow glance, without moving my head, and I saw Joan standing there in a nightdress. She waited a minute or two, while I kept still and made a heavy breathing noise.

"Oh, there you are," cried Elizabeth, whisking me forward twenty-seven years. "Lunch is in, and we haven't too much time."

"Sorry, Liz," I said, and followed her out of the bar. When we were settled in the dining-room, I said: "Why haven't we too much time? What's the hurry?" Though I knew at once that Elizabeth was now full of plans, for she was wearing her special busy look, which I knew of old.

"That's why I've been telephoning to the hotel," she replied. "I've been asking them to pack for me. I've decided to take the afternoon train to London, darling. No soup, thank you." This, with a brilliant smile, to the waitress, who was shaking with excitement and glory.

"Sudden decision, wasn't it?"

"Well, not really, Greg. You want to finish the script—and we all want you to finish it, as soon as possible—and I've nothing to do here and several things I ought to be doing in London—talking about clothes for the part, for one thing; and then Brent rang me this morning to say he wants to give a big cocktail party for me—and—you know what it is, darling."

I did know, but I also knew that I hadn't heard the real reason why she was going. Something I had told her on the way to this place had done it. And it was clear too that now there was quite a distance between us. We hadn't really been close since she came up to my room late at night; there had been a widening space between us; but this new and more definite retreat was her doing and had happened during the last hour.

"There's some nonsense going round in that exquisite head of yours, Liz," I grumbled.

"Not at all. But you see why we mustn't be too long before we get back to the Royal Ocean. I'll just have time to pick up my things, pay the bill and tip people, and then I'll have to take this car on to the station. And you can get back to work, can't you, Greg?"

"Why the sweet malicious tone, Liz? What am I supposed to have done? And if I do get back to work—well, it's a job I'm doing for both of us, isn't it?"

She nodded, smilingly, not giving anything away. She didn't ask me to finish my Alington reminiscences over the lunch-table, and I was glad because the room was almost full and we were very much in the public eye and ear in there. We exchanged a few remarks as we ate—Liz beaming beautifully—and left it at that. But once we were back in that Minerva drawing-room, very much alone behind its steamy windows, we had hardly left the cove before she opened fire. "Which one of those girls was it you said you met just once again? Was it that sweet little Bridget?"

"No, it was that sweet little Joan. I ran into her by accident, early in 1919, just when I was finishing with the army. I took her out for the evening—she was teaching in a girls' school and wanted to see some gay metropolitan life—and she had a drink or two at a night club, and then was queer and hysterical."

"What about?"

"Eva's death. I asked her a question or two, and then she said it wasn't an accident but suicide."

"How horrible! That sounds as if you stayed up very late with her. Were you making love to her?"

"No. I had a bed in the sitting-room of the flat she was staying in, but that was all. As a matter of fact I never said good-bye to her, because I left next morning before she was stirring. And I never saw her again."

"What did she tell you about Bridget?" And the question came out rather too casually.

"She told me Bridget had just got married to a fascinating Irishman—though Joan didn't like him—called Connally, and had gone to live in Ireland. What was left of the family—Mrs. Alington and young David, who was then up at Cambridge, doing something brilliant—had moved from Bruddersford. And that really is the end of my story, Liz. I've never seen or heard of any of them since. As it's life and not the movies, the last sequence is a miserable little jumble, all anti-climax. No good producer would tolerate it for a moment. But I warned you it might be disappointing."

She shook her head, and looked very wise. Then, catching my eye, she carefully produced an enigmatic little smile.

"All right, Monna Liz," I said, in an offhand grumbling tone that was as careful as her smile, "I've told you all I know. Now, if all this sagacious nodding and smiling and general knowingness mean anything, you tell me something."

"Don't be beastly, Greg." And I knew that I really had offended her.

"Sorry, Liz, I didn't mean to be. It was only an act. If there's anything you want to say, I hope you'll say it. As a matter of fact I could do with a bit of help."

This pleased her. "That's the first time I ever remember you saying that to me, Greg," she cried with some warmth. "Why do you feel that?"

Yes, why did I? I had to think for a moment or two. "Of course I couldn't tell you the story with all the detail I've been remembering," I began slowly. "And a lot of colour—and emotion too, I suppose—has been dropped out of it. Still, there it is, and it doesn't seem to me to amount to very much, to add up to anything very significant. And yet, Liz, to me it has done. In a way I feel that just remembering it has changed me. Unless of course the change was really there first, and started me off remembering."

"No, it's the other way, I think," said Elizabeth gravely. "Because you remembered, then you were different. I told you when we first met again that you were. You seemed different to me. I asked you if you had fallen in love with somebody—you remember? And it's got worse, Greg. Look at us now, and then think how we schemed and plotted for me to come over here and for us to be together again. And we haven't really been together, haven't even been the friends we were years ago in Hollywood. And it isn't me, it's you. No—don't say anything or I shall cry, and I don't want to. And refusing to go back to Hollywood, and all the queer things you've been saying—that's all part of it, Greg. I think a lot of very important buried stuff has come out, and that you're discovering part of yourself—no, please, Greg, don't interrupt. You asked me to tell you something now. So I will—just two things. And one of them will certainly surprise you."

She stopped at that point, not for dramatic effect but because the car was in one of the deep narrow lanes and there were some cattle in front of us and another car behind, so that there was a great honking and bellowing. "Go on, Liz," I said as soon as we were moving quietly again.

"I met one of your Alingtons about eighteen months ago," she announced coolly.

"You were quite right, my dear girl. You certainly *have* surprised me. Are you sure? And if so—which, when and where?"

"I told you when. And it was in Washington, at a party. I was introduced to a rather nice shy Englishman, who was over there doing some mysterious scientific war work. Atom bomb, of course—that's obvious now. And his name was Sir David Alington."

"Sir David Alington? Yes, I've seen that name in papers—he's a well-known physicist. But, Liz, I don't think that's the boy I knew."

"I'm sure he is. This man and I talked for about half an hour. He's several years younger than you are—though he doesn't look it—but I remember him saying something about being born in 1900. And he was at Cambridge—and when he was a boy he lived in Bruddersford." She looked at me in triumph.

"Then it must be. Good lord! I can still see him—a calm clear little boy, buried in a book. And now he's Sir David and has been helping to make atom bombs, to finish us all off. Liz, I can feel cold fingers creeping up my spine—not because of atom bombs —but just thinking how Time, Chance or Destiny—or is it God?—keeps shuffling the pack and laying out the cards again. If we could only step back far enough to take a good look at the changing pattern—"

"Yes, darling. But let me finish what I was going to say. I remember now that this Alington man and I talked about Britain and food—the usual thing—and I remember that he said he'd been sending some food parcels to his sister in England, and that she was a widow with two or three children. And I got the impression that this widowed sister was all that was left of his family. And you see what that means?"

"Well," I began cautiously.

"It means," she swept on still triumphantly, "that though the others may have all gone, your Bridget is still alive. In fact I'm nearly sure he called her Bridget once or twice."

"You're probably right. Except that she isn't *my* Bridget."

"But that's the point, Greg. That's the beginning and end of it all. Of course she isn't your Bridget, but you feel she is."

"Now wait a minute, Liz. It's thirty-two years since I set eyes—"

"I don't care," she cried, "and I don't believe it matters. It's quite obvious to me that behind all this fuss is the simple fact, quite obvious to any woman, that when you were a boy you fell in love with this girl and that deep down, unknown to you until just now, you've stayed in love with her ever since."

"I don't believe it," I said sharply. "That's much too simple

altogether. I may have been fascinated—held in a kind of spell
—by a certain quality of life—"

"Oh, quality of life my foot! You just stayed in love with her
and didn't know it. And that explains a lot of things about you,
Greg. And it also explains the change in you I found when we
met again, the other day. You couldn't really bother about me
because you were so busy remembering little Bridget. And if it
wasn't for her you'd never have started thinking about that miserable Lord Harndean and his wife, you wouldn't have thought
they were worth five minutes of your time—as anybody could
see they aren't. It's all Bridget—and nothing but Bridget."

"It won't do, Liz. It really won't do."

"Look, Greg, don't let's talk any more about it now. Please.
Only just think over what I've said. What time is it? He seems to
be going very slowly, and I must catch that train."

After looking at my watch I told her that she wouldn't lose
the train, as long as she didn't linger in the hotel.

"It won't take me more than ten minutes. Do you think you'll
miss me, Greg?"

I looked at her steadily. "Yes, my dear, I know I shall. And all
the more because I'll feel—as I do now—that I didn't make the
most of you when you were here. I know it'll be damned dismal
in that hotel when you've gone. However, I'll just slog away at
the script and get it finished."

She had been smiling while I told her I would miss her, but
now she gave me a sharp accusing look. "You're bored with that
story now, aren't you? George Adony hinted that you were. And
the way you talked to Leo Blatt made me feel uneasy."

I answered her carefully and earnestly. After all, she was not
only my friend but she was also a great star, and it was largely
through my persuasion she had come over here, and there was a
great deal of prestige and money tied up with this engagement.
"You're confusing several different things, Liz, and not being
quite fair to me." And I reflected that she wouldn't have dared to
talk like that to me a few years ago, when we were in Hollywood
together and I was still the old hand who had helped her. "It's
quite true I'm bored with this kind of film. Probably I've written too many of them. It's also true that at this late stage, when

I'm on the final sequences of a shooting script, I'm apt to find myself getting bored. And why not? The idea's been talked over and chewed over for months; the story line has been planned and plotted over and over again; and naturally the interest goes. I'm tired of this blasted beautiful lady who hits back. But that doesn't mean, after nearly twenty years of it, that I won't finish the job properly. You'll have a good script—don't worry. And don't let's talk about this any more, either."

She placed her firm square hand, which didn't really belong to the exotic mask of a face she had acquired now, over my hand, which was resting on my knee; and she said: "I'm sorry, Greg darling. I wasn't really worried about the script. Only about you."

We arrived at the hotel in a silence that had more sympathy in it than most of our talk had known. She begged me to go straight up to my room and work, and not to bother about seeing her off. "We'll meet in a few days in London," she continued. "I'm staying at the Dorchester. But I may ring you up very soon."

She gave this last statement rather more emphasis than it needed, and I guessed then that she was up to something. But I didn't say anything. I just nodded and smiled and said I hoped she'd have a nice journey, and then left her at the hotel office, demanding her bill. Up in my room I found myself feeling uncertain and rather depressed and not anxious to do any work. The cure for that, I discovered long ago, is to compel yourself to do some work. What you do, at first, is nearly always bad; and you realise it's bad, tear it up, and then without further effort really settle down to the job. And this did the trick once again, so that I worked steadily and successfully until about eight o'clock.

Down in the dining-room, alone once more, I realised that I had been quite right when I had assured Elizabeth that I would miss her. It looked as if half the lights had gone out. Both the place and the people seemed dreary, hopelessly unpromising. The evening before me stretched out like a long wet street. I couldn't hurry back to my room to recapture that Bruddersford time. I'd had it. And no Elizabeth; though, ironically enough, when she had been here, I'd neglected her to go Bruddersfording. But then that reminded me, and I looked across at the Harndeans, who smiled at once and gave me the impression that they must have been trying to catch my eye. I had thought about them enough, as the Nixeys, but I had never really talked to them; and then I remembered that just after I had recognised them as the Nixeys they had told me that they had been talking about what he called "the old Bruddersford days." Well, now that I had done my remembering, this was the time when we had better have our chat about those days.

They left the dining-room before I did. I went up to my room for a cigar, and then came downstairs to find Lord Harndean sitting alone, finishing his coffee, in a corner of the lounge. It seemed odd to join him there, for I had left Malcolm Nixey still standing in the Alingtons' long room, in July, 1914.

"Ah, Dawson, come sit down," he said, pleased to see me. "Eleanor's gone up to do a little packing. We're leaving in the morning. I promised Lincing to join in a final rubber or two of bridge tonight, but they aren't ready yet. Has the famous Elizabeth Earl deserted us now?"

"Went back to town this afternoon," I told him. "By the way, you remember the Alingtons—in Bruddersford. Well, she told me today she met the youngest of them in Washington last year—he's now Sir David Alington, one of the atom bomb men."

"Really? Done well, eh? Now which of 'em would that be?"

"The young boy who was at school when we knew them," I replied.

"Can't remember him. Remember the girls—very pretty. One fell off a cliff, didn't she? What happened to that family?"

"Dead, mostly." I looked curiously at him, this brittle elderly man, still very spruce in his dinner jacket. This was Malcolm Nixey, with the same restless eyes. A lot had happened to him: he had been very successful in business, had made a fortune, had been useful in some way to the Chamberlain Government, and had received a peerage: quite a success story. Yet I felt at that moment, staring at him, that really nothing had happened to him, that he'd never known vital experience, neither the sweat nor the savour of life, that ever since I left him in Canal Street he'd only been calculating, telephoning, and attending board meetings, all in a glass case. My intuitive feeling about him when he first came to us at Hawes and Company, that he never really experienced anything, had been right.

"I've been thinking a lot about those two years I had in Bruddersford," I said. "Remembering things—and people—I hadn't thought about for years."

"Have you now? Well, as I think I told you, my wife and I were talking about that time. It was meeting you, of course, that started us off. Have a drink, Dawson?"

"Not just now, thanks. Tell me something." I waited a moment. "When you were sent up, by your uncle, to the Bruddersford branch of Hawes, ostensibly to learn the business, had you and your uncle planned to push Alington out? I know it's a long time ago—and doesn't matter now—but I'm interested."

"Quite. Let me think." And clearly the question didn't disturb him. "My uncle had met Alington at the London office and didn't think much of him—the wrong type, as he was, you know. Ought to have been a professor or schoolmaster or something of that sort—not a business man. Eh?"

"I dare say you're right," I said drily.

"Undoubtedly. My uncle knew that war was coming, absolutely inevitable, but Alington wouldn't believe it, chiefly because the Germans he knew were old-fashioned Liberals, whereas my uncle and I knew the other kind. Well, my uncle's idea—mine too, as a matter of fact—was to sell as much as we could to Germany, while there was a chance, but at the same time to build up the home market quickly, so that when the war came the firm could take advantage of the situation. Our idea wasn't to stay in the business—we'd no particular interest in it, and of course I didn't want to stay in Bruddersford any longer than was necessary—but to build it up quickly and then sell out at the top of the market. Which we did—but that was after your time, of course."

"Yes, I remember old Joe Ackworth saying that that was exactly what you would do."

"Ackworth? Oh—that was the old wool-buyer, wasn't it?" He laughed. "Couldn't stand me, and used to be damned rude at times. But if he'd been running that show instead of Alington, who really wasn't much good, we might have had more trouble. But that daughter of his being killed like that finished off Alington. Queer business that, I always thought."

"The sister who was with her told me some years afterwards that it was really suicide," I said slowly.

"I wouldn't be surprised. A bit unbalanced, I always thought, that family. The youngest girl charged in once—last time we ever went there—and went for Eleanor and me in the most ridiculous and hysterical fashion."

"I know. I was there."

"Were you? Oh yes—I believe you were. Well, you remember how the girl went on at us—quite unbalanced."

"And yet, you know, Harndean," I said quite pleasantly, "what she told you was perfectly true."

"I can hardly believe that," he said stiffly. "I've forgotten what she did say. But I remember that her manner was hysterical and very objectionable."

"She'd had a nasty time, what with one thing and another —sister being killed, father ill."

He relaxed now. "No doubt. Now tell me about this film business. I had a little interest in one of the companies here but didn't care for the way it was being run."

"I'll tell you about the film business," I said. "But I'd like to ask you one more question. You'll probably think it a peculiar question, but I'm a writer—and we writers are peculiar people and full of curiosity about other people."

He liked that, which is why I slipped it in. If we scribbling fellows are probably barmy, then the Malcolm Nixeys are all right. As soon as England accepted the business man's outlook—and even trade union leaders have usually spent a good deal of time with business men—then all creative artists and their like were pushed out to the eccentric fringes of society.

"Tell me," I continued, throwing in a whimsical look, "what you've got out of it all?"

He frowned, more in bewilderment than in distaste. "I don't see what you mean."

"Well, Malcolm, he means—what have you got out of it all?"

And this of course was from his wife, who had arrived unseen behind Harndean's chair.

"Oh there you are, my dear," he cried, with some suggestion of relief. "Finished packing?"

"I've done all I'm going to do tonight," she said as she sat down. "I thought you were going to play bridge with the Lincings."

Harndean remained standing. "I'm waiting for Lincing. Dawson and I have just been chatting about that wool firm in Bruddersford. Ah—there's Lincing. What are you going to do, my dear?"

She settled down into her arm-chair. "I'll stay here and talk to Mr. Dawson—and tell him what you've got out of it all. Then I shall go to bed—I won't wait for you—I'm tired." And he left us.

"Join me in a drink?" I asked her, ringing the bell.

She said she would, and then accepted a cigarette. We said no more until the girl who brought the drinks had gone. The trio was playing softly; our corner of the lounge was deserted; she was rather tired and had been feeling rather bored, and now could relax; and there was an odd and unexpected suggestion of intimacy about us.

"What made you ask Malcolm that question?" she asked, smiling a little.

"Because I wanted to know. We'd been talking about Bruddersford, and I remembered how I felt then, particularly once when I had an evening out with him, that he didn't really experience and enjoy anything. Well, he's been busy and successful ever since, but I wondered what he'd really got out of it all."

"I don't think I ought to try to answer that," she said, still with a little smile. "But perhaps I should tell you that Malcolm's parents were quite poor, but he was taken up by a rich uncle, who completely dominated him. Incidentally, I hated this uncle, and he disliked me. Then Malcolm went on and on, still pleasing his uncle long after his uncle wasn't there to be pleased. Apart from that, nothing much has happened to Malcolm." She waited a moment, then looked at me. "You've been thinking a lot about that Bruddersford time, haven't you?"

"Yes. How did you know?"

"Well, to begin with, I've noticed that you've looked at me several times, during these last few days, in a queer questioning sort of way. As if saying to yourself, 'Is this the woman I knew then?' Um?"

"Right. But I didn't think you would have noticed."

"Oh, I notice things like that. I'm not Malcolm, you know. And then again, your friend Miss Earl told me that you were busy brooding over your distant past. She told me in the middle of a poker game last night. There was a peculiar American, who arrived, made us play poker, and then vanished."

"He's a Hollywood agent," I explained. "They're like that. So Elizabeth told you, eh?"

"Yes, and then asked me what you were like then. I said that you were a rather clever cheeky boy, who obviously thought that Malcolm and I were a pair of rather sinister interlopers. Like the furious child who denounced us—do you remember?"

I looked hard at her. She smiled, all cool and easy. I felt she could do with a jolt or two. "Yes, I remember that evening very well. Your husband mentioned it, and I told him that I thought everything Bridget said was quite true. I also told him that the sister, Joan, who was with Eva Alington on that ledge on Pikeley Scar, told me some years afterwards that it wasn't an accident but suicide."

She wasn't smiling now. "Did you believe that?"

"Joan seemed queer and hysterical when she told me," I said carefully, "but I can't see why she should have said that if it wasn't true. Obviously the whole thing had been very much on her mind—as well it might have been. And she'd had a bad time, for this was in 1919, and her brother had been killed in the war—and Jock Barniston, the man she was in love with—and her father died. They'd had no luck from that morning when we went to Pikeley Scar."

"And they were a happy family when Malcolm and I first arrived, eh?"

"Yes, I think they were," I said, meeting her steady gaze. "That's how they looked to me. I know that I was happy with them. It was all a long time ago, of course, but it happens that I've never felt like that about a family since then."

"I've never felt it about any family at any time," she said crisply. "But then I don't like families. And what happened to those Alingtons was no worse than what happened to millions of other families, all over Europe. They're not the only people who suffered. And, you know, you're not the only person here with a memory."

I looked at her expectantly, but decided not to say anything. I could hear the trio playing a Waldteufel waltz and making a very ragged job of it. One of the bridge-players at the other end of the lounge began guffawing. We still had the corner to ourselves, and, if she really wanted to tell me something, the place and the time were right. So I waited.

"We're leaving in the morning, and probably you and I won't meet again. So I'm going to risk telling you something that nobody else knows." There was no warmth in her tone, no hint of any emotion in her voice: she was cool and incisive. "It's all ancient history, but as we seem to have been thinking about it, we might as well get it straight. You still think—as that Alington child said that night—that I deliberately took Ben Kerry away from her sister for a little amusement, just grabbed him to pass the time, don't you? Of course you do. I've seen it in your eyes these last few days, every time you've looked at me. And you're quite wrong. It wasn't like that at all."

She stopped, and I was afraid for a moment that she would leave it at that. I looked enquiringly at her, and she met my glance for a couple of seconds and then, without any suggestion of embarrassment, stared down at the little table between us.

"That's the kind of thing I might easily have done at that time. But this was quite different. There wasn't any grabbing and amusement. I was in love with Ben. It was the first and last time I ever was in love. That girl—or any other girl that age—couldn't have begun to understand what I felt about him. I was ready to give up everything for him. When he was killed, just after we spent his last leave together, I thought I'd go mad. And I've never really forgotten a single second of the time Ben and I spent together. That's why I said you weren't the only person here with a memory. Good night, Mr. Dawson—or perhaps we'd better say—Good-bye."

And I found myself still standing, gaping after her, at least a couple of minutes after she had gone.

ELEVEN

During the next few days, with nobody in the hotel I wanted to talk to and with no more remembering to be done, I tore into the last two sequences of *The Lady Hits Back*. Probably I worked all the better because I felt so bored and empty when I wasn't working. And it rained a good deal, so that I wasn't tempted to lounge about on the cliff walks. On two of the days I kept at it from morning until late at night, giving myself a break only for lunch and dinner, and as usual when I worked at this pace, took no exercise and smoked far too much, I slept badly, waking between confused but disturbing dreams. This gave my temper an edge, and twice when Brent rang up I was very short with him and inclined to snarl. But I told him the work was going well and nearly finished, so he didn't mind.

Then—it was rather late on the Monday evening—Elizabeth, with whom I hadn't exchanged a word since she left the hotel, rang me up from the Dorchester. She sounded very pleased with herself, and rather grumpily I told her so.

"And you sound very cross, darling," she said. "What's the matter? Brent said you were pleased with what you've done."

"It's all right," I told her. "And either late tonight or sometime in the morning, it'll be finished."

She made excited noises. "And when will you be coming to London then, Greg?"

"I'll catch the afternoon train tomorrow."

She said that was perfect. "For two reasons," she continued, her voice bursting with plans and excitements. "Now listen, darling. First, Brent's giving a huge cocktail party for me at Claridges on Thursday—and you must be there, and now you can be. And the other thing is this. Could you come and see me on Wednesday—say, at tea-time? It's very important."

I said that I could. "And of course I'd like to, Liz. But what are you up to?"

It wasn't a very good line, but nevertheless I could hear a little gurgle, and I knew she was having a lovely time. "That's a date then—tea-time on Wednesday. And it's not just me, but somebody you're longing to meet."

"Liz you know I hate fun on the telephone. Who is this?"

"You'll see," she crowed. "Wednesday, then. Good-night, darling."

I was left with that forlorn feeling which follows long-distance calls from people I am fond of, and to get rid of it, before settling down to work again, I hurried downstairs to the lounge, where I was just in time to catch the trio as they were packing up for the night.

"Hoy!" I said. And old Zenek, the pianist, looked up and smiled.

"Hoy yourself!" said Susan, who was the little cheeky one. The other girl, Cynthia, was tall and very shy. "I thought you'd forgotten all about us."

"Certainly not," I told her. "But I've been working hard these last few days, and before that I was rather tangled up with people."

"Beautiful film star," said Susan. "We saw you. And we don't blame you—gosh, talk about glamour—though of course she's a bit old now."

"No, she isn't," I said. "It's just that you are almost straight out of the egg."

"That is what I have tried to say!" said old Zenek, sighing.

"I'm leaving tomorrow afternoon—returning to London."

"I am sorry," said Zenek. "But they want a dance band here for the summer season, so we also leave at the end of next week."

"And a jolly good job too," cried Susan.

And here the silent Cynthia, who had been staring at me with great fearful eyes, looking like an elongated doe, now surprised me by producing a huge grin.

"Well, the point is—can you three lunch with me tomorrow?" I asked them. "Not here, but at that nice little place—you know—the *Lobster Pot*." This was a small hotel at the other end of Tralorna, and it could on occasion, the rumour ran, conjure forth an excellent lunch.

Zenek had to refuse: every Tuesday he gave lessons in a neighbouring town. But the two girls accepted with joy and acclamation. "When Cynthia's father came down," said Susan, "we had a wizard lunch at the *Lobster Pot*. But you've got to ring them up first—and say it's very important, and all that. Don't forget, Mr. Dawson."

"I won't. I'll ring them up in the morning and tell them it's terribly important. And I'll see you there about one, then." Feeling better now, I went back to work and stuck at it until I reached the final fade-out. This was about half-past two in the morning, and felt like it. Something approaching a spring gale had hit us, and the night outside my turret was howling and shuddering. I lingered at the table, staring at the last page of my script.

I found this rather a solemn moment. *The Lady Hits Back* was finished, and with it, I felt, a whole long chapter of my life. I couldn't help thinking about the beginning of that chapter, when I first left New York for Hollywood, in what seemed now another age, another world. It hadn't been a bad life—and certainly quite unlike the nightmare of wasted effort and frustration that so many writers have given us as records of their film careers—but now, I knew quite definitely, I had done with it. Exquisite ladies would have to hit back, Elizabeth and the other glamour-queens would have to find scenes and words to fit them, the Sam Grumans and Brents would have to herd their customers into dreamland, all without any further assistance from me. I'd had it. All the money there was in this gigantic doped jam-puff industry couldn't tempt me to go back again. If you were sufficiently experienced and artful, as a few of us knew, you could score a point or two in the dark without frightening anybody by a glimpse of reality; but I was no longer young and couldn't enjoy any more the first fine flavours of cynicism. I was growing old in a tragic world, and if I had anything to say I wanted to be able to say it, even if most of the customers ran screaming from the box office. I'd done my share of administering the anesthetics; it was time I moved into a consulting-room, even if I hardly ever saw a patient. So the script and I between us, at that late and lonely hour, had to play a farewell scene. "Exquisite, lovely, glamorous Lady," I murmured, "who couldn't draw two breaths in the real, thick, sweating, suffering world, go and show them in ten thousand darkened halls how you hit back and yet found your way to happiness. And, for Elizabeth's sake, Brent's sake, all our sakes, I hope you won't do it for less than a gross of a quarter of a million sterling. Be a Big Success, Darling. And good-bye for ever."

I hadn't a lot of sleep but the quality was good. I awoke to a typical leaving-a-place day, with everything maliciously looking its best. There was still a high wind and the sea thundered and foamed angrily, but the sun shone out of a clear sky, the gorse along the cliff was a golden flame, and the fields and hedges might have been newly made that very morning. After clearing up and packing, I had ample time for a stroll before lunch. Looking about me for the last time, I was troubled by a sense of regret, mysterious and incommunicable, originating below the level of words or even definite images. It was, I felt, as if this Tralorna, bright and burnished to see me go, had offered me something, and that I would leave, never to return, without even knowing what it was I had missed.

Susan and Cynthia were waiting just inside the door of the *Lobster Pot*, all tidy and sitting very close together, demure but excited. "Did you remember to telephone?" Susan asked in a fierce whisper.

"Yes," I replied, giving a fair imitation of the same whisper, "and told them it was very important. Come on."

We had a little bay window to ourselves in the dining-room, and the lunch wasn't bad and was far more plentiful than the hidden mathematicians of the Royal Ocean Hotel ever allowed us to have. The girls ate heartily, and drank cider.

"Jolly good," said Susan, through a mouthful of treacle tart. "We've been hungry all the time down here, haven't we, Cynthia?"

"Yes," said Cynthia. "We've had to keep buying buns," she explained to me, looking at me with her huge sad doe's eyes.

"We're just bunged up with starch," said Susan. "And the woman where we stay tells us miserable stories all the time. Her husband is in bed all day with heart disease, and she's got arthritis, and all their children died. And every time we try to complain about anything, she starts all over again—how her beautiful little girl of three screamed for two days and then died, and how nice she looked in her little coffin—and we cry and cry, and forget about complaining, and then she gives us nothing but horrid bits of calf's head and carrots for dinner again—and it's miserable. This is jolly good, though. Super."

I asked them what they were going to do, and they explained that they had decided to return to the Royal College for two or three more terms. Susan would have another go at the Brahms Concerto, and Cynthia was to try for the Elgar 'Cello Concerto. They talked for some time about the Royal College and the students there. "The two best when we left were a boy called Forshaw, who's a pianist and only eighteen but huge and a bit mad—marvellous, though—plays the Brahms *B Flat* and anything," Susan rattled on, "and a girl called Sheila Connally, who's a violinist, about my age, and she's just played with the London Symphony—only the Mendelssohn, but still—proper concert and everything—lucky pig!"

"Where does she come from?" I asked.

"I don't know. Do you, Cynthia?"

"No, I don't," said Cynthia in her shy dreamy fashion. "I hate her."

"Cynthia hates her," Susan explained to me. "I don't like her much either. Not jealousy or anything like that. She's got marvellous technique, and she's obviously going to be very good."

"What's wrong with her then?"

Cynthia murmured something, and Susan, who frequently acted as Cynthia's interpreter, said: "Yes, that's right. Cynthia says Connally's too self-centred. She never joins in anything or has any fun or talks to anybody. She's all wrapped up in herself, and I think—and so does Cynthia—that it comes out in her playing. Very cold and correct. I'll bet her Mendelssohn was terribly dull, but of course they'd all clap because she's so young and looks quite nice on the platform."

"Is she Irish?" I asked.

"She doesn't talk in an Irish way," said Susan. "Just ordinary. She has queer eyes, but some people think she's rather glamourous. Wizard lunch we've had, Mr. Dawson."

"Let's have our coffee outside," I suggested. "It should be warm out there, and I'd like some air before the train journey."

We sat full in the sun and out of the wind, and it was very pleasant. I asked them if they had enjoyed playing at the hotel.

"No," replied Susan, "it was fun at first, but after that we hated it. Cynthia nearly chucked it, didn't you?"

"Was that because you had to play such silly stuff?" I enquired.

"No, not really—though I suppose that helped—but it was the people. We didn't like them. And neither does Mr. Zenek."

"Stinkers," Cynthia murmured.

"That's right—stinkers," cried Susan. "Not you of course. Or Elizabeth Earl—she came over and spoke to us—and was sweet. But none of the others ever looked at us or really listened or seemed to be really alive at all. They just sat and jabbered in a dull sort of way. I wouldn't stay in that sort of hotel with people like that—no, not if I was paid just to stay there. I know now I just don't like these oldish people who are rather rich. There's something the matter with them. Mr. Zenek thinks so too. They must be all peculiar inside—half-dead or something. I never want to play to people like that again. You can't, really. They don't want music—or anything that's exciting. Gosh! And they're frightening in a way too. Like those wooden dummy people in the fairy story by George MacDonald—they'd just knock you about without even knowing they were doing it. I'm always jolly glad to get away from them." And she stared, half in scorn, half in apprehension, at some vision of the wasteland of the English comfortable classes; and I could almost see Malcolm Nixey in it.

Cynthia murmured something about her father.

"That's right," cried her interpreter. "Cynthia's father—he's very nice: you'd like him—says they've spent their lives starving their imagination, just starving it to death. And now they're zombies. Yes, you can laugh—but how would you like to play to zombies every tea-time and evening?"

And Cynthia now produced her sudden startling grin. "Some are zombies. Some are stinkers. Two different kinds."

"I hate 'em all," cried little Susan fiercely. "Well, I suppose we ought to go now. And you have to catch your train, haven't you?" And they thanked me very nicely for the lunch.

"I enjoyed it as much as you did," I told them. "Perhaps more. When you're back at the Royal College you might like to come and listen to some music with me." I gave them my address; and then remembered something.

"By the way, about that Connally girl. What colour are her queer eyes? Greenish?"

Susan thought they were, but Cynthia said she wasn't sure. So we left it at that; and I hurried back to the hotel, remembering that I had meant to send a wire for a car to meet me at Waterloo, where the afternoon train from this part of Cornwall didn't arrive until after midnight. Actually it didn't arrive until one-fifteen that night; but the car I had ordered belonged to a man who did regular work for Brent's studio, and it was there, waiting for me; and at about quarter to two I was in my flat in Cavendish Square. It wasn't a bad flat and I had been there for nearly three years, but that night it looked about as much like home as a telephone-box. There was a long cable from Sam Gruman, repeating the offer that Leo Blatt had urged me to accept. And I'll admit that for a minute or two after I'd read this cable my resolution about not going back to Hollywood weakened considerably. It wasn't the job or the money that made this sudden appeal to me. It was a distaste, which arrived quite unexpectedly, for the vast shuttered gloom of London, for this mournful flat, for the stewed tea and imitation sausages that the grumbling woman would bring in the next morning, that nearly carried the assault. On the Coast, I told myself, there would at least be sun and air and colour, to say nothing of coffee and fruit and some real food. And there was nothing to keep me here: I didn't know what I wanted to do, hadn't the faintest sketch of a plan. I fancy that if Sam or Leo had come through on the telephone at that moment, had been persuasive for just one minute, I'd have agreed to go. And Elizabeth in person could probably have done it in half a minute. As it was, I tore up the cable, using an unnecessary amount of energy, left a small pile of letters unopened, and went to bed.

I slept late, and it was Brent on the telephone who wakened

me. I agreed to take the script round to his office and then stay on and lunch with him. George Adony was there when I arrived, and the three of us spent the next two hours talking over the script. There were several things in it that they were doubtful about, and I gave my reasons for doing what I had done with these things and persuaded them both that I was right. But there was a scene in the final sequence in which, they proved to me, I had gone wrong, and I promised to put it right within the next twenty-four hours. This made Adony happy, and after reminding me that I was to dine with him soon, he went off smiling. Brent was pleased too. I had a feeling that they had expected me to be very difficult, ready to fight all day to keep in new scenes they didn't like, and that they were now immensely relieved.

"It's a dandy job," said Brent, as we went out to lunch. "And I doubt if you've ever done a better. And George has some very good ideas, and what with you and him and our beautiful Elizabeth, we've got a picture. And you were quite right about her, Gregory. That's a nice sensible woman, very co-operative and easy to handle. At first I wasn't sure, but now we're getting along famously. I'm throwing a big party for her tomorrow at Claridges—her first official appearance—and Jake's roping everybody in—you know."

"Yes, I can imagine it," I said with a great deal of absent enthusiasm.

"Anything wrong, old boy?"

"No, not a thing," I replied. "Unless I'm hungry. Where are we eating?"

It was another little club he had discovered, where they gave him very special attention. In another minute we were there, with the special attention flying all round us. I will say this about film producers—they still have prestige in a world in which nearly everybody else has lost it. If there has been a managerial revolution, then films must have been put at the top of the list of manufactured goods. Brent could always get everything he wanted; not excepting intelligent audiences, because he didn't particularly want them. Now he wanted rich food and sound liquor, and they arrived.

"Trouble about these places, of course, is that they can't keep it up," he said. "Somebody gets found out, I suppose. The thing to do is to make the most of 'em while the going's good. You'd better let 'em put your name down at once."

"No, thanks, Brent. I'm enjoying this lunch, but I don't like these places. I've gone off them."

He gave me a quick look. Brent is no fool, though he sometimes talks like one. "Been working too hard? Or was that hotel too much for you? Or has anything happened? You were in fine form at the story conference this morning—"

"I wanted to get on with the job," I put in, rather impatiently.

"Of course. But now—well, old boy, to tell the truth, you seem a bit disgruntled. If there's anything I can do—all right, then, let's forget it. I hear that Sam Gruman's been making you a big offer to tempt you back there."

I didn't ask him how he heard. They always hear. Probably somebody was calling Sam in Hollywood to tell him I was lunching with Brent. "Yes, Leo Blatt talked to me, and I've had a cable from Sam. I've turned it down."

Brent looked delighted and didn't pretend not to be. "That's fine. I thought you might be still considering it and getting worried." He waved a hand at some people who were approaching our table, probably to have a word with him, and he made the single movement at once a greeting and a dismissal. It is this sort of thing that sets producers above mere directors and writers, who simply don't know how to make their hands say "Hello! Keep away." Now he leaned across the table. "If this picture does only half of what I think it'll do," he said, "I'm still going to be very grateful to you, Gregory. Not only for the story but for getting Elizabeth over here. Give me a week or two—I'll make it sooner if you like, but you know how it is when you're going into production quickly—and we'll talk plans. Eh?"

I shook my head. "I haven't any plans I want to talk about."

"Naturally, when you've been up to your neck down there with this script. But I've some ideas—one or two dandy ideas —and I think I can prove I'm grateful to you for staying with our organisation—you'll see, old boy."

Well, I could have told him—and nearly did tell him—that I'd no intention of staying with his organisation and had ceased to have the slightest interest in his dandy ideas. But it didn't seem fair at the moment. He was enjoying himself and we were having a wonderful special-attention lunch. And there was another thing that stopped me. I still hadn't the vaguest notion what I was going to do, or even what I wanted to do, in place of shaping and dressing up his dandy ideas, and so I felt it would be better to wait until I did know a little more.

"Thank you for the lunch, Brent," I said as we were leaving. "Wonderful meal. I feel that you and I ought to be taking a turn down a coal-mine this afternoon—"

"None of that stuff, Greg. I can't help it if—"

"No, I know, I know. I only meant that at least we'd have been stoked up properly. In fact, I feel a bit over-stoked. I have to see Elizabeth this afternoon at the Dorchester, and I'd better walk there—the longest way. See you tomorrow. And I'll re-write that scene tonight."

I walked along Piccadilly and then as far as Knightsbridge, turned into the park and kept moving briskly there for half an hour or so, taking with me a slight but persistent headache that was the result of Brent's hospitality. I felt irritable and not ready to cope adequately with any delightful surprise that Elizabeth might be now preparing for me. My guess was that she had discovered that Sir David Alington was back in England and willing to take tea with her at the Dorchester. But I found it hard to believe that any distinguished Cambridge scientist would regard it as a great treat to meet a man who merely knew him as a small boy. This was just one of Elizabeth's silly ideas, I concluded, as I took my little headache and my irritation across Park Lane.

As Elizabeth admitted me into her suite, I could see that she was still alight with triumph. Some wonderful daft plan had now succeeded. She was wearing a corn-coloured suit and an absurd tall hat blazing with scarlet feathers, and she looked ten thousand times better than anybody or anything I had so far seen in London.

"Now what's happening, Liz?" I began; but she shook her head, smiled, and led the way into the sitting-room. There was a little middle-aged woman on the settee in there. I couldn't see her face, because she was wearing a shapeless old felt hat, but she was a shabby little figure and gave me the impression that she was there to enquire about some sewing or to take some message to the costume people. So I ignored her, and turned to look enquiringly at Elizabeth, who was now standing near the door, as if ready to go out. She pulled a face at me as I started to speak.

"Well, now," she cried, still looking triumphant, "here you are. And tea'll be up in a minute. I've ordered it. I have to go out for an hour or so, but I'm sure neither of you will mind about that." And the radiant creature, to my astonishment, smiled meaningly, first at the woman on the settee and then at me. This made me give the shabby little middle-aged woman a second and longer look, and this time, as she lifted her head and there was more to be seen than that awful hat, I saw her face. I wouldn't have recognised her in the street, and I think it was only because of what Elizabeth had said that I did recognise her. Thirty-two years are half a lifetime, and it was close on thirty-two years since I had seen her last. For of course it was Bridget Alington.

"Tea's here now," cried Elizabeth gaily, sparkling away. "That's perfect, isn't it? If there's anything else you want, please do ask for it. And have a lovely talk." And then she vanished, like a golden summer, and there was a waiter fussing about with tea-things; and this was a dull place with three middle-aged silent people in it. But I didn't feel sad, I felt annoyed. And Bridget wasn't smiling or looking encouraging; she kept her face buttoned up, as I imagine it must have been ever since she entered the hotel. Not a word was said until the waiter left us.

"Well, Bridget," I said, trying hard to look delighted, "this is a great surprise."

"Yes, it is," she said, not even making any attempt to sound enthusiastic. "I suppose I'd better pour out."

I pulled up a chair, accepted a cup of tea, passed the sandwiches, and took another and closer look at her. The greenish eyes were the ones I'd known in Bruddersford, but they looked out of a square and weathered face, rather hard and not the kind of face I like. I felt that the flame and fire I remembered had burnt out long ago and had left behind some toughened metallic deposit. This was a woman who had had a lot more trouble than fun, and was still grimly battling her way through. My Bridget was as far away now as Eva and Oliver.

"How did Elizabeth—Miss Earl—get hold of you? Through David?"

She nodded. "I live in London now—in Ealing—and so it was easy."

"Do you live in London because you have a daughter called Sheila, who's a violinist?"

It was as if I'd flicked a switch: she lit up at once. "Yes, because of Sheila. Have you heard about her?"

"Yes, I heard about her the other day. Sheila Connally. I met Joan years ago and she told me then you'd just married an Irishman called Connally and had gone to live in Ireland. I want to know all about it, but first—tell me—what happened to Joan?"

She frowned. "She died—about ten years ago. There are only David and I left. I was still in Ireland then—and my husband was very ill—and I never quite understood about Joan. She became —well, she was rather unbalanced and queer and had to stop teaching—and used to take a lot of things to make her sleep. But," she added rather defiantly, "they said it was her heart in the end. More tea?"

"Thank you," I said politely. I might have been wrong but it did seem to me that we were meeting on those terms: two strangers really who happened to have had once some common friends and acquaintances—oh, long ago. "Did you ever go back to Bruddersford?"

"No. Did you?"

"No. I was in London some time and then went to America and came back during the war. But I've just met the Nixeys— you remember them?—and they set me thinking about Bruddersford."

"Yes, Miss Earl told me that." And it was as if she had been told I had started collecting Roman coins or Chinese porcelain or had taken up salmon fishing. I took my cup, and then passed her a plate of cakes.

"Tell me, Bridget," I said, trying to sound a little more intimate, "what's been happening to you?"

Her story, which came out as a series of replies to questions I had to put to her, didn't surprise me. I think I could have guessed most of it. The marriage to Connally wasn't much good—though she didn't say so—and he was clearly an extravagant and shiftless fellow, who was an invalid for several years before he died, which was sometime about 1936. They had three children: Michael, who was still in Ireland, in an estate office; Sheila the violinist; and John, who was now in the sixth form at St. Paul's, doing very well and, I gathered, a protégé of his famous Uncle David. Bridget, it was clear, had kept the family going, by playing in orchestras, giving lessons, and cooking and mending and nursing and generally mothering at all hours. After the worst of the bombing was over, and with some help from David, she had come to London for the sake of Sheila and John, who had to have their chance.

"They sound a fine pair," I said. And I couldn't help feeling that if Sheila and John had been there I might really have had another glimpse of Bridget Alington.

"Oh, they are," she cried, and told me more about them and what the maestros and critics had said about Sheila's playing and what David and his masters thought about John. Once or twice there was the old green flash in her eyes, and she was Bridget again. But not for long.

"Well, you're right to be proud of them," I said. "And you've had a tough time and come through." And I wondered where Elizabeth was and what she imagined we were saying. Probably she saw us in each other's arms, sobbing above a forgotten and shattered tea-table. With some swell incidental music dubbed into the sound track. Liz from Hollywood!

"Yes, it's been hard at times," she said with a touch—a justifiable touch—of complacency, "but I think we're through the worst of it. I still give lessons, but I don't play any more. Of course I never could play like Sheila. Sometimes when John's in a silly mood, he reminds me of Oliver—you remember Oliver?"

"Yes, I remember Oliver." Then I risked it. "I was thinking, the other night, about the evening you and Oliver and I spent at the Leatons'—you remember the queer lanky chap who played the piano—and how we came back in the moonlight, talking nonsense." And I smiled reminiscently.

She smiled too, in a small polite way, but her eyes looked blank. "It's such a long time ago, and so much has happened since then. But I remember we did all talk a lot of nonsense, just as the children do now sometimes. You're not married are you?"

I offered her a cigarette, and to my surprise she took it. After that we looked cosier, even if we weren't. "No, I'm not married. Somehow I've never got round to it."

"You talk like an American," she said, staring at me reprovingly.

"I picked it up over there." I made this a statement and not an apology. "And even here we film people often talk like Americans. It makes us feel that our pictures will probably play to more money."

"I don't see that."

"Don't bother about it," I said hastily. "Just a joke."

"I don't often go to see films," she announced.

"I don't blame you."

"Michael—my elder boy—thought once of trying to act in films. He's like his father—tall and very dark—and good-looking. More Irish than the other two. He didn't believe in the war at all."

"What did he believe in?" I asked sharply, having taken a dislike to handsome young Michael from the first. "Dachau and Belsen? All right, let's not talk about it." Then I plunged in. "Two nights ago I was talking to the Nixeys—now Lord and Lady Harndean—about that Sunday evening when your father was ill and they called, and you came down and told them what you thought about them. Don't tell me you've forgotten that."

"No, I haven't. But I can't imagine why you think it's worth bothering about now. Why, I was younger than Sheila is, and not much older than my John."

"I have an idea that doesn't matter," I said. "But why I mentioned it is that Eleanor Nixey told me something that surprised me. She didn't take Ben Kerry away from Eva out of devilment, as we thought. She was madly in love with him."

"Was she? From what I remember of her, she couldn't have been madly in love with anybody except herself."

"I think she was telling me the truth. I'd given her a jolt or two. You see, Joan told me—that time when we met in 1919 —that Eva hadn't fallen down Pikeley Scar by accident but had deliberately thrown herself off that ledge."

"Oh rubbish!" she cried contemptuously. "Joan would say anything, if she felt like it and wanted to attract your attention. You never understood what Joan was really like. In fact, I don't think you really understood any of us. We often used to laugh at you—I don't mean we disliked you or anything like that—but I suppose because you were a lonely boy and rather sentimental and romantic, and enjoyed making things up—because you wanted to be a writer, I imagine, you never saw us as we really were. That's one reason—" And she stopped abruptly.

"One reason what?" I demanded.

"Well, you wrote to me once, after you'd joined the army, and I didn't reply. And that's one reason why I didn't. I've just remembered, though I haven't given it a thought for years and years. I've had too much to do to bother about what happened when I was still in my teens and didn't really know anything." And the glance she gave me suggested that if I was a sensible man of my age, I wouldn't be bothering either but would be telling her now how well my son had done in the Air Force and how my daughter was working for a Girton scholarship.

"Well, Bridget," I said, probably with some heat, because I was annoyed, "you may be right. I knew nothing about you then. I'm wasting my time now. That's it, isn't it? But my guess is as good as yours—and it might possibly be better, just because I've had a little time to waste thinking about the past. And I think that what you were then and all that happened to you then have made you what you are now. Same with me, of course. At some point, probably about the time Oliver was killed and your father died, you stopped looking back because you daren't look back—it was all a ruin. Then you married a man who—and you knew this instinctively—would soon throw the whole burden on to you. And the fact that he came from another island, even rummer than this one, probably helped too. You gave yourself a grand obstacle race, with a devoted happy family as the prize. And you might remember, next time you want to say that you've too much to do to bother about what happened when you were in your teens, that your Sheila and John are living in much the same sort of world I've been trying to recall—"

"No, they're not," she cried. "It's quite different."

"Yes," I said, "it is different. But if you don't remember the other one, you won't even know where the difference lies."

She gave me an angry look, pushed back the settee, and stood up. "I don't understand what you mean, and I think it's silly arguing like this when it's over thirty years since we last met. We don't really know each other. I'm quite different now, naturally."

"Naturally," I murmured.

"I'm not sure you are," she went on, more amiably and with a certain maternal condescension that came easily to her. "I think you're still just making things up. Probably, being a writer, you can't help it."

"There may be something in that," I told her rather wearily.

And then Elizabeth sailed in, a galleon from the Golden West. "You're not going, Mrs. Connally?"

"Yes, I must," said Bridget, a shabby little middle-aged woman again, awkward, defiant. "I said I couldn't stay very long. I ought to have gone earlier—it takes such a time to get to Ealing. Thank you for the tea, Miss Earl. And good-bye—er—Gregory."

I was still standing in the middle of the room when Elizabeth returned. "Well?" she cried gaily. "Sit down, darling, and let's talk."

"No."

"You're furious with me, aren't you?"

I looked at her. "No. Though it was a damned silly scheme, Liz. And I'm surprised she accepted your invitation."

"She wasn't very keen to come. And I have a sort of idea," Liz continued, sparkling mischievously, "that the chief reason why she did come was that she wanted to be able to tell her daughter what a film star was like at close quarters. I may be wrong, but I fancy that came into it."

"I should think you're quite right. Sheila and John will have it for supper tonight. Well, Liz, I must go."

"No, don't. There are some people coming in for a drink and then we're dining somewhere, but they're mostly people you probably know, so why not stay? It'll do you good, Greg. I see now you're not furious—you're just depressed."

"That's nearer. And I don't want to stay, Liz. I'm not in the mood for some bright chat about our celluloid dream trade, and besides I want to re-write a scene later tonight."

"I see. Well, you're going to have one drink. Don't move—though I'd rather you sat down."

But I didn't. I stood there, rather mulishly, and slowly filled a pipe. Elizabeth came up with a large whisky. "Now drink that." And then she kissed me lightly on the cheek, sank gracefully into a chair, and looked at me with bright expectant eyes. "It must have been most peculiar meeting her again after all this time. Tell me."

"This was your idea, Liz, not mine. Of course she wasn't at all like the Bridget Alington I remembered. Some people probably don't change much, but she's quite different. And I'm not sure it just happened—that there was no choice about it—though of course for a long time now she's been one of those tigresses at bay in a cave with their cubs. They're all brave devoted women, I suppose, but I've always had my doubts about 'em, even from the point of view of their children."

"Still, you talked about your distant past—eh?"

"No, that didn't work. She wasn't interested. Nice of you to take the trouble, Liz. I must go."

"Just a minute, Greg." She came towards me, no longer looking triumphant or mischievous but grave and concerned. "I don't like you going like this. You're miserably disappointed, aren't you?"

I considered this carefully for a moment or two. "No, I'm not. I just happen to feel flat—empty—at a dead end."

"A dead end of what?"

"No, Liz—sorry. But there are too many different things mixed up in this—it's more complicated than you think—so let's leave it now. I'll see you tomorrow at Brent's party."

It was only quarter to six and I didn't want to go to my flat. That scene I had to re-write could wait until after dinner or if necessary until the morning. A bus took me down Park Lane and along the Green Park end of Piccadilly, and then I walked as far as the Hippodrome, went up Charing Cross Road, and then at Cambridge Circus I turned down Shaftesbury Avenue. I did this with some vague idea of seeing a play or a film, but there didn't seem to be anything new I wanted to see. The early evening crowds were swarming, especially along Coventry Street. London looked horrible, like the shabbier side of some third-rate American city. What were once decent shops were now bogus wine stores, fun fairs, and places selling shoddy knick-knacks and pornographic drivel. Half the women looked like cheap tarts and the men like Black Market touts. There was neither dignity nor genuine high spirits. The atmosphere wasn't English, wasn't Continental, wasn't honestly American: it was a dreadful rancid stew, the combined swill of war factories, Yank camps, stuffy little flats, bad-tempered or bewildered suburban homes: it was a hellish huddle of nasty trading, of tired pleasure-seeking, of entertainment without art, of sex without passion and joy, of life buzzing and swarming without hope and vision. London could take it. But how much more of this could it take?

And how much more could I take? After turning away from all the lighted vestibules and the box offices, walking towards my club, where I might dine later, I realised that I felt finished and done for, hands and feet touching the wall at the dead end. I had gone back to my youth, to the Alingtons and Bruddersford, on some daft treasure hunt that I'd never really understood, and had come out empty-handed. I had drifted away from Elizabeth. I didn't want Hollywood, didn't want Brent; although the only thing I could do was to write and help to produce films, for I had no illusions about turning novelist or playwright again after all these years. From now on, it seemed, I didn't know where to go to work or even—assuming I needed a rest—where to go to play. I'd had bad times before, been broke in London and in New York and out with everybody in Hollywood, but always before there had been plans humming in my head and glimmers from landing-fields and harbours in the future. But now—nothing; nothing inside or out, here or somewhere else, now or next Christmas. Although I was on my way to the club and might soon have a drink there and order dinner and make conversational noises with the rest of them, nevertheless, as a real man, as a planning, struggling, hoping, loving human being—I was dead.

And I was still dead, perhaps even a bit deader, the following afternoon, when I haunted Brent's cocktail party for Elizabeth at Claridges. The large room there on the ground floor was crowded with representatives of the British film industry and the press, together with some of those people who are invited to everything, although nobody knows why. Golden and amber streams of Martinis and sherry and whisky were cascading down distinguished or useful gullets. Jake West, almost sober, was sweating with triumph. Brent, who loves this kind of thing, was behaving as if the notion of giving a cocktail party had just been thought of for the first time in his office that morning. I saw George Adony, amorous but pessimistic, muttering darkly to a tall fair girl who looked like a consumptive somnambulist. I saw everybody, and felt I never wanted to see any of them again. Except Elizabeth, of course, who was queening it magnificently in black with a glitter of diamonds. But even the few moments I had alone with her were melancholy.

"'Hopeless to try to talk here, of course, Greg," she gabbled. "I'll be taken away in a minute. And I know I sound rather tight but actually I've only had one tiny drink. It's the people who do it."

"I know. I wish they did it to me," I said. "I find they have quite a different effect."

She ignored this; probably didn't hear me. The old ghost would have to start howling and clanking chains. "But I did want to tell you, darling," Elizabeth continued at full speed, "that Brent sent round the final sequences for me to read at lunch-time. And, Greg, you're marvellous—you really are. You know just what I can do, and everything's just right and there needn't be any arguing. You don't know what a relief that is. I've done nothing but argue and argue about scripts since you left Hollywood. But this one's perfect. I am grateful." And she meant it, every word, even though it did sound like an actress talking at a cocktail party. There was a real warmth behind the trite professional phrases and in the velvety look she gave me.

While I mumbled some sort of reply I was wondering

whether to say: "Look, Liz, I feel empty and miserable and bang up against a blank wall. You don't owe me any kindness, not after what's happened between us lately, but I need some. Walk straight out of here with me—and then let us talk quietly." And I have often asked myself since what she would have done, and, if we had walked out together, what would have happened to us afterwards. But I didn't say it.

"Don't go, Greg," she said hastily. "You look as if you want to put your head down and charge out. But most of them will have gone soon, and Brent and I and one or two more people are dining here—"

"And you're invited," said Brent, who arrived at that moment, smiling and proprietorial. "Now don't say no. Elizabeth, there are some nice people here who are clamouring to be introduced—"

"You pop off, Liz," I said. "I'm going. And I'm glad you like the script."

"Greg," she said. And then we looked at each other for a moment, and Brent and his party, just for this one moment, weren't there. And it was good-bye, and we both knew it. One of us was waving from the ship's rail and the other from the receding quay. Then I smiled at her—or at least I hope I did, for I tried hard enough—and turned away, my heart a lump of lead. I heard her exclaim sharply but then Brent cut in with something easy and reassuring and I heard her laughing as she moved away with him. But she knew what had happened.

"Sorry!" I muttered as I bumped into somebody near the doorway.

"Dawson, you're just the chap I'm looking for," he said.

I was staring at the mechanical little smile and the restless empty eyes of Malcolm Nixey, Baron of Harndean or whatever it was. I made a noise that was a kind of truncated laugh.

"So you're here, are you?" I said.

"Got a card from that fellow West," he said. "Eleanor's in there somewhere." For now we were moving into the corridor. "But you're the man I want. Tried to get you on the telephone earlier but I couldn't."

"Let's go down there," I suggested. And then when we had

nearly reached the main entrance of the hotel and we had a quiet space to ourselves, I stopped and looked enquiringly at him. "What is it?" I said. "Apart from its being a nice pattern."

"Pattern?" And he stared.

"Don't bother about that. I'm just rambling. That's what these parties do to me."

"Yes, don't care for 'em myself these days. But Eleanor enjoys 'em—you know."

I said I did know. What I didn't say was that the sight of him at the Tralorna hotel had set me diving and groping into the past, that I had come out empty-handed and empty-hearted and was neither my old familiar self nor yet a new one, and that if he couldn't perform a miracle, if only for the pattern's sake, then he was nothing but the last flick of irony.

"But why were you looking for me?" I asked him.

TWELVE

"I'm on a committee," Harndean began. "It got going in the war—the Ministry of Labour set it up to deal with conditions of women's employment—and I've been meaning to resign from it. But I attended a meeting yesterday, and I was talking to a woman there—a Mrs. Childs—who represents some of the big women's trade unions. She's one of those personnel experts —and the usual hard-bitten Socialist type. Well, this Mrs. Childs was asking me if I knew any film people, and so I told her I'd just been meeting some down in Cornwall, and I mentioned your name and said you were a first-class fellow who'd worked in Hollywood and all that sort of thing. Then she said at once —all excited, you know how these women are—that I must put her in touch with you. I said I didn't know your address or anything but that I might be running across you—and so she gave me this." And he handed me a card with a telephone number scribbled across it. "Would you give her a ring, soon as possible, at that number."

"I see." I put the card in my pocket. "Well—thanks. And I'm sorry you've had so much trouble."

"Not at all, Dawson. I must go back and find my wife. Hope you'll dine with us one night." And he trotted off.

It was still too early for the dinner crowd and the place was fairly quiet. I sat down in one of those chairs facing the entrance, feeling that I didn't want to go across for my hat and coat before I knew what I was going to do with myself. I forgot about Harndean and his Mrs. Childs; I thought about Elizabeth. I could see that widening space of mist and tide between us. She was beautiful and kind and a great star in the only sky that would ever drop manna on me; she had been my friend for years, and we could earn fortunes together and laugh while we were doing it, and she had been ready to be more than a friend; and I had given her up—for what? To sit and wonder what the hell to do next. As if I'd been thrown out of that party and hadn't walked out of it. I'd jeered at Bridget, but Bridget was now busy as a bee shaping and colouring the evening for her Sheila and John, and delighted to be so engrossed. And what was I doing? Even Lord Malcolm Nixey Harndean, whom I'd denounced to myself as a fellow who'd never lived at all, at least could attend committees and trot his wife to and from cocktail parties. I pulled out the card he'd given me and glanced idly at it. Probably the woman had a niece in the Burnley Amateur Dramatic Society who only needed a chance to be just as good as Elizabeth Earl or any of those other film stars. Or she thought that something that happened to her brother once in New Zealand would make a wonderful scenario. And I never could have cared less. My fingers closed round the card and, as if they had their own anger, tore it in two. And then, perhaps because that bit of anger had been released and I felt better, I put the card together again, and made sure of the number as I walked along to the telephone desk.

"Mrs. Childs speaking." This was a business-like woman, and she had a crisp voice and a slight North Country accent—an unusual combination.

"I'm Gregory Dawson. Lord Harndean has just told me you wanted to talk to me. Something about films."

Business-like, crisp, North Country, she might be, but there was some suggestion of excitement at her end of the line. "Oh yes, I do. It's really very important. I'm so glad you've rung up."

"What's it about?" I demanded. "Because I must warn you that if you've got a beautiful niece who wants to be a film star—"

Her laugh cut me short. "No, it's nothing like that. No beautiful nieces. We're discussing the formation of a new film group, quite a big thing. I've got some film people, mostly keen young technicians, coming here tonight for an informal meeting. Could you possibly join us, Mr. Dawson?"

"Well, I don't know," I replied dubiously. I could see these youngsters—baby wizards of the documentaries, assistant camera men and cutters, and an untidy script girl or two—all sitting on the floor and telling one another how to make a smashing Left Wing film for fourpence. "I'm a cynical old motion picture hack, you know. And I doubt—"

"No, I know about you," she said. "And you're just the person we need. Do come and talk to us—please."

Well, it seemed that somebody wanted me somewhere, if only for a bit of nonsense. So I said I would look in; and she gave me an address in Hanover Square—thank heaven!—instead of Golders Green or Blackheath. It meant that when I had had enough of their vague planning I could walk home from there in a few minutes, and wouldn't have to linger on hoping for transport.

Eight o'clock was the time she had suggested, but it must have been about half-past when I arrived in Hanover Square. Mrs. Childs appeared to be a compact woman about forty with reddish hair and a rather heavy face; but I had no chance of taking a good look at her because she hurried me into her sitting-room, which was filled with smoke and with youngsters of the type I had imagined would be there, all sprawling around and arguing and guffawing. And at the sight and sound of this foggy monkey-house I cannot say my heart leapt up. However, I recognised one of the noisiest talkers, a very useful and enthusiastic lad called Hinchcliff, who had been working for Brent as chief cutter. He bounded up and shook my hand.

"Now look who's here," he shouted. "Quiet, everybody! George—Hilda—turn it up. This is Gregory Dawson, and this is just the bloke you wanted, Mrs. Childs. Tell him how far we've got."

I was given the largest chair, though there were still two fierce young women perched on the arms of it; and for the next twenty minutes I sat back and listened. Mrs. Childs and young Hinchcliff did most of the talking, though there were interjections and little elaborations from a few of the others. What I heard brought me an agreeable surprise. So far as it went it was sound sense, and was a nice change from what I'd heard so often from Brent and Adony and Leo Blatt and the rest of them. Mrs. Childs, who was as crisp and business-like as she had appeared to be on the telephone, explained that she and others in the trade union movement were worried about the kind of films their people saw—and paid for with their shillings at the box office. The outlook and values of most of these films, she

said, were all wrong. They didn't want films to be so much political and economic propaganda, but they did feel that the screen
should show how real people behaved in a real world. If a new
producing unit was organised, ready to work along these lines,
the necessary capital would be forthcoming, and certain of the
unions would put all their weight behind the task of distributing
its films. Hinchcliff said that a great many of the best younger
technicians were tired of helping to produce mischievous nonsense and he could guarantee more than an adequate staff of
good camera men, sound men, cutters and the rest. No new
studio could be built for some time, but he understood that
the Government was about to de-requisition the old Willesden
studio, and he and Hilda and Ted had sneaked in to have another
look at the set-up and though it was rather out-of-date and
smallish, it would do, if everybody used their heads, until there
was a chance of building again. And he called on Ted to give his
report on equipment, which of course presented a tricky prob-
lem. Ted was a huge youth in a dark blue sweater and a beard,
who looked more like a fisherman than a film technician, except
that film technicians always look like something else. He read
out his report on equipment, and a very sensible little summary
it was, even though he blushed and stammered when a high-
spirited damsel, who was apparently with us in the character
of a Spanish gipsy, chaffed him from her smoky corner. Then
about half a dozen youngsters began talking at once, but they
were silenced by Mrs. Childs and Hinchcliff, who turned to me.

I talked first about the two awkward problems: finding reasonably good equipment when even the big rich studios were
still short of it, and obtaining adequate distribution outside the
two powerful combines; and then I came to my own angle. "I'm
a writer, although I've been an associate producer and director
in my time. And I naturally take the writer's point of view. Any
other writers here?" At this the fierce girl sitting on the left arm
of my chair announced firmly and proudly that she was, and was
promptly cheered by two of her boy friends across the room.
Mrs. Childs gave me a grin that lit up her rather heavy face at
once, and I was troubled by some obscure recollection that I had
to dismiss. "Well, I'll talk for both of us, shall I?" I said to the

fierce girl, who nodded violently and nearly fell across my knees. "Now I've argued for years that the basis of good film-making is first a soundly constructed story—for if the story's bad then all the acting and directing and fancy camera work in the world won't amount to anything—and then an absolutely fool-proof shooting-script that doesn't waste time and money." And I gave them some instances, both from British and American studios, and couldn't help feeling pleased when they all listened eagerly and enthusiastically agreed with me. "If you can get this unit into production," I continued, "obviously you'll have to work economically at first. Now some costs are just there, and there's nothing to be done about 'em. Skimping them is fatal. But huge packets of money are always being thrown away simply because a bunch of people, who are responsible for the finance, don't know what they want but insist upon wanting it, often finally make do with a poor story, and then go into production with a shooting script that's never been planned to the last detail. You people know how it is, eh?" They did, most vociferously; and Mrs. Childs grinned again, and once more disturbed me.

After insisting upon the importance of a first-class scenario department, to be given full cabinet rank in the government of the unit, I warned them against throwing out what was good in the Hollywood A pictures as well as what was bad. "That's a mistake that's been made before. Hollywood values—all right, get rid of 'em. But Hollywood technique—with entertainment if possible all the way, smooth continuity, no suggestion of the-atre about the small character parts, a glossy finish on the job, and visuals and sound that'll stand up to poor projectors in small town theatres probably using worn prints—don't try to throw any of that away, get as much of it as you can, until you've found something better. And now about finance." That set us going. Most of their estimated costs for feature pictures, using a name or two in the cast, were much too low, even when all allowance was made for sensible economical methods of production; and I had to argue with them, finding myself hemmed in and almost suffocated by these vehement youngsters. But some of them had bright ideas, new to me and very useful, as to how time and money could be saved in their own particular departments.

While we were still exchanging these ideas Mrs. Childs and two of the girls arrived with beer and coffee and cake.

Hinchcliff took me on one side. "They'll be all going soon. Can you hang on? I want to have a little talk with you, and so does Mrs. Childs. Okay?"

I said it was, but I added that I saw no signs of the party—and it looked like a party now—breaking up. He winked and said that he and Mrs. Childs, who knew all the tricks, would look after that. And after about a quarter of an hour or so, during which I talked to the fierce girls and the Spanish Gipsy and Fisherman Ted, the two dispersers went into action, amiably but effectively. Ten minutes later there were only the three of us left, and I found myself opening windows to clear the air while Hinchcliff and our hostess rushed cups and glasses into the kitchen. I had a chance now to take in the room, which had a few nice little water-colours above the low open bookshelves; and I liked the look of it. The next thing to do, I decided, was to form some definite impression of its owner, who, apart from that sudden grin which seemed to disturb me, still remained a rather vague figure, though she was obviously anything but a vague type of woman. Then the three of us sat round the fire, with that sense of release and intimacy which almost always follows the departure of a crowd.

Hinchcliff turned to me. "I heard this morning you've just turned down a big offer to go back to Hollywood."

"Yes, I have."

"Is Elizabeth Earl staying on here after she's done your picture?"

I raised my eyebrows at him. "I've no idea, Hinchcliff. But I should think it's very unlikely. She's still under contract over there, and Brent only borrowed her for this one job. Why?"

"I just wondered," he said. He didn't exchange any glances with Mrs. Childs. "Are you going on with Brent?"

"He wants me to, and I haven't told him I'm not. But as a matter of fact I'm not going on with him."

"Look—I hope you don't mind my asking—but what are you going to do?"

"No, I don't mind. And the answer is—I don't know what I'm

going to do. I only know what I'm not going to do. It's like that."

"Is there any particular reason?" This was from Mrs. Childs, speaking quietly from the depths of her chair.

"No, I don't think there is," I said slowly. "Except that I've been at it a long time—and I'm feeling bored and rather stale. I've been down in the country—working hard on a script—and thinking about myself."

"Go on," she said to Hinchcliff, who gave a quick glance at his watch, jumped up, and then stood over me.

"Why don't you come in with us?" he said eagerly. "You'd make all the difference. You've had just the experience the rest of us haven't had. Let's make some real pictures. I know we can't offer you anything like the money—"

"Never mind about the money," I told him, cutting in. "It only annoys me, anyhow, paying out most of it in taxes. And I've nobody but myself to keep. So leave out the money. What have you to offer?"

"A seat on the board," said Mrs. Childs.

"Write—show other people how to write—produce—find some directors—some new stars—do whatever you've wanted to do before, and do it in the right way," cried Hinchcliff. "I'll have to go—I'm living out at Harrow and I promised not to be late. You talk to him, Mrs. Childs. Give him the works. No, don't move—I'm off."

We heard two doors slam and then exchanged uncertain smiles across the silence that followed.

"You must be tired," I said, turning in my chair to suggest that if necessary I was ready to go too.

"I'm tired of listening and talking to a roomful of people," she said. "I've had three lots today. But I'm not sleepy, if that's what you mean. Actually it's quite early. You didn't have any beer or coffee, did you? Neither did I. Wouldn't you like some tea? I haven't any whisky. Tea? I left a kettle on."

While she was in the kitchen I began trying to decide what to say first to her. My mind was untidy, uncertain, confused. But I was alive again, and very much alive.

When she came back with the tea-things I had my first long look at her. She wasn't pretty at all, couldn't even vaguely be called handsome; but there might be times when people who knew her well would think her beautiful, not as Elizabeth with her exquisite golden mask, the dream creature shining in the dark, was beautiful, but in a strong plain fashion, rich in thought and experience, daily bread and weather. For a moment or two she returned my stare, a half-defiant gleam in her darkish amber eyes, as if to say: "Well, here I am. Think what you like." But what she actually did then was to switch off the top light, leaving us with one standard lamp, on her side of the fireplace, cosily illuminating us.

"Lord Harndean," she began, as she passed me a cup of tea, "said he'd probably meet you at a grand film cocktail party at Claridges, and Hinchcliff also said you'd probably be there earlier this evening. I was wondering what you'd think of this noisy gang here after that."

"I'll tell you." But I took a sip or two of tea and then carefully put down my cup, giving myself time to think. "To begin with, I'm tired of those studio publicity department's parties—I've had too many of 'em. They're not work and they're not fun, but something in between that doesn't matter. As for your gang here—well, rather to my surprise, I liked being with them. Of course I've met some of these youngsters in the studios—they're nothing new—but tonight I met them in a different way, all in a bunch, with their bosses well out of sight and hearing, ready to speak their minds, eager to get on with something worth doing and at the same time enjoying one another's company. And I not only liked it, but also it did me a lot of good." There I stopped, feeling that I was talking too much.

"Go on. Tell me," she said softly.

"It made me realise that although these youngsters are probably different from what I was at their age—and I'm thinking now particularly of the younger ones, the mere kids—yet something—oh!—a mixture of eagerness and warmth, enthusiasm and companionship—that I thought had gone is still about if we know where to look for it. But you don't want all this stuff."

"Yes, I do. You forget I have to persuade you to join us—you heard what Hinchcliff said. Important business, you see—part of my job."

"I see. But you're working late, aren't you? Long past good union hours."

She laughed. "But I want to know anyhow. What you said earlier—to Hinchcliff—about refusing all these grand offers and feeling bored and rather stale—and I think you meant even more than you said—well, naturally that made me curious. So, if you don't mind my saying so, I've been wondering what's been happening to you."

"So have I. You won't think it amounts to very much. But down there in Cornwall, where I've been working, I ran into some people I once knew years ago, and I began remembering —often very vividly and not always quite coolly—my life in my late teens, just before World War One." She made a sudden movement but checked herself; and, anxious to get on and be done with it, I continued with some haste: "This going back didn't do me any good. No, of course, why should it? I came to a kind of dead end, even though there were one or two surprises. And then it was a dead end, so to speak, all round. Probably I'd really been feeling stale and dissatisfied for some time, but these midnight returns to the past took the colour and flavour out of my present. I didn't want to go on with the same jobs. I didn't want to work with the same people. And it even made a hash of a very genuine personal relationship—"

"Elizabeth Earl?"

"Hell's bells!" I cried. "Does everybody know everything that happens in the film world?"

She laughed. "I hardly know about anything that happens there. But this was an easy guess. Both Harndean and Hinchcliff told me that you and she were great friends and that this party was being given for her. Well, seeing that you left the party early, obviously didn't like it, and don't want to go on working with these people, and then said that about a personal relation-ship—"

"Yes, it wasn't a hard guess. Well, that's how it's been— though it probably sounds a lot of nonsense to you—and that's why I said it had done me good coming here. For the last two days I've been feeling like a weary old ghost. And I rang you up, after walking out of that party, not because I imagined for a moment that you'd say anything I wanted to hear about films, but because I was wondering what on earth to do with myself."

She nodded, looked curiously at me for a moment, not smiling but with an air of grave kindness, and then went across the room and took a picture off the wall. She held it under the lamp and I joined her there. And then I stared through a little window at another world, at a bright morning lost for ever, until tears blurred my eyes. For this was the very water-colour sketch that Stanley Mervin showed Jock and me in the pub at Bulsden, on the morning of that Sunday when the Nixeys first arrived: here were the glinting stream, the stone arch of the bridge in morning sunlight, the moor and the hills.

"He showed it to Jock and me in the *White Horse*," I cried. "He'd just done it that morning. And he said: 'Ah've been out since early on 'aving a go at that little bridge at Broadstone Beck End. An' if Ah've had one try at that little beggar Ah've had a dozen. Never could get bloody tone right. But Ah think Ah've got it this time,' he said. And I told him it was a little miracle. And it is—it is. It's all that's left of that great gold Maytime—and Jock striding like an Indian—and the hot Sunday noon in Bulsden and the dark cool bar of the pub—and old Mervin grinning over his pint—and the Alingtons at their cottage, Eva and Joan and Bridget, and the cricket we played on the green—another world and another time; and now all gone, lost, forgotten."

I was back in my chair now, looking towards the fire but not seeing it.

"You've not forgotten," she said. She must have followed me, and was now standing near the fireplace and was looking hard at me. I found myself wishing she would look somewhere else. "And it's the same world," she continued in a quiet level tone. "Even the little bridge is still there. I saw it last summer. But you must stop going back like that—it's the wrong way. I felt like you when I lost my husband ten years ago. We'd been very happy together, and it was for such a little time—and I said, 'Lost, lost, lost—everything gone, everything lost' until I made myself stop, made myself realise that life goes on—and if people die and things change, that's all part of it—and that the worst thing to do is to turn your face away and hold yourself rigid and not let life go flowing through you. Do you see what I mean, Gregory?" She checked her eager rush of words, and then added in a very different tone: "Your name slipped out like that because I knew you once, a long time ago. You won't remember."

"You can't say that. I'm the one who does remember. And from the very first," I told her, "there was something about your eyes and that sudden grin you gave me that set me wondering. I know now. You were Laura Blackshaw, weren't you?"

"I was only ten," she cried, "and you never saw me again after that dreadful Sunday at Pikeley Scar. I never imagined you'd remember me." She held out both hands and I took them and we did an extra-long double handshake, smiling at each other. And she seemed to me to look quite different now from the woman who let me into that flat, altogether lighter and more vivid. "I used to follow you around at Silverdale in the most shameless manner. I must have been a little pest, but you were very kind in a rather lordly way. And then I insisted upon you taking me with you to Pikeley Scar. That horrible ghastly hot Sunday. Though I can remember now how happy I was going with you and your friend Jock in the train. But I think it took me years to get over the rest of it." And she sat down and began staring at the fire.

"I'm sorry," I said. "It was a miserable business for a child to be mixed up in—all that screaming and confusion. I remember thinking when I took you home—"

"You were sweet to me," she cried, smiling at me now. "Wonderful for a boy of—what?—eighteen? I adored you for years afterwards."

"Well, I remember thinking then you'd had a bad shock. It's all been much in my mind lately." And then I told her how I remembered meeting Joan in '19, when Joan insisted, in a queer hysterical fashion, upon telling me that Eva had really committed suicide. "And the funny thing is," I continued, "that only yesterday I met Bridget—you remember Bridget?—and when I told her what Joan had said she jumped on it at once, full of scorn, and said that Joan would say anything."

"What became of that one—Joan?" asked Laura in a rather odd cautious way.

"Bridget told me she died some years ago. Went off her head,

I gathered. She was a bit unbalanced even in '19 when I met her."

"What's Bridget like now?"

I told her a little about Bridget, and then added: "We were really strangers who didn't particularly take to each other. It was a silly idea our meeting, but it wasn't my idea—nor hers. Somebody else thought of it."

Laura nodded, and, to my relief, didn't ask whose idea it had been. She merely observed: "I'm not sure it was a silly idea."

We were both looking at each other, I fancy, in the same way—half-smiling, half-curious. She was on the point of saying something, but checked herself. I raised my eyebrows at her. She smiled and shook her head. The fire hissed softly. A dance band on the radio in a neighbouring flat came thud-thud-thudding through the walls. I think we both had a sense of heaviness and slow motion and waiting.

"Well, Laura," I said, breaking the spell, "I'm wondering why you asked me about the Alingtons. There's something. What is it?"

"I'm past forty now," she said slowly, "and I was only ten then. It's hard to believe it could matter all this time. But it does. I suppose it's because I bottled it up, pretended to forget it, for so long."

"Do you mean—something that happened that day at Pikeley Scar?"

"Yes, and it's something I've never told anybody. But you've been thinking about that time, and it was you who looked after me and comforted me then, and now I feel I ought to tell you."

And then I seemed to see an extraordinary thing. It was almost as if I were back on that little train returning from Pikeley to Wabley station, and was glancing apprehensively at the silent frightened child. I felt that the release of some secret deep feeling of horror, long buried away, had temporarily cancelled all the years between, so that the face of this woman wore the frozen look of the child. And my heart went out to her.

"You see, after it happened," she was saying, "nobody noticed me or asked me any questions. And I was too terrified to say anything. But, you remember, I'd wandered away from you and

Bridget, chiefly because I felt you didn't want me with you, and where I was I could see those two girls, Eva and Joan, on that ledge. I could even hear their voices, although I couldn't tell what they were saying. But they began quarrelling, and I watched them. Eva slapped Joan's face, and then Joan flew at her. And then—oh I tried so hard to pretend that I hadn't seen it, that somehow I'd just made it up; but I *did* see it—Joan pushed her off the ledge."

"So that's what really happened?"

"Yes." The tears rolled down her cheeks, and she exclaimed in annoyance at them. But as I went across to her I felt that the child Laura, who had never shed a tear that afternoon until she remembered, walking up from the station, her lost little haversack, had returned for a moment to dissolve away at last her horror and pity.

"I'm sorry," she said. "I didn't think I'd be so stupid. But I can't help it."

"Oh—blast the Alingtons!" I cried, standing over her and wondering how to comfort her. "Joan must always have been a bit mad anyhow. Well, you've told me and you're rid of it. All over and done with, Laura. So let's forget it all—and march on."

She turned away for a moment, then came up, smiling. I had stepped back, and now we were facing each other across the fireplace. "I was saying something like that to you a few minutes ago," she murmured.

"Well, that's how it is. People have to keep on saying these sensible things to each other. Sometimes it's your turn, sometimes it's mine." I waited in the hope she would reply to this, but she didn't, although she still looked at me expectantly. I grinned. "Even my old office chum, Malcolm Nixey—your Lord Harndean—has his moments."

She laughed, and I knew then that she and I wouldn't differ much about his lordship. "Why do you say that?"

"One day, if you want me to, I'll try to explain the whole thing. But—let us say—I found myself up against a great black wall. All right, probably I'd spent years secretly building it, just quietly walling myself in, but it wasn't until I recognised Malcolm Nixey at that hotel in Cornwall that I began running round in the dark and became aware of that wall. And then, this evening, just when I'd decided there wasn't even a peephole in the wall, Harndean popped up, said you wanted to talk to me, and gave me a card with your telephone number on it."

I was staring down at the fire now, wondering whether I'd said enough. But she murmured something that suggested I ought to go on.

"That card was a crack in the wall," I continued, warming up. "And for the last two hours the crack's been widening and widening, with more and more light streaming through, and I know now there's a world on the other side. It's not as secure and cosy as the one I'd been remembering—it's a bit hungry and tattered and bomb-dazed—but if I could live and work in it properly I might soon find it the same rich warm world."

I looked at her and saw that she was frowning, and I thought that what I had said was distasteful to her.

"I mean it," I told her, "although it may sound to you rather corny. I've written so much screen hokum—"

"Then stop it," she flashed out, quite angrily. I might have known she'd have a temper, but this was the first glimpse I'd had of it. And there was nothing heavy about her now. "If there's one thing I'm tired of and despise and detest—it's the attitude of people who deliberately do work that brings them plenty of money and easy living and privileges, but who are elaborately bitter about it all in private to prove how superior and noble they really are. Socialists who write Tory columns. Working-class leaders who forget their origins until they've had some drinks late at night. Soulful women who run rackets for the smarties. Writers—"

"Yes, yes, Laura, I've got it," I said, cutting in firmly enough but speaking quite coolly. "You're right to feel so exasperated, although it's not so simple as you think. I mean, there's more drift and less decision."

"Yes, I can see there might be," she said. "And that's something else you can explain. But not tonight," she added quickly.

"No, not tonight. And I'm going. You're tired. But seeing that lovely little water-colour of old Stanley Mervin's—by the way, how did you come across it?"

"Mrs. Mervin gave it to me. When I was at college I used to go and stay in her cottage in the summer vacation. But what about Stanley Mervin?"

"When he and I were walking across the fields, the Sunday that Eva Alington was killed," I said, "he told me that if I'd anything in me that demanded to be let out, then I ought to drop everything else to get it out, and if I didn't, then it would go bad in me. But after the war I thought I knew too much to remember any advice from old painters who spoke broad Yorkshire. By that time I thought I knew it all."

She nodded. "I apologise for the outburst, Gregory. And I didn't think what you were telling me was hokum, as you called it. I was just puzzled about the wall and the crack and the light coming through. I've got rather a literal sort of mind." She waited a moment. "Are you going to join our film venture?"

"Yes, if you really want me to."

"Badly." And then she couldn't help yawning. "I'm sorry. But we do need you badly."

"Then we'll have a thundering good try. I'll have a word with young Hinchcliff sometime tomorrow. I've a lot of ideas that couldn't be mentioned tonight. Is there any chance of your dining with me tomorrow, Laura?"

"I have a meeting, but I'll try to get out of it, Gregory. What's your telephone number? I couldn't find it in the book."

Two minutes later I was out in Hanover Square, where there was a fine night with a glimmer of stars through thin moving veils of cloud. I didn't feel sleepy. There was in my mind a little brilliantly illuminated stage on which ideas paraded and excitedly capered; and all round the stage, where timeless eyes watched in the shadows, was an atmosphere of solemn tenderness for life. I hadn't known that mood, that theatre of creation, for years and years. Something good might come out of it.